the idea of you

AMANDA PROWSE

LAKE UNION
PUBLISHING

This is a work of fiction. Names, characters, organizations, places, events, and incidents are either products of the author's imagination or are used fictitiously.

Published by Lake Union Publishing, Seattle

www.apub.com

Amazon, the Amazon logo, and Lake Union Publishing are trademarks of Amazon.com, Inc., or its affiliates.

ISBN-13: 9781503942332
ISBN-10: 1503942333

Cover photography by Tin Moon Limited

Cover design by Debbie Clement

Printed in the United States of America

the idea of you

OTHER BOOKS BY AMANDA PROWSE

The Food of Love
Poppy Day
What Have I Done?
Clover's Child
A Little Love
Christmas for One
Will You Remember Me?
A Mother's Story
Perfect Daughter
Three-and-a-Half Heartbeats (exclusive to Amazon Kindle)
The Second Chance Café (originally published as The Christmas Café)
Another Love
My Husband's Wife
I Won't Be Home for Christmas

NOVELLAS BY AMANDA PROWSE

The Game
Something Quite Beautiful
A Christmas Wish
Ten Pound Ticket
Imogen's Baby
Miss Potterton's Birthday Tea

PRAISE FOR AMANDA PROWSE

'A tragic story of loss and love.'

Lorraine Kelly, *The Sun*

ating, heartbreaking and superbly written.'

Closer

eply emotional, unputdownable read.'

Red

lifting and positive, but you may still need a box of tissues.'

Cosmopolitan

u'll fall in love with this.'

Cosmopolitan

'arning: you will need tissues.'

The Sun on Sunday

'Handles her explosive subject with delicate care.'

Daily Mail

'D eply moving and eye-opening.'

Heat

'A perfect marriage morphs into harrowing territory . . . a real tear-je er.'

Sunday Mirror

'Powerful and emotional drama that packs a real punch.'

Heat

The Idea of You is dedicated to every woman who has known the pain of miscarriage, who has felt her hopes and dreams of motherhood end without warning.

Maybe she is like me and is unsure of how to grieve, how to mourn something that was never whole, and yet touched her soul in a way that is difficult to describe. I still think of all my little miracles who brought me joy and sadness in equal measure, and undoubtedly shaped the woman I became.

I send all these women and their partners love and this reminder that helped me head towards happiness: 'It is always darkest before the dawn; don't give up.' X

FROM THE AUTHOR

I started writing at the age of forty, having always been an avid reader. Every book I read I would put into a category of either 'I wish I had written that book' or 'I can do better than that'!

I didn't have the confidence or courage to put pen to paper, fearing my lack of grammar and limited understanding about the world of publishing might hamper my efforts.

It was only after beating cancer that I looked at the world in a different way, figuring that if this was my one time around the block, what did I really want to do? And what I really wanted to do was write stories! I have been writing for four years now and have written seventeen novels and six novellas.

I am pretty much average at everything. I'm a rubbish cook, useless at sport, and can never manage to get the duvet into the duvet cover. They say everyone has one thing that they can do, and I have discovered my one thing: I can write stories very quickly. They play in my head like a movie, and all I have to do is write down what I see. I am truly thankful every single day for this gift.

I write about ordinary women, women who find their lives disrupted and need to find strength to overcome the obstacles in their path. I find it amazing when a stranger tells me that they have enjoyed one of my books; that stranger and I are linked by something that germinated in my imagination. If that's not magic, I don't know what is.

Soaring higher than I could ever reach.
Leaving nothing, but the perfect idea of you,
a space where a heart used to beat,
and hopes and dreams of the better world that hovered
in your tiny palms.

I cannot forget the frail longing for time,
time to hold you skin to skin and to watch you take
shape,
the solid you, made of love and pride and things that
were no match for the wings that you grew too soon.

AJWP

PROLOGUE

'Are you nervous, sweetie?'

She whipped her head towards the kindly voice of the woman who had entered the room, and nodded. Her breath came in short bursts. Her fringe was stuck to her forehead in fine, damp wisps.

The woman smiled, her slow, patient manner welcome, calming. 'Well, it's easy to say, but don't be. We have done this a million times before.' She patted Lucy's narrow shoulder before walking away with a squeak to her shoe and a swish of her skirt.

Lucy would have liked to reply, but at that moment her voice had disappeared, hovering beneath a plug of fear that sat at the base of her throat. How could she begin to explain? It wasn't only a fear of what was about to happen, but also the sadness that, after this, she would be changed. And she didn't want to be changed. She liked being like this. She liked it very much.

Lifting her fingers, she placed them on her heart, which was beating so hard she was convinced it was forming a heart-shaped bulge in her skin, like the love-struck cartoon characters she liked to watch.

'Is there anyone you would like me to call for you?' the woman called from the doorway, holding the handle and looking back over her shoulder.

Lucy shook her head.

'There's no one you would like to have here by your side – a friend, a relative?'

Lucy took a deep breath as a single tear fell down her cheek. There was no one she wanted to call because no one knew, apart from one person – her mum – whom she definitely didn't want to see and who was at that very moment sequestered in another room at Lucy's demand. And this was the way it would be. A secret. Always.

'I . . .' she managed.

The woman cocked her ear, bending her head to enable her to hear better. 'What is it?'

'I . . . I miss my dad.' She paused to wipe away her tears with the back of her hand. 'He died a little while ago, and I really miss him.'

The woman smiled sympathetically and gave a small nod of understanding, just as a fresh wave of pain caused Lucy's body to convulse.

ONE

Today, Lucy felt a little like an imposter in the house of God. Christenings made her feel especially uncomfortable. Being asked to be a godparent was, however, an honour, a great responsibility, and one she hoped she would shoulder well. She glanced at Benedict, the beautiful baby boy in his mother's arms, on this, his special day. As she smiled at his gummy face, self-doubt hammered inside her head. Supposing this baby grew up to be a reprobate; would that be her fault? Surely not. It had always been her belief that how a child turned out was down to three things: parents, environment and schooling. This, she felt, would exonerate her nicely should the need arise. Not that she could picture him being anything less than wonderful. He was far too cute.

Her discomfort also came from the fact that she was yet again single at an event that screamed coupledom. On a day-to-day basis, she tried not to give her single state more than a passing thought, tried to ignore the image of Richard's face that leapt into her mind unbidden. But it wasn't always easy, and at any party or event where she was encouraged to bring a plus-one, she became a little more aware.

Today was no exception.

Everywhere she looked, people stood cosily in twos like bookends or matching pairs, one gently holding the elbow of the other, or subtly resting a hand on the small of their back, or grazing their palm against their partner's. She found the displays a little nauseating.

She shifted her feet inside her wedge sandals and adjusted her dress sleeve, lest she might be revealing more flesh than was deemed appropriate in this setting. Trying to smile sanguinely and nod occasionally, she hoped it looked like she was paying full attention. Her mind tuning in and out of the Reverend Anthony's words, she stared at his face.

'And today on this – Benedict's special day – we should think about the words that Jesus said: "Let the little children come to me and do not try to stop them, for the kingdom of heaven belongs to such as these."'

It might of course have been her imagination, but she was certain that the vicar saved his hard stares and meaningful pauses for when he was looking directly at her.

Her imagination . . . now there was a rampant and illogical thing – that is, if she listened to Richard. 'You are imagining it! You need to control this ridiculous unfounded jealousy!' had been his exact words. And her particular favourite, which she conveniently remembered word for word, shouted at her as they drove up the motorway on a rainy Sunday morning: 'If I was going to leave you for anyone, Lucy, it *certainly* wouldn't be your cousin Davina – she's bonkers! Wasn't it she who locked you in the garden shed and told your parents you'd gone out with friends? An utter nut.'

And as it transpired, Davina was an utter nut whom Richard would be marrying in a few weeks' time on a sultry Caribbean beach with a handful of Lucy's very own family present. All unsuitably dressed for the environment, no doubt, with grit in their sandals and sweat stains on their shirt collars.

One thing she certainly hadn't imagined was the scrolled gold-on-white invitation that was currently propped up on her mother's mantelpiece. She suspected her mum had given it pride of place as a sharp rebuke, letting her know what she could have won if only she had been more like cousin Davina.

This she already knew.

Lucy had taken the invitation into her hands and held it against her chest as she cried. It wasn't that she wanted Richard, not now that he had made his choices clear, but the rejection of her for another, no matter how justified, hurt just the same. She had loved him, and it was so nearly her name on the invitation, and this realisation only made her tears fall harder. This rectangle of fancy card was a reminder that she was losing a race she didn't know she had entered; she hadn't heard the starter pistol, and by the time she looked up, everyone she knew of a similar age seemed to be halfway around the track.

It was a self-inflicted pressure, but whenever she looked at her peers she automatically totted up their age and their achievements, instantly working out how far behind she was. For example, Helen, forty-two, owns a holiday home in Portugal and has three kids, of which the oldest is eighteen – *eighteen*! Which meant that she, at thirty-nine, was already at least sixteen years behind Helen, who had married at the age of twenty-three – there was no way she could catch up! The realisation that she wasn't even set for a bronze medal was disheartening. In fact, forget the medals – Lucy didn't even know if she was going to be able to finish the race. If she did, everyone else would have left the arena long ago, meaning there would be no one there to witness her achievement, and so what would be the point?

She glanced at Tansy, who looked lovely in her duck-egg-blue, fifties-inspired frock, as she rocked the sleepy Benedict in her arms, cooing 'Shhhh . . .' with a look of abject fear that if she stopped rocking, or indeed cooing, he might wake up fully and yell. And that would never do – not in a church on this auspicious day, when he was the star of the show.

Tansy had what Lucy considered to be mum-like proportions: an ample bosom, sturdy arms and a broad back. Quite unlike her good self, who had for as long as she could remember been best described as scrawny. This was much to the chagrin of her friends and colleagues, who spent an age in the gym trying to emulate the very slender, lanky shape that she had been born with.

Mum-like proportions or not, it was Tansy who stood with her beautiful, sleepy child in her arms, her teenage son Michael by her side and Rick, her tall husband, standing with an arm draped around her. Lucy saw the way he looked at his wife and then his boys with something beyond love. She felt the bunch of emptiness in her stomach, trying to imagine what it might feel like to have someone look at her that way.

And just like that, she was once again acutely aware of her singledom.

She swallowed and tried to concentrate, but as the Reverend Anthony spoke, her thoughts refused to stay anchored to the buffed flagstone floor and the old pitch pine pews. Instead, she stared over his head at the stained-glass windows high above.

Richard and Davina . . .

If she was being completely honest, his leaving had been coupled with an enormous and instant sense of relief. In the year since they had split, she had been able to breathe properly and laugh heartily and commit more fully to her job, which hadn't gone unnoticed in her quarterly appraisal, where a directorship had been mentioned.

She and Richard had clearly been mismatched, not least of all because she was a stickler for little things like fidelity and he, rather obviously, was not. But it was more than that. Richard wanted the finer things in life: a twin-engine speedboat, a Breitling watch, a VIP pass for a major sporting event and a healthy cellar bursting with burgundies. Whereas all she wanted was a baby. Not that she would ever mention this in the office, having been party to discussions with her male superiors who had spoken openly about other women they were nervous to promote, knowing there might be childcare issues. She hated the hypocrisy and flagrant disregard of the law that didn't seem to bother them a jot.

She found it quite ironic that her friends who leant on the window ledge and admired the view from her swanky London office, and who flexed her company credit card longingly between their fingers before trying on her enviable collection of Choos, the same ones who sat at home surrounded by a mess of baby paraphernalia, floors cluttered with baby gyms and soft toys, and whose worktops were crammed with sterilisers, bottles and baby wipes, *these* were the friends she yearned to trade lives with. And she would have done so in a single heartbeat.

As her girlfriends bemoaned their lack of sleep and whined about cracked nipples while hunting for a semi-clean mug in which to make tea, with baby vomit smeared on their shoulders and their hair escaping in greasy tendrils from grimy scrunchies, trilling 'Don't look at me! I haven't even had time for a shower!', Lucy felt a surge of something in her gut that came very close to envy.

Arriving home to her beautiful, spacious, neutral-toned apartment after any such visit, she eyed her immaculately plumped pillows with disdain. The smear-free, cold, hard, dark granite surfaces and the neat TV remotes, lined up on a dust-free shelf, were solid proof of her childless state. This was an environment that no big family could maintain, and she hated what it said about her.

At these times, when loneliness threatened to engulf her, Lucy consoled herself with the thought that this life and this home were all temporary, and that her real life would begin when she met someone to love and became a mum. This would enable her to leapfrog her way around the track, putting her back in contention for a podium finish. It wasn't that she didn't appreciate what she had achieved in her career – she did – but she knew that total fulfilment would come when she could juggle this career with parenting. She would show her little girl how, with a bit of careful planning and a whole lot of hard, hard work, she, like her mum, could achieve anything.

This she could never share – not while she was being held up as a shining example among her peers of how a woman could break through the glass ceiling and have it all.

Only she didn't have it all, not quite.

As she neared forty, Lucy was starting to think of alternative ways to make her dream of motherhood a reality and was considering all avenues, from getting her already slightly dated eggs harvested, to looking into adoption. She hadn't given up hope, not at all, and loved nothing more than to read articles in the downmarket, thin-papered magazines that lined the racks at the checkout with headlines like 'My Baby Miracle!' or 'Gran Gives Birth to Quads Shocker!' These stories she read with a pinched mouth and a visible headshake of disapproval, just in case anyone might be watching. But the reality was, stories like these gave her hope. If an octogenarian virgin living on a remote Italian hilltop was able to pop out a whole gaggle of bambinos after nothing more than bathing in the local magic stream, then all hope was not lost for her.

'Lucy!' Tansy whispered from the side of her mouth. Tansy's sister giggled and the well-groomed middle-aged man with a close beard next to her gave a small cough and blushed a little on her behalf.

She looked away from the window and down at the crescent of people gathered around the font with their hands clasped and a measure of expectation in their stares, all directed at her.

'Well, do you?' Tansy prompted, her sigh indicating that she might be starting to regret her choice of godmother – and this before they had even left the church. It did not bode well.

'What?' she whispered, dry mouthed with embarrassment at what she might have missed, before tucking her long, dark hair behind her ear.

'Do you?' the Reverend Anthony repeated.

'Oh yes.' She nodded. 'Yes, I do. Absolutely. I do.' She beamed and stood up straight, wishing she had been paying better attention, hoping that she hadn't agreed to something hideous, while simultaneously wondering when she might be able to get her hands on a glass of wine.

◆ ◆ ◆

That was the trouble with being a work friend of the child's mother: it wasn't like she knew the family that well, and there wasn't anyone else from work here. She guessed it was a compliment of sorts, but right now, as she hugged the wall with one hand behind her back and cradled a passable chilled white with the other, she wondered what was the shortest possible amount of time it would be considered acceptable to stay after the ceremony. By her reckoning she could leave in about thirty minutes. After all, what was she going to miss? The cake would be cut with minimal speeches and her generous gift was already nestled in an envelope marked 'For Benedict' inside a white basket festooned with blue and white ribbons and placed, non-surreptitiously, at the end of the buffet. She smiled across the room at Michael, Tansy's elder son, who looked just as awkward as she felt, pulling with his fingers at the shirt collar that sat stiffly against a neck that was more used to wearing T-shirts.

'Forgive me, I'm a little bit out of practice at christenings, but is it the same as a wedding where the usher and bridesmaid have to dance and make out?' The man's question caught her a little off guard.

'Excuse me?' She twisted around, instantly recognising the blushing guy with the trendy beard from the church. She leant forward, wondering where this conversation might be going.

'You know.' He placed his hands on his hips inside his well-cut navy suit jacket and stood directly in front of her, smiling to show off his neat white teeth, which crossed ever so slightly in the centre. 'It's the rule at weddings, isn't it? And the only reason so many ne'er-do-wells agree to take on any duty in a wedding party. It's because they are almost guaranteed at least one smooch with a good-looking, tipsy bridesmaid.'

'Really? I did not know that.'

'Yes.' He nodded encouragingly. 'It's practically the law.'

'The law?' She cocked her head to get a better look at him, noticing how he didn't feel like a stranger. Taking in the spaces between his features on a face that was unfamiliar, she searched her mental database to see whom he reminded her of, matching him to faces she knew and loved. He had her dad's sincere stare, her first love's face shape, and George Clooney-esque eyebrows. This was all boding very well.

'At least, it was the law at *my* wedding,' he continued.

And just like that she felt her balloon of happy anticipation deflate.

'Oh! So you're married.' She took a sip of her wine, sucking in her cheeks, aware of the slight frost that laced her words, as if he had in some way misled her, which was ridiculous. He was only being polite; she had after all been hoping for someone to talk to. Her neediness and disappointment both angered and embarrassed her. She took another glug of her wine.

Tansy whooshed past with a crying Benedict in one arm and an unfurled nappy under the other, on the way to the bathroom. 'Don't bother trying to chat her up; she's my boss!' she managed, as she passed by in a whirlwind of perfume, champagne and baby powder.

He threw his head back and laughed quite loudly. 'Charming.' He bent his head towards her conspiratorially. 'And for the record: no, I'm not married.'

'So you just had the wedding to provide an afternoon of distraction for the ne'er-do-wells in your life?' Lucy drained her glass, deciding there and then that the right time for her to leave was, in fact, now.

Again he laughed before taking a step closer to her. Her face hovered under his chin.

Just the right height . . .

She had to look up to see his face.

'No. I had the wedding because when it was in the planning stage, I didn't have the faintest idea of how things would unravel. It was a big wedding – huge, in case you are interested.'

'I'm not,' she lied, folding one arm across her chest and holding her wine glass in the air with the other.

He continued as if she hadn't spoken. 'And I mean *huge*, with all the bells and whistles, just as you might expect after hours and hours of discussion and no expense spared. A skyscraper of a cake, a crystal-strewn designer dress and doves. Oh yes, doves.' He shook his head. 'But it was just that, a wedding, and what I didn't get at the end of it was a marriage. We lasted eighteen months.'

And just like that her balloon reinflated.

'I'm sorry to hear that,' she lied again.

He seemed to be studying her face, drinking her in, and she felt as if time were suspended as she stared up at him, feeling his presence wrap around her like a warm blanket on a cold night. It was a second or two before he lowered his face towards her and spoke, not an inch from her ear. His words sent a shiver of delight along her limbs.

'I promise you that when we get married, it will be a simple affair. Just you and me, without distraction. No bridesmaids, good-looking or otherwise, no gift list, no toasts, no doves released from a box, no three-tiered cakes and no fancy frocks. How does that sound?'

She smiled. 'It sounds perfect.'

He reached up and placed his hand in front of her, putting it in the small gap between them. 'And your name is?'

'Lucy,' she whispered.

'And I'm Jonah, Jonah Carpenter.'

'Hello, Jonah, Jonah Carpenter.' She beamed and sighed, deciding, as he gently held her elbow, that there was nowhere else she would rather be than right here.

So here it is, my letter to you. A letter you might never see, but one which I shall take great joy in writing nonetheless. Where to start? I suppose with a snippet of my current life. Every aspect of my existence changed when I met my husband. Up until that point, my life had been ordered, neat, a little sterile I guess, in retrospect, and this was how I pictured it continuing. If I looked ahead, I saw no break to the established norm of working hard and marking time, with pockets of happiness dotting an often hectic calendar. Day trips, glasses of wine and leisurely lunches with my girlfriends, even holidays to locations that provided perfect postcard-worthy landscapes to capture with my camera lens, snapping images in the hope that these pictures might help me bottle the wonderful moments of distraction. These were the things that I looked forward to: events that placed a big, joyous dollop of motivation on the darkest of days and helped quash any suggestion of loneliness. And then I met him, Jonah, and the picture I had carried in my mind for so long changed. And I liked the way that this new picture looked. I liked the new me. This man I met – a wonderful man – picked up the snow globe of my life and gave it a really good shake, and just like that I started to enjoy 'today'.

TWO

The one-year anniversary card sat on the mantelpiece. Lucy had kept it there for the last three weeks and was loath to put it away. Every time the thin wedding band on her finger caught her eye, it still sent a jolt of happiness right through her. To be this happy felt good.

Their wedding had indeed been perfect. The whole event had been delivered exactly as promised, devoid of bridesmaids, gift lists, toasts, doves and three-tiered cakes, and not a fancy frock in sight. The temporary receptionist at work, Delia, had given up her precious lunch hour, along with a man from the accounts department at Jonah's car dealership. Delia had been sworn to secrecy about her whereabouts, particularly if Tansy asked.

The four stood awkwardly in front of a lady with a pair of spectacles resting on her pointy nose, who neatly filled out the blank rows on their marriage certificate before offering a perfunctory 'many congratulations' and tearing the numbered sheet from its gluey stays. The happy group exited the Camden Register Office in Judd Street, London, and hovered, as if uncertain what duty or tradition demanded.

Jonah, who had very little interest in duty or tradition, shook hands with his witness, kissed Delia heartily on the cheek like she was an old friend, and grabbed his new wife by the hand. It was very clear that the two strangers were being dispatched.

'Where are we going?' Lucy had giggled, tripping along the pavement in her heels, which clattered over the flat, discoloured blobs of chewing gum that littered the path. He had looked back and grinned at her, speeding up, as if aware that they both had to be back at work in a wee while. Both had agreed that there was something exciting about taking only an hour or two out of their day to perform this life-changing act. Like a proposal in a busy street or dancing cheek to cheek in a crowded square, it was this slice of magic among the mundane that added to the thrill.

They crossed roads and ducked through traffic, while Jonah masterfully held up a hand to cyclists and couriers, intent on slowing them down. She looked up and recognised the entrance to St Clement's Gardens.

Jonah shrugged his arms from his jacket as they made their way along the meandering path, eventually laying it on the grass under a spreading plane tree before settling back and inviting his bride to sit. Lucy crouched and took a seat on the pale silk lining of his jacket.

'I'm worried your suit will get dirty.' She ran her hand over the shiny fabric. The new platinum band on her finger glinted in the sunshine.

'I'm not.' He retrieved a packet of sour strawberry laces from his trouser pocket and pulled one out, handing it to her.

'My favourite! Strawberry laces!' She clapped before lowering the sour, worm-like liquorice into her mouth with Jonah sat by her side. 'This is lovely.' She looked around at the weathered graves, impressive statues, moss-covered obelisks and faded grandeur of the Regency era, nestling on the beautifully kept grass. A leafy oasis in central London where the sharpened edges and shiny glass of modern architecture encroached on the space if she let her gaze wander too high over the walls.

'How do you like being married?' he asked, leaning over to graze her mouth with a light kiss.

'I like it very much so far.' She looked at her watch. 'All twenty-two minutes of it.'

Jonah kissed her again. 'I wanted to bring you here not only because it's beautiful—'

'Which it is,' she interrupted, speaking as she poked the remainder of the sour strawberry lace back into her mouth from where it had escaped.

'But it's also good to be among the dead.'

'Oh.' She pulled a face. 'Not quite the wedding speech I'd envisaged, but do carry on.'

He took her hand into his. 'I love you, Lucy Carpenter.'

She smiled at this, and felt quite coy at the first use of her new name.

'I love you,' he continued. 'You are the very best thing that has ever happened to me. You're like a prize for the best raffle in the world that I didn't even know I had entered.'

'Thank you. I think. Although right now I feel like a prize – a mid-week steak dinner for two.' She laughed.

He closed his eyes briefly. 'What I am trying to say is that you are like a glorious second chance that I didn't think I had any right to, and I will treasure you every day, because, as all these people know' – he circled his hand around them – 'since they are long dead and buried, time passes in a blink. They were us once, sat here, and now they're not.'

His sobering words made her wish she wasn't chewing on the childish waxy candy that she couldn't seem to swallow. She nodded.

'I love you, Lucy, my wife, and I want us to make the most of every single brilliant day that we get together. Deal?'

'Deal,' she managed, swallowing the sour treat before her husband leant in for a kiss.

◆　◆　◆

'Look at you, sitting there smiling,' her husband teased her, as he walked into the sitting room.

'Sorry. I shall try to look more miserable.' She gave a mock frown and turned down her mouth.

'That's better.' He took in her stern face. 'You know, there is something very sexy about watching you knit.' Jonah slumped down on the end of their oversized sofa in his jeans and sweatshirt, sinking into the squidgy cushion with a mug of tea in his hand.

'I don't see how.' She laughed, curling her feet in her bedsocks up under her legs. 'It's what most people associate with their granny.' She paused, laying the needles in her lap with the wool still looped around her fingers. 'Probably because it is often our granny who teaches us how to knit; at least it was mine who taught me. It's partly why I love it; makes me feel close to her. I can hear her tutoring me if I get stuck or make a mistake.'

She'd been only seven the day her gran taught her, and by then the old woman's voice had borne the crackle of age: 'You need to concentrate, watch me and then you can do it for yourself. How does that sound?'

'Good.' She nodded, huddling closer to her gran on the stiff-backed sofa where a lace cover hung down to protect the never-seen green velour. Lucy's nose twitched against the peculiar smell of her gran's house – a mixture of mints, cologne, lavender and something vaguely medicinal.

'Here we go.' Her gran looped a long tail of wool over her little finger before winding it around her index finger; working quickly with the knitting needle and her finger, she popped tiny loops on to the metal rod. 'This is called casting on,' she explained, 'and these little woollen lines are your stitches. We need to keep them nice and even.'

Lucy nodded, wriggling closer still to get a better look over her gran's plump yet dexterous fingers.

'And just you wait and see, something magical happens, Lucy, just by adding more loops, and with more twists of the needle you can make all kinds of wondrous things!'

'Like what?' she had whispered.

'Like scarves for people you love, and most important' – she had bent down and almost mouthed her next words – 'baby clothes,' giving them an almost sacred significance that had stayed with Lucy.

'Good Lord,' her husband's words drew her to the present. 'When you put it like that, I must admit all sexy thoughts have indeed vanished from my mind.' Jonah curled his top lip. 'I am now only able to picture your grandma.'

'How dare you pull that face? You never met my gran. For all you know she might have been very sexy.' She laughed.

He cradled her foot in his hand and rubbed her toes inside the pretty sock, gently shaking his head. 'Maybe sexy was the wrong word; I know I'm certainly regretting using it. I think the word "sweet" might be better; watching you knit makes you look nurturing and homely. I like watching you do it,' he admitted. 'It's like the alternative you, the true you, the one who doesn't wear a suit and worry about budgets and advertising campaigns. When you knit, you are my Lucy.'

Lucy flexed her foot against her husband's palm. 'I am always your Lucy. And I like the end result of my knitting very much. Look at this.' She held up the slender needles, from which dangled a half-formed white matinee jacket; the lacy scalloped stitches were delicate and pretty.

'It's beautiful, you clever old thing.' Jonah's compliment made her smile.

'For my gran, knitting for the new babies of the family was almost a rite of passage, a way of welcoming them. My mum and aunts used to pass the little garments around, so we all wore Gran's knitting at some point. We have endless pictures of Fay and me, my cousins and their kids too, in the same cardigans, bonnets and tiny booties with lace or ribbon threaded through the top. And since she died, all of those items have become so much more precious. I think that when you knit for someone, it takes so much time and concentration, it's literally impossible to make a garment like this without love.'

'That's a great thing,' Jonah agreed.

'I can't believe our little bunny will be wearing this, can you?' She beamed, holding it up once again and feeling another wave of pride at her handiwork.

Jonah shook his head and blinked as if a little overcome at the prospect. 'And just so we are clear, I will only let you dress him in this girlie stuff until he is a few months old; then I will most definitely be stepping in and insisting that he wear denim and army camouflage and football shirts.'

'Is that right?' She looked at him quizzically. 'Anyway, we don't even know if it's a boy – might be a little girl.' She smiled at the image, caring little about the sex of her baby, knowing that when it arrived it would miraculously be the exact baby she had been hoping for.

'I just picture a boy. I don't know why,' he confessed.

'Maybe because you already have Camille?' She nodded towards one of several pictures of Jonah's willowy teenage daughter, who lived with her mum, Geneviève, and stepdad, Jean-Luc, in La Charente, France.

'Possibly, or maybe it's just my instinct.' He reached across and rubbed her still flat tum. Lucy felt a kernel of warmth beneath his touch; it bloomed inside her into joy. Here she was, married, happy at work and pregnant. She was winning the race.

'Well, one of us will be right.' She smiled. 'Did I tell you what I read today?' Without waiting for an answer, she reached down and placed her knitting on the scrubbed wooden table by the side of the sofa and picked up the book that was never far from her fingertips – a pregnancy manual.

She had vowed not to read ahead, knowing that the excitement would be more than she could contain. Instead, she awaited every marker, reading and learning each milestone. Today was one of those days.

Flipping open the pages, she let her eyes rove the illustrations that fascinated her and smiled before lifting the book closer to her face and reading deliberately.

'At week eleven your baby is growing well and is now about the size of a chicken's egg but it is much tougher, with quite sturdy bones. It will now weigh up to fourteen grams.' She lowered the book. 'Can you believe that? Fourteen grams and already so tough. Isn't that amazing?'

'It really is.' He chortled. They were both so happy. She knew that for Jonah this pregnancy was a chance for him to experience all he had missed with Camille.

'When do you think we can start telling people?' she asked eagerly, biting her bottom lip.

'Well, we agreed that twelve weeks would be a good time, so any-time from now on I guess, but I think you should bear in mind that, once you do, it'll set in motion a whole chain of events.'

'At work, you mean?' She pictured the half-smiles of her bosses, their congratulations tinged with sourness at the inconvenience her absence would cause, but that was just too bad. She knew they were very good at talking the talk when it came to flexibility and accommo-dating maternity leave, but the reality behind closed doors was a little different, sadly.

'Yes, at work.' He released her foot and sat up straight. 'It won't be easy for them to lose someone in your position; it will create ripples.'

'It won't be forever.' She kept her eyes low.

'Lucy.' He laughed. 'I have a strong suspicion that when you get your hands on this baby, hell or high water will not drag you back to that desk. You will be besotted – you are already! And the idea of you handing him over for someone else to look after is laughable. I know you are leaving all options open and I think that's the right thing to do, but I would bet my Hawaiian shirt on you wanting to stay home.'

'And you love that shirt!' She smiled, beaming at the seed of truth in his words. From the second she had found out she was pregnant, her excitement had bounced like a rubber ball in her mind, distracting her from every task in hand and demanding her attention. It took all of her strength not to run the length of every street with her arms spread wide, shouting 'I'm going to have a baby!'

'I do. But I can't see you hotfooting it back to the world of advertising anytime soon after, can you?' Jonah asked earnestly.

Lucy chose to ignore the shard of panic that pierced her thoughts. She was undoubtedly looking forward to becoming a mum, but the idea of giving up a job she loved and a role that she had worked so hard to attain caused a ripple of self-doubt.

'I don't know,' she admitted, slouching down on to the cushions and putting her head on his shoulder. 'I am hoping that I can find a balance. I've worked too hard to just walk away from all that I've achieved in my career, plus I love it, I really do and I don't want to give it up. I guess I'm hoping that a middle ground will appear somewhere. Millions of women manage to strike that balance – Tansy, for example, and Fay has always worked. I think it'd make me a better mum if I kept my dreams and aspirations alive. Maybe I'm being greedy, but I don't think I need to choose. And talking of Fay, I'd quite like to tell her. She will of course tell my mum straight away. But I was thinking maybe this weekend?'

'Of course! Let's do it. And I get it; it's exciting.' He kissed the top of her scalp. 'But remember that once you tell your sister, she will tell the whole world; she won't be able to keep it secret.'

Lucy nodded, knowing this would be true. She felt a shiver at the prospect of breaking the news to her mum, Jan. She rubbed the top of her arms to ward off the sudden chill that shot up her spine and settled on her shoulders.

'Mummy, mummy? I think I'm having a baby . . .'

Jonah's voice was low. 'You okay? You look miles away.'

'Yes, I'm fine. Of course.' She nodded with more enthusiasm than she felt.

Jonah continued: 'You know, don't you, that Fay will start to harass you with a gutful of good intentions and a headful of experience about what it was like when she was pregnant with Maisie and Rory, and that will drive you mad, and you will then start to avoid her or argue with her or both.'

'You're very good at this,' she remarked.

'Good at what?' he asked.

'You know, sussing out the whole family dynamic. Considering you have only been saddled with us all for just over a year, you've got your head around it very quickly.'

'You make it sound like a compliment.' He chuckled.

'It is! Goodness me, you are impressive, Mr Carpenter.' She wrapped her arms around his arm and held it to her. 'But I also think that somewhere in your rationale lies a reluctance for this little bit of news to get out, because once it has, you will then have to talk to Geneviève and Camille, and if I had to guess I would say that you are trying to avoid it.'

She felt a deep sigh leave his body.

'Oh, I hate that you might be right,' he confessed.

She knew there was no 'might' about it.

Both instinctively let their eyes wander to the photograph sitting in front of a collection of books on the overstuffed shelves. It was of their wedding day, an image snapped on a phone that Jonah held at arm's length as they stared up at the screen.

The planning for their wedding was the first time Lucy had fully understood the impact of Jonah's first marriage on their lives. Not only was he wary of his feisty ex-wife, whose tendency towards hysteria had not been tempered by her marriage to a French farmer, but he was also like a rabbit caught in the headlights when it came to his sixteen-year-old daughter, Camille.

'The thing is, love, the longer you leave telling them about the baby, the more you will dread it and the worse it will be. And that takes a bit of the gloss off your happiness, which isn't fair on anyone,' she rationalised, running her hands over her stomach. 'You might be pleasantly surprised – Geneviève might actually be happy for us!'

'I know. She *might*,' he agreed. 'But on the other hand, she might not, and I can't stand the idea of more conflict; we can't talk like normal humans. She's impossible, twists everything I say and has this knack of making me feel like the bad guy all the time. It was bad enough when I told her we'd got married. Instead of congratulating me, she huffed loudly and muttered "Typical". She's just mean.' He pinched his nose.

'It's difficult sometimes when an ex moves on.'

'It's been years!' he reminded her.

'I know, and it's hard to explain, but sometimes, even though you don't want that person any more, and no matter how you have split, acrimoniously or otherwise, it's still a bit jarring to hear that the person you once loved has moved on. I think it's the fact that someone has taken your place. None of us like to think we are dispensable.'

'But surely that's not always the case? I was happy she had Jean-Luc, the poor man, delighted for him to take my place as you put it, and more than glad that she became someone else's headache.' He laughed.

'Ah, don't be mean. Plus, things are different now; you've got me here to fight in your corner.' She nuzzled against him.

'I have, and you've given me confidence. I mean, you don't think I'm an idiot, do you?'

'Not *all* the time.' She smiled.

'And I joke about it, but I know she must influence Camille,' he continued, 'and that gets me more than anything, like there's this big debate going on and I'm not there to defend myself. She gets more airtime than me.'

Lucy understood. She had been eager to meet her stepdaughter from the get-go, badgering Jonah to make it happen.

'Soon. Soon,' had been the familiar, muted response, before he found a way to distract or silence her, usually with a kiss or cake.

'Won't she mind not coming to the wedding?' she had asked more than once as they booked the registrar, selected matching wedding bands and woke on the day itself. The girl's absence had bothered her.

'Isn't it far easier if we don't invite anyone?' he had suggested. 'I think it should be just the two of us and a couple of anonymous witnesses. We'll do it and then announce to the world, "Hey, guess what we just did!" That way no one gets offended. A blanket ban on guests means we get the day we want.'

'So you're not even going to tell Camille?' She had struggled with this, knowing that her sixteen-year-old self would at least have liked to know about it. It rankled her still that the announcement had been made after the event, done over the phone without her involvement in a rather unceremonious 'and by the way . . .' manner. She felt it devalued their big news.

'Trust me; it's fine. She'll only tell Geneviève and, you know . . .'

Lucy didn't know, but she was beginning to understand that Jonah was more than a little anxious where his ex-wife and child were concerned.

'Do you think Camille will be happy to be getting a little brother or sister?' This thought, spoken aloud, drew her back to the present.

'Possibly.' He shifted in his seat on the sofa. 'But I think we should also be aware that she might feel a little envious. It's only natural that she will have worries about her nose being put out of joint, particularly as this baby gets to live with her dad, something she has never done.'

It was a reminder that Geneviève had told him of her pregnancy only when the ink had dried on their divorce papers.

'Then we will just have to make her extra welcome, really get her involved,' Lucy enthused. 'Maybe I could teach her to knit?' She sat forward, enlivened by the idea.

Jonah threw his head back and laughed. 'I love you.'

'I love you too.'

The two looked at each other, still, after one year married, thoroughly smitten.

◆ ◆ ◆

The next morning the alarm let out its shrill ring, and Jonah groaned as he hit the snooze button on the top with the palm of his hand.

'Five more minutes,' he pleaded – with whom she wasn't sure, and she smiled as his dark, curly hair disappeared under the duvet, as if he might be able to hide from the day. Quite the opposite of her, he wasn't a morning person.

Lucy lay back against the soft pillow and let the light creeping from under the roman blind wash over her. It was still a wonderful surprise for her to wake in this Victorian terraced house in Windermere Avenue, Queen's Park, London, a mere hop, skip and a jump from where Jonah had grown up, an only child. His parents had died quite recently. She was sad that she never got to meet them, knowing it would have been lovely to know the other woman in the world who loved this man as much as she did.

Their bedroom was scruffy and the bed low to the ground, with dust bunnies gathered in the spaces between the floorboards. Framed vintage posters of fast cars snapped at the Le Mans rally in the sixties hung either side of the bed, and none of the bed linen matched. She had, when she moved in, simply amalgamated her things with his, and the result was this mismatch of homely and functional.

She had to admit that she rather liked it, all of it – the piles of magazines, the imperfect paintwork, the nests of discarded shoes at the bottom of wardrobes, the abandoned, broken sports equipment clogging any available corner, the creaky doors, the dodgy plumbing and the high, ornate ceilings where cobwebs lurked. This solid three-bedroom house with its waxed pine floors, tarnished brass door furniture and split-level cook's kitchen – where jars of herbs and spice tins jostled for position on the dusty wooden open shelves – felt like home. There were blackened skillets and pots hanging on menacing-looking hooks above the well-used range. The uneven terracotta floor listed slightly towards the French windows, as if keen to encourage you out into the busy garden, which boasted either a tangle of fragrant, climbing jasmine or a bundle of rather sorry-looking brown twigs, depending on the time of the year. The whole house and everything in it seemed to have been waiting for her. To live like this felt carefree, relaxed. Every surface and every object had a tangible history, making her feel closer to Jonah and all that had gone before. It was a house with roots that she nurtured and made her own.

It was a world away from her previous home of four years, in which everything was considered. Her waterside apartment in a purpose-built block on the Thames Path in East London had sat empty for a long while, until she had been persuaded to rent it out to Ross, a fastidious friend of Tansy's, for an initial six-month let. She hoped he would renew the lease, agreeing that it was better to have someone in it than to let it stay empty. Initially her reluctance to hand over the keys had been down to her own insecurities – supposing she needed a fallback? Jonah laughed, explaining to her in simple terms that marriage didn't work like that. It wasn't a 'try and see' situation, there was no 'free sample' on a tiny spoon, no 'return it within twenty-eight days, no questions asked'. This was it! The very next day, she had rung Ross and organised his lease. It felt like progress.

Life in their marital home was comfortable, and once she had got used to the overground train ride and her extended commute to and from work, and familiarised herself with all the good stuff along the bustling Salusbury Road, including the delicatessen, baker's, gastro pub, organic supermarket and vintage hardware store, it felt like a trip out to the suburbs every day. This feeling might not have been solely down to the location of their house, but also the blissful state in which she now lived, with her man by her side and her baby in her tum. Lucy had never felt this happy, had never known she *could* be this happy.

She turned on to her side and placed her head on her husband's pillow; the sight and smell of him still filled her with a bubble of joy.

'Time to get up, sleepyhead,' she cooed, kissing the side of his head.

'No. Go away,' he snapped, drawing the duvet even tighter around his form, as if this feathery defence might be all it would take to keep the day at bay.

If only.

Lucy stretched out her foot and placed it on his calf, sliding it up and down. She felt his body shift beneath the covers.

'Don't.' He laughed, pulling the duvet beneath his chin, his smile giving the opposite message. 'It's not fair to tempt me with your delicious bod, not when I could be sleeping. I still have a few minutes left.' He let his eyes wander to the clock that was on snooze.

Wriggling closer, she placed her leg over his thigh and rested her face on his shoulder, palming circles on his hairy chest. Jonah gripped her wrist. 'Okay, we have a serious dilemma,' he growled.

'What is it?' She threw her hair over her shoulder and dipped forward to kiss his chin.

'I have approximately four and a half minutes before I have to jump up and into action. There's a training session today for all three sites and they want me there to rubber-stamp the day, hand out certificates and give the nod to the top sales teams, and if I don't get up and get out my whole day will be thrown out of sync.' He reached up and kissed her. 'On the other hand, if I miss this opportunity for a bit of quick, fuss-free sex with my beautiful wife, I just might regret it for the rest of the day. Meaning I wouldn't be able to concentrate at the training event. You see? A dilemma.'

Lucy rolled on top of him and kissed him full on the mouth.

'So what's it going to be?' she purred.

Jonah pushed her into a sitting position and manoeuvred her legs either side of him as he held her by the waist, 'I am going to see just how much progress we can make in four minutes.' He grinned, impatiently helping her undo the flimsy ribbon that held her pyjama bottoms in place, as she wriggled to be free of the candy-striped cotton.

'Shit! Oh my God!' His sudden shout alarmed her.

Jonah tried to sit up, pushing her a little too quickly to one side, as he eased his legs to the edge of the mattress and sat with his back curved and his shoulders heaving, as if his breathing were laboured, heavy.

Lucy gave a small giggle, born of embarrassment and fear. 'Are you okay?' She raked her nails over his back.

He turned to her, his expression one of shock, his mouth opening and closing as he seemed to struggle to find the right thing to say. She noted that his face had taken on a greyish hue.

'Jonah? You are scaring me. Please speak to me. What's the matter?' Her mind raced. What had he remembered? Or was it his heart? He was a good seven years older than her, and his love of cooking with wine, cream and butter worried her. 'Jonah? What is it? Talk to me,' she repeated, as she too sat up in the bed.

And then she looked down at his shaking hand, raised in front of his chest, and then at the patch on his stomach where she had sat only seconds before.

Her eyes widened and her tears sprang, as she touched her fingers to her sodden pyjama bottoms.

The alarm pipped its shrill, invasive sound. She watched her husband reach out and slam the button on the top with a palm that was bright red with her blood.

I often wonder what your voice might be like. I think about it progressing from baby sounds and gurgles to a burbling lisp of repetition – mumma . . . mumma . . . mumma . . . – until your true voice emerges and you speak clearly and coherently, sharing all the wonderful things that you have learned, and telling me of all the amazing things that you have seen in your sweet, sweet tone. I hear you, when you are older, ending a call with 'gotta go, I love you, Mum!' And my heart lifts at the very idea of you in a rush to crack on with this busy, wonderful life of yours. I wonder if you might sound a bit like me? This idea makes me smile; I like it very much. I also think about your first steps. What a thing! Your first ever steps on the planet! I imagine me there, smiling on one side of the room, and my mum or my sister on the other. I pull away my fingers that you have been gripping and watch as you sway a little like a drunk and then almost run, maybe on tippytoes, towards the warm embrace that awaits you on the other side of the room. I clap and cheer, full of joy. My tears hover on the surface, overcome by the emotion of the moment. I would be so, so proud of you. You are off! And then you take maybe four or five wobbly steps before you are scooped into a safe pair of arms and lifted high! I think about this incredible skill that will stand you in good stead for your whole life, the start of your adventures. I think about your chubby little feet that will carry you far and wide and I want you to know that if I had my way, I would always be by your side, ready to catch you if ever you should fall.

THREE

Lucy could only breathe with her mouth open and she did so with her eyes closed, trying to block out where she was and why she was there. She didn't care how it looked to the other patients or their visitors or indeed the numerous medics who hurried across the shiny floor with clipboards resting on their forearms and fixed half-smiles of reassurance and regret. She figured it was far better to sit propped up in this exposed bed in this very public day ward with her mouth open, keeping as calm as she possibly could, rather than have to explain that if she breathed through her nose, she could smell the iron-laden scent of her loss. It was especially strong to her, the earthy, blood-tinged odour of her baby leaving her body, as it wafted upwards. She knew that one strong inhalation might be all it took to push her over the edge.

. . . about the size of a small chicken's egg . . . It will now weigh up to fourteen grams.

That might be true, but this baby was not as tough nor nearly as sturdy as she had thought.

I am so sorry that I couldn't take better care of you. I'm sorry that I couldn't keep you. I wanted to, more than you will ever know.

Jonah was talking. She turned to face him and took in snippets of his speech, allowing the odd word to permeate her own thoughts, liking the comfort of his warm tone, but at the same time praying for silence.

He sat forward on the blue plastic chair and, with her one drip-free arm dangling down, he thumbed the skin on the back of her hand as he spoke: '. . . that's what the sonographer said, sometimes there is no good reason. It just happens . . . We can try again . . . when you are ready . . . no hurry . . . just a little procedure, you won't feel a thing, that's what the doctor said . . . then I can take you home . . .'

She screwed her eyes more tightly shut and pictured the little girl who lived inside her mind.

I'm sorry, darling. I am so sorry.

◆ ◆ ◆

They were right; the procedure was strangely mundane. She was left with a feeling not dissimilar to period pain that a couple of co-codamol tablets almost instantly diluted, and when the pain had gone she wished for it to return, deciding that it was better to feel something. With her pyjamas nestling in the bottom of a plastic bag, along with a leaflet on what to do when she got home, Lucy sat in the front seat of the car wearing the jeans Jonah had packed in haste. She watched as he clenched and unclenched his fists on the steering wheel and sighed and exhaled repeatedly, trying to expel whatever lurked inside.

It was a feeling new to her, this awkwardness and the accompanying silence. As a couple they chattered aimlessly for hours about anything and everything, sharing their inner monologue and humming at will; their noisy interaction provided the background music to their lives. This cloak of quiet dampened their already dented spirits. This mute withdrawal was in itself enough to make her feel sad.

Lucy stared out of the window as dusk fell on the houses en route. When the traffic slowed, she gazed into windows and glimpsed the evidence of family life. She saw pink bunting strung up in bedrooms where little girls would lie under princess-inspired canopies. Tricycles that lay abandoned in front porches, and trampolines with high safety nets taking up too much of the garden, left idle for the night. And then a dad, pushing open a gate, holding the hand of his small curly-haired son, as they wearily trod the path towards home.

Lucky. Lucky people. Why couldn't that be me?

'Are you okay?' Jonah asked for the millionth time that day, as the engine purred at the traffic lights. And for the millionth time she could only nod her response, anaesthetised by the shock of what had happened, still trying to comprehend that this morning she had woken up pregnant and now, as she travelled home, she was not.

How can that be? What did I do wrong?

Jonah helped her from the car, despite her protestations that she could manage. He opened the front door and flipped on the hall light and then, one by one, the three lamps in the sitting room. Yet no amount of lamplight could help tonight. The house seemed to have lost some of its magic, as if in their absence it had dulled the mirrors, kept the corners dark and the air a little too warm in respect of what had passed. And she was grateful that the atmosphere reflected her sorrow.

'Are you okay?' he asked again, and she swallowed the instinct to snap; he was, after all, only being kind. Lucy reminded herself that he didn't know what to say, just as she didn't know what to do.

She nodded.

'How about a cup of tea?' He rubbed his hands together and headed for the kitchen. Both were glad of the distraction of the task for very different reasons.

Lucy dumped the plastic bag on the sitting room floor and made her way to the sofa. She sat back on the soft cushions and kicked off her trainers, staring at the ashes in the hearth. On the cushion next to her sat her baby book, cast aside with the corners of its pages folded over so she wouldn't lose her place. But she *had* lost her place and was now no longer in the queue for motherhood. It felt like being sent back to the starting line just as she got on to the home straight. She opened the book and scanned the index, turning to the page where she read:

Miscarriages are quite common in the first three months of pregnancy. Around one in five confirmed pregnancies sadly ends this way. The reasons for miscarriage are many and varied. Early miscarriages (up to ten weeks) can happen because there is something wrong with the baby, such as a chromosomal abnormality, or it could be due to other medical problems. A miscarriage in the first few weeks can often feel like a period, with spotting or bleeding and mild cramps or backache. This can progress to heavy bleeding, with blood clots and quite severe cramping pains.

'What's that you're reading?' he interrupted her. 'Shall we put this away?' he asked, making the question redundant and treating her like a child as he reached down and took the book from her grasp. He placed it on the bookshelf, hiding it behind a row of books on the French Revolution. He placed her tea on a coaster on the table by her side.

'Thank you.' She gave a weak smile, her voice still croaky from lack of use. As Jonah sat on the seat beside her, she picked up her knitting and positioned her hands, looping the wool around her fingers and scanning the pattern, continuing to click the needles and wind the wool.

'What are you doing, darling?' he asked with a catch to his voice.

Lucy looked up at him, as if it were odd that he was asking the question. 'My knitting. It's not finished.' She held up the lacy matinee jacket for him to see.

'You don't have to finish it, Lucy.' He spoke softly. 'It doesn't matter.'

'Of course I do. It does matter.' She looked at him quizzically, as if the suggestion were ridiculous. She fixed her eyes on the wool and carried on. 'I'm sorry you missed your training thing at work.' She never lifted her eyes from her task.

'It's not important. Nothing is as important as being here for you when you need me.' He placed his arm along the back of the sofa, resting it on her shoulders in a loose hug.

'Thank you.' She smiled, briefly.

'Are you—'

'Please don't ask me if I'm okay.' She cut him short, pausing from her craft and speaking with a little more of an edge than she had intended.

There was a beat of silence while she stilled her needles and stared at the floor.

'I'm sorry, Lucy. I guess I don't know what to say to you. I feel useless. I want to make it better, but I don't know how,' he confessed.

'You don't have to say anything. Nothing at all,' she stated, calmly. 'But it's nice to have you here by my side while I get this finished.' And just like that, she once again found the rhythm and began to knit.

'Okay, then.' Jonah nodded and stretched his legs out in front of him, as if settling in for the evening at the end of any ordinary day.

It was only minutes later that Lucy noticed the slight slump to his posture and the way his head tipped back in a doze.

She worked industriously, as the evening slipped into the night, feeling the ache to her bones and grit beneath her eyelids. It was a little after midnight that she slipped the left needle into the front of the first stitch, inserting it from left to right. She then pulled the first stitch over the top of the second stitch, and using her left needle she worked her way along the hem, finishing off.

Sitting back with a tired sigh, an aching back and a cramp in her fingers, she laid the little garment on her lap and ran her fingers over the delicate matinee coat, pleased with her work. It still needed the ribbon threading through the bodice and the three little white buttons attaching at the top, but that could wait; there was no rush, not now. Lifting it gently, she laid it on her arm and raised it to her face, imagining the tiny newborn that might dwell inside it smiling back.

Slowly, without disturbing her husband, she stood and carried the knitted coat in her palms, up the stairs and into their bedroom. Reaching up to the top of the wardrobe, she pulled down the wicker and leather hamper. Carefully, she laid the coat on the bed and placed the hamper on the duvet next to it. She loosened and released the leather straps from their brass buckles and smiled as the lid opened with a creak. Inside she had taken the trouble of lining the base with crisp white tissue paper, which she now opened, and in the centre she gently laid the little knitted item, carefully covering it in an envelope of white tissue before fastening the leather hamper straps and reaching up to put the basket back on top of the wardrobe.

She placed her hand on her stomach. Her body was having difficulty catching up with proceedings. She felt the shock wave of nausea as she stood up straight, and her boobs were still a little tender. She swallowed as she approached the bed and clicked on the bedside lamp. It was as she pulled back the duvet that her head spun, her legs buckled and her breath caught in her throat.

There, in a large, butterfly-shaped stain, were the rusty remains of her loss.

'Jonah!' She screamed out his name. 'Jonah!' she cried again, louder this time, as she sank down on to the mattress, burying her face in her pillow as she howled. Her grief filled her up and took her over. Her body coiled against the once red mark, now brown and nothing more than a darkened crust against her skin as she wept.

She heard his footsteps thunder up the stairs and then in an instant his arms were around her, holding her tightly as she wept.

'I wanted my baby so badly!' she cried. 'I wanted her with me!'

'I know. I know my love.' He held her close to his body, rocking her, as if this might help.

'I don't know what I did wrong, Jonah.' Her words came in short bursts, struggling to get out between her breaths, fractured with sobs. 'I took my folic acid, I napped, I ate right, I did it all, I did everything it said in my book, but I lost her anyway. I'm sorry, Jonah . . .' She sobbed until speech was impossible and all she could do was lean into him and close her eyes.

'You don't ever have to apologise. You did nothing wrong, my darling, nothing. And we will try again – when you are ready we will try again and the next time it will all be fine. We have to put it behind us and carry on. We've got each other and that's all that matters right now. I love you, Lucy. I love you so much.'

Lucy gripped his shirt with both hands, her fingers trembling, as if afraid to let go.

Three days later they sat at the breakfast table in the kitchen, both dressed for work and munching on wholewheat toast, hers smeared with marmalade and his dripping with butter and jam, and both sipping tea. The rain lashed the French doors and a neighbour's dog howled in protest at something or other.

'Are you sure about this?' Jonah asked again. 'Because there is no rush. You must take the time you need.'

'Yes! I shall be fine. I am fine. But I *won't* be if you confine me to barracks for another day. I might possibly go nuts, so let me get back to work and carry on with my life. The sooner I can do that, the sooner I can get back to normal.'

'You know, don't you, that if you don't feel up to it at work or you change your mind, you can just call me and—'

'And you will come and rescue me. I know. You have already said.' She bit her toast and blinked slowly.

'I'm fussing,' he admitted, as he placed his empty mug in the rattling dishwasher, 'but that's my job, to fuss over you, in case you had forgotten.'

'I had not forgotten.' She took a gulp of her tea. 'And I love you for it.'

He gave her a quick kiss before dashing to clean his teeth in the downstairs shower room that lurked under the stairs.

Lucy laid the remainder of the toast on her plate and closed her eyes, leaning on the breakfast bar to stop the tremor in her hands, as she breathed deeply.

You can do this, Lucy. You'll be okay . . .

Mercifully the rain had stopped by the time she hovered on the platform at the train station. Her eyes drifted to the billboard in front of her. It carried an advertisement for baby formula with a big blue-eyed baby staring down at her. She looked away and straight at the news stand, where every other magazine featured a young, beautifully coiffed celebrity beaming into the lens as they held up their precious bundle for the world to see. It might have been her imagination or a new sensitivity to the topic, but it sure felt as if every advertisement, every newspaper, every programme and every song featured babies. She saw an incredibly high percentage of pregnant women, and nearly every other person on the street seemed to be pushing a buggy. It was all she could do not to scream or turn on her heel and run back down Salusbury Road, all the way home.

Tansy was her first visitor of the day. She walked into her office and closed the door behind her, launching without preamble into her line of questioning.

'It's not like you to have a couple of days off; in fact, in the six years that I have known you, I've never known you to have one day off. I told everyone it must be the bubonic plague or a lottery win. They are the only two things I could think of that would keep you off work.'

'You got me!' Lucy held her hands up in submission. 'I got the bubonic plague and then with my lottery win used the money to fund a cure. Hence my two days out of circulation.' She concentrated on opening her email, flinching at the hundreds of messages that had accumulated in her short absence and feeling a stab of guilt, wondering how this feeling might be magnified were she to be off on maternity leave.

'Well, it's good to see you back. Benedict said to me the other day how he would love to see his godparents, and I said, "What a coincidence! Because Daddy and I would like to see them too." And so I figured you guys need to come over for supper and kill two birds with one stone. How does that sound?'

Lucy looked up at the expectant face of her friend, who rarely asked anything of her. 'Sounds like a plan, and how amazing that he is talking so well!' she managed, ignoring the throb in her stomach and groin where her body continued to try to fathom what had occurred.

'Well, okay, I admit he's still not talking, but I can tell you that if he was, that is most definitely what he would be asking.' She grinned as she made her way back to her desk, her parting words, 'Good to have you back, by the way.'

Lucy felt the need to visit the bathroom, where she hastily removed the evidence of her miscarriage that continued to come from her and popped it in the sanitary bin, trying not to look at the tiny stains. Reminders. All that was left of her dreams of motherhood.

◆ ◆ ◆

The next couple of weeks were hard. Lucy felt torn. In some ways it was a blessing not to have told the world that she was pregnant; it meant she avoided the embarrassment of having to set people straight when they asked how she was doing in that knowing way, sparing them both the ordeal. But at the same time, not having the support of those who loved her to help her through her loss left her feeling isolated. She spent a chunk of her working day secretly looking at thousands of threads online written by women who were in similar situations, and it helped a little. There were of course the odd one or two comments that left her reeling and confused; one was from MsNinjaZx6R: 'It's only like a heavy period, a bunch of cells. Get over it! Talk to someone who has lost a child; now, *that's* hard.'

She sat on the train that night with her bag clutched against her chest and her mind whirring. Maybe MsNinjaZx6R was right; was she overreacting? How could she be grieving for 'a bunch of cells'? But she was, and that grief was real. As she strolled the length of Salusbury Road, smiling nonchalantly at the mums pushing their buggies or clutching the hands of their toddlers, she felt her resolve weaken, her armour loosen and her smile fade. By the time she arrived home, without the will to search in her purse for her key, she rapped with weary knuckles, waiting to be let in. Jonah answered the door. And there she stood, aware of her mascara-laden tears running in thick streaks down her face, leaving a sticky, dark smear across the back of her palm; her nose and throat were clogged with distress and her heart and womb pulsed with longing.

'Oh, my Lucy!'

He stepped forward and pulled her towards him, shutting the door behind her, as she cried into his chest. 'I wanted our baby, so . . . so badly,' she managed.

'I know, and it will happen for us, darling, it will. Just you wait and see,' he whispered. 'I promise.'

Again she clung to him, wanting so desperately to believe him.

I like to imagine all the pictures and cards that you would have made at nursery school. I know that our kitchen cupboards and walls could only benefit from being covered in things that you had made and designed. It would bring me joy every time I looked at them. Oh! To see your little handprints smeared across a page in red or blue paint and to be able to frame the first Christmas card you made! I think that would be the most wonderful thing. I picture a badly drawn Christmas tree, coloured in with sparkles and glitter all over it. I bet you would love to get your hands covered in glue and pom-poms and bits of macaroni, and I think it's these pictures, these glorious creations, that turn any house into a home, don't you? And that's a house I have always wanted to live in.

FOUR

Lucy learned to move on; at least, that was the face she presented to the outside world. It wasn't that she hid her feelings from Jonah as such, but she was certainly aware of presenting an outer persona that was often stronger than she felt, as if this was the person he expected her to be. When in the house alone, she did on occasion pull the baby book from behind its French Revolution barricade and flip to the page where she would be, if nature hadn't played its cruellest trick on her.

She held the open book to her face and read.

> At week thirteen, were you able to see your baby you would probably recognise it as a baby. It has nails on the ends of its fingers and toes and can move its neck and head. It is approximately the size of a large clementine and can open and close its mouth.

'Wow!' she spoke aloud. 'Little nails on the ends of your fingers, imagine that!' She ran her hand over her flat stomach before reading on.

> At week fourteen your baby is now moving around a lot. It is 8–9 cm in length. If it's a boy, his penis will

be visible on a scan.

Lucy closed the book and popped it back in its hiding place, just as the phone rang.

'Lucy, hi. Fay and I were thinking of coming to town on Saturday for a bit of a stroll and a spot of shopping – are you around for an early supper?' Her mum's tone was, as ever, a little clipped, impatient, as if there were somewhere else she needed to be or something else she needed to do and this call was a complete but necessary inconvenience.

Like her mother, her sister, Fay, younger than her by three years, loved to shop. It was a total mystery to Lucy, who could find no joy in ambling along crowded pavements or scooting around sanitised malls with a desire to buy stuff, any stuff. For her, shopping was an unpleasant necessity and it had to be done fast, like ripping off a plaster or getting a jab. Food, bar the odd special item, was largely delivered. Clothes were selected from websites and bought with an impatient click, and furniture was sourced and then bought online. The very word 'stroll' made her shudder. Who had time to 'stroll'?

'It would be lovely to see you both. Why don't you come here?' she suggested, a little reluctantly.

'Will Jonah cook?' her mum asked nervously.

'Yes,' she laughed, 'don't worry, I won't.'

'Thank goodness for that.' Her mum gave an exaggerated sigh. 'I'm still reeling over your chicken Kiev. Honestly, I don't think I've been the same since.'

'Please don't drag that up again.'

'That's easy to ask, Lucy, but I shan't ever forget it. It's still a mystery to me how you managed to get the outside charred and keep the middle still frozen. Oh God, I'm feeling queasy just thinking about it.' Her mum's voice trailed off. Lucy pictured her in the hallway with her hand at her throat, trying to quash the urge to be sick. She suppressed her wicked desire to laugh at the image.

'Well, don't think about it then. And at least I tried.' She recalled how everyone around the table had gone silent, including her new husband, each wondering how to broach the subject that was going to wipe the very satisfied smile of accomplishment from her face.

'Can I bring anything? A cookbook? A takeaway?' Her mum still found it hard to believe that she could do anything without her assisting in some way, without interfering or suggesting a better way of doing things.

'Very funny. Nope. Just yourselves.' She spoke with a false brightness.

'See you Saturday then.' Her mum ended the call abruptly.

◆ ◆ ◆

The sound of Jonah's key in the door made her smile. She swallowed the strawberry laces she snacked on illegally before supper and pulled a cold beer from the fridge, popping the lid before meeting him in the hallway.

'Well, this is the kind of welcome I could get used to.' He shrugged off his jacket and hung it on the newel post before taking the beer bottle into his hand and crushing her to him with his free arm. Lucy reached up for a kiss, and within seconds this kiss had bloomed into something more. They leant against the banister, kissing like teens. It was lovely, unexpected, carefree and cathartic. It had been weeks since they had slept together – her fragility and their joint loss had been a gatekeeper for anything more – but here in this instant, as he held her close, it felt like the most natural thing in the world. Jonah paused from kissing her and tentatively took her hand, leading her up the stairs to their bedroom. She avoided looking at the wicker hamper on top of the wardrobe as he lay her down and they slowly began the process of reconnecting.

Lucy lay with her head on his chest while he twirled her long hair between his fingers.

'How was your day?' he asked.

'Well, it's got a lot better since you came home.' She smiled against him.

'Mine too!' He laughed. 'But I meant at work.'

'Good, busy, the usual. We are all frantically working on this pitch for the green energy company. It's interesting.'

'I do hope you get it.' He kissed her.

'Me too. Oh and Mum called, she and Fay are popping in on Saturday for an early supper. I said you'd cook.'

'Great idea – can you give me your recipe for those chicken Kiev ice lollies that you made the last time they came to eat?'

'Don't you start! I've had my mum reminding me about that already. Sheesh, a girl makes one mistake! She turns it into a joke but I know she is genuinely worried about me cooking.'

'Yes, but it was a pretty memorable mistake.' He laughed, wrapping her in his arms and rolling her on top of him. 'Luckily I didn't marry you for your cooking skills.'

'Funny, because that's the exact reason I married you.'

'I thought it was because you found me irresistible.'

'No, it was because I thought, now this looks like a man who can whip up a mean grilled cheese sandwich.'

'And you were right.' He kissed her before pulling away. 'You seem a bit . . .' He looked up to the ceiling, clearly searching for the best word.

'Better?' she volunteered.

'Yes.' He held her gaze. 'Better.'

They were silent for a second or two before Jonah spoke. 'You don't have to be brave all the time, you know. You can tell me how you are feeling and I will try to make it better if I can.'

'I know.' She smiled, declining the subtle offer to open up to him. It was hard for her to explain how she handled things best: by keeping a lid on certain aspects. She had trained herself to be this way, living alone and being single for long periods.

'I spoke to Geneviève today.' He shifted his position until they were lying facing each other across the mattress, as if this topic required a more remote stance. Reaching out, he continued to run the ends of her long hair through his fingers.

'Is she okay?' Lucy pictured the woman she had only seen in photographs, the petite blonde with the deep tan, pixie crop and slightly aggressive stance.

'She's having a bit of a tough time with Camille. I told her it's probably normal teenage rebellion, which she took as an excuse to remind me how fortunate I was to be able to diagnose this from afar and not actually have to suffer the slamming of doors and open hostility that she's been subjected to.' He tsk-tsked.

'It must be tricky. I was never a door slammer, and I think my only act of rebellion was to sneak sweets before bedtime – that was, until I became a teen, and then I really went off the rails.'

'Sour strawberry laces by any chance?' He laughed.

'If they were available, yes.' She nodded, swallowing and trying to refocus her attention on the present. 'I think you are right, though; it's probably normal and healthy that Camille shows a bit of rebellion – all part of testing the boundaries. Fay was a right handful, really put my mum through the mill, and she levelled out pretty quickly once she'd left home.' She pictured her lookalike little sister, a great mum and a good teacher, happily married to another teacher, Adam.

'I'd like to see Camille more, I really would,' he mused. 'And it gets me that Geneviève has a go at me about not being there when I would love nothing more than to be involved in her everyday life. But she just doesn't see that.'

'I've already told you to get her over here. I'd really like to meet her! It's weird for me that I haven't.'

'It's weird for me too, but it's just kind of how it is. She has her life in France, school, friends, and her mum and Jean-Luc, and I have always been this shadowy figure on the outside. I feel more like an uncle sometimes, except when Geneviève can't find anyone else to scream at and then of course she calls me.' He looked skyward.

'It must be strange that you've never lived with Camille, not properly,' she thought aloud.

'It is odd to the outside world, but it made perfect sense for us. By the time she was born, Gen and I were divorced and she was already seeing Jean-Luc. To ask for anything more made me feel like I was imposing on their new life, messing things up, or certainly making it more complicated than any of us could cope with.' He took a deep breath. 'And if I'm being honest, it suited me.' He looked down at the mattress. 'I don't think I've told anyone that before. Don't get me wrong, I love her, I do, but I was able to carry on with my life, working hard to get the business established, and not having a small child in tow made it easier. Sometimes I don't feel like I really know her and that makes me sad. I worry sometimes that it might be too late to properly rectify that. I don't want her to be a stranger.'

'Well, only seeing someone once a year for the odd week of the holidays doesn't give you enough time to get to know someone; it's like starting from scratch every time, and that's not your fault. But what would be your fault was if you didn't try to put it right. It's not too late to get to know her better. It really isn't.'

'I guess.' He swallowed.

Neither voiced the fact that Camille had declined to come for her regular visit earlier in the year. She had mumbled some vague excuse about an assignment for school and keeping her friend Alice company. It all sounded rather ambiguous and had made Lucy feel horrible, as if her presence meant that Jonah had to miss out on this precious event. Not that Camille had been this explicit, and Lucy didn't want to suggest it in case she were wide of the mark, but nonetheless this was how she felt.

'It was hard to know what to say to Geneviève earlier, though I hate arguing with her, and it feels like for every suggestion I make she has this acid-tongued rebuttal lying in wait.'

'That's a shame.'

'It is. We had this amazing courtship, she was such great fun, and it saddens me how quickly it all faded to dust after our marriage. When I talk to her, I always feel like she's a woman on the edge.'

'Maybe she's unhappy?' she suggested.

'Yes. Maybe.'

'Well, I've said what I think. You should definitely invite Camille over to stay again. I can give the spare room a quick tidy, remove all those boxes of clutter—'

'Erm, hardly clutter, my precious collection of comics and vinyl,' he pointed out.

She ignored his justification. 'It'd be a lovely chance for me to get to know her, for you to spend some quality time with her, and it would give her mum the break she says she needs.'

'I actually think things would be easier between Camille and me because you are here – less pressure to think of what to say or how to act. It'd be so much better with the three of us together. I've often wished there had been an interpreter present, having never been a teenage girl myself.' He smiled.

'The summer holidays are coming up, in a few months; that might work?'

'Yes, she gets a long break – nine weeks, I think.'

'Perfect, then. She would be more than welcome to come here,' Lucy confirmed.

'I didn't want to suggest it, not with everything that's been happening.' He again averted his eyes.

'Don't be silly. It's fine, Jonah. She's your daughter.' She dug deep to find a smile that might mask the hurt at having to again confront the fact that he was a parent and she was not. She ignored the punch of envy to her gut, knowing it was misplaced.

'Let's have a think about it,' he concluded, reaching out for her and pulling her towards him, clearly now thinking about something else entirely.

◆　◆　◆

The house was calm in the lull of a Saturday afternoon, as if the bricks and mortar knew there was no need to rush, not today. There were no trains to dash for, no deadlines to make and, unlike the working week-days, they were not on a timer.

The sound system jumped between the two playlists and, as always, it made her chuckle. Her love of eighties pop, interspersed with Jonah's favoured soft rock, meant that they switched from Depeche Mode to Bon Jovi in a blink. He beamed as she sang along, clearly delighted that she had, after a year of forced indoctrination, picked up at least some of the lyrics.

'They're here!' she called over her shoulder up the hallway, towards the kitchen where Jonah chopped peppers and onions and stirred his homemade passata which had been bubbling for a while.

She opened the door to Fay, who inhaled the rich, garlicky aroma. 'Oh, thank God! Jonah is cooking. Amen!' She kissed her sister on the cheek.

'Lovely to see you too.' Lucy smiled, as her sister swept past.

'Hello, dear,' her mum called.

Lucy felt a little winded at the sight of her mum walking up the path with Fay's one-year-old daughter on her hip. She hadn't realised that Maisie was coming too. Not that it wasn't lovely to see her, the little darling; it was. But the way her stomach folded with longing that felt a lot like hunger took her quite by surprise.

'Take her, please. I need to visit the bathroom.'

Jan unceremoniously thrust Maisie into her arms and made a dash along the hallway. 'Hey, Jonah!' her mum offered quite warmly. 'I shan't be a mo; get ready for my greeting hug,' she called, before closing the cloakroom door behind her.

Maisie gave a dribbly smile and reached up to grab a fistful of Lucy's hair, wrapping it around her chubby fingers. 'Mama,' she cooed, before laying her head on Lucy's chest and settling in for a hug. To be addressed by that word was so beautiful it took her breath away. Lowering her face towards her niece's scalp, she inhaled the scent of childhood, a glorious mixture of baby powder and sweetness. 'Thank you, Maisie,' she whispered. 'Where's Rory?' she called out to her sister.

'He's having a daddy day. Adam was delighted, let me tell you. I wish I had snapped a picture of his face when I told him the girls were having a day shopping and he was looking after Rory. I could tell that up until that point he could see nothing ahead but a golf course and a few beers at the nineteenth hole.'

'Poor Adam!' Jonah voiced his brotherly support.

'Poor Adam? They are *our* children, Jonah. Don't make me give you the same lecture I gave him – when's my day off to play bloody golf?' Fay yelled.

'I concede!' Jonah waved his wooden spoon in the air.

'Not that I play golf, but you get my point.' Fay opened the fridge in search of wine.

As Fay chatted to Jonah, making him laugh with tales of how she had nearly lost her mum in the vast Westfield shopping mall, Lucy walked up and down in the hallway, rocking the little girl gently from side to side, marvelling at the beautiful abandon with which Maisie edged towards sleep. The act of trust was implicit, as if Maisie sensed she would not let her fall.

'I've got you,' she whispered into her scalp.

As Maisie grew heavier in her arms, her full weight sinking against her and her body drifting deeper into slumber, the skin of her bare legs touched against Lucy's arms and reminded her so powerfully of the contact she would never have with the baby she had lost that it rendered her still, while her heart continued to race.

'Look at you!' Fay called, coming up behind her, removing her lightweight jacket and popping it over the newel post. 'You're a natural. Looks like she's nodding off. How marvellous!'

Lucy laid her head against her niece's and walked slowly into the sitting room, where she stood in front of the large, ornate mirror above the fireplace and watched herself rocking back and forth.

I like the way I look holding you, Maisie. I think I look like a mum, a good mum . . .

'Oh dear,' her sister called loudly behind her, 'stay away, Jonah, nothing to see here! But if I had to guess, I'd say someone might be getting broody.'

Lucy looked up as her mum, sister and husband gathered in the doorway. She stared at their faces reflected in the mirror.

'I think there must be something in the water.' Fay sighed. 'Did you hear Davina is due any day, apparently? I got a call from Auntie Joyce; they are beyond excited, already opened a bank account for school fees and drawing up a list of names. Good luck to them, though; you can't blame them for being thrilled. It is such an incredible thing when you have a child, not only for yourself, but it's a wonderful gift for the whole family.'

I know this, Fay! And believe me, I would like nothing more than to bring that gift to you all! I want it more than you know!

Lucy tried to order her thoughts, noting that her sister had felt she couldn't mention Richard when she spoke of Davina, and the way her mother had visibly coloured at the whole topic. It was ridiculous, this awkwardness, quite without foundation; everyone had moved on a long time ago. The omission of her ex in her sister's chat made it an issue when it really wasn't. The fact that they all mentally filled in the gaps with his name elevated him to a point of interest that he had no right to.

'I'm right, you know, you are a natural,' Fay chimed. 'You should seriously start thinking about swapping your fancy career for a few years of good old-fashioned mothering; after all, you aren't getting any younger.' She lifted her glass of wine towards her big sister.

Lucy got the message loud and clear and felt her chest cave with hurt. Her sister's words left her feeling hollow. In her mind it already felt like she was letting everyone down, knowing they would feel at best that she was slow off the mark, and at worst that she was deliberately choosing to remain childless. Which, if she were, would be nothing to do with anyone but her and Jonah. It was as if they had a right to the grandchild or niece or nephew they had been expecting, and the weight of that expectation sat on her shoulders, dragging her further down.

Jonah pushed past them, his expression determined, like a first-aider who has been called into action from the sidelines. He stood by her side. Raising his hand, he stroked Maisie's head before gently resting his palm on his wife's shoulder.

'All in good time,' he whispered, giving her a knowing look.

She did her best to keep her tears at bay, trying not to think that if things had turned out differently, today might well have been the day that she told them of her happy news, that she had indeed decided to have a few years of good old-fashioned mothering.

They were right, after all; she wasn't getting any younger.

There are a couple of lovely schools around here. I tend to slow up as I walk past them on my way to and from the shops and I can't help but beam at the little children who run around the playground like busy wasps. The noise they make collectively is glorious! It's a high-pitched burble of words, suffused with laughter and squeals. I always think that if angels chattered, it would sound something close to this. It's the sound of innocence, the sound of happy. Their little shoes are scuffed and they have the remnants of lunch on their cuffs and collars and splotches of paint and glue on their shirts. Even now, I envy the mums standing in clusters at the school gate, that disparate group from all four corners of the globe with only one thing in common: that they stand patiently waiting to wrap their hand around the smaller hand of their child and skip them towards home, where a cosy tea waits in a warm kitchen. I picture myself standing and chatting with those mums. 'Oh she's doing really well, she loves books! Takes after me like that, a proper little bookworm . . .' and suddenly, there you are, smiling at me at the day's end, ready to take my hand and let me lead you home.

FIVE

Lucy felt the beginnings of a headache as Tansy banged her palm on the table. 'I am *not* being deliberately difficult and I refute the suggestion. I think what you need to understand, John, is that pitching is what I do! I have successfully won the JBBD account, which is still our second-biggest grossing client, and the Met diversity campaign.' She counted on her fingers, as she reeled off the details.

'Are we going to have to sit and listen to a complete list of your achievements and accolades, Tansy?' John interrupted. 'Because if that's your intention, it might be quicker if you simply gave us a copy of your CV. I wouldn't want to miss any crucial detail that might clearly indicate your suitability over mine. I mean, did you for example ever get a citizenship award at school or have you run a half-marathon? I would like to take this opportunity to point out that I came second in a Rubik's cube timed assessment when I was fourteen.'

'Very funny.' Tansy glared at her male counterpart across the board-room table, with the twitch of a smile on her lips. John was popular and funny, and in any other circumstances she probably would have been on his side, a friend.

'Okay. Okay.' Lucy sat forward and took a deep breath. 'This isn't getting us anywhere.' She had hoped that by bringing into the board-room the two top candidates to lead on the green energy project, they might be able to discuss the best way to proceed, allocate tasks, identify the first point of contact for the client and get moving. It had, however, quickly deteriorated into this mock gladiatorial display. Both were more than capable of heading up the pitch, and she was acutely aware that she had to bury her favouring of Tansy based purely on the fact that they were friends outside of the workplace, even though having her on the pitch would make the long hours and lengthy rail and car journeys travelling to and from meetings so much more bearable.

'We are getting quite close to the first deliverable; it's mid-May already.'

'Yes, thank you, John. I'm aware of the date.' Lucy gave him a small smile. This was actually a lie; she hadn't been aware of the date, not at all. 'Let's take a break for lunch, I'll give it some thought and then we can come back in here in an hour and decide how we go forward.' She closed her laptop and reached for her handbag.

'But . . .' Tansy pulled a face of irritation, fumbling for words, as Lucy left the room.

Mid-May, mid-May! The words rattled around her brain as she swept down the stairs and out into the bustling crowds on Victoria Street, where workers and tourists filled the pavement, some clutching small brown paper bags that contained their lunch, eager to get back to their desks, and others holding cameras aloft. Each group travelled at a quite different pace, proving an irritation to the other. Lucy didn't seem to notice; with a spring in her step she tripped up and down the kerb, dodging crowds and keeping a determination to her stride that meant idlers made way for her in the throng. She paused as she entered the store, pulled a basket from the stack by the front door, and closed her eyes briefly.

April the seventh, so add on seven days, April fourteenth, April twenty-first, twenty-eighth, May the fifth, twelfth, nineteenth, and now twenty-second . . . makes it six and a half weeks since my last period.

Her heart skipped as she did the maths, stepping forward into the aisles, her eyes searching for what she was looking for.

◆　◆　◆

It wasn't that they had planned to try, far from it; they had simply neglected to be overly careful, trusting Mother Nature to do what she thought best. They had been told that it might be a while before her cycle regulated itself, and she had thought any lack of menstruation might be down to that. It had felt like a relief not to make the decision and go with the flow, as it were, but now, with the pregnancy testing kit safely ensconced inside her handbag as she made her way back towards the office, Lucy was beyond excited.

She was also delighted that the bathroom at work was empty. She locked the cubicle door and hung her bag from the hook on the wall before trying, as silently as possible, to peel the cellophane from the packet. Her fingers twitched in anticipation as she opened the box and ripped impatiently at the foil-wrapped spatula with her teeth. Holding the white plastic stick above the toilet bowl, she closed her eyes, not daring to think about the possibilities.

Calm down. Take a breath.

'Lucy? Are you still in here?' Tansy's voice bounced off the tiled walls. 'I saw you walk in; I was waving across the foyer, but I don't think you saw me.' She sounded a little put out.

'Good God, Tansy. Can't I have five minutes' peace?' She extricated the little stick and balanced it on the tissue dispenser.

'Sure, I just wanted to say—'

'Tansy! Honestly, I should be able to use the bathroom without being harassed by you.' She laughed, in spite of her frustration. 'Please go away!'

'Okay. Shall I come back in five minutes?' her friend pushed.

'No! Don't come back in five minutes. I'll see you back in the boardroom as we agreed, sheesh!'

'Was that a "sheesh, I am going to make you lead on this project" or a "sheesh, I'm giving it to the inexperienced, youthful John who has a horrible habit of running his tongue up around his gums, hoping he might find a snack"?'

'It's "sheesh, go away, Tansy!"' She shook her head and placed her elbows on her knees and her head in her hands, looking up only when she heard the bathroom door close.

It was hard to monitor how long she had waited, but she figured it was long enough by the time she had restored her clothing, flushed the loo and gathered the stick into her sweating palms.

Lucy squinted at the pregnancy test, holding it up to her face to confirm what she thought she saw in the little results window.

Pregnant 3+

She read it again. *3+*

And again. *3+*

3+

This meant that she was more than three weeks pregnant!

Closing her eyes, she silently pogoed up and down inside the cubicle holding the test to her chest.

Taking a minute to compose herself, Lucy washed her hands thoroughly and practised her neutral expression in the mirror, which was difficult. A wide grin kept splitting her face, which instantly caused her tears to prick. She coughed and opened the bathroom door, ready to face the world.

'Or maybe we could share the role.'

'God, you made me jump!' She darted back as her friend continued to hassle her, having only managed to make it to the corridor by the bathroom door – hardly the space Lucy had been hoping for.

'Yes! That's a brilliant idea. Share the role.' She nodded. 'Decide between yourselves where your strengths lie and lead on those areas. Let me know who's looking after what. Great work, Tansy!'

'Oh, thank you.' Tansy looked a little taken aback, as if she had fully expected her suggestion to be rebuffed. 'Where are you going now?'

Lucy looked back over her shoulder as she hitched her handbag on to her arm and made for the stairs. 'I need to see Jonah; shan't be too long.'

'Is everything okay? Please tell me it's not a resurgence of the bubonic plague?' her friend called across the rapidly filling reception, as elevators disgorged workers, bike couriers and delivery drivers into the open space.

'No! You are quite safe,' she shouted, taking the stairs two at a time.

◆ ◆ ◆

'Jonah Carpenter Motors': the shiny chrome letters seemed to twinkle in the glint of the sun.

'Hello, Mrs Carpenter.'

'Oh, hi!' Lucy dared not confess that this greeting was one that still threw her a little off balance, as much as it thrilled her. *Mrs Carpenter . . .* She instinctively ran her thumb over the little platinum band on her left hand, smiling at the smartly dressed, bubbly girl on reception. 'Is Jonah free? If he's busy, please don't disturb him,' she gabbled, suddenly feeling a little self-conscious about turning up at his workplace. 'I was passing, so . . .'

'He's on a conference call right now, but will be done in about five minutes. Can I get you a drink or anything while you wait?'

'No, but thank you. I'll just sit here, if that's okay?' She pointed at the ultra-stylised black leather couch that sat behind a chrome and smoked-glass table.

'Sure.' The girl nodded and turned her attention to her computer screen.

In front of Lucy on the table sat two iPads, each with a gallery of stunning photographs of the cars at the three garages across London. She picked one up and let her finger scroll right to left. Even she had to admit the close-up pictures of hand-stitched scarlet leather, chrome accelerators and a brushed aluminium gearstick made her want to grab a ride in one of these sleek high-priced machines. She placed the iPad back in its place and let her eyes rove the spotless showroom. The white floors were polished to a high shine, the picture windows were immaculate and there wasn't a speck of dust to be seen. That 'new car' smell hung tantalisingly in the air. The streamlined vehicles themselves shone under a myriad of spotlights and uplighters with neon strips glowing from the floor. It made the place feel space-age, and it was a million miles from the cluttered soft wooden surfaces and wonkily fitted drawers of their home.

Lucy looked up and there he was, walking towards her across the showroom in his navy suit and open-necked white shirt. His expression carried a worried little crease between his eyebrows. It was unusual for her to turn up at his workplace.

'Everything okay?' he asked as he approached. He placed his hands on her shoulders, as if she might be in need of this instant physical comfort.

She felt a jolt of love in her gut for this handsome man. She nodded quickly. 'Everything's fine. I just wanted a quick word.' She eyed the receptionist and the slick-looking young sales duo, who were busy tapping into keyboards at their desks in the corner.

'Of course.' Gripping her hand, he trailed her behind him until they were safely in the confines of his office, where he pulled the cord until the venetian blinds obscured them.

'This is a lovely surprise.' He smiled at her, before kissing her on the mouth.

Lucy pulled away. 'Jonah.'

'What?' He looked concerned.

'I'm pregnant.'

'What?'

'I'm pregnant.' She smiled, speaking a little more slowly this time.

'No!' He gasped.

'Yes!' she squeaked.

He pulled her towards him. 'Oh, Lucy!' He held her close. 'You haven't said anything. I didn't know whether to bring it up, or what to ask . . .'

'I didn't know what to say!' She laughed. 'And it honestly didn't occur to me that I might be, not really. I've had a couple of periods since, you know.' She shook her head, not wanting to sully the moment. 'And then nothing, and I thought that was my body resetting itself, and then this morning I was in a meeting with John and Tansy and we were talking about the date and it fired something inside me. I realised it had been a while since my last period and here we are!' She bit her lip.

'Are you sure?' He searched her face, needing confirmation.

She shrugged free of his embrace and rummaged in her handbag, locating the plastic spatula; she held it up towards his face. Jonah pulled his head back on his shoulders and narrowed his eyes, which, after a second or two, misted. He cupped his palm over his mouth and nose.

'Yes!' She beamed. 'I'm absolutely sure.'

'Oh God, Lucy. I knew it. I knew that we'd crack it.' He again pulled her towards him in a tender hug, as if she were already in an advanced state and needed careful handling. 'Clever girl.' He kissed her head.

'Clever us,' she corrected.

She felt him exhale against her body. 'We can put what happened behind us and enjoy this.'

She nodded against his chest. 'Yes, we can.'

'How do you feel?' he asked.

'I feel great! Really great, excited, bit nervous,' she confessed.

'No, don't be. These things just happen, that's what the doctor said, and he said that there was no reason why we couldn't try again when we were ready – and here we are, ready!'

'More than ready. I'm really excited!' She squealed with her fists clenched.

'Me too. We'll have to celebrate tonight. I love you, Mrs Carpenter.'

'I love you too.'

'You are going to be a mum!' He beamed.

'I am.' She closed her eyes, relief and joy washing over her. 'I'm going to be a great mum.'

Later that night, Lucy was nestled on the sofa when she heard the sound of Jonah's key in the door.

'Where are you?' he called out, crashing and bashing his way through the front door. By the sound of it, he was laden with bags. This meant a nice supper, and her mouth watered at the prospect.

'Ah, and we have some decent music playing!' He chuckled as Def Leppard's 'Pour Some Sugar on Me' blared from the sound system.

'Not intentionally.' She laughed. 'It's that blasted shuffle system. If I had my way, there would only be my tunes on it.'

She smiled at the sound of Jonah dumping the groceries in the kitchen before he poked his head around the door. 'How's my girl?'

'I'm good.' She sighed, resting her busy hands in her lap.

'And she's off already! What are you making?' He knelt on the floor by her feet, letting the soft strands of white wool slip through his fingers.

Reaching for the pattern, she abandoned the needles. 'Look at these.' Opening up the page, she held up the image of a pair of delicate booties, fastened with a tiny loop over a pearl button and a matching hat with a little bobble-like blob that sat on the top of it. 'How cute are they?' She wrinkled her nose.

'They are brilliant.' He kissed her nose. 'Feels like we are back on track, doesn't it?' He smiled.

'It really does.'

'So how pregnant are you? How can we tell?' he asked, his face full of excitement.

'I should have an appointment at the hospital in a few weeks; they are giving me an early scan because of everything.' She swallowed, not wanting to dwell on that time, as if this second chance wiped out all the bad. 'They'll give me a date and work out how far I am and everything then.' She shrugged. 'The pregnancy test doesn't go any higher than three weeks plus, but if I had to guess, I think I'm probably about six weeks, so still very early days, but I feel *so* great!' she emphasised. 'I have already had a little glimpse at my baby book, and even at six weeks what's going on is just amazing. The ectoderm is in place, which will form the baby's brain, skin and nerves. And the endoderm, which will become the lungs and liver. And the mesoderm, which will become the baby's bones and muscles.' She sat upright, smiling as if she had passed a test.

Jonah laughed loudly. 'It sounds like you might have accidentally swallowed that textbook.'

'I can't help it.' She leant forward. 'I find the whole thing so fascinating – that at just six weeks all that is already in place and it's still only so teeny!' She held her thumb and forefinger out, showing a very small gap between the two.

There was a moment of quiet while the two looked at each other, letting their new joyous state wash over them.

'I'm going to take really good care of you.' He stood, dusting the knees of his suit trousers.

'You always take good care of me.'

'Yes, but I mean *properly* take care of you. I want to make sure you don't have an ounce of stress or worry and that you can take it easy. Don't suppose you fancy giving up your job, do you?' He closed his eyes and raised one shoulder, cowering away from her, as if preparing to take the force of her response.

'No, I don't. But I will slow down when the baby arrives. I don't want to miss a second, Jonah. I'll take extended leave and enjoy every bit of it.'

'Deal.' Jonah clapped. 'And now I shall make you a delicious supper. How do you like the sound of stuffed ballotine of chicken with fresh asparagus and pomme purée?' he asked, as he left the room.

'Sounds fancy and delicious!' Lucy picked up her needles and resumed knitting.

'Oh, meant to say . . .' He popped his head back around the door frame. 'I spoke to Geneviève today and she is all for Camille coming over for the summer. Not a word of protest. I was amazed.'

His expression told her that this made him happy, and she felt her heart swell at the prospect of welcoming the girl into their home. She so wanted to get it right, picturing day trips with Camille to museums or maybe jaunts out for lunch. This excitement, however, was tinged with sadness; it was rare for Jonah to show his absolute love of being a dad, and at that moment she wanted more than anything to have this baby enriching both of their lives.

He tapped the door frame, as if having a thought. 'Unless of course we should say our plans have changed? I mean, we are in a different position now.' He looked a little concerned.

'No! Of course not. It will be lovely to have her here. I can't wait to meet her. But I do think we need to decorate the spare room, make her feel really welcome, and she can be part of this pregnancy from the outset and that will make her feel more connected to you and the baby.' She rubbed her hand over her tummy. 'A lovely little family.'

'God, how did I get so lucky?' He stared at her.

'I think it was largely down to the fact that we'd both had a little too much wine and everyone else at the christening was taken.' She laughed and turned her attention to the pattern with a feeling of warmth spreading over her. She had almost forgotten how much she loved being pregnant.

I often think about how I would dress you. And to be honest I change my mind a lot! I think when you were little I'd have put you in traditional clothes, all the knitted things that I have made, of course, and some made by my mum and my gran too. I love the idea of cradling you in something that has been touched by the hands of all those generations of women. Then if I think of you as a toddler, I picture you in dungarees with striped T-shirts underneath and cute little bow barrettes in your curly hair. Or sometimes I see you in a really over-the-top party dress with a net petticoat and flowers, the full works. I think you'd hate it, but would look adorable.

I bought you a dress once. It makes me cry to think about that, but I did. I can't really explain why. I was in a department store looking for a bread bin and I found myself in the children's clothes department. The place was crowded with parents and their children, most looking like they wanted to be anywhere else, irritated by the outing. I stopped at a display and saw these tiny little dresses in red and white gingham. They had a beautiful smocked yoke and a dainty Peter Pan collar edged in red ribbon. A woman came over and asked me what size I was looking for. I saw you so clearly that I smiled and said, 'It's for my daughter; she's nearly ten months.' I stood back and watched, as she worked her fingers nimbly through the display, looking for the size I wanted. She called out then to her colleague across the floor, as she held the dress up. 'Do we have this in ten or twelve months for this lady's little girl?' My heart swelled! It was oh so wonderful! That she thought it possible that I could have a child, that I could be a mum! I smiled at her and in her eyes I was just like every other woman in that department at that time. I was someone who had had a baby. And it felt . . . it felt incredible. I paid for the dress they had located, and watched as they wrapped it in tissue, before placing it inside a little bag. I didn't want to bring it home, in case anyone found it, so I carefully laid it on the wall of the car park where I had left my car. I hoped, I still hope, that someone found it and a little girl got to wear it. A little girl like you.

SIX

'Fay, I need your help.' Lucy placed the phone under her chin and stared at the colour swatches, spread into a fanned rainbow on the worktop in the kitchen. It took all of her strength not to blurt out to her sister that she was pregnant, but she knew it was wise to wait until after her first scan, when she could tell the world!

'Oh God, it's not money, is it? Because I can tell you that whatever you in your fancy advertising agency and Mr Porsche are earning, it has to be a darned sight more than Adam and I bring home as teachers.'

'No! It's not money.' She tutted. 'I'm trying to pick out colours for the spare room; I want it to be as nice as possible for Camille, but I'm not very good at this. I have always gone for white walls and bold-coloured accessories, and that works for me, but she's a sixteen-year-old girl and I want it to be pretty and funky and I don't know what sixteen-year-old girls are into.'

'Seventeen-year-old boys,' Fay quipped.

'Very funny. I don't think Camille is that kind of girl – according to Jonah she's had quite a sheltered upbringing.' Lucy lowered a tangle of red sour strawberry laces into her mouth.

'That's what all dads like to think!' Fay laughed.

'Are you going to help me or not?' She pushed her long hair out of her eyes and stared at the array of colours.

'Are you eating?' Fay asked accusatorily.

'Yes, only sweets.'

'How come you eat that rubbish and stay so skinny, whereas I only have to look at a bar of chocolate and it's miraculously attached itself to my hips?'

'Just lucky, I guess.' She chewed the candy that she loved. 'Should I go for pink?' she asked, returning to the task in hand.

'No, definitely not; pink is risky. She might not be a girly girl and might hate pink. I always hated pink. If I were you, I'd go for something that's trendy, grown-up, sophisticated and a bit quirky, cool.'

Lucy sighed. 'Okay, so what colour is trendy, grown-up, sophisticated, quirky and cool?' With only a small window of time in which to get the room ready, she was losing patience.

'How about something neutral, but not cold, like a linen or a light khaki, and then accessorise on a theme like, I don't know, Old Glory? You could have the flag on one wall and then a vintage chest, tapestry rugs, a faux-fur throw – it might be nice.'

'Okay, I shall google some pictures, but that sounds quite good. I'm off to source paint.'

'You are really getting into this. Are you a bit nervous about meeting her?' Fay knew her well.

'Not a bit, a lot,' she admitted, swallowing the sweets.

'It'll be fine! You live in a trendy part of London where she can go and explore. You are cool and fab and she will have a lovely time. Don't stress.'

'Thank you for saying I am cool and fab.' She smiled into the receiver.

'I didn't mean it. I was just being nice.' Fay laughed.

'Go away, Fay.'

'Go away, yourself. Love you!'

With that her sister ended the call. Lucy laid her palm on the waistband of her sweatpants, feeling the slight bloat to her stomach and looking forward to the day it became a pronounced bump. There was something wonderful about the prospect of losing her boyish, flat physique and becoming fully rounded; she couldn't wait. Fay was right, though. *Hear that, baby? Don't stress . . .*

Lucy had earlier turned to her trusty baby book, knowing that nine to ten weeks would be her next big milestone.

At week nine your baby is approximately 3 cm in length. It has recognisable eyelids, a jaw and a nose. It also has small pads on the ends of its fingers.

This information helped her picture her growing baby and helped her communicate with her. She was again convinced that it was a little girl she was carrying.

Her fear had not left her entirely. In fact, the first thing she did upon waking each morning was to snake her hand under her bottom and feel the mattress beneath her. She would then surreptitiously bring her hand up to her face for scrutiny, and when she saw it with her own eyes, clean and dry, she could then start her day with a huge sigh of relief and a surge of optimism that the day she got to hold her baby was getting closer and closer.

Jonah had finally, after much nagging, cleared the spare room of all the furniture and clutter. He piled the dismantled bed and pine chest of drawers in the hallway and stowed all the sagging cardboard boxes full of his ageing collections in the attic for sorting or throwing out another day. Lucy suspected that day would never come – not that she cared. Out of sight was all she had wanted.

The dated peach-coloured carpet had been ripped up and offloaded at the municipal dump. She had whooped with joy at the wide, aged timbers that were revealed, and she promptly skim-painted them with a pale-blue floor paint, which clung in some areas and yet skirted the knots and dips, making the floor look worn and yet contemporary at the same time. With the wallpaper stripped and the walls primed, she was now ready to start painting.

'Can I help you?' Jonah asked, arriving in his overalls and looking ready to get involved.

'Sure.' She smiled, tucking the loose wisps of her hair up into the scarf that she had tied in a front knot on her head. She dipped the long-handled roller into the tray and ran the soft spongy head vertically up and down. The thick paint made a delightful sucking sound as it clung to the wall, leaving a beautiful, pale, natural raffia-coloured stripe on the orange-tinged plaster.

'What do you think?' She stood back to admire her work.

'I think it looks great!' he enthused. 'Good colour choice.'

'I hate to admit that it was Fay's idea and not mine. She's so much better at this stuff than me. I'd have gone for a pink feature wall and apparently that is a massive no-no.'

'Camille will love it. She'll be happy to be here no matter what; a newly decorated room will be a bonus.' Jonah dipped the short roller into the tray and ran the paint along the base of the wall, above the wooden edge.

'Don't let it drip,' she instructed.

'You are so bossy.' He laughed. 'I have painted something before.'

'I'm not bossy. I'm helpful, confident,' she corrected him. 'I just want this to be perfect for Camille. We'll have to do all we can to make her really welcome, encourage her to invite friends over and get her out into Queen's Park; she'll want to hang out with people her own age, I'm sure.'

'Are you saying we are boring?' Jonah pulled an expression of mock hurt.

'No.' She shook her head. 'I'm saying you are boring.'

'Oh God.' He stopped painting and stared at her. 'I've just had a thought.'

'What?' She stopped laughing, any amusement halted by his rather concerned expression.

'When this baby is sixteen, I will be sixty-three. That's really old!'
He pulled a face.

'It's only old if you let it be. And for the record, I don't think you'll
ever be old, no matter what age you reach.' She walked over and stood
on tiptoe to kiss his stubbly cheek.

'Do you think . . .' He paused.

'Do I think what?' She kissed him again.

'Do you think that our baby issues, the miscarriage, was anything
to do with my age?' He avoided eye contact.

'No! No, I don't. No one has suggested that and you mustn't think
it. Plenty of men a lot older than you father babies.'

'I know.' He shrugged. 'But I would hate to be to blame for what
you went through.'

'You are not!' she asserted. 'You are young in body and mind and
will be a great dad to this little one.'

'It certainly helps having a hot young trophy wife living in the
house to keep me on my toes.' He winked.

Lucy laughed. 'Oh, that's me!' She leant in and kissed him again. It
was mere seconds before their ardour built. 'Not here.' She placed the
rollers on the floor and grabbed his hand, leading him from the room.

'What do you mean "not here"?' He chuckled. 'There's only us in
the house!'

'We can't do it in Camille's room. That wouldn't be right,' she chas-
tised, leading him past the stack of furniture, now propped along the
banister, and into their room.

◆ ◆ ◆

As Lucy sat on the edge of the mattress, coiling her hair into a loose bun
and retying her scarf that had worked loose, she caught her husband
gazing at her profile.

'You look beautiful.'

'There's no need for flattery. Not now you have already had your wicked way with me.'

'I mean it. You are so beautiful. Being pregnant really suits you.'

She blushed with happiness.

'I hope our baby looks just like you. A little girl, just like you,' he whispered. 'That would be amazing.'

Lucy turned to face him on the mattress. 'I do think it's a girl, Jonah. I don't know why. I just have this feeling.' She placed her hand on her stomach, as if this might help her communicate with her baby.

'Well, I place a lot of stock in a mother's instinct. What are we going to call her?' He reached for her arm and pulled her back to him, where she lay against his form.

'I don't know. But I do like the name Daisy.' She smiled.

'Daisy? As in *Daisy*?' he questioned.

'Yes.' She ignored his ribbing. 'I love daisies and I like the word and the name and the way it sounds. Daisy Carpenter – that's a good name. She'll be bright and pretty, Daisy.'

'I think we'll park that and come back to it.' He squeezed her shoulders.

'What name do you like then?' She leant on her side, propping her head on her hand with her elbow planted on the mattress.

'I quite like Iris. A bolder, stronger flower.'

'Oh, I quite like Iris too,' she mused.

'You do?' he asked with what sounded to be more than a small element of surprise.

'I do.' She sat up and pulled on her old T-shirt that would do for decorating. 'But not as much as Daisy.' She blew him a kiss and made her way back down the landing.

It was a full week later that Camille's room was finally finished. Having worked hard every evening after work and over two weekends, Lucy stood back and admired her handiwork. The fresh, clean newly painted walls gave the already generously proportioned room a feeling of even more space. At the large sash window were heavy blue linen curtains. The antique wooden bed with its wooden head and footboards was now covered with a vintage-inspired quilt that boasted a myriad of blues and whites with the slightest hint of red. The patchwork of fabrics had been artfully placed together. The ditsy florals, faded stars, weathered stripes and muted checks worked well together, creating the illusion that this bedcover might be a family heirloom, sewn with love and made from offcuts of fabric from generations past. The scrubbed pine chest of drawers in the corner now had cream aged frames on top, in which Lucy had placed photographs of Camille with her dad throughout the years. The sweetest ones were of him holding the relatively newborn baby, and the most recent showed the confident teen staring into the lens and looking a little awkward about having her dad's arm cast across her narrow shoulders.

A battered leather trunk sat at the foot of the bed, and in the middle of the floor was a vibrant handwoven striped wool rug in red, oatmeal and blue with a thick fringe at either end. By the bedside was a simple rusting navy metal table that she hoped might be familiar to Camille, like the kind that you might find sat outside any French bistro on a lazy afternoon, usually adorned with a carafe of pastis, a jug of cool water and an enamel stovetop pot of garlicky mussels. On the table was an oversized pewter lamp base with a wonderfully tactile hammered pattern and an oatmeal coolie shade with a red stitched edging and a faded printed pattern of the stars and stripes.

She had placed a bulky mirror above the wrought-iron fireplace. Its weathered frame of reclaimed timber dotted with blackened horseshoe nails was a dominant feature in the room. On the back of the door was a set of resin and metal hooks, made to look like antlers.

71

'Okay, you can come in!' She pushed the door wide and watched Jonah's face as he stepped inside. She noted the way his eyes wandered from surface to surface, taking in every detail.

'Lucy!' He shook his head, staring around the room. 'This looks absolutely incredible!'

She felt a blush of pride at his compliment. 'Do you think Camille will like it? I didn't want it to be too babyish or too girly. I just hope I've got it right.' She wrung her hands together, clearly a little nervous.

'She'll love it.' He shuffled on the spot. 'At least I think she will. The truth is, I don't know her that well, do I? I'm a bit nervous,' he confessed.

'What about?'

'I suppose I'm worried that she might not like me or might not like it here away from her mum and friends.'

'It's only natural that you are anxious, but we will make sure she has the best time,' she reassured him.

Jonah stared at her. 'I love that you have gone to so much trouble for her. Thank you, honey.'

'I liked doing it, good practice for the nursery.' She folded her arms across her chest.

'The nursery? By my reckoning, we only have three bedrooms in this house. I have a sneaking suspicion that you might be referring to my study!'

'How can you study in there? You can barely *get* in there with all the clutter you have.' She pointed down the landing where the room lurked, lined with semi-industrial-looking shelving units that sagged under the weight of all manner of stationery, photograph albums, shoeboxes and files.

'It's still my study,' he almost pleaded.

'Did you hear that, Daisy? Your dad won't give up his junk room so you can have your own pretty nursery. Instead, we shall have to let you sleep in a drawer in the corner of the room like your grandma did during the war.'

Jonah laughed out loud. 'Okay! You win. I can't have our little Iris sleeping in a drawer. I admit defeat – she can have my study.'

Lucy beamed. 'I got my scan appointment through from the hospital. It's next Friday at three-fifteen.'

'Oh shoot!' Jonah flicked his head towards her. 'That's when I'm collecting Camille from Paddington; she's jumping on the Heathrow Express.'

'Oh, that's okay. I can manage.'

'No, let me see if I can get someone else to fetch her. I'm sure one of the lads from work won't mind, or I'll ask her if she can get a later train; there's plenty to do at the airport.' He looked towards the window, trying to figure out how to solve the clash.

'No! Don't be crazy. I'll be fine. It's only a scan, not like I haven't had one before, and I promise to remember everything they say and report back in full.' She walked over and pecked him on the cheek.

'I don't want you to go on your own, not after—'

'Jonah,' she interrupted him. 'I promise you I'll be fine. I'll jump in a cab and meet you both back here. We can't let anything get in the way of making Camille feel welcome; it's too important.'

'Will we get a picture?' he asked, looking younger with his eager, open expression.

'We might!' Lucy squealed with joy and beamed brightly at the thought.

Early one Saturday, I sat in Gail's bakery on Salusbury Road with a cup of coffee and a slice of carrot cake. I was comfortable in the way that you can be at the weekend, in my jeans and a T-shirt and trainers. Jonah was having his hair cut around the corner and was going to meet me there afterwards for a catch-up. I grabbed a newspaper from the rack and took a seat in the corner at a little square table by the bathroom. The place was busy and I liked being among people and yet at the same time in my own private bubble. I took a sip of my latte and opened the paper, skimming articles about the plans for a new hospital ward, bits of celebrity gossip that I was only a little bit interested in and adverts for things to do in London, new releases at the cinema and a great recommendation for a pop-up Cuban café opening on the South Bank. I forked a chunk of moist cake into my mouth and savoured the taste and texture. Then I turned the page. And there it was.

I swallowed the cake that had turned to ashes on my tongue and laid my fork on the plate. I ran my finger along the column, devouring each word in the same way that rubberneckers stare at an accident, unable to withdraw their gaze from the sights that might well haunt them as they chase sleep around their head in the dead of night. The woman pictured on the page looked hard, her thin-lipped mouth was set in a slight sneer and her eyebrows were over-plucked on a shiny forehead. The image of the little girl next to her was cute; she had a button nose and a big smile. I leant closer to the text, as if this might help my understanding. The words leapt from the page, 'catastrophic injuries' and 'one of the worst cases of violence in a domestic setting.' And worse, the judge's summing up, 'beating her over the head with a heavy object or throwing her against the floor or wall.'

I didn't realise I was crying. Didn't realise I was making a noise at all. Quite unexpectedly, I felt a hand on my arm and when I looked up, an older lady was smiling down at me from where she stood. 'Are you okay, dear?' she asked and I gave a small nod. It was then I noticed that lots of other people at nearby tables were staring at me too, gathering their children closer to them and shrinking against the walls in case my distress was catching or worse, a precursor to something far more troubling. 'They broke her bones,' I explained. 'They hurt her and she died,' I managed, as my tears clouded my vision and filled my nose and mouth. And then in the next instant, Jonah was there. I watched the smile slide from his face and he almost ran when he saw me crying, with the stranger touching my arm. His expression was one of curiosity. 'Jonah!' I called out to him. 'Jonah, these terrible people, they wasted her, wasted that chance to be parents, they killed their little girl! They didn't deserve her! I would have loved her . . . I would have been a good mum and they had that chance and they killed her! Why did they get her and not me? It's not fair, it's so unfair!' He took me by the hand and helped me stand, cradling me against him, as we walked out of the café and on to the street. I didn't care that people were staring at me, at us. I didn't care about much. I couldn't think straight, couldn't see beyond her little face.

SEVEN

Lucy paid the cab driver and stepped from his taxi, gripping the key in her hand. She tried to swallow the nerves that fluttered in her chest, exhaling through her open mouth and digging deep to find a smile while trying to steady her hands.

It will all be okay, Lucy. Just take a deep breath and get through this, she reasoned, as she put the key in the lock.

The first thing she heard was raucous laughter coming from the kitchen.

'Hel-loo?' she called out, turning to close the front door; she shut her eyes briefly, as if in prayer.

'Hey, love! In the kitchen!' Jonah called out.

Leaving her jacket and bag in the hallway, she pulled her hair free from the collar of her blouse and trod the steps down into their cosy kitchen. The first thing Lucy noticed was the way Camille stopped laughing and sucked her cheeks in slightly, as if posing for a photograph. Jonah was, as ever, holding court from the stovetop, where he stirred a deliciously fragrant curry with a wooden spoon in one hand and a large glass of red wine in the other. He leant across and gave her a fleeting kiss as he abandoned his stirring. He looked happy.

'Here she is!' he boomed, indicating the girl, as if he had magicked her from thin air.

'Hey, Camille, you made it!' She stepped towards her with her arms open wide. 'I'm sorry I wasn't here to meet you.' She briefly glanced at Jonah, both knowing where she had been and why.

Camille nodded, failing to walk forward or accept the offer of a hug, keeping her willowy arms in their thin cotton cardigan by her side and her feet in their slouching suede ankle boots firmly planted on the terracotta floor.

'S'okay. Dad was there,' she offered dismissively.

Lucy hadn't quite expected the girl's accent. She let her arms fall to her sides and bunched her fists. 'You sound American, not French!' she said, pointing out the obvious.

'I go to an international school, I always have, and my tutors are all American and most of the pupils, so . . .' She kept her gaze down and widened her eyes.

'Is this as strange for you as it is for me? I'm married to your dad and here we are only just meeting now! It's quite surreal, but I am so glad that we are. And Jonah has told me all about you. I feel like I know you already,' she gushed.

Camille nodded and twisted her mouth.

'Have you had something to drink?' Lucy walked towards the fridge, about to recite the list of juices and sodas that she had got in specially.

'I'm all good, thanks.' Camille held up a mug of coffee.

'Great. Great.' Lucy closed the fridge door, again feeling a little uncertain of how to treat this child-woman. She let her eyes sweep the form of the beautiful girl. She was tall for her age and whippet slender, yet shapely, with chestnut hair that sat in a long, blunt bob on her shoulders. Her eyes and eyebrows were without a doubt those of her father, but her wide mouth and aquiline nose belonged to her diminutive mum. Lucy felt a stab of inadequacy at the sight of this striking, confident teen who seemed to take up more space than she actually filled in their little kitchen.

Camille reached up and opened the cupboard above the fridge. 'Do you still keep the cookies in here?'

'Ha! No, we are now a cookie-free zone.' Jonah seemed delighted that the layout of the kitchen was familiar to his child; it made her less of a stranger, whereas Lucy felt it was a sharp reminder that this was Camille's place long before it was hers. The atmosphere was not that of people who did not get along, which was the picture Jonah had painted. This was in fact quite the opposite – they seemed at ease, leaving her to feel like the interloper.

'Anyway' – he beamed as he resumed stirring the pan – 'you don't want to spoil your supper.'

'It smells delicious.' Lucy tried to enthuse about the dish even though she had no desire to eat it; all she wanted to do was fall into bed and hide under the duvet. 'What is it, exactly?'

'Thai red curry, vegetarian of course, with sticky jasmine rice and a vegetable tempura of carrot, red pepper and courgette, with a sweet chilli dipping sauce.' He winked at her, knowing that he sounded like a pro.

'Wow!' Lucy remembered to smile. 'That sounds yummy, but why no meat? I bought the chicken fillets you asked for; don't tell me you are going all vegetarian on me?' she asked.

'I'm a vegetarian, actually,' Camille informed her with a slight sigh.

'Oh, Camille, I didn't know.' She felt a blush at the base of her neck, silently cursing Jonah for not knowing this or, if he did, for not informing her. 'How long have you been a vegetarian?'

'About six weeks,' she answered stiffly. 'I refuse to eat anything that has a face.'

'Well.' Lucy looked at her husband. 'Good for you. We could certainly do with cutting down on red meat and stuff, so it sounds like you will be a good influence on all of us.'

Jonah turned and smiled at his wife. A smile that told her she was doing great.

'Did you see your room?' Lucy wondered if she liked it, hating how desperate she was for the girl's approval.

'No, not yet. We only got here like a while ago.'

'Would you like to come up and see it now? We can get your stuff unpacked and get you settled. I can help you if you like?'

'Sure.' She gave a small shrug of indifference and slowly placed the half-full coffee mug on the worktop.

'Don't be too long, you two; supper is literally ten minutes away.' He concentrated on lowering the vegetable batons into the light batter that sat in a bowl.

'Can you manage?' Lucy asked, as Camille lifted the large wheeled suitcase and bumped it up the stairs.

'Yep.' The girl nodded.

Lucy walked in front of her, treading the stairs to match her pace and hoping that her stepdaughter wasn't studying her rear.

She recalled the smell of the little room in Hammersmith Hospital where she had been only hours earlier and shook her head, ridding her mind of the image.

'So how was your journey?' Lucy asked over her shoulder, with artificial jollity. She couldn't remember if she had already asked her this.

'Easy. Cab, plane, train, cab, here,' Camille offered dryly.

'I guess you are used to travelling. When I was sixteen I don't think I had travelled anywhere on my own. I might have gone on a school trip to Barcelona, but that doesn't really count, does it? All I had to do was sit on a coach for what felt like an eternity and then try and not get lost on the ferry.'

'Am I in the same room as usual, or has that been moved too?' Camille arched her head to look around the wall and on to the landing. Lucy wondered what else had been moved.

'Yep, same room, but I think you'll like it a lot more. I've spruced it up a bit.'

She walked ahead and opened the door, glad of the fresh scent that wafted from the freesias she had placed in a glass vase on the table by the bed.

Camille gave a big sigh as she left her bag in the doorway and walked around like an inspector, officiously, touching her fingers to the bedspread, the mirror and finally the antler hooks behind the door.

'Do you like it?' Lucy cupped her hands together, holding them against her chest.

'Is it . . . ?' Camille placed her hands in her jeans pockets and lifted her shoulders. She appeared to be struggling to find the words.

'Is it what?' Lucy cocked her head, looking for a clue in the girl's expression.

Camille shook her head. 'Nothing.' She went to retrieve her case and laid it on the double bed, unzipping it before flipping it open to reveal clothes, stuffed into every available space. 'Is there a wardrobe?' She looked around, although it was obvious there wasn't one.

'No, gosh! I didn't really think about a wardrobe.' She felt her cheeks colour.

'Clothes are my thing,' Camille explained, addressing the depths of her suitcase. 'I love fashion. It's what I want to do when I leave school.'

'I did not know that. We'll have to get you into town to look at some of the designer stores, and there are some brilliant markets for unusual pieces.' Lucy wished she were better informed on this stuff.

'So, the wardrobe?' the girl prompted with an overconfident tone.

'I thought you could use the chest of drawers for clothes and the travel trunk at the end of the bed for shoes. I didn't think it through, but I can see now you have things to hang up.'

I've been a little distracted . . . She swallowed the thought.

'So, can I, like, put things on these deer horns or whatever they are?' She hooked her finger over one and gave it a tug. 'They don't seem that strong.'

Lucy looked at the design piece on the back of the door that she thought made a bold statement, embarrassed by Camille's obvious disapproval of her choices.

'No, they're not that strong. I think you are right. Maybe you could hang light things on them, your nightdress and things.'

'Pah!' Camille let out a loud burst of laughter. 'My nightdress? Okaaay.' She returned to her suitcase with wide eyes.

'We can get you a rail from Ikea if you'd like, just a simple rack that you can hang things on – would that be better? You could put it here.' She pointed to the space against the wall between the fireplace and her bed.

'That would be great. Thank you.' Camille smiled, briefly, and Lucy was glad of the thanks.

'I want you to have a really good time here, Camille, and I want you to relax and I want us to get on. I want you to ask me anything and be able to say anything and I want us to get to know each other.'

That's a lot of wants, Lucy girl . . .

'Sure.' Camille nodded and gave another tight-lipped smile.

'Do you need anything right now?' she asked, as she made for the door.

'Nope.' The girl spoke from the confines of the suitcase in which she delved.

'Well, I'll see you in the kitchen in a few minutes for dinner.'

'Sure,' Camille muttered again, as she extracted pairs of socks balled together and an armful of charging cables and wires.

She closed the bedroom door behind her and fought her desire to cry.

'Supper's ready!' Jonah called up the stairs.

Lucy sat with her back to the wall on the wooden pew on the far side of the table. Jonah sat at the head of the narrow table with Camille to his right. The conversation between the two was animated, and Lucy did all she could to keep up, nodding in the right places and smiling at their jokes. It wasn't that she wasn't happy for the two to be reunited; of course she was. It was just that tonight she wanted nothing more than a hot bath, solitude and the comfort of her husband's arms around her.

'So I told her' – Camille filled her mouth with rice and chewed before swallowing quickly and refilling her fork – 'I can't be the only girl in my year without an iPhone 6S and she was like . . .'

Lucy watched as she waved her fork in the air like a baton, pulling expressions of disdain as she discussed her mother, and tucking her hair behind her ear. It was hard to believe she was only sixteen.

'. . . she was like, you don't need a phone like that! *Tu es seulement une enfant, une enfant!*'

The girl's quick-fire French threw her a little. Jonah threw his head back and laughed. Lucy felt the prick of tears at the back of her eyes.

She placed her fork on the plate and sat back. 'That was delicious, Jonah, thank you.'

'My pleasure. Are you done? I've made pudding.' He placed his hand over the back of hers and gave it a gentle squeeze.

'I couldn't eat another thing. Now, if you will both excuse me, I have a very busy day tomorrow and need to do a bit of work before I fall asleep. Camille, is there anything you need before I go up to bed?'

Camille raised her eyebrows and raised her palms, as if trying to think of one thing that she might possibly need.

'In that case, I shall love you and leave you. Sweet dreams both.' She kissed Jonah on the head as she passed.

'Don't nod off.' He grabbed her hand. 'I shan't be too far behind you. We'll have our pud and then I just need to get these dishes done.'

'Okay.' She smiled and left the room.

Hovering on the bottom stair, she looked at the slice of light that crept from under the kitchen door and heard the echo of their laughter. Now alone in the semi-darkness, Lucy gave in to the tears that she had held at bay for the evening. Gripping the banister, she climbed the stairs slowly and closed the bedroom door behind her. After peeling off her skirt and blouse, she stepped into her pyjamas and climbed beneath the thin summer duvet. The curtains fluttered in the warm evening breeze and the beeps of cars and the shouts of revellers, making their way home from the pub no doubt, filtered up through her window.

Life goes on.

This was her final thought before sleep offered her a blissful avenue of escape.

'Hey.'

Lucy was aware of a hand on her shoulder, rousing her from sleep. She sat up and rubbed her eyes to find Jonah lying next to her in bed.

'Hello, my darling.' He beamed, reaching over to take her in his arms. 'I told you I wouldn't be far behind you.'

'How long have I been asleep?' She felt a little out of sorts.

'Twenty minutes, max.'

'Gosh.' She shook her head, trying to reach a state of greater alertness. 'Feels like longer.'

'Isn't it great having Cam here?' he marvelled. 'Isn't she wonderful? I can't believe she is here.'

She nodded.

'So, come on, I want to hear all about it. Did you get my picture?' He sat up, bouncing a little on the mattress and rubbing his hands together like an excited schoolboy.

'I . . .' She tried to figure out how to start. 'I got there easily enough and the lady was really nice.'

'Good. That's good.' He smiled.

'They already knew what had happened to me. Before.' She looked up at him.

'I guessed they would. They have your files and everything. It means they will take extra good care of you,' he whispered.

Both were acutely aware that there was now another person in a room along the landing and they kept their voices low accordingly.

'Did they say how far along you were?' He ran his hand over the curve of her shoulder, over her breast and down to her stomach. On any other night this would have been an invite to progress to sex, but tonight it only made her shiver with something close to revulsion.

'I would be ten weeks, but' – she took a deep breath – 'there was no heartbeat.'

'What?' He sat up straight, sitting in front of her now; he took her hands into his own.

Lucy shook her head as her tears fell, coming now in great gulps that made speech almost impossible.

'She had no heartbeat, Jonah, and she hasn't had one for a long while – a couple of weeks, they said.' With her head hanging forward on to her chest, she cried, feeling wave after wave of sadness, as the woman's words echoed in her mind.

'I am so very sorry, Mrs Carpenter. Sometimes we can't give you a reason and I know how hard that must be . . .'

'Did . . . did they say why?' he asked, pushing her hair back so he could see her better.

She shook her head. 'They said it just happens. That's what they said the last time, but there must be a reason. There must! I know these things just happen, but why do they keep *just happening* to me?' She looked at him, crying harder when she saw her tears reflected in his own. 'I thought . . . I thought this time it would be fine,' she stammered.

'Shit.' Jonah sighed.

'Are you . . . are you angry with me?'

'Angry with you? Oh, my darling, no! No, of course not.' He held her tight and cradled her head into his chest, holding her as she sobbed. Her tears left a damp patch on his T-shirt. 'My Lucy, I am so sorry I wasn't there for you. And I'm so sad for us. But we can try again. If that's what you want.' He kissed her head.

What I want? Isn't this about what we want?

'I can't think that far ahead,' she managed, sitting up a little to face him, unwilling to admit that his words sounded hollow and offered no solace at all. At that point the thought of trying again was more than she could cope with, if it was without his full and unwavering support.

'Of course, of course.' He had a look of anguish, clearly unsure of the right thing to say to placate her. 'Do they have to . . .' He paused, struggling to find the right phrase. 'Do we have to go back in for a procedure like we did before?' he asked gently.

She shook her head. 'No. They have given me some medication, a pill, because I'm not bleeding or anything. I take the pill and it will help speed things along. Then I'll miscarry, usually within a few days and it will be like having a period. She said that some women might have a heavy period and not even realise that it's an early miscarriage. So it should be fine.'

Her tears came again, and both knew it was anything but fine.

'Oh, Lucy. I am so sorry, my darling.'

'Me too.' She sniffed.

'Have you taken the tablet?' he asked.

'No.' She shook her head. 'I wanted you to be here when I did. Which is crazy because this little thing is already gone.' At her words, her tears fell afresh. 'But I still didn't want to take it when I was on my own.'

'I understand.' He kissed her hand.

'Dad?' The shout from down the hall made them both jump.

'Yes, love?' he called out over his wife's shoulder.

'Can I get a blanket? I'm really cold.'

'Yes, of course.' He jumped up. 'I shan't be a sec,' he whispered, as he left her alone.

Lucy sank down on to the pillows and thought how very lucky her husband was to be called Dad. She placed her hand on her tummy.

I'm sorry, little one. I am so, so sorry. I know it's my fault. I should have listened to Jonah. Maybe I should have called you Iris. They are stronger than Daisies, that's what he said. Maybe I should have called you Iris instead.

Sobbing, she closed her eyes, waiting for the morning.

After my second miscarriage I had a dark recurring thought that, try as I might, I couldn't suppress. I fully understood that Jonah had Camille, that she was his baby girl and always would be. But I realised that the scene I had imagined for so long, that beautiful, life-defining moment when our baby was lifted from my body and handed over to him, would only ever be a rerun of what he had already experienced. And even that thought made me feel so sad. Like this might all be pointless. I was feeling the cloak of depression throw itself over my head. My failure to become a mother, the grief at my loss, it was all a little more than I could bear.

EIGHT

Over the following weeks, Lucy recovered, to a degree. She placed her baby book back behind its French Revolution wall and found that it helped to bury the hurt somewhere so deep inside her that even she couldn't see it. The challenge of working with Tansy and John on this vital project served as a good diversion. It was a campaign to make business users aware of innovations in green energy and it would be a much-needed cash boost for the agency.

It was just as much of a challenge as living in a house where, on occasion, she felt like a stranger. Camille filled her days in a horizontal fashion, waking late and sloping to the sitting room, where she took up residence on the sofa. A collection of coffee cups, biscuit wrappers and empty crisp packets would gather around her, until she got bored of her latest box set and sloped back upstairs to the bathroom, where she would lie in the tub for hours, soaking in a scented bubbly marinade and listening to music. Then she would slide back to the bedroom, ready to sleep and repeat the next day.

'I had a thought yesterday,' Lucy chirped after a pleasant dinner of vegetarian nut loaf with couscous and a spicy tomato and basil dressing. She had laughed surreptitiously at the way Jonah searched the plate, hoping to find some meat lurking under the veg. 'Why don't you try and get a little job while you are here?' She spoke as she stacked the dishwasher and Camille and Jonah dipped spoons directly into the ice-cream tub on the table.

Camille shot her father a look, as if waiting for him to jump in with a thousand reasons why she should be spared this ordeal.

'Do you know, I think that's a great idea!' he chimed.

She saw Camille's shoulders sink and her top lip flex slightly.

Jonah continued: 'It would be a good way for you to meet people; it would give you a social life. Even if you are only here for a couple of months, I think it might help you get the best out of it. I worry you aren't busy enough.'

Lucy loved that he echoed her thoughts on this; it felt good to know they were on the same page.

'It's hard for me to be busy; there's nothing for me to do here.' Camille ran the spoon along the edge of the ice cream, bringing a large curl of soft strawberry gelato up to her mouth which she devoured in a second.

'Nothing to do? How can you say that? You are in London! One of the greatest cities on the earth; there's so much to do here.' Lucy kept her tone jovial, wary of further alienating Camille, the girl whose approval she continued to seek.

'But I don't know anyone, and so there's no point in doing anything.' The girl slumped over on her arm. Her thick hair lay in a fan across the tabletop.

'That's exactly why a job would be so good for you.' Jonah nudged her. 'You'd get to meet people – not only the people you worked with, but if you were in one of the shops, customers as well.'

Camille rolled her eyes.

'And in the meantime, if you want me to take you to any of the sights, I'd be very happy to do that, Cam – we could go exploring one weekend?' she offered brightly, planning days out in her head.

'Like where?' Camille sat up and stared at her.

'I don't know . . .' Lucy thought hard. 'The Tower of London, or the London Eye, or Harrods?'

Camille snorted her laughter. 'Dad has dragged me around those places a million times. It's all we used to do when I came to stay.'

'I thought you liked our trips?' He looked more than a little crestfallen.

'I did, when I was like ten, but I don't want to do them again. What else, Legoland?'

'Ooh, I'd love to go to Legoland. I was a big Lego fan in my youth.' Lucy gathered from Camille's stare of disbelief that she had, of course, been joking.

'I'm going to FaceTime with Alice.' Camille let the spoon clatter to the surface and left the table, off to seek out the quiet of her room to natter to her school friend who lived in Poitiers.

Lucy closed the dishwasher door and took a seat next to her husband, who offered a spoonful of ice cream which she refused with a shake of the head.

'Do you think she's having a nice time here?' She kept her eyes downward.

'Yes! Definitely,' Jonah enthused.

She looked up at him. 'I'm not sure she likes me,' she whispered. It had taken all of her courage to say the words out loud.

'Of course she does. She thinks you are great!' He used the same tone that she had heard him use to try to enthuse Camille.

'I'm not so sure. She's a bit cool with me. And I feel a bit . . .' She paused, tapping her nails on the table, trying to phrase her words carefully. 'I feel like she'd prefer it if I wasn't here, as if I'm intruding, and that makes me feel a bit crap if I'm honest.' She exhaled, feeling slightly better for having voiced it.

'That's not true, Lucy. It's great with the three of us here.'

For you maybe . . . She kept the thought to herself.

He continued. 'I think she's still settling in and I think your idea of a job is the best one, something that will get her out of the house, and once she meets people her own age, everything will fall into place.'

She nodded. 'I hope so.'

'I know so.' He placed his hand over hers. 'And also . . .'

'What?' She sensed his hesitation.

'I think you are still reeling a little from what's happened.'

And you are not? You think we can all just laugh over supper and carry on as normal?

She buried the thought; maybe he was right.

'And that is perfectly understandable,' he continued, 'but I think you are holding back a bit with Camille, not shining your brightest, and that's not a criticism, my God, you are doing amazingly well. Lots of people would have caved, but not you – you have just dusted yourself off and carried on. You are quite something.'

'Maybe you are right.'

'I think I am.' He smiled at her.

Lucy met his gaze. 'I know that we have been very relaxed about contraception and everything, taken it in our stride, but I think it's a good idea if we actively wait before trying again. Maybe put a bit of space between my associations with being pregnant and trying for a baby, if that makes sense? I don't think I could cope with another disappointment, not for a while.'

'It makes perfect sense, love. I think that's probably wise.' He let the chair scrape on the wooden floor as he leant forward to kiss her cheek.

'I think I might go and read or knit.' She stood from the table and grabbed a glass of water from the tap to take with her. She took a sip, trying to swallow the bitter taste of disappointment at the fact that Jonah had agreed so readily. At the back of her mind, she had hoped that he might have fought a little harder to have a baby with her, or at least try.

As she trod the stairs she heard Camille laughing loudly. '. . . *veux-tu aller à Legoland? Vraiment!* No, I swear to God!'

Lucy switched on the lamp and sank on to her bed, taking refuge in her knitting, concentrating on the click-clack of the needles as she crafted the tiny socks, checking the pattern for the right dimensions. She smiled, thinking of the little feet that might one day sit inside these tiny striped things.

It was a hot day in late June. Lucy had the air conditioning on full blast in her office and concocted many excuses not to have to leave its cool confines. Tansy knocked and entered, speaking as she did so.

'So, John has arranged to go and see the CEO, the eco guy, and I find out via an email?' Tansy ranted, as she leant on Lucy's desk. 'Why didn't I know about it?'

'This is the first I have heard of it, but I suggest you talk to John, sort it out.' She massaged her temples with her fingertips.

'There is no talking to him! He railroads me at every turn and then acts all innocent in front of you.' Tansy actually pouted. 'It's driving me crazy.'

Lucy stood and stared at the busy London street below her window. 'Do you know what? I think if you can't sort out who is leading what aspect and communicate like adults, we will go back to plan A and I will give one person control, and it sounds like that person should probably be John if he's the one having secret lunches with the CEO.' She turned on her heel to watch Tansy's mouth flap, fish-like, as she clearly struggled to think of her next move.

Lucy hated the tone she had used, reminding herself of her mum when she and Fay had once battled over the remote control to the big TV in the lounge. She could no longer remember what they had wanted to watch, but recalled the incident. They had rushed home from school, bickering and racing to see who could get back first. Once there, they tussled on the sofa, each holding tightly to an end of the remote control and shoving the other in an attempt to gain an advantage. Shouting petty insults, they used their feet to try to push each other on to the floor. Their mum had waltzed into the room and very calmly walked over to the corner unit where the TV sat. She unplugged it from the wall and produced a pair of scissors from behind her back, which she then used to snip the cable, cutting the plug away.

'But? Mum?'

'No way!'

'Are you crazy?'

'God!'

The girls had quickly relinquished their grasp on the now use-less block of plastic and sat back against the cushions, united in their grievance against their mother. Lucy's mouth twitched into a smile as she recalled the hours that felt like days with no TV, until her dad deemed it time to put the plug back on. Lucy was certain it was noth-ing to do with the fact that he considered they had been adequately punished and everything to do with the fact that he didn't want to miss the rugby.

'You're right, Lucy. I'm sorry. I shouldn't have brought it to you. We are grown-ups; we can sort it out.'

'Good.' She sat back down behind her desk.

'The thing is, I'm struggling a bit,' Tansy began.

'Oh, how?' She was concerned for her friend.

'Michael is playing up a bit, pushing his boundaries, and Rick have locked horns over everything from bedtimes to allowances. I feel more like a referee than a mother. It's driving me nuts. And Benedict's cutting a tooth and he's so clingy, you know how they get, it's "Mummy, Mummy, Mummy", every five minutes, and if I let him he'd be permanently sat on my hip with his hands clamped around my neck, his face an inch from mine. I hope he grows out of it soon. I need some me time back.' She closed her eyes and sighed. 'I guess this is my punishment for having such a big gap – teenage rebellion and teething to cope with.'

Oh, Tansy! What wouldn't I give to have a little one that close to me and to be called Mummy. That would be the greatest privilege . . .

'You okay?' Tansy looked at her with an expression of concern. 'You look like you're miles away.'

'I'm fine.' She turned her attention to her keyboard, trying to give the hint that she was busy and wanted to be left alone.

'Oh God!' Tansy suddenly gasped and leant on her desk. 'You're not pregnant, are you?' she whispered.

Lucy stared at her.

'I mean, there has been talk.' She winked. 'You've been married for over a year now and those tubes are about as willing as they are ever going to be. You are, aren't you? You're up the spout!' Her eyes were wide with excitement. 'You can tell me. I shan't tell a soul!' she gabbled.

'No.' Her tone was curt, and she avoided looking at her friend. 'I'm not pregnant.'

'Are you sure? I think you might have a look about you and I'm usually a good judge of these things.'

'Positive.'

'Oh.' Tansy straightened. Both tried to ignore the slightly awkward atmosphere that lingered. 'Still,' Tansy continued, 'I guess you don't need one of your own; you've got Camille there now. How is she getting on on this side of the Channel? Settling in okay?'

'Was there anything else work-related? It's just that I am really up against it.' She pointed at her screen. Her slight was unusual, and Lucy knew that with that sentence came a shift in the dynamic of their friendship.

◆ ◆ ◆

She decided not to tell Jonah about her and Tansy's conversation, unwilling to relive her friend's admission that there had been 'talk'. The idea of everyone debating her decision not to have children was more than she could bear. What business was it of anyone's but hers and Jonah's? The fact that she had tried and failed made the idea of their gossip even more unpalatable.

Camille was prostrate on the sofa and Jonah was not yet home. Lucy hated to admit that she always felt slightly awkward when it was just the two of them, preferring Jonah's presence as an oblivious, amiable mediator.

'Hey, Camille!' she called through the open door. 'How was your day?'

'Fascinating,' came the rather drawled response.

'Any luck on the job front? Did you drop your letters off?' She did her best to keep a note of positivity to her questioning, remembering her husband's suggestion that it might in fact be she who needed to try a little harder.

Camille and Jonah had spent the previous evening concocting a letter of introduction and a brief CV. They had stressed her multilingual talents, her punctuality and her willingness to work hard. Lucy had suppressed the many comments that sat on her tongue, deciding it best not to point out that inside the house the girl was unwilling to bring her dirty laundry down a set of stairs or to put her coffee mug in the dishwasher, preferring to leave it by the side of the sofa to be collected by the maid – Lucy herself, of course.

'I didn't get a chance, but I'll do it tomorrow.' Camille yawned, stretching her arms over her head.

'I tell you what, why don't we go and do it right now? It's a lovely evening and we can walk the main road, pop letters into any place you like the look of and stop for ice cream at the other end? What do you say?'

'Actually I thought I might wash my hair.'

Camille stood and Lucy smiled at her. 'Camille, you look amazing. Your skin is like peaches and cream and your hair is shiny. I honestly think you are good to go. I think it's important we get these letters out now if it's going to happen at all.'

'Fine.' Camille stomped up the stairs without a hint of a smile, as she went to reluctantly get her boots on.

Lucy washed her hands in the kitchen and took a glug of orange juice. It had been a long day, and the last thing she felt like doing was trudging up and down the Salusbury Road. But it would be good to spend a little bit of time with Camille alone and try to break down some of the barriers, and it might just help her get a job and get out of the house.

'This is nice,' Lucy commented, as the two turned left at the end of the road and walked side by side. 'I like living here close to where your dad grew up. He's seen a lot of changes, I bet.'

'I used to visit my nan here when I was little, only a couple of times because I didn't come over here when I was really small, and then she died, but I remember it a bit.'

'What was she like, your nan?' Lucy was intrigued.

Camille sighed. 'She was okay. A regular nan. I didn't like going to visit her, though.'

'Oh! Why not?'

Camille shrugged. 'It wasn't that I didn't *like* her; her house was really funky, interesting. She had these fussy lampshades trimmed with tassels, and every surface was crammed with stuff.'

'Ah, well that explains a lot. I've decided your dad has the potential to be a hoarder.' She laughed.

'I remember her neighbour had this hissy cat, which was sometimes nice and wanted a hug and at other times was not and tried to scratch me. But it was Connor that had made me scared. I think he was my nan's neighbour's son.'

'Yes, that sounds right.' Lucy nodded, trying to remember and knowing that she had heard the name mentioned – the son of one of Jonah's school friends, or something similar.

'My nan's house was overlooked by Wormwood Scrubs, the prison,' Camille explained, as if Lucy might not know what Wormwood Scrubs was. 'I was only real small, like, maybe five, and I was playing in the garden with Connor and he pulled me to one side and pointed at the brown high walls, and these pretty towers, and he asked me if I knew what the big building was. I just shook my head, because I didn't. If I'd had to guess, I might have said that it was a church.'

'I can see why.' Lucy pictured the somewhat ecclesiastical design.

'He whispered to me, like it was a secret, he said, "It's a prison. Do you know what that is?" And I remember him looking towards the kitchen window. He knew that if he was overheard one of the adults would probably tell him off for trying to scare me.'

'How mean!' Lucy gave a small laugh of understanding, happy that they were sharing this chat, this insight.

'I know, right? Anyways, he told me that was where they sent all the baddies. Murderers, muggers, robbers and worse! I couldn't even think of what might be worse. But Connor was eight so I figured he must know all about life. He pointed at the windows and said, "Did you never wonder what all those bars were on the windows for?" I think I just stared at him. I was already feeling afraid, and it was the way he whispered. And then he told me it was because if they got out, they would jump over my nan's back wall and mug and murder and rob me, until I was dead!' She turned to Lucy and shook her head. 'I was so scared. And as I was working out what to do next, the neighbour's hissy cat jumped into the back garden from the side fence. God, I screamed so loud, even Connor was scared! My dad came running out and Connor got into trouble and I was crying, and even though my dad told me over and over that no one could get out and, even if they did manage it, they couldn't get over my nan's wall, the damage was done and I never wanted to go there again, just in case.'

'You poor little thing!' Lucy pictured the scared little girl, and her heart flexed. 'And your poor nan.'

'I got over it. I told my mum when I got home that I'd been in a prison – I got a little confused – and she of course flipped out!' Camille laughed at the mix-up.

'Are you and your mum close?'

'Yes. Very. We really are.' Camille nodded vigorously and held her eye. 'Everyone says we are more like best friends. We go out together all the time and we hang out with my mates, who all think she's great, and we go shopping and stuff. She's very beautiful and funny and we go to the movies or we just sit by the pool if the weather's nice. She's *very* cool.'

'Wow, she sounds it.'

No wonder you find me so boring. I hate shopping and I don't have a pool that we could sit by . . .

'Have you spoken to her much since you have been here?' Lucy tried to sound casual, hiding the fear that she might be reporting back to her mum just how boring it was here and how rubbish Lucy was at cooking and how she fared at being a stepmum. A stepmum . . . she didn't feel like anything of the sort. She felt redundant, surplus to requirements.

'Not really. She's busy remodelling a barn in the garden, and her and my dad, Jean-Luc, he travels a lot to suppliers and markets and she goes with him. But we talk occasionally. She makes me laugh so much.'

Lucy saw the way her cheeks coloured at having called the man who raised her 'my dad'; she wanted to tell her that it was okay, that you could never have too many people who had your back, but she didn't feel able. It was interesting to her that the reason for Camille's visit was to get this unruly teen away from her poor mum who was at breaking point, yet this was far from the picture that Camille now painted. She knew, however, that to raise it with Jonah would only make it seem like she was complaining about Camille's presence, which would not be the case. It was just a little confusing.

'This one?' Camille pointed at the newsagent, the first shop they came to.

'Yes, great, and then we'll work our way along. Do you want me to come in with you? Give you a bit of moral support?' she offered.

Camille's eyebrows met in a confused *V* above her nose, as if the idea were laughable. 'No, I'm good.'

Lucy watched as the girl flicked her bouncy hair over her shoulder and walked confidently inside.

I like to think that we would be great friends and that we would want to spend time together, just hanging out. I like to think that I would be able to fix every little thing that worried you and make it better, smoothing your path through life, be your go-to gal for everything from a spider under the bed to a bad dream. I would hold you and tell you everything was going to be okay, and it would have been okay, because I would be your mum and I would never let anything harm you. Never.

NINE

It was a mere three days later that Lucy arrived home to a distinct hubbub in the kitchen. She was glad of the distraction, the change of tempo, a refreshing change from the whine of the television and the sight of Camille slumped on the cushions that usually greeted her. This was different, and she welcomed the sounds of laughter that filtered under the door of the kitchen.

Her boss had hauled her over the coals not an hour ago; he was, apparently, less than happy at the lack of progress on the eco company job. Tansy and John, it seemed, were so busy bickering about their roles that they were failing to get things done, and this, she rightly understood, was her fault.

'You only get to wear the big-girl shoes, Lucy, if you are willing to make the tough decisions. That's what we pay you for, right?' her boss had asked, sitting behind his desk with his legs splayed and his overpowering cologne stinging her nose and the back of her throat.

She had nodded, deciding not to reply that she was tempted to whip off her big-girl shoes and whack him around the head with them, the sexist pig. She couldn't begin to imagine him talking to one of her male peers in the same condescending manner.

I hate my job, she thought as she left the building. But this wasn't true; she only hated her job today. In fact she loved her job. It gave her a huge sense of fulfilment every day to make her way across the foyer to the office with her name on the door, proof that she had broken through the ranks and made a mark. Her goal now was to promote others who were struggling with that glass ceiling; she wanted to help them smash through and would then encourage them to give her boss a virtual kick up the butt with their very own pair of big-girl shoes.

Pushing open the door, she took the two steps down into the kitchen, where there was the distinct mood of celebration. Jonah stood with his back to her, prepping two fat steaks with olive oil and salt and pepper, while seasoned vegetable kebabs of peppers, onions, mushrooms and courgettes awaited the grill, and Camille danced around the kitchen with music Lucy didn't recognise playing in the background. She swayed from side to side with her eyes closed and her arms stretched, trance-like, in front of her. The beat was loud and irregular, and Lucy smiled at the thought that she would actually rather be listening to Bon Jovi; at least then she could sing along. She knew if she shared this with her husband he would be delighted at how far she had come.

'Hello!' she called with a sense of embarrassment that she found hard to justify; she was, after all, only returning home to her husband and stepdaughter at the end of a busy day.

'Hey! Hello, you.' Jonah leant backwards and she pecked his upside-down cheek.

'This is some music.' She gave him a false bright smile, showing all of her teeth.

'Tell me about it.' He grimaced. 'It's Foals apparently.'

'Of course it is.' She nodded, none the wiser.

'Guess what?' Jonah smiled at her, as he set the steak aside and began to cube yet more onions and courgettes on the chopping board.

'What?' She was eager to catch up and join in.

'I got a job!' Camille jumped up and down and actually grabbed her by the shoulders for a second. It was a rare and welcome display of physical contact.

'Oh, Cam, that's great! I am so pleased for you. Where will you be working?'

'At Bill's; you know, the retro store? It's amazing; you know how much I love fashion? Well, they sell vintage pieces and reproduction vintage pieces and it's really cool and they could do with the help, part-time, for a few weeks, and they said that if it works out, whenever I come back I can go in and help out, just casually. I've got a job!' She began jumping up and down again, hugging herself.

'That is just brilliant.' Lucy was pleased, not only to see the girl's joy at securing her first job – she remembered how good that felt – but also that Camille had hinted that she might like to come back after this trip, meaning that her stay with them couldn't be that bad, not if she was planning to repeat it. 'You should be so proud of yourself. Getting a job, any job, is a real achievement and it shows gumption and drive. Well done, Camille. I see a lot of job applications and it's always those people who have worked hard, used their gumption and got out there that interest me the most.'

'That's pretty much what I said,' Jonah piped up from the counter where he was working. 'I figured we needed to celebrate, hence the finest fillet steak, twice-cooked chips and a ratatouille to accompany. And for you, this.' He reached behind the fruit bowl and produced a large glass of red wine, which he placed into her hand.

'Ooh, I don't mind if I do.' Lucy took up a seat at the kitchen table, deciding to join in rather than go and change into her comfortable clothes and miss out on the bonhomie that filled the room, bounced off the ceiling and fell to the floor like a sparkling mist.

'I called Mum. She's so happy, and *very* proud, like off the scale! She said that if she were nearer she'd take me out for a manicure or a massage, or some other treat. I miss her so much.' Camille pouted.

'Oh, that's a great idea! I can take you out for a manicure if you like? There's a great place on the Kilburn High Road. Would you like that? Your mum's right – we should celebrate. Your first job is a big deal,' Lucy enthused.

'How about that, Cam?' Jonah encouraged, in the way Fay did when trying to get Maisie to eat her greens.

The girl shook her head and sank down on to the bench. 'No, it's okay.' She studied her nails and drummed her fingers in time to the slowing beat of the song.

And just like that, Lucy was again reduced to the role of outsider. She sipped the wine, which had become strangely sour on her tongue, and could think of nothing to say as Camille and Jonah criss-crossed banter from one side of the room to the other, planning how she would spend her first pay packet and what new clothes she might need to complete the right look for the store.

'I can see this is going to end up costing us a fortune, eh, Lucy?' he guffawed.

Camille gave a mock sigh and threw a dishcloth at her dad, while Lucy nodded meekly and sat watching, feeling like a spectator who had been put in the cheap seats, far from the action, with something immovable blocking her view.

◆ ◆ ◆

She was more than happy when the time came to climb between the sheets. She was tired, but still decided to attempt a little bit of knitting before she fell asleep. It helped her switch off. Unfurling the new pattern, she smiled at the picture of the tiny pale-pink wrap-around ballet cardigan before picking up the loose ball of wool and rubbing it across her cheek. It was gloriously soft, and she got goosebumps imagining a baby girl wearing it in her arms. She cast on with the same enthusiasm she always felt when starting a new garment, buoyed by the thought that with nothing more than this long twist of delicate yarn and these two narrow metal sticks, she could create something beautiful and practical.

It still thrilled her, the idea that one day her baby might feel the touch of this wool against skin. By knitting she felt that she was keeping the dialogue open between her life now and her future life, as a mum. She let her mind get lost in the rhythm of the click and clack and the slow count of stitches: one, two, three, loop, three, two, one, loop . . .

'You're still awake?' Jonah's question, as he crept into the room, sounded a little accusatory, as if she might be hiding. Or maybe that was just her guilt being pricked, as his words probably held more than an element of truth.

'Yes. Thought I'd nod off, but I seem to have got into my pattern.' She held up the picture and saw him take a big swallow, as if even to see the picture, a reminder, brought him a measure of sadness. And for this she was glad, happy to see that his often jovial banter and seemingly easy acceptance of their childless state was not as clear cut as it seemed. It gave her comfort to know that he was still on board.

'Great news about Camille's little job, isn't it?' He changed the topic as he placed his cufflinks in the little pewter dish on his bedside table.

'It really is.' With the rhythm of her craft broken, Lucy finished up for the night, wrapping the wool around the needles and the half-made garment before stowing the bundle on the shelf in her bedside cabinet.

'She's feeling very pleased with herself.' He smiled as he unbuttoned his shirt and rolled his cuffs, rubbing his neck with his palm where his collar had irritated.

'It was a good idea of mine to go and distribute the letters with her; otherwise I think they might still be sitting in a pile in the sitting room, gathering dust.' She spoke a little curtly.

'Did she say thank you?' he asked, taking her cue that she had played a part.

'At the time, probably, yes. I don't remember exactly.' She pulled her knees up under the duvet and sat back against the headboard.

'Well, all right then.' He placed his watch on the bedside table and opened the drawer to remove one of the oversized T-shirts that he slept in. They nearly all bore the logos of motor companies, freebies given out at various events. There was a beat of expectation, heavy in the air, that this was not the end of the conversation.

'I do find that generally, though, she *isn't* that thankful, more expectant if anything, confident that things are going to get done for her and that's just the way it is! I suppose the word I am trying to avoid is "lazy".' She let her hands rise and then fall against the duvet.

Jonah pulled the cotton top over his head and placed his hands on his hips. 'Are you trying to start a fight?' He walked over and sat facing her on the edge of the mattress. 'This doesn't sound like you.'

'Well, maybe it *is* me and I've just been swallowing all the things I wanted to say for the last few weeks for fear of telling the truth,' she blurted, feeling her cheeks flame.

'What are you talking about?' He shook his head in confusion. 'What things?'

'I don't know.' She looked to the ceiling, trying to put into order what bothered her the most, aware as she drew up her mental list of how minor they sounded. 'Little things, like the fact that Camille should be putting her coffee mugs in the bloody dishwasher and not leaving them all over the house so we actually run out of mugs and I have to go foraging for one before I can make a hot drink. Or the fact that she has an inability to throw her dirty laundry in the basket, and she stores wrappers and packets under the sofa!' She beat the duvet in exasperation.

'She's a teenager; I think they are oblivious to that kind of thing.' He tried out a small laugh, as if he might be able to turn the air of tension into one of joviality with a bit of well-placed humour. It didn't work.

Lucy continued. 'And when I came home tonight, she has her music playing loudly, but we have a set thing, we play each other's music and it's funny and she comes along and whacks on whatever that was and we just put up with it!'

Jonah stared at her. 'Are you being serious right now?'

She continued. 'Yes! Yes, I am. It's like there's this little Jonah and Cammie club and I haven't been invited to join. I'm not part of the gang. She makes me feel like an outsider and this is supposed to be my home, but it's clearly her home and I don't know where I fit in. Or even *if* I fit in!'

'I honestly cannot work out if you are being serious.' He cocked his head to one side. 'I don't know where this is coming from or what's going on.'

'Yes! I'm being serious. She won't let me get close to her, not even a little bit – and trust me, I have tried. She verbally beats me with how wonderful her mum is and that makes me feel like crap, like it's a competition.' It was as if her thoughts had been uncorked, and once she started speaking, the words frothed from her, spilling over and leaving their mark.

'Every time I take a step towards her, invite her out, try to chat, anything at all, she takes two steps in the opposite direction, and I'm running out of space. She's up against a wall and I'm running headlong into it!' She was aware she had probably raised her voice, and this was confirmed by the way Jonah darted his gaze towards the closed bedroom door, a silent reminder that Camille was only a few feet away along the landing.

'Listen to yourself, Lucy – coffee cups and biscuit wrappers, it all sounds so petty!' he spat.

'That's me, petty,' she answered sarcastically. 'Do you have any idea what it has done to me? Losing my babies? Have you any concept of the emotional roller coaster that I am riding without a seat belt? I am bruised, I am hurt and I am scared, Jonah! I want a family, and as if that wasn't hard enough to contend with, I'm not sure you feel the same. And Camille . . .' She looked away. 'She knows how to pour salt on to my wounds. That's how it feels.'

He took a deep breath while they both reloaded, and she hoped for a change of tack. His words when they came were delivered slowly and quietly.

'She's a little girl who is a long way from home and is probably trying her very best to fit in,' he whispered.

She noted the tension to his jaw. It was interesting to her that he only chose to address this one aspect of her outpouring.

'Oh please, Jonah! She might only be sixteen, but she is very aware of what she does and how she does it.'

'Have you any idea what you sound like?' He narrowed his gaze. 'You sound jealous, horribly jealous, and it is very unattractive.'

Lucy took a sharp breath, wounded by his words. 'Well, I am sorry if you feel that way. But if I am jealous it's because I've been pushed out and I have tried every which way to find a gap, to wriggle into the inner circle, but she won't let me.' She cursed her tears that now fell, finding their way into her open mouth.

Jonah edged forward on the mattress. The sight of her tears seemed to have stirred something inside him. 'I think you are very tired and I think you are still grieving; your body has been through a lot and your hormones are still all over the place and that is only to be expected.'

'Don't you fucking dare!' It was a rare use of bad language in their home. 'Don't you dare try to blame the state in which we live on my hormones! Don't you dare!' Her voice squeaked, her throat taut with emotion.

Jonah paused and blinked. She got the overwhelming feeling that her outburst might only be confirming to him that he was on the right track, and this idea made her cry harder.

'Maybe having Camille here is a reminder of what we don't share, but I promise you, Lucy, it's ridiculous to feel that way. We can share Camille. You need to drop your guard and give her a chance.'

She sniffed at her tears, her body longing for him to place his arms around her and her mind wanting him to leave her alone. She gave a small nod.

He wasn't done. 'I also think it might be an idea if we go and talk to our doctor, see if he has any advice on how we get through this and just have a chat.'

Lucy looked up through her tear-filled lashes, nervous of seeking outside help, yet tempted by the possibility. 'Do you . . . do you think he might be able to do something that would help me keep a baby?'

Despite agreeing that the best thing they could do was wait, this faint glimmer of light on a dark horizon was something to which she was instantly and powerfully drawn.

'I think it's worth a chat,' he whispered. 'I was also thinking that he might be able to give you something that might help you mentally – do you think you might be a bit depressed?'

'I am not depressed,' she whispered. 'I am sad, and there's a world of difference.'

Jonah reached out and wrapped her in his arms. She placed her hand on the flat of his chest, feeling his heart beat against her fingers.

'It's okay, Lucy,' he murmured.

'I . . . I love you,' she managed through her tears. He kissed her head and her tears fell anew. Rather than the kiss, she had wanted to hear his response, the three little words of reassurance that would make everything feel a little better.

Camille sat with a small smile on her mouth as she tucked into her cereal. It was rare for the girl to be up this early, joining her and Jonah as they drank their morning coffee and prepared for their day. It was as if she didn't want to miss out, almost like she was enjoying the tension. Lucy shook this from her mind; maybe Jonah was right and she was being petty.

'So when do you start your new job?' she asked, as she took a seat opposite Camille at the table.

'This afternoon. But it's only to watch and learn how to work the cash register,' Camille answered with a mouth full of cereal.

'You'll be great. I'm sure.' She sipped her coffee. 'Would you like me to walk up and meet you? What time do you finish?'

'Six-thirty.'

'Okay, well, I'll come straight from the station if you like and we can walk home, two working girls together.'

Camille nodded. Lucy felt Jonah's large hands on her shoulders before he bent low and spoke into her ear. 'I love you, Mrs Carpenter.'

And the fact that this felt like a reward for doing and saying the right thing made her skin bristle.

◆ ◆ ◆

Lucy thought about what Jonah had said, and after careful consideration she dialled the number. She knew she would find it easier to go and talk to Dr Millard alone. She would then, of course, give Jonah a full rundown of what he had said. She managed to get an appointment early afternoon and left work early.

She sat in the waiting room watching the screen for her name to pop up. Sitting in the small room surrounded by new mums and expectant women was its own form of torture. Rather than engage with them, she buried her face in her phone and counted down the seconds until she was called. It was a huge relief to see her name flashing on the screen.

'How can I help you today?' The older man's officious manner made her speak quickly, aware that time was of the essence. She clutched her handbag on her lap.

'I have had two early miscarriages in the last few months, both quite early in the pregnancies.' She tried to focus on a chart on the wall, looking at the pyramid of numbers, anything other than give in to the emotion that threatened.

'Yes, I see from your records that conceiving is not the problem for you.' He paused and smiled at her.

She felt a thin film of cold sweat cover her skin, and her arms ran to goosebumps. 'No. Conceiving is not the problem.'

'So, recently,' the doctor continued, 'we have had one conception that resulted in an ERPC after severe bleeding and the other was deemed to have failed at scan, so' – he ran his finger over the screen – 'you took a pill and administered a pessary.' He read from the screen to his right through his thick-lensed glasses. Of course, her hospital visits were linked to her medical records, so Dr Millard was well aware. Of everything.

Lucy stared at the chart on the wall, watching as the numbers fogged into one another. She remembered how the first time she had heard the phrase 'ERPC' she had had to ask what it was. The busy nurse had given her a leaflet, and that was where she read the definition for the first time: 'Evacuation of Retained Products of Conception.' It was so horrible, so jarring, that she had to read it again: 'Evacuation of Retained Products of Conception.' Lucy had looked up at Jonah, both a little traumatised by this grotesque, mechanical description for what would be happening to her. He had gripped her hand as she read further: 'This means the removal of the remains of the pregnancy and surrounding tissue.'

The nurse had looked a little sheepish, offering in a kindly tone, 'I know it's a horrible term, we're not supposed to use it any more, but some of the literature is a little out of date.'

'Then perhaps you should get new literature,' Lucy had suggested, as she flicked the corner of the page back and forth with her thumb.

The nurse had nodded her agreement.

Jonah had squeezed her hand. She stared at him, not knowing how to put into words just how devastating it was to think of her baby as a retained product of conception. A thing. A product. Waste.

'This can't have been an easy time for you,' the doctor spoke, drawing her into the now.

'No, it hasn't.' She smiled at the understatement. 'We were wondering' – she coughed, trying to maintain her composure and move the discussion along – 'if there was someone we could go and talk to for advice. Maybe I'm doing something wrong?' She took a sharp intake of breath; speaking these words aloud caused a pain in her chest.

The doctor smiled at her and his face changed from stern to kindly. He removed his glasses and placed them on his desk before folding his hands over his ample belly.

'This is a conversation that I have too often, sadly. And I wish it were as simple as giving you the one golden solution that would make things work, but that isn't the case.' He paused. 'There are so many reasons for early miscarriage; it could be down to abnormal development at a very early stage, hormones or even a minor infection and a whole host of other things.' He waved his hand in an arc. 'You haven't done anything wrong, Mrs Carpenter, trust me. I see hundreds of women who experience the exact same thing as you and then go on to have a perfectly healthy full-term baby. In fact, this is usually what happens.'

'I do hope so.' She gave a faltering smile. 'Should I maybe go and see a specialist anyway, just in case?'

The doctor gave a single nod. 'That is your prerogative, of course, but we wouldn't be able to organise it for you until you had experienced at least three, or maybe more, early miscarriages.'

'So I would have to go through it again before I got a referral?' She found this unbelievable.

'Yes.' The doctor nodded and looked down, indicating that he too found the policy regretful. 'That is the process, largely because of the reasons we have discussed – that usually women who have two or three early miscarriages do then go on to have perfectly healthy babies. And it makes the investigation and any treatment redundant.'

'I don't want to go through it again, and I'm too scared to take the risk.'

'I understand that is how you feel right now, but please do take heart that just because of your experiences, this is by no means an indicator that it won't be possible for you in the future. There is no reason for you not to try again, if that is what you decide, as and when you are ready.'

'I wish I could do something more proactive than just wait and see.' She sniffed.

He nodded. 'And you *could* go and see a specialist, but I should warn you that about half of the couples who have investigations, which can be timely and expensive, don't ever find out why they miscarried. And I understand how frustrating this must sound but, on the positive side, this is because it reinforces what I said earlier, that there is a good chance of the next pregnancy being successful without any treatment at all.' He sat back in his chair.

Lucy looked at the man who seemed so full of optimism that she herself did not feel. 'Thank you, Dr Millard.'

'Not at all. I hope that what I have told you has offered you a ray of hope, of sunshine.'

'Not really,' she answered honestly, as she stood. 'I did want to ask you one thing.' She hesitated, nervous.

'Go ahead.'

'I . . . I have a picture in my head of my little girl,' she began.

Dr Millard nodded. 'Yes.'

'I talk to her and I feel like she's waiting somewhere for me, and I am worried that it's not normal to behave like that,' she stated, as she gathered her bag on to her shoulder, preparing to leave.

'Oh, Lucy, what's normal? I think you have been through a lot. A lot.' He paused. 'And that takes its toll. Do you have someone to talk to?'

She nodded.

'Keep talking – that's key. And for the record, I don't think you need to worry about your behaviour; it's just another sign that you are a mum-in-waiting.' He smiled.

❖　❖　❖

Lucy left the surgery with a hollow feeling of disappointment lining her gut. She had hoped for more, a silver bullet, a magic cure, anything. She now trod the pavement, off to meet Camille from her first day of work. She heard the doctor's words and hoped and prayed that this was not her destiny – to always be a mum-in-waiting.

◆ ◆ ◆

Camille came bounding out of the dark interior of Bill's with such exuberance it surprised Lucy. This was the most animated she had ever seen her. The girl landed on the pavement in front of her, having almost leapt Tigger-like from the doorway. Lucy was a little taken aback by her short shorts, denim cut-offs that showed an ample amount of her bottom and which she had teamed with a thin off-white cotton T-shirt that was a little sheer. It was tricky; Lucy would have felt far too self-conscious to leave the house looking like that, even if she did have the curves. The voice of reason in her head told her that Camille should be a little more covered up at sixteen, but it was a minefield and one she was wary of entering. She didn't want to mention anything that would give this stunning girl an ounce of self-doubt over her beautiful figure, and similarly she felt awkward about raising the fact that she felt Camille's clothes were a little too sexualised. Maybe it was her that was out of touch? She smiled broadly as the conversation flowed from her step-daughter, watching as she tucked her hair behind her ears and flapped her hands around to demonstrate what she was trying to describe. It made a pleasant change from the monosyllabic or reluctant responses that Lucy had to tease out of her ordinarily.

'. . . and I'm working with Emily and Dex, and Dex is so cute! He's seventeen and part-time like me and the rest of the time he's at college and he's going to be a DJ and he already does, like, really big club nights. And Emily is really cool too. It's her parents' store and she's full-time, but she's also a tattoo artist.'

'Don't let her practise on you; your dad would flip!' she managed to interject.

'Her tattoos are really beautiful; she's got like roses with thorns and other little flowers growing off the vine and they are these really pretty shades of pink and orange and she wears this awesome clashing bright red lipstick and her hair is like amazing!' She stopped to draw breath. 'And the clothes in the store are incredible. Leather jackets from the fifties – is that like before the war?'

'Almost.' Lucy smiled, thinking it might be a good idea to invest in a history book for Camille to take back to school.

'And Dex said he'd teach me to drive. I told him I was seventeen in three weeks.'

'So you are!' Lucy blushed, having quite forgotten the girl's birthday was looming. 'Although I'm not sure it's a good idea to get driving lessons from someone you have only just met; he might be a really bad driver.' She laughed, her message semi-serious. 'And in fact I don't think it's a good idea to drive in central London at all, not until you have found your feet.'

'Dex said it's easy; he had to learn to drive and get an old car because he's always had to rely on himself. He has no one looking after him. It makes me sad. He's got no dad, no family, apart from his mum, who is like a complete bitch, and it was the only way he could think to get away from her.'

'Camille!' Lucy stopped walking and looked at the girl.

'What?' Camille stopped walking too; she turned to face Lucy, shielding her eyes from the sun with her hand.

'I detest that word. It's horrible. And you can't talk about someone like that, especially not someone you have never met, *and* someone's mum.' She was aware of her authoritative tone, but the girl was only sixteen and was in her care.

'What do you care? You don't even know her!' Camille shouted.

'And neither do you, but that's not really the point.'

'Lighten up, Lucy. Here's a newsflash for you: not all mums bake cakes and help you with your homework; some are in fact complete *bitches*!' Camille emphasised the last word in absolute defiance. This not only shocked Lucy, but hurt her too. She had the distinct feeling that this was directed at her.

Lucy opened her mouth to respond, preferring that they didn't have this altercation in the street, but, as she did so, Camille turned and broke into a run, disappearing around the corner at the end of the road. It was such a sea change from the jovial chat they had been enjoying only seconds before that it left her a little stunned. She looked up and down the pavement to which she was rooted, almost as if looking for a clue as to what had just happened.

I think it's fair to say that I never think about the negative aspects of you. I never picture telling you off or feeling pissed off with you in any way. I can only ever see you as a smiling, beautiful, happy girl. I think about you and I sitting at the table in the kitchen and poring over prospectuses for colleges and universities, trying to decide over a mug of tea what might be best for your future. I watch you tap the pencil against your teeth, still undecided between architect, veterinary surgeon and lawyer. We weigh up the pros and cons of each and, exhausted by the task, we take a break for a tea refill and a piece of flapjack. And I feel like your friend as well as your mum, and that feels amazing.

TEN

Lucy took her time, walking home slowly with a layer of upset and confusion sitting on top of the emptiness she had felt since her visit to Dr Millard. She closed her eyes and offered up a silent prayer for strength before putting her key in the door. The first thing she heard was Camille's crying, huge gulping sobs that came from the sitting room, interspersed with the sound of Jonah cooing his words of comfort.

'Don't cry, Cam! Don't let anything spoil your first day at work; this should be a happy day,' he soothed.

'It was a happy day!' Camille shouted.

Lucy let her bag fall to the floor and walked into the sitting room with a feeling of dread. Jonah's expression was one of confusion. He looked torn. His body twitched, as if he wanted to jump up and talk to her but knew that when Camille was crying his rightful place was by her side. She felt the cold creep of exclusion wash over her once again and it wasn't pleasant.

Camille looked up at her with tear-stained eyes and sank further back in the cushions with her mouth set in a pout.

'I didn't expect you to run off, Camille.' She looked at the girl, who avoided her eyes.

'I think she's got herself a bit flustered.' Jonah's smile was fleeting. It disturbed her to see how quickly he tried to justify Camille's actions without speaking to Lucy first. It made it very clear in whose corner he stood.

'I don't doubt it. I was a bit flustered too. I'm not used to being spoken to like that, and equally I would never *talk* to anyone like that, especially in the street, but I can see how upset Camille is right now, so—' She was in the middle of offering an olive branch, about to suggest that the histrionics were attributable to a lot of excitement in a strange environment, a way for the girl to save face and for them all to move on, when Camille sat forward and spoke over her.

'You just don't get it, Lucy! Not everyone has a perfect life!' The petulant outburst was that of a little girl, a stark reminder to Lucy that she was just that. This was not a disagreement with any intellectual parity between the two.

'I know that, Camille, and I wasn't making a judgement on anyone's life or anyone's parenting.' She looked skyward at the near absurdity of the conversation and how quickly it had deteriorated into this fiasco.

Jonah's words floated into her mind: *Geneviève's having a bit of a tough time with Camille. I told her it's probably normal teenage rebellion . . .* 'Suddenly, she understood all too well what the woman might have been referring to. She chose a softer tone of reconciliation. 'What I objected to was the word you used, in public, very loudly, in my neighbourhood. A word that I find reprehensible.'

'What word?' Jonah looked at Camille.

Lucy looked at the girl, waiting for her to speak, wanting her to come clean. She was now certain, after hearing Jonah ask the question, that Camille's account could not have been that full or accurate.

Camille shrugged.

'What word, Lucy?' He looked at her. She understood he was seeking clarification, but couldn't shift an underlying resentment at the fact that she was being questioned in the same vein as Camille.

She ran her fingers through her hair. 'Do you know what? I have had a bit of a day, to put it mildly. I am going to go and have a long soak in the bath and leave you two to chat. If you want to talk to me when I am done, Camille, you know where I am.'

◆ ◆ ◆

Lucy lay in the bath, listening to the drip of the ancient plumbing and casting her eyes over the jumble of bottles that littered the top of the medicine cabinet in the corner. They were mostly old cologne bottles that were wrapped in a thin, sticky film of dust and needed throwing away. This was just one collection of Jonah's that drove her crazy, from the disused, defunct sports rackets and bats that filled a shelf in the wardrobe to his shoebox full of beer mats that clogged precious drawer space in their bedroom. There had been a time when she first moved in when she found his clutter endearing, homely; now she simply wished she could spring-clean without feeling guilty or being accused of destroying his heritage. She closed her eyes and lay down in the hot water, letting the warm foam of her bubble bath cover her skin. With her ears submerged, she could hear the distorted burble of the conversation in the sitting room, as high squeaks and low baritone responses reverberated up underneath the tub and hit her ears. For the first time in as long as she could remember, she let her mind wander to the cool, calm interior of her apartment on the Thames Path. She pictured neat and tidy Ross over on the other side of town, running his hands over the clutter-free surfaces and walking into the spacious wardrobe, and she wept with envy. At that moment in time she would have liked nothing more than to go there for a break, to revel in the solitude and dance barefoot on the tiled floors while drinking wine and wearing a face pack.

Don't be stupid, Lucy, she reprimanded herself. *This will pass. You are just tired. Too tired.*

◆ ◆ ◆

She had fully intended to go downstairs after her bath and grab a drink with Jonah, observing the old adage that you should never go to bed leaving things unsaid. The lure of the soft mattress had proved too much, however. Lucy had slipped seamlessly from her bathrobe into her pyjamas and under the duvet. Flitting in and out of sleep, she lay with a small inch of pink cotton fabric nestled in her palm, finding comfort in the contact, as she always did. She looked up at the ceiling through narrowed lids, as the last of the evening sun filtered through the leaves of the silver birch by their window, casting a dappled gold across the room. The pattern shifted in the gentle breeze. Birds perched on the telegraph pole tweeted up a cacophony that to her tired ears sounded a lot like bickering. The bedroom door opened slowly.

'I thought you were going to come back downstairs. I've been waiting for you.' His tone was a little accusatory, suggesting she might have been deliberately hiding out.

He might have been right.

'I thought I would too, but I got rather comfy and seem to have taken root.' She smiled, patting the mattress and pushing the pink cotton item up under her sleeve to retrieve later. Jonah kicked off his shoes and, still in his suit trousers and with his shirt sleeves rolled up, he lay next to her on the bed, his head resting on the stack of pillows that he always threw on to the floor, one by one, as the night progressed. The two lay side by side on their backs, both looking up at the beautiful display across the ceiling. It was certainly easier to talk when not sitting face to face.

'How's Camille?' Her concern was genuine; she hoped she had stopped crying.

'She's good. Had a little weep then spoke to her friend in Poitiers – Alison?'

'Alice.'

'Yes, that's it, Alice; and then she went up for an early night with a box of crackers and tub of cream cheese. I don't think any amount of distress could dampen her appetite.' He laughed.

'Oh, Jonah, what a horrible day. I don't really know what happened with her. One minute she was gabbling, happily talking about work and the people she had met and I genuinely felt like we were making friends.' She looked across at him briefly, aware of how shallow that might sound; she was, after all, the girl's stepmother. 'Then she used the word "bitch" so casually and aggressively and I told her that was not okay and she got so mad. I certainly didn't want to take the gloss off her first day at work. I think I was alarmed at how easily it slipped from her mouth and the fact that it was aimed at a woman she had never met, but then I was more alarmed at how quickly it escalated. Maybe I over-reacted.' She paused, waiting for him to offer an insight. In truth, she was hoping for reassurance that she hadn't been in the wrong.

Jonah took a deep breath. 'I think it's different for her generation. I think they do swear more—'

'No, you misunderstand me,' she cut in. 'It's not swearing I have a problem with – I mean, I'd rather she didn't, of course – but if it had been just that I would have given her a look of disapproval, a bit of a jokey reprimand to keep the peace and we could have moved on, but it was more than that. It was that particular word. I meant what I said to her – I detest it. There is no male equivalent; it's vicious. I find it judgemental.'

She had rocked on the mattress, trying to erase the words, which were not meant for her ears. Two male orderlies snickering outside her hospital ward: 'How old? Dirty little bitch!' followed by their lascivious grunts of laughter.

Lucy shivered.

'I suppose it is.' He spoke as if in thought.

'I don't want to be the censorial maiden aunt in the background, but I guess I find it difficult sometimes to know where the lines are drawn. I definitely hold back where she is concerned. I know I do, and that makes it hard for me.'

'In what way do you hold back?' he asked.

'Lots of ways, but a good example would be that if Maisie, when she was older, dressed how Camille did today, in a very revealing way, I would have no hesitation in telling her, nicely, that I think she'd be better off wearing something a little more conservative. I mean, yes, I would encourage her to celebrate her body, of course! She's beautiful. But there was something a bit raunchy about Camille's clothes that I didn't think was right. It was her first day of work and I understand the need for her to be in fashion, but I don't think it sent out the right message. God, listen to me. I sound exactly like that maiden aunt.'

'No, I think you have a point, but it's a hard one to broach,' he confessed, and she was glad they appeared to be on the same page, something she had missed of late.

'For me it's about keeping her safe,' she continued. 'She has that amazing body, but she is only sixteen and I think sometimes, when you have a body like that, it can be a while before your mind catches up, even if you think it has. Does that make sense?'

'Yes.' Jonah turned on to his side and stared at her. 'Why do you think you hold back with her?' He went back to that point, clearly still curious.

Lucy turned her head towards him and they held hands. 'I think I am very aware that I don't want to tread on Geneviève's toes. I'm conscious of the fact that she has a mum and for me to jump in with my amateur parenting would feel odd for us both. I guess also I don't have the confidence because I have never done it, but I think above all I want Camille to like me, I know that will make you happy, so I tend to hold back, trying to be nice all the time so she likes me. That's it, I guess.'

She watched his eyebrows knit together, as if she were speaking a foreign tongue and he was trying to figure out the meaning. The clipped tone that followed was not what she had expected after her own impassioned confession.

'We will only ever feel like a proper family if we can all relax; it's important. It doesn't need to be the big deal you are making it, Lucy. She is only here for a few weeks, don't forget, and then she's back in France to start a new course or get a job, whatever. I just want her to have a nice break while she is here. You don't need to parent her; you need to be her friend, a guide, that's it!' He made it sound so obvious.

'I know that, Jonah, of course I do! But firstly, it doesn't matter that it's only for a few weeks; it is laying the foundation for all future visits. And secondly, it's not as easy as having a plate of pasta and whacking on some music and giggling until dawn; these things take time.' Her blood pressure rose as she struggled to make herself understood.

'Exactly,' he gestured. 'These things take time, and there are huge gaps in my knowledge, don't forget. We shall figure it out together.'

'That sounds good.' Her words were both appeasing and resigned; she didn't want to keep going around in circles. 'Camille and I have to get to know each other, and I feel she puts up barriers that make that harder than it needs to be.'

'Look, she's probably nervous as hell; I don't buy all that bravado. She might be sixteen but I think she's still a little scared of losing her dad.'

Lucy looked back towards the ceiling as a steady stream of tears fell along her temples and into the mattress.

'Don't cry, my Lucy!' He leant forward and kissed her face; his mouth was soon wet with her tears.

'I can't help it.' She sniffed. 'I sometimes wonder if I lost a little bit of myself when I married you, and that scares me. Don't get me wrong; I love you. I love you so much, but I get scared too. I know it sounds selfish, maybe it is, but I want us to come first and I think we've lost a bit of that recently.'

'No no no no, Lucy.' He laid his arm across her in a loose embrace. 'You can't look at it that way. You do lose things when you get married, it's true, but what we gain far outweighs what we have lost. My life was so empty without you in it. That day I saw you in the church, your beautiful face and your manner . . . I fell for you, hook, line and sinker, and I realised that you were my missing piece. I am happy with you by my side and without you I am not. It's that simple.'

'Is it that simple?' She wiped her eyes.

'Yes! It really is. I know I can make you happy, always. And we have to try not to overcomplicate things.' He kissed her face again.

The two lay like that for some minutes, feeling the world settle around them until their heart rates dropped and the natural rhythm returned to their breathing. It was Lucy who broke the silence, as she tried to paper over the crack in her thoughts.

'I had an appointment with Dr Millard today, just before I went to meet Camille.'

He sat up on the mattress and faced her. 'You should have said. I would have come with you.'

'I know.' She patted his arm and smiled. 'But I wanted to go on my own.' She sniffed again.

'What did he say?' His chest heaved.

'Pretty much what everyone else has said, that these things just happen sometimes and that there was no real point in investigating why as, more often than not, people who experience early miscarriage go ahead and have healthy babies.'

'Well that's really good news!'

She was certain his open expression was meant to reassure her.

'I guess, but there's a part of me that would like to know why, not only so that I can try and guard against it, but also because it would help me understand. I think it might make me feel less sad if I knew,' she whispered. 'He said there was no reason not to try again when we were ready.'

Jonah's face broke into a wide smile. 'Lucy, this is good, good news! If it's just a case of keep trying, why don't we? I know that I certainly haven't changed my mind. I want nothing more than to have our baby.'

'Really?' She looked into his eyes.

'Yes, of course, really!' He kissed her again.

'I've been worried that you didn't seem that fussed when I suggested we wait. I thought you might have been a little relieved and it threw me completely. I thought we might have been on different paths.'

'Relieved? Not at all. We are on the same path, my love. But I didn't want to put any more pressure on you than you were already trying to deal with. I still don't.'

'I do want our baby,' she cried. 'I want her so much. I feel like she's waiting for me somewhere.'

'I want our baby too.' He held her tight. 'I do.'

The two fell into a deep slumber, wrapped in each other's arms with the promise of a brighter day tomorrow. Lucy slept soundly, exhausted and at the same time relieved to have spoken her mind; she felt wonderfully unburdened.

Both stirred as the light of dawn peeped over the horizon, flooding their bedroom with light.

Jonah wriggled. 'My arm has gone numb.' He laughed, trying to work his limb free from under her side.

'I feel happy.' She smiled, snuggling closer into him under the duvet.

'Me too.' He pushed her hair from her face. 'I'm sorry about the whole Cam thing yesterday. I didn't know what to do. I felt caught in the middle and I didn't like it one bit.'

'Me either,' she admitted.

'I guess we have to figure these things out together, but one thing I do know is that you shouldn't hold back, Lucy. If you want to say something you need to be able to. This is your home and you need to be free to speak; otherwise things will get bottled up and that's no good. No stress, remember?' He smiled.

'Yep, no stress.' She nodded against him.

'How about we organise a bit of a family day, take Camille out to meet Fay and Adam and your mum? Cam might like that.'

'Really?' She wrinkled her nose.

'Yes, really. It would be great for her to feel she is part of something bigger than us rattling around in Queen's Park. Let's take her out to Kent to meet the wider family.' He spoke with growing enthusiasm.

'If you think so,' she agreed.

'I do. And in the meantime, I am very excited about us trying again for our baby, and you know what they say . . .'

'What?' She yawned, glad that there was still more sleep to be had before the alarm went off.

'No time like the present.' He kissed her, before pulling the duvet over their heads and rolling her on top of him.

Things between us were strained. I knew I loved Jonah, that he made me happy and that I wanted to be married to him. I also knew he would be the best dad ever, I saw evidence of his kind nature every day, but it was like someone in the distance was slowly banging a drum that only I could hear. It was a low, slow, deep, heavy boom that resonated in my mind, reminding me of the passing of time and distracting my thoughts. I could only focus my mind on one thing, the fact that I was desperate to be a mother. It was an overwhelming, all-consuming sensation that flavoured my food, coloured my opinions and influenced my choices. I was also battling with the thought that Jonah didn't feel the need for a child as strongly as I did and I didn't know how to manage that.

And this will sound extreme, ridiculous even, but when I got my period it was with such a sense of sadness that I would lock the bathroom door and howl, as surely as I had when I miscarried. These two events were, quite obviously, inextricably linked. The blood lost in both cases might have been for different reasons and in differing amounts, but both were proof of one thing: I was still a mum-in-waiting. And that made me sadder than I can say.

ELEVEN

The car journey out to leafy West Malling was pleasant. Camille sat on the luxurious back seat of the off-road Porsche. It was one of the perks of Jonah's business, being able to rustle up a fabulous car when the need arose. With her headphones plugged into the sound system, her stepdaughter alternated between snacking on sweets and singing out loud. Every time her tuneless caterwauling filled the small space, Jonah laughed and Lucy joined in. She felt like they were any other family out on a jaunt, creating memories that would inevitably help build their shared history, and that could only be a good thing. Lucy tried to ignore the stir of concern that Camille might be rude or offhand in front of her family, not quite knowing how she would handle that.

'This is so pretty!' Camille sat forward and looked out the window. Lucy was glad that the traditional English high street – with its ivy-covered buildings, timber-beamed pubs, Georgian terraces, double-bay-windowed shopfronts and cobbled area where the war memorial lived – was making the right impression. Jonah again caught her eye with a smile that boasted success.

The peace of the historic market town where her sister and family lived was shattered the second Fay opened the front door to their extended cottage. The original part of the house was over three hundred years old, with exposed aged brickwork and an inglenook fireplace. It was peppered with history: blackened hooks in the ceiling where meat had once hung to dry and the remnants of an ancient bread oven, now used as a rather natty bookshelf. There was a modern extension at the back, added in the seventies, where the big square kitchen opened out on to the garden, letting the light into what would have been a rather dark space.

The sounds of Maisie crying, Rory shouting, Adam calling from upstairs, nursery rhymes playing and Duster the large mongrel barking filled the air.

'It's like a portal to the underworld! Please don't make me go inside!' Jonah pulled a face at Lucy, and she placed her hand on his arm in a small gesture of reassurance.

'Fear not – I'll protect you. I know their ways.' She laughed.

Camille showed none of the reticence that Lucy had envisaged. Instead, she climbed down from the back of the car, in her high-waisted jeans that stopped just above her ankle and a pretty sleeveless floral shirt, and trod the path to the house confidently.

'Hey, Camille! Welcome!' Fay stepped forward, wiping her hands – which were nearly always covered in paint, glue, flour or something equally as messy – on her jeans, and reached up. Lucy watched in surprise as the two wrapped their arms around each other in a warm, easy hug, as if they had been doing so forever, both parting with a smile. She found it hard not to recall the awkward introduction that had been made in their kitchen only a few weeks before, remembering what it felt like to have to lower her arms and retain her grin while her face flamed.

'It's so lovely to finally meet you! I have heard so much about you,' Fay enthused. 'Welcome to the madhouse!' She stood back, gesturing with her arm for Camille to go on in, which she did.

'How are you?' Fay kissed her sister on the cheek.

'Good, you?' Lucy replied.

'Great!' She smiled.

With the formalities out of the way, Lucy and Jonah followed Fay inside, handing over the bunch of flowers, box of chocolates and bottles of wine they had retrieved from the car, along with two brand-new children's books whose illustrations had called to her when she had popped her head into Queen's Park Books. She had thoroughly enjoyed choosing them.

'You shouldn't have!' The gifts filled Fay's raised arms. 'But I'm very glad you did. Thank you for our goodies.' She beamed as she deposited the booty on the dresser, to be dealt with later. Lucy felt her shoulders tense, worrying that the summer bouquet of pink stocks, sunflowers and orange antirrhinum wouldn't get into water in time. They were already looking a little wilted after being incarcerated in the back of the car for an hour or so.

They trooped in, and, without instruction, Camille turned left into the cosy sitting room and immediately sat on the rug where Rory, still in his Superman pyjamas, had laid out a rather elaborate car track that filled most of the floor space. He was busy running cars and rescue vehicles along it with sound effects as he shouted instructions. 'You can be a lorry driver.' He put the little green lorry into her palm. Camille immediately lay on her front, kicking her long legs up behind her. With the track at eye level, she whizzed the lorry around making an impressive engine noise, until it came bumper to bumper with Rory's tractor.

'Beep beep!' she called out. 'Hey! Move that tractor, Superman. I have important deliveries to make, you know!'

Rory's face split into a wide grin, clearly delighted with his new friend who was not only pretty but also great at playing cars.

Fay pulled a downward mouth and nodded approvingly to Lucy, as if to acknowledge how well the girl had dropped into the house and become Rory's playmate. It was almost as if she was challenging the picture Lucy had painted.

'Hi, all. Sorry, got in a muddle with the days. I was convinced you were coming next week for some reason!' With Maisie in tow, Adam looked as if he had only just jumped out of the shower, as was apparent from the wet hair that curled against his neck. This was not a shock. Adam lived his life at a permanent jog, undertaking every task with his arms set at right angles by his ribs, as if this half-running stance might help him claw back some of the time that he inevitably lost as the day unfolded. He was on constant catch-up. Lucy would have found his lack of punctuality and his forgetfulness hard to live with, and even as an occasional visitor she was tempted to shake him by the shoulders and suggest he set his alarm a little earlier and write stuff down. She and Jonah had privately wondered how he managed to deliver five sixty-minute lessons a day, picturing him as a haphazard tutor whose marking was sloppy and organisation poor. Lucy loved him regardless; he made her sister happy and was a great dad to her niece and nephew, and that made everything else seem a little irrelevant.

'Maisie is teething.' Fay pointed at the plump baby girl with red cheeks who now hovered on her dad's hip, her dribbly fist shoved in her mouth as she hiccupped tears.

'Poor little thing.' Lucy touched her finger to Maisie's cheek and smiled at the little beauty.

'Poor little us,' Adam corrected. 'She's been up half the night.'

'Do you want me to take her?' Jonah stepped forward at Adam's grateful nod and scooped Maisie into his arms, jiggling her up and down as she sat on his forearm. Her crying stopped, suggesting she was either glad of the change or a little shocked. Either way, no one minded the quiet that crept over the kitchen. Even Duster the dog seemed to sigh, as he lay with his greying muzzle on the cool floor by the back door.

Lucy smiled at her husband. There was something quite wonderful and bittersweet about seeing her man holding this baby girl, and she wondered if he would ever get to hold their own.

'Adam, as you are now hands-free, could you fire up the barbecue?' Fay smiled at her husband, sweetly.

'This is what she does.' Adam shook his head in Fay's direction, speaking about her with fondness, as if she were absent. 'If she thinks I have a second in the day that isn't allocated, she fills it up with a pressing chore.'

'No, you are right, honey. Don't bother,' Fay mocked. 'I'm sorry to have troubled you. Why don't you go and put your feet up and I'll give everyone a raw hamburger and a bit of salad. It'll be fine. Or a frozen chicken Kiev, à la Lucy!'

Lucy pulled a face at her sister.

'Okay, okay, I'm going!' Adam loped out to the kitchen, winking at the wife he adored, admitting defeat. Jonah and Maisie followed him outside.

'So, how's you?' Fay asked, as if she might get a more honest response now they were alone.

'Fine.' She nodded, giving a small shrug.

'Whoa there with all that information!' Fay briefly placed her hands over her ears.

'Well, what do you want to know?' She leant against the worktop and pushed the sleeves of her cotton jersey over her elbows before folding her arms and watching as Fay popped on the kettle to make tea.

'I don't know . . . How's your fancy job? What's it like having Camille to stay? Why do you look so skinny? And why does your smile only go as far as your nose?' She turned to her sister with her hand over her eyes. 'It's like everything below my hand is smiling, but when I do this' – she removed her palm – 'your eyes look a bit sad.'

'You do realise I am not one of your eight-year-old pupils, right? You can talk to me like a grown-up,' she snapped, irritated not only by the question but by her sister's insight.

'Okay, you want grown-up talk? I'm worried about you. You don't seem yourself and it's not only me – Mum called me and said the same, and we want to know if there's anything we can do to help. Happier to have it phrased like that?'

'A bit.' She was thinking of how to explain how she felt, the pressure she was under and her desire for a child, as well as how difficult it was trying to bond with Camille, when the girl herself appeared in the kitchen.

'Hey, Camille!' Fay alerted her sister of her presence, in case she hadn't noticed. 'When you've had enough of playing with cars, feel free to escape. Rory would be more than happy to keep you captive there all day if he had his way.'

'No, it's okay. I like playing with him. He's so sweet. And he said I could be Supergirl, which is like the biggest compliment ever!' She laughed, reaching up to pull her hair into a ponytail, anchoring it with the thin red band that lived on her wrist and revealing her taut, flat tummy as she did so.

'God, it is,' Fay agreed. 'I've been playing cars endlessly for years and I've only ever made it to Superman's assistant. You should consider it the highest honour.'

'Oh, I do.' Camille chuckled.

'And Lucy told me you have a job in a shop in Queen's Park?'

'Yes!' Her eyes lit up. 'It's part-time, just while I'm here, but I really like it.' She hunched her shoulders, looking simultaneously happy and coy.

'What does the shop sell?' Fay asked, as she filled the teapot with hot water to warm it.

'Amazing vintage clothes and retro pieces, like belts and funky rings, all sorts, and nearly every piece is a one-off,' Camille explained. 'They get a lot of stuff imported from all over the world. It's exciting. I love the clothes!'

'I'm not surprised – it sounds great!' Fay enthused. 'Bit different from life in France I bet?'

'It is, and I work there with my boyfriend, Dex, who is a DJ and at college too, so pretty busy.' Camille kicked the toe of her navy canvas Toms against the red tiled floor.

'Oh, wow! I didn't know you had a boyfriend.' Fay smiled. 'Fast worker!'

Lucy knew she looked startled, and she concentrated on finding a more neutral expression. The ease with which Camille divulged the information to Fay, a complete stranger, took her by surprise, coupled with the fact that she had been kept in the dark about this development, the kind of thing she hoped a girl might share with her stepmum.

'Yeah, I guess, but when it feels right.' Camille shrugged, seeming way older than her sixteen years.

'So what's he like; is he nice?' Fay was enjoying the teenage topic.

'He really is. He's smart and good-looking and he's had to kind of look out for himself. His mum was . . .' Camille turned and looked at Lucy, as if she had been waiting for a chance to use the new and improved phrase. 'Let's just say she was not such a great mum.'

Lucy couldn't decide whether the girl's pointed choice of phrase was an olive branch to appease her or a verbal stick with which to prod her, reminding her of their row.

'Oh, how sad,' Fay commented.

'It is, really.' Camille smiled at Fay's sympathy. 'But he's happy now and I guess that's what matters.'

'Who's happy now?' Jonah asked, as he came through the back door with a very happy Maisie still bouncing on his arm.

'Camille's boyfriend,' Lucy fired, happy to see the look of confusion on his face, making her feel like she wasn't alone in being kept at arm's length.

'Boyfriend? Goodness me! Who is this young man and why has he not asked for my permission?' Jonah joked, and Fay and Camille laughed.

Lucy looked from one to the other; was it only her that felt a little put out by the revelation?

'Hel-loo!' Her mum's voice filled the hallway, drawing their attention as she called through the letterbox. All looked towards the door.

Lucy felt a second of awkwardness wash over her, hoping Camille didn't embarrass her or showcase her poor stepmothering skills in front of Jan.

She watched as the girl stepped forward and took the teapot from Fay's hands. 'You go and open the door. I can make the tea.' She smiled sweetly. 'Where are your cups?'

'In the cupboard above the sink. And thank you, Camille. That's so kind.' Fay gave Lucy a double thumbs up, clearly very impressed with her stepdaughter.

It was quite incredible. She looked from the girl to Jonah, who beamed with pride at Camille's impeccable manners and confident air. Lucy, however, was intrigued as to how Camille could have lived with them for all this time without so much as putting a cup in the dishwasher or making her bed, and yet here, in a house where she had only just set foot, she was a model visitor and obviously feeling very at home.

Lucy's mother swept into the room, dotting kisses on everyone's cheek as she made her entrance, adding to the party atmosphere.

'Camille! How lovely for me to have a teenage granddaughter.'

Lucy felt the blood drain from her face and her legs wobble. She gripped the nearest chair. How easily her mum spouted the words.

'Please call me Gran or Granny, whichever you prefer. And look at you; you are very beautiful!' her mum offered with typical gusto, appraising the girl who smiled in front of her.

No sooner had Jan put her basket on the table than she and Camille stood swapping small talk about her journey from Surrey. The front doorbell rang again.

'I'll go,' Lucy called out, but since Fay stood with her hands in the sink, the men and babies had gravitated towards the barbecue and Jan and Camille were laughing like old friends, she wasn't entirely sure that anyone had heard.

She opened the front door and stared, feeling her legs sway beneath her.

'Lucy!' Richard looked equally as taken aback to see her on the other side of the front door. He instinctively placed his hand on the tiny down-covered scalp that peeped from inside the baby sling he wore so comfortably on his chest. 'I didn't expect to see you.' He looked a little flustered.

It was odd for her too, to come face to face with the man for whom she had shed so many tears and feel nothing more than a flicker of attraction and a whole heap of awkwardness.

'I promised to drop the keys off for Joyce's caravan, think Fay and Adam might be going for a long weekend.' He rushed, as if hoping that by speaking quickly he could get the whole interaction over with as soon as possible and at the same time wanting to show he had a legitimate reason for turning up at her sister's house. 'H-how are you?' he stuttered.

She watched the nervous bulge of his Adam's apple rise and fall.

'I'm good.' She looked again at the purple sling from which dangled the two tiny spaghetti legs of a newborn.

'I believe congratulations are in order; you got married!' He rocked on his heels as if this alone was a miracle.

'Yes, I did. And congratulations, yourself; you've had a baby.' She pointed, awkwardly, feeling the usual hot swarm of tears at the back of her throat, a reflex when in close proximity to a new baby. It felt so unfair.

'Yes!' He smiled and pulled his head back on his shoulders to get a better look at the infant. Turning, he pulled the sling aside to reveal a sleeping bundle swaddled in a white blanket. Its little nose was squashed and the tiny fingers rested on its rounded cheek.

'This is Dominic Drake, who arrived eight weeks ago, weighing seven pounds three ounces.' His voice echoed with pride and a little shock, as if he still couldn't quite believe that this incredible miracle was his. This she understood.

Lucy looked from the baby to his dad, who placed his hands protectively on the sling. He looked tired, but utterly, utterly besotted, as if he held in his hands everything he had ever wanted, and not a Breitling in sight.

Her mind flitted to the conversation they had shared during their relationship. Lying on his sitting room rug in the early hours with tongues lubricated by Prosecco, she had felt emboldened.

'I want a baby, Rich!'

'No, you don't. They are noisy, smelly, inconvenient and expensive. Get a cat.'

'I don't want a cat! I want a baby. I think it would be wonderful.' She nuzzled his neck. 'Let's just go for it.'

'No! You have a great career; do you know how many people would kill for a position like yours? You can't give it all up to have a baby.'

'I can have both.'

He had sat up then, placing his wine glass on the coffee table; it was a second or two before he spoke. 'Even if that is true, I think we might be on different pages, Lucy. I mean, I love you, of course, and I think we make a great couple, but babies?' He shook his head. 'They are not in my plan, not at all.'

It occurred to her then, as she studied the man on the doorstep, that when he had said he didn't want a baby, he had actually meant he didn't want a baby with her. And now, as she looked back down the hall in time to see Camille opening the drawer to locate a teaspoon and lining up the cups on the worktop, so relaxed in this house, it made her wonder if maybe her miscarriages were nature's way of telling her she couldn't do it. Maybe she wasn't cut out to be a mum – maybe Richard saw that and maybe Camille sensed it too.

'He's lovely,' she managed, smiling at the infant, feeling a bolt of loss fire through her gut.

'We think so.' He beamed, establishing himself in a couple, as if she needed any reminder. It irritated her that he might think she harboured any feelings for him other than indifference. 'Anyway, I shan't come in, but can you take these?' He dangled the keys at arm's length. Lucy took them and nodded.

'You look well, Lucy,' he added before turning around. She watched as her ex-fiancé made his way back down the path and off to a life with cousin Davina.

Lucy walked into the kitchen, listening to Fay quiz Camille about what she might like as a gift for her upcoming birthday. She placed the keys on the dresser and tried to remember a time when Richard had looked that happy, and couldn't.

'Penny for them?' Jonah whispered in her ear, standing close to her.

She painted on a bright smile. 'I was thinking we should invite Camille's boyfriend over for supper on her birthday; what do you think?' she lied.

'I think that sounds like a splendid idea.' He smiled and bent down to kiss her cheek.

◆ ◆ ◆

Except for Richard's visit with his beautiful son, the day had been a great success. Everyone had laughed and eaten too much, and Camille, Fay and Rory had even had a dance in the garden. Lucy was well aware that it was only her that seemed to feel a little on edge, as if waiting for something to be said or done that might reveal the cracks in her relationship with her stepdaughter.

As Jonah drove them out of the countryside and back towards town, he twisted his head and asked the question over his shoulder: 'So, a boyfriend, eh? That seems a bit sudden.'

Lucy was glad that he had broached the subject.

Camille beamed. 'I like him.' As if this phrase might be all it took by way of explanation.

'You can't have spent that much time with him; you've only been at Bill's for a couple of weeks,' Lucy pointed out, keeping her tone as gentle as she could muster, aware that anything more accusatory might inflame the situation. The last thing she wanted was to spoil what had been such a lovely day.

'It feels like a lot longer,' Camille whispered. 'We talk all the time. I've never got on so well with anyone in my whole life, ever.' She addressed the darkening shadows outside the car window. One quick glance told Lucy that the girl was in an almost dreamlike state. 'I just know.'

Jonah leant across and placed his hand on top of Lucy's. 'I know that feeling, and we can hardly comment, can we? I practically proposed within minutes of meeting you.'

She smiled at the memory, but knew that it was not comparable. Camille was a child of sixteen who needed steering in the right direction. It bothered her that Jonah wasn't seeing that.

'I do think you should take things slowly, Cam.' It was the best way she could think of to hint that she probably knew very little about this seventeen-year-old boy. Camille nodded, but Lucy doubted she was giving her words a second of consideration.

When they arrived home, Camille retreated to her room, no doubt to FaceTime Alice or speak to the enigmatic Dex.

Jonah filled the kettle.

'Are you worried at all about the whole boyfriend thing?' she asked tentatively, as she yawned.

'No, not really.' He wrinkled his nose. 'I figure they're just kids having a bit of fun, and it might be just the distraction she needs. It was certainly lovely to see her so relaxed and amiable at Fay's today. I think she was quite a hit. Especially with Rory.'

Lucy nodded. 'Oh absolutely.' That she was. Jonah's summary, however, did little to reassure her, but one thing Lucy did know was that she didn't have the energy for another altercation over what was best for Camille. It was one more example of how she felt unable to fully express her concern, relegated in the parenting stakes.

◆ ◆ ◆

She kicked off her sandals and showered, letting the warm spray wash away the dust of a strange day. After changing into her pyjamas she pulled the little wicker hamper down from the top of the wardrobe, smiling as the lid creaked open to reveal the stunning, ever-growing collection of baby clothes. It gave her comfort and caused her heart to ache as she ran her fingers over the tiny cardigans, little jerseys and mini socks that she had made. Some she plucked from the tissue and ran over her cheek, loving the feel of the soft wool against her skin. She pictured Richard, recalling his expression of pure joy as he laid his palms on the baby that slept against his chest.

'I hope I can do it, baby. I hope I can find you and I hope I can keep you. I want it more than anything,' she whispered into the still night air, as the familiar sob built in her chest.

Her telephone buzzed on the bedside table.

'Hey, you got back okay then?' Her sister was drinking, no doubt topping up on her tea fix, as was her habit.

'Yes. By the way, before I forget, Richard dropped off the keys for Auntie Joyce's caravan. I shoved them on the dresser.'

'No way! You saw him?'

'Yes, it was no big deal,' she lied. 'He showed me his little boy; he was beautiful.' She swallowed.

'Who, Richard or the baby?' Fay quipped.

Lucy tutted, ignoring her jibe. 'Thank you for a great day.' She meant it; both Fay and Adam had gone to a lot of trouble.

'Oh, we loved it. We were just saying that Camille is so lovely.'

'Yes.' She decided not to elaborate.

'Rory was very taken with her,' Fay enthused. 'He asked if she could come and play again soon.'

Lucy nodded. 'It's funny, Fay. I saw a different side to her today. Usually she's not so . . .' She tried to find the right word.

'Not so what?' Fay prompted.

'I don't know, not so appeasing. She's a little cool with me.' Once again she pictured her and Fay's comfortable hug, a small thing, but a big thing to her.

'Well, firstly you don't know what her mum has said about you, and kids are very easily influenced, don't forget. I once mentioned in front of Rory that my department head had been unreasonable, and when we bumped into her in the street, he practically snarled at her! I was so embarrassed, but it's that protective gene; it's strong.'

'Good point.' It was the first time Lucy had considered this – that it might be a straightforward case of Camille taking sides and of course she was going to pick her mum's side in whatever imaginary war Geneviève had discussed.

'Secondly I'm not sleeping with her dad.'

'I should certainly hope not!' She giggled.

Fay tutted, choosing to ignore her. 'And therefore I am far preferable to you on that score; it might make her feel a little uncomfortable and that might be reflected in some of her behaviour.'

'Okay, another good point. Anything else?' She was grateful for her sister's wisdom.

'It might be a bit of old-fashioned jealousy.' The sound of Fay taking a gulp of her drink filled her ear.

'Really? I don't know what she would feel jealous about. I have tried really hard to make her feel special. I went to so much trouble with her room and she never really said if she liked it. In fact, she just pointed out that there was nowhere for her to hang her clothes!' Lucy eyed the bedroom door, making sure it was closed, as she kept her voice down.

There was a second or two of quiet before Fay spoke again. 'Of course, there is another explanation.'

'What?' Lucy sank back against the pillows.

'It might not be Camille that's the problem or Camille who is jealous. It might be you.'

Lucy could only stare at the phone in her hand. 'That's ridiculous! What a thing to say to me.' She felt an intense frustration that Fay had suggested such a thing. To her it smacked of disloyalty. She wondered how quickly she could end the call.

I sometimes think about my future and realise that not being a mother isn't a temporary sadness, something that will pass. Without you, I never get to see my child graduate, never get to sit at the front of a church when you marry, never have the chance to lay my arm across your back whilst trying to figure out how to fix your broken heart, and I never get to hold my grandchild.

In later life, probably as the pain has subsided a little and I have patched the holes in my life that you would have filled, with work, with Jonah, with holidays and all manner of happy distractions, I will then have to go through it all again. Not only have I had to watch my friends and family holding their babies, but I will then want to slope off to a dark place while they press pictures of grandchildren into my palms and regale me with the achievements of the cleverest, cutest kids ever born, beaming with a pride that I can only dream of.

It's as if the punishment for me will go on and on until my dying day. The little ripples of not having you here with me will get bigger and bigger, as the years pass, until I can no longer see the point at which it began, but will live in the middle, trapped by the rolling rings of consequence from that one thing: losing you. You will always remain the one thing that I crave. The one thing I want. And that thought, this realisation, makes me sadder than I can ever say.

TWELVE

Lucy stood in the shower, lamenting the arrival of her period, soaping her body with vigour and disliking her inability to do anything about the situation. She considered this monthly event, knowing that for some it brought sweet relief. For others it was just an irritation to be suffered, an inconvenience during any holiday or special occasion. But for her, it was a tangible sign of her failure, and it was hard not to let it get her down.

You've got to be patient, Lucy! Her little pep talk did little to alleviate her disappointment. She watched her loss snake along the shower tray in a thin, dark, winding tributary, and cried quietly into the deluge.

Dressing quickly, knowing that time was of the essence, she towel-dried her hair, creeping down the stairs before Jonah woke and Camille surfaced, happy that Camille's birthday had fallen on a Saturday. She had decided to go to town. This was a chance to build a bridge, and not just any bridge, but one that sparkled with pizazz and fairy dust! Fay's comments had troubled her, and this was a chance to show just how grown-up she could be about the whole situation.

The two helium balloons that had been collected the day before and had spent the night hiding in her wardrobe were now standing in pride of place in the corner of the kitchen, hovering on long blue ribbons that were weighted at the bottom. A large shiny silver number one bobbed next to a large shiny silver number seven. They made quite a statement. The cake, which she had ordered from the snazzy Pru Plum's bakery in Mayfair, was stunning. Knowing that Camille wanted something a bit different, she had chosen this magnificent creation that now sat in pride of place on an ornate glass cake stand on the breakfast table. Sitting on top of a dense, rich base of buttery shortbread crumble was a pristine New York baked cheesecake that had been artfully decorated around the border with a wealth of glazed halved strawberries, blueberries and raspberries, all finished with a dusting of powdered sugar. In fine dark chocolate script were the words 'Happy Birthday Camille'. It looked beautiful and was just the perfect dessert for the tea party they had planned for this afternoon.

Jonah's card sat propped against the wrapped gifts, and hers sat beside his. They decided to send one each, wanting Camille to have as many cards as possible to adorn the shelf. There was one that had arrived in the week from France, and this too now stood proudly with the others, including one from West Malling, Kent, and one in Lucy's mother's instantly recognisable handwriting.

Lucy made the pancake batter and set it to rest on the side before painstakingly coring, peeling and chopping an array of ripe fruits, including nectarines, apples and pears, which she placed into a glass bowl. She then prepared virgin cocktails of cranberry juice, freshly squeezed lime and sparkling mineral water, poured them into long glasses, garnished them with a rip of mint, and left them to cool in the fridge. A batch of plump, buttery croissants was warming in the bottom oven, and a bowl of glossy strawberry compote was ready to be served. Fresh coffee had brewed, sending its heady aroma out into the atmosphere, and now all she needed was the birthday girl.

Jonah bounced down the stairs, arriving in the kitchen in his bare feet. 'Oh my! This looks and smells wonderful; you have been busy.'

'I thought it would be a nice thing to do.'

'It really is. You are lovely. You should have woken me up.' He yawned. 'I'd have helped you.' He rubbed his eyes and fastened his cotton dressing gown over his T-shirt and plaid lounge pants.

'Jonah, you can hardly stay awake now, let alone if I'd got you up any earlier!' She laughed. 'Anyway, I wanted a little bit of time alone.'

'Oh, not working on the weekend again? Do I have to confiscate your work laptop?' He narrowed his eyes. 'You know the rule.'

'No.' She concentrated on pouring him a cup of coffee. 'I got my period today.'

'Oh, Lucy.' He walked over and took her in his arms. 'We just need to keep practising – that's the good news, right?' He kissed the top of her head. She knew he was trying to turn the sad moment into a humorous one, and he nearly succeeded. Lucy knew deep down, however, that these words were not enough of a sticking plaster to keep her dark thoughts at bay.

Suddenly they were aware of the thump of footsteps on the stairs, and they parted.

'Happy birthday to you . . .' they both sang loudly and out of tune, each bolstered by the other's carefree performance. Camille stepped down into the kitchen looking freshly risen with her hair mussed and her skin glowing. She covered her eyes in mock embarrassment, before beaming broadly at the sight that greeted her.

'Oh, wow! Look at my balloons – they are so cool!' She stood with her pyjama sleeves pulled down over her dainty hands, hands over her mouth, looking at the stack of gifts and inhaling the rich aromas of what promised to be a lovely breakfast. 'Oh, and look at my cake!' she squealed, noticing the stunning centrepiece for the first time.

'It's from Pru Plum's,' Lucy pointed out, wanting Camille to know she had gone to the trouble to make things as perfect as they could be.

'Thank you, Lucy. It's gorgeous.' Camille unexpectedly walked across the room and placed her arms around her stepmother. Lucy felt a surge of something close to love as the girl held her tightly.

'You are very welcome,' she whispered, as she held her in a warm embrace. 'Happy birthday, Camille.'

As the two women parted and Lucy turned her attention to retrieving the cocktails from the fridge, she noticed Jonah had turned his back to them both at the sink. If she didn't know him better, she would have sworn that he was crying.

The birthday breakfast was a feast of mammoth proportions. With her and Jonah's playlists shuffling on the sound system, Camille saw fit to mock both of their tastes in music, and by the time the pancake course was cleared away, croissants polished off, cocktails drunk and the fruit salad ladled into bowls, they had conceded, and Camille put her phone into the docking station, filling the kitchen with the heavy guitar and monotone, indecipherable crooning that she favoured. She and Jonah put their heads in their hands and laughed.

'It's not my fault you guys are so old!' Camille mocked lovingly.

Lucy pushed the little stack of presents towards her stepdaughter. 'Come on, open your gifts!' she urged. 'Before we get any older.'

'I'll start with my cards first.'

Lucy smiled, remembering doing the same when she was younger, wanting to savour every second and make it last.

She and Jonah sipped coffee and forked mouthfuls of fruit into their already full tummies while they watched Camille, with a bright spot of colour on each cheek, carefully extract every card and read the messages slowly, holding each one up to show who it was from. It was a task she undertook with humility and evident joy, which was heart-warming.

The card from Geneviève and Jean-Luc was short and sweet, depicting a large, glittery gift tied in a bow. Inside were three short lines and a whole bunch of kisses.

'From my mum!' She smiled and placed it on the shelf. Lucy couldn't help but notice that the card was the generic kind she might grab in a hurry from a convenience store, bought in a rush along with milk and plastic-tasting white bread and without too much consideration of the recipient. She buried the thought; maybe she was just being mean and again the lack of gift could be explained because it was hard to send things over that distance, and costly too. Lucy knew without a doubt, however, that if it were her daughter it wouldn't matter where she was in the world. That girl would receive a gift and a card with the words 'For My Daughter!' emblazoned on the front and a carefully chosen reminder of home.

Happy Birthday, this is for you, a single kiss to mark your special day, my darling . . .

'Oh, thank you both! That's great. I can get that blouse that's just come into Bill's! Thank you!' Camille fanned the two twenty-pound notes that had been placed inside her card and slowly read the message from her dad.

Lucy felt her stomach bunch in anticipation as Camille then pulled from the envelope the cream, hand-cut card she had chosen. On the front was a sketch depicting a vintage handbag, the kind she hoped Camille would like.

'I love this!' Camille raved. 'I can get it framed! Can we get one of those little frames from Ikea?' Her enthusiasm brought a lump to Lucy's throat.

'Of course we can.' She smiled; it was a great feeling to know that she had chosen well. The message she had written was simple and well considered: 'To Camille, I wish for you nothing but wonderful things in your coming year. May your dreams come true and may the path that leads you to them be without bumps! With love, Lucy x'.

'Thank you.' Camille smiled again before attacking her gifts with childlike abandon. Holding up the tan leather anklet with a beautiful turquoise stone that Fay had sent, Camille beamed. 'Oh my God! I love it!' She immediately placed it around her ankle and admired the way it looked by twisting her leg to the side and photographing it in close-up on her phone and sending the image to her friend Alice for good measure. Lucy reminded herself to let Fay know just how delighted she had been with her gift.

The grey cotton waffle robe Lucy had chosen for her was similarly well received, along with a box of chocolates, two spiral-bound notebooks for school and three disposable purple fountain pens, which Lucy had chosen on the basis that she would like the gift herself.

'Oh these are so cool! I love stationery!' Camille enthused.

'Me too!' she echoed, ridiculously happy to have unearthed another connection.

Both flicked through the empty notebooks, agreeing, much to Jonah's bemusement, that there was nothing quite as nice as a fresh, clean notebook, awaiting the touch of an ink pen and the endless possibilities of what it might contain.

With all her presents unwrapped, Camille sat back on the bench and surveyed the detritus of gifts and food and wrapping paper.

'I've never had such a lovely birthday morning, ever!'

Lucy doubted this was true, not when Camille and her mum were so close, but she loved her for saying so nonetheless.

◆ ◆ ◆

She and Jonah cleared the kitchen, stopping to kiss and chat, as the radio burbled away in the background and the sound of Camille, singing happily in the bath, filtered through the floorboards from above.

'I think she's having a great day,' he commented, raising his eyes towards the ceiling. 'Thank you. She got some lovely gifts. You are so good at this stuff. I can't remember the last time I saw her on her actual birthday, but I know it was years ago. And I didn't do half as good a job as this. I think we went out for a wander around the Victoria and Albert Museum if I remember rightly.'

'It's been easy and fun! My mum and dad always made a big deal of our birthdays when we were small, and I remember how lovely it was to feel like I was special on a day that was so ordinary for everyone else. And for the record, I would have loved a day at the V&A. Still would.'

'I find it a bit strange how you and your mum don't seem that close, and yet you had this idyllic childhood. What happened?' He sounded curious.

Lucy shrugged as she placed the birthday cake in the fridge. 'I don't know. I think things changed for me after my dad died, and they certainly changed for her.' She busied herself inside the door, organising the bottles and jars that had been shoved in rather haphazardly.

'Your father would be so ashamed!'

'But not for Fay? I mean, she and Jan seem to get on really well,' he pushed.

'I don't know, Jonah. Maybe she just likes Fay more, or maybe Fay is just a goody-goody!' She tried to employ his favoured method of layering humour to ease the situation.

'I don't see Fay as a goody-goody, not at all. I don't know, just something I was wondering about. It always feels like there is a little bit of an edge to the way you and your mum interact. It's like you've just had a fight. I know that sounds crazy.' He laughed.

'I don't know what more to say, Jonah; why don't you ask my mum?' She closed the fridge door a little forcefully. *Please don't push me on this.* Her thoughts were loud and intrusive in her mind.

The two were quiet for a second or two. Lucy gathered up the discarded shreds of wrapping paper and scrunched them into a ball before pushing it into the recycling box.

'I'm looking forward to meeting the elusive Dex this afternoon.' Jonah sucked in through his teeth and straightened his back as he dried the cocktail glasses with a dishcloth.

She was glad of the change of topic. And was similarly excited about meeting the boy who apparently took her stepdaughter out to lunch, introduced her to his friends who visited them at Bill's, and took her for a spin on his BMX around Queen's Park. It would be good to finally put a face to the name. 'Really? You are looking forward to it? Your words say one thing, but your body language screams the exact opposite!' She laughed.

'I'm trying.' He winked. 'It's an odd feeling. I still think she's a little girl and yet here she is, old enough to drive a car, God help us all.'

She high-fived this; her fear of Camille on the road was just as real.

'And as if that is not enough to petrify me, she's bringing home a boy she's dating. I mean, if you can call it that. I think it's more of a friendship.' He sighed. 'I wish I could put the brakes on the world and keep time at bay for a few more years. I knew how to handle her when she played with My Little Pony and all it took to make her day was a Happy Meal with her dad.'

She hated that he might never get to do these things with their baby.

'It'll be fine. And you know that you will always be able to make her day with a Happy Meal if she's eating it with you.'

'Minus the hamburger now of course.' Jonah laughed.

'Of course.' She rubbed his arm. 'And as for Dex, he will probably be feeling more nervous than we are. We shall make him welcome.'

'Oh, Lord above – now I am nervous. Supposing he's horrible, arrogant?' He put the cloth on the drainer and stared at her.

'Again, we have to remember that this is Camille's choice. Plus, if he is, we can take comfort from the fact that it's purely a little holiday fling and she will be abandoning us for France in a month or so. These little romances are good practice. I had one with a boy once.' She paused, thinking of Scott . . .

'Oh, do tell me more!' He laughed.

Lucy opened her mouth and sought a reasonable substitution in her mind. 'Let me see . . . we met at a caravan park in Tenby, he let me braid his hair, and I thought that was a great recipe for future love and happiness.'

He laughed again. 'How old were you?'

'I think about nine.'

'Okay. My jealousy has faded, and for the record if you want to braid my hair you can.'

'That's so sweet, darling, but you haven't enough to braid.'

'Ouch!' He ran his hand over his thinning pate. 'That was brutal.'

Lucy had thoroughly enjoyed her interaction with Camille that morning and had loved preparing for her birthday. Their conversation, however, reminded her that in just a few weeks they would have the house to themselves again and she would no longer feel the need to tiptoe around Camille, craving her approval.

This would also be the best time to get back on track with trying for a baby, and at this thought her spirit felt a lift of joy.

◆ ◆ ◆

With Jonah out for a run, no doubt trying to jog off the three crois-sants and two pancakes he had devoured, Lucy took advantage of the quiet lull in her day. It had been an early start, and she was glad of the opportunity to sit on her bed with her latest knitting pattern spread out in front of her, running over the instructions with her finger on the text, reading out loud: 'Place the needle under the top stitch and bring the yarn back over the first stitch. Twist around in a loop and repeat . . . What? That makes absolutely no sense!' She scratched her head with the end of the needle and read it again.

She felt the beginnings of regret that she had chosen to make an intricate blanket, with a raised pattern and a soft, feathered, lacy edge. She had only managed a few rows, and now her only hope was that as her familiarity with the pattern increased, so too would her confidence and then her speed.

Lucy looked up as Camille slowly pushed open the bedroom door, half knocking and calling out 'Hello?' as she did so, offering plenty of time to afford Lucy some privacy should she need it.

'Hey, Camille. Just having a breather.' She always felt a little guilty for taking time out to relax.

'What are you doing?' Camille sat on the edge of the bed with one leg beneath her and ran her hand over the pattern.

'I'm knitting.'

'I didn't know you knitted!' She laughed with a little disdain to her tone.

'You can laugh, but it's the most relaxing thing I know. I can sit for hours and knit and I get lost in it. I forget my troubles and think about nothing other than the wool between my fingers, and sometimes when I stop knitting, I find that solutions pop into my head. It's like pressing my reset button. It stops me overthinking.'

'That sounds good.'

'It is. And at the end of it, I have made a beautiful garment that I am always really proud of,' she admitted. 'And although this doesn't look like much at the moment, it will become something really lovely. If I ever get the hang of it. I must confess I'm struggling, but I won't let it defeat me.' She held up the measly few rows that sat in a thick cluster on her needles.

'Is this what you are knitting, this blanket?' Camille closed the page and looked at the picture on the front, a photograph of the finished article; the blanket was folded in half with the lace edge dangling down and a small brown knitted rabbit perching on the top of the woolly mattress.

'Uh-huh.' She nodded.

'I like the little rabbit. Are you going to do one of those too?'

'I hadn't planned on it, no.' She saw the flicker of disappointment on Camille's face, as if she might like such a thing.

'Is it a blanket for Maisie?'

'Not really, she's a bit big for this now.' She felt a flush of embarrassment creep over her chest, wondering what Camille's next question might be.

'It's for a baby,' Camille stated.

'Yes.'

There were one, two, three beats of silence. Lucy silently prayed that the girl wouldn't probe too deeply, knowing she would sob if she were to have to recount her attempts at becoming a mum.

'Do you think you and Dad might have a baby?' she asked, keeping her eyes downward as she toyed with the anklet that Fay had sent her.

Lucy shook her head and took a breath. 'I don't know, is the honest answer.' She felt the sudden knife-like stab of period pain to the left of her belly button, a reminder of just how far away that dream was. 'I think I would like to have one.' She hesitated, knowing this was best, this watered-down version of her all-consuming desire to become a mum. 'But I guess it's up to nature. I can only do so much.' She coughed, realising that she was talking about sex – and not any old sex, but sex with this girl's dad. Camille pulled a face at her and they both laughed.

'I think you'd be a good mum.'

Lucy stared at her; the words tripped so lightly from her stepdaughter's tongue, she could have had no clue as to just how much they meant.

'Really?' Lucy whispered, swallowing the rising tide of joy that almost choked her.

'Yeah, I mean, you do great birthdays!' She smiled. 'That was awesome this morning. My balloons are so cool.'

Lucy took Camille's hand into hers; it felt like the most natural thing in the world.

'I'm having the best day.'

'Good.' She gave a small nod, as she released her grip.

Camille stood, a little embarrassed by the display, and thumbed towards her room. 'I'd better go and get ready. Dex will be here in a couple of hours.'

Lucy nodded, and she tried to imagine a time when she had taken two hours to get ready for a boy. She picked up the needles, reopened the pattern and resumed her knitting with a bubble of joy in her gut that buoyed her.

◆ ◆ ◆

'I'm a bit nervous,' Jonah confessed, as Lucy popped a bottle of champagne in the fridge and laid a cloth over the individual tarts she had warmed, the aroma of goat's cheese, scorched scallion and melting Gruyère wafting up her nose.

'Don't be. It'll be fine. Imagine being a weedy seventeen-year-old, off to meet the parents. He must be petrified. The poor lamb.'

'I guess so.' He seemed to relax a little.

With everything set, they took the opportunity to sit and read the newspaper. Jonah pulled the Saturday edition in half, keeping the sports and handing her the news and celebrity gossip. They sat in amiable silence at the table with their thighs touching, both lost in the fine, opinionated print. Their peace was eventually shattered by the sound of the front doorbell. The two exchanged a knowing look and hastily folded the newspaper away before leaping into action.

Before the faint echo of the bell had receded, Camille thundered down the stairs. 'I'll get it!' her voice screamed in panic at the prospect of either Lucy or Jonah getting to the door first.

Lucy stood on tiptoes and kissed her husband on the cheek before removing the Pru Plum creation from the fridge and placing it once again in the centre of the table, turning it so that the words were facing the door. She heard the high-pitched laugh of infatuation leave her stepdaughter's mouth. It was one she recognised, a heady burble that told anyone within earshot that she was completely enamoured. She remembered emitting something similar with her first love, Scott, as they walked to his house during lunch break. She knew it was a glorious release for the fireworks of happiness that fired within. The memory of that time made her stomach bunch; it had felt wonderful. She had revelled in that happiness, blissfully unaware of what lay ahead.

Camille opened the kitchen door and with a blush to her cheek, smiling widely, announced, 'Dad, Lucy, this is Dex.'

Lucy had been wrong on a couple of counts. Dex certainly didn't appear to be nervous, he wasn't the least bit weedy and he was certainly no petrified lamb. She felt Jonah's stare bore into the side of her face, but she refused to acknowledge it, keeping her eyes resolutely fixed on their guest.

Stepping forward, she smiled at the hulk of a boy standing before them in his black skinny jeans and scruffy Vans. His ripped muscles, visible in his tank top, gleamed beneath a slick of moisturiser. His dark curly hair was artfully styled into a short but fierce Mohawk and his face was beautiful. Lucy could see the attraction. She reached out her hand to shake Dex's, as he hastily swapped hands, placing his large, unwieldy skateboard in his left and shaking with his right.

'It's good to meet you, Dex.' She smiled.

'Yep, same.' He returned her smile, to reveal an impressive set of straight white teeth. Lucy looked at Camille, who stared up at Dex with a doe-eyed expression that looked like something beyond love. The atmosphere around the two crackled with a level of intensity that fired a bolt of concern through her gut. Her instinct told her that this relationship was way more than just a couple of kids having fun.

'And I'm Jonah, Camille's father.' Jonah coughed.

Lucy watched as he stepped forward and gave the boy a brief but firm handshake. She noted that he had rejected the less intimidating word 'dad', and it made her heart flip with love for her man who, she could see despite her earlier reassurance, was more than a little out of his depth.

'Can I park that for you?' Lucy pointed at the skateboard.

'Oh yeah, thanks!' He handed it over with both hands, as if it was a thing of a delicate nature, a precious object, and she realised that to him it might well be.

'Happy birthday, Cam.' He handed her a slender tissue-wrapped package that he had pulled from the back pocket of his jeans.

'Oh wow, thank you. I told you not to get me anything,' she scoffed, clearly beyond delighted that he had ignored her. Camille turned the gift over in her hands and carefully ripped one end of the tissue, as if trying to be contained and grown-up in every action. 'No way!' She hugged the two strips of dark card to her chest before throwing her arms around Dex's neck with abandon. He placed a strong arm across her back, anchoring her close to him.

Jonah coughed again.

'Tickets to see Foals! Oh my God! Thank you!' Camille waved them at Lucy, as she broke free from Dex's hold.

Their close physical proximity told Lucy that this was not the first time they had been this intimate; there was no hint of awkwardness, no first-time nerves, no fumbling hands or respectful distance. They slid together in a well-rehearsed dance. There was an obvious ease between the two physically as their bodies aligned, demonstrating a comfortable familiarity. This single action made a mockery of Jonah's suggestion that the two might just be friends.

She decided this would be one insight that would need very careful handling; she would have to choose her phrases well. She considered the prospect with a measure of dread. How was she going to broach the fact that, in her opinion, Camille and Dex were enjoying a lot more than a spin around Queen's Park on his bike?

As the four took seats at the kitchen table, she and Jonah chose chairs on one side and Dex and Camille sat close together on the pew by the wall with their thighs touching, just as she and her husband had done earlier, despite the bench having adequate space for three.

Jonah poured four flutes of champagne.

'Oh wow! Do you do this every day?' Dex grinned, holding the delicate stem between his fingers.

'Yes, every day we stop whatever we are doing for champagne and cake!' Lucy smiled. 'Actually, wouldn't that be lovely? I think we should introduce it as a house rule.'

'In that case, I shall see you at the same time tomorrow,' he quipped.

'And you would be most welcome,' Lucy said.

Camille gave her a look of such warmth that she seemed to be lit up from within, and Lucy basked in the reflection.

'Actually,' Dex said after taking a small sip of his fizz, 'I think if you did this every day it would become normal, and that would be such a shame if an occasion like this didn't feel special.'

'You are absolutely right.' Lucy smiled at the boy, warming to his easy manner and smart insights.

'So, Dex,' Jonah began, 'Camille tells me you are at college?'

'Yes.' He chewed and swallowed the mouthful of crumbly tart, placing his hand over his mouth as he spoke. 'I'm at the City of Westminster College doing a course in Music Tech.'

'So do you play instruments?'

She watched Jonah's face light up at the prospect; given his love of music, this would definitely elevate the boy in his opinion.

Dex shook his head and took a sip of his drink. 'No, I don't. I wish I did. I'm learning the piano, but I'm pretty rubbish. What I do is more around music technology.'

'Right.' Jonah nodded, clearly having no more of an idea than she did.

'What does that mean, Dex?' she asked, on their joint behalf.

'Okay, so it's like basically using computers and technology to compose music, edit stuff or improve someone else's composition,' he explained with enthusiasm. 'You need the ear of a composer, the rhythm of a musician, but you also need to know how to program.'

'Gosh, it sounds complicated.'

The boy shook his head. 'Not really.'

'Dex had a gig in Ibiza at the beginning of the summer, just before I met him,' Camille added brightly, as if trying to bolster the boy's CV. 'His stuff is really good. It's all over YouTube and he gets asked to do sets all the time!' the girl continued with her PR offensive.

'Were you playing at a party in Ibiza?'

Lucy loved how Jonah was trying, feeling a swell of affection for her man.

Dex's smile was one of warmth, without the condescension she might have expected in someone of his age. 'It was a bit like a party, yes. It's a huge outdoor nightclub that holds around five thousand people.'

'Five thousand?' she queried. 'Goodness me.'

'Yes, I know, it's mad,' he agreed. 'There are different dance floors and huge terraces – it's crazy. But I can earn more there in a couple of nights than in a whole month of my regular jobs here, so it's worth it,' he explained.

Lucy remembered Camille's description of how Dex had no family to speak of and no support. It tore at her heart to see this young man who was self-sufficient, without the wonderful network that she or indeed Camille enjoyed.

Dex continued: 'People think it's just a case of standing in the booth and pressing a few buttons but it's so much more than that. It's not enough to just pitch up with your playlist. You have to feel the tempo of the room and respond to that, making sure you don't drop a beat, fading one tune into the other in a way that builds and builds. It's like you are taking people on a journey. And if you get it right, they are dancing, lost and they don't realise that you are on to the next tune or the next. You carry them along on a wave of sound.'

Lucy noted the slight glaze to his eyes. 'Do you really love it?'

'I do!' He nodded. 'When you look out and there are thousands and thousands of people dancing to your music, it's like you're a puppeteer, making them all jump.' He shook his head, as if reliving it.

'And then after you finish your set, you slip into the crowd and no one recognises you, but you know inside what you have just achieved and it feels amazing.' He paused, and Lucy got the distinct impression that he was going to share a confidence. 'But what I really want to do is write scores for films; that would be the dream.'

'Well, I think if you have passion for something that is half the battle.' She nodded and finished her glass of champagne.

'Plus, he's really good. He's going to have a brilliant career,' Camille gushed. Lucy would have been willing to bet that the girl saw a flash of his future and, if her fervid manner was anything to go by, she was certain that Camille saw herself in that picture too.

'So how much longer do you have at college?' Jonah steered the conversation into less emotive waters.

'I'm just about to go into my final year, which will be cool, as I get to pick the modules that I really want to study and I may even get a placement within the industry, although they are rare, but also, I get at least one year with Camille. It'll be really nice.' He smiled at the birthday girl.

Both she and Jonah, still with their smiles fixed, looked from Dex to Camille and then each other.

'I'm sorry?' Judging from Jonah's expression, he, like her, was more than a little confused. Lucy was wondering if Dex was planning to go to France, and tried to guess what Geneviève would make of that.

Camille sat forward. Her fingers fidgeted against each other on the tabletop, her cheeks blushed and her posture was that of someone who wanted to flee the room.

'I was going to say,' she began, shooting a quick look at Dex – whether to gain confidence or in reprimand, it was hard to tell – 'I am applying to Dex's college to study fashion design. It's a two-year course. I wasn't sure what I wanted to do in France, but this makes more sense. I only applied a few days ago, but they've already offered me an interview.

So I may as well go and see what happens. I'm really excited.' She eyed Lucy with obvious nerves.

There was a second or two of silence while Jonah stared at his daughter and Lucy felt the flutter of anxiety in her chest. It was one thing having the girl here for a break, and she had to admit the last couple of days had been more than pleasant. But, as unpalatable as it was, she was certain that the reason for this was that she knew Camille's time here was coming closer to the end.

'Well, I never!' Jonah sat back in the chair, looking a little winded.

'What do you think, Lucy?' Camille asked, looking up at her through lowered lids.

'I think we need to eat this birthday cake!' she offered with more gusto than she felt, as she went to fetch a sharp knife.

Oh, your birthday! What a day that would be. I would make you a cake and decorate the house with banners, before creeping into your room with a fistful of balloons and confetti and a cupcake with a single candle in it. This would become one of our traditions, so no matter how old you got, you'd always wake to a cupcake, with pink frosting of course, and a single candle. If for any reason I couldn't be with you on that day, you'd make one for yourself or someone you loved would buy you one, and holding that cupcake would make you feel close to me wherever you were in the world. Your birthday would be a day for great, great celebration, the day my life changed. The day I got you, the day I gave my heart away . . .

THIRTEEN

Lucy took her time in the bathroom, spending an age cleaning and flossing her teeth, removing her make-up, cleansing and toning her skin, and even giving the toilet a good bleaching. She did anything she could to delay having the next conversation with her husband. She knew that for them, when it came to Camille, it was a bit like being friendly supporters of two neighbouring teams that never played each other, making amicability and gentle ribbing possible. But boy oh boy – when they did eventually meet on the field, she knew they could expect a good fight.

The birthday tea had been nice, the fancy cake a great success, and Dex very good company. The second bottle of champagne that she and Jonah had shared before the kids left the house for the late-night cinema also helped their Saturday pass in a slight haze of fuzzy happiness. But the effect of the alcohol had long since dulled. It was now bedtime, and they were going to be alone, free for the first time to discuss Camille's announcement. Lucy dotted moisturiser onto her face and neck before rubbing it in. Unable to think of another thing to do short of polishing the tiles, she pulled the light cord and made her way into the bedroom. Jonah was already in bed, sitting up and reading the headlines on his tablet.

'I think everyone's had a good time today.' She smiled, tucking the lightweight duvet over her legs.

'You did her proud, you really did. What do we make of young Dex?' He swiped the screen and put the tablet face down on his bedside table.

'I thought he was lovely. Not what I was expecting at all.' She whispered this confession as she massaged hand cream into her cuticles, even though they were alone. Whispering made the gossip seem more palatable.

'In what way?'

'I suppose if I tried to picture a seventeen-year-old, I thought he'd be like a boy, but he's clearly manly, grown-up. And very mature.' She trod with caution.

'Yes. I didn't know whether to be happy that she was in safe hands – I'm sure he can look after her should they ever run into trouble – or devastated because she's still my little girl.' He yawned.

'I like him. I do,' she confessed, 'and Camille seemed very happy. I liked the way she was around him – relaxed – and it's good for her to feel like that. When it's reciprocated it can make you feel like a million dollars.'

'Well, I hope you feel like a million dollars, because I adore you.' He slipped down on the mattress and lay with his head on her stomach. 'How's your tum?' He placed his hand on her pyjama top, which covered her stomach.

She stroked his dark, curly hair. 'It's fine.' Running her hand over his naked shoulders, peppered with the freckles of past tans, she considered how best to launch the topic that swirled in her mind, kicking up a dust storm that made it hard to see anything else clearly. Despite her reticence to discuss the issue, she knew that it would hover until she did, making sleep impossible. 'So what do you think about Camille staying here on a more permanent basis?' She tried to keep her tone casual, hoping it belied the frenzy of anxiety she felt.

'I'm really surprised!' He snorted. 'She hadn't mentioned anything to me, but I don't think she's serious. I wouldn't have thought she'd choose this inner-city life over a spacious farmhouse with a pool in France, where she's not only got all that space and sunshine but her mates and her mum too. It's all she's ever known.'

Lucy nodded, thinking for the first time that a pool, a farmhouse and the pretty French countryside were no match for the buzz of inner-city London for a seventeen-year-old girl with a love of fashion and music – especially an inner-city London with the lovely Dex residing in it.

'I'm not so sure, Jonah. They say the grass is always greener on the other side, and I think she might want to stay because she wants to be with Dex.'

'No!' He laughed, shifting until his head rested on his hand above his elbow. 'Surely not? That's just a little holiday fling. I mean, I don't dislike the boy, he clearly has had to carve his own path and that's admirable, but I don't think he's for Camille.'

'Ah, but that's just it. You don't get to choose who's for Camille. She does,' she reminded him.

I can see your future! I can see it, as surely as if I had a crystal ball! You are a child! A child!

Lucy shook her head to rid it of the words that had sprung unbidden to the front of her mind.

'I know that.' He chuckled. 'But I can tell you it's not DJ Dex or whatever his name is.'

'Jonah, I am not kidding. Did you see the way she *looked* at him? I can tell you, this is more than a fling,' she reasoned. 'They had chemistry and seemed very at ease with each other.'

She pictured herself at a similar age, draped over the boy she had loved, desperate to feel his skin against her, intoxicated by his scent.

He sat up and scooted back to his side of the bed and the support of the padded headboard. 'Really?'

'Yes, really!' She tutted, a little irritated that he was so oblivious.

'Well, I guess if she wants to stay and it's a course worth doing . . .'

Jonah let his words linger, and Lucy felt a swell of something close to panic in her chest. He was clearly not opposed to the idea of having Camille in their home as a permanent fixture – far from it.

'I know she's not terribly academic. I don't think she's that interested in higher education, not really. Geneviève and I have had words about it before. Cam scrapes by on her grades, and so maybe it wouldn't be such a bad idea. We'd have to discuss it with her mum, of course, the logistics and so forth.' He shrugged and sank down on to the pillows, clearly readying for sleep, as if the decision were pre-approved, straightforward, and merited little more than a stamp of approval and the buying of an extra pint of milk.

'I think we should talk about it a bit more,' she urged.

'We can, but not now, Lucy.' He gave a loud yawn, reaching out a flailing hand to pat her. 'I'm too tired.'

Lucy flicked off the bedside lamp and lay in the dark with her knuckles joined across her stomach. Her eyes lingered on the outline of the wicker hamper on top of the wardrobe, and her spirits sank. She was of the belief that having Camille as a permanent fixture under their roof would leave little room for her to pursue her dream of becoming a mum. It was almost as if one child would be enough, no matter that she had arrived in her life fully formed, as a teen. Lucy cursed the tears that gathered and trickled down her face. As Jonah snored, she had the uneasy feeling that things were changing . . . and she wasn't sure they were changing for the better.

◆ ◆ ◆

Over the next two weeks, events moved at pace, leaving Lucy feeling like she was being swept along by the current.

'I've got my interview today,' Camille reminded them, as she applied mascara at the kitchen table, holding the small magnified mirror in her palm.

'You'll do great.' Jonah nodded, as he gulped his coffee and grabbed his suit jacket from the back of the chair. 'Time has beaten me this morning. See you both later. Lucy, have a good day, and Cam, let me know how it goes.' He blew kisses from his palm and swept from the room.

Lucy shook her head. 'This house is complete chaos every morning. It drives me nuts! Don't get me wrong, I love our life – I love being in this house with Jonah – but I don't understand how there's only the two of us and yet nearly every morning ends in this supreme rush to get out of the door. It mystifies me!' she babbled, as she wiped down the crumb-laden surface with a cloth.

'Three of us.' Camille held her mascara wand still and stared at her through thickened lashes.

'Yes, of course, three of us!' She tried to laugh off her faux pas, silently cursing herself for having let her guard down and made this Freudian slip.

Camille's expression changed as she stood up from the table. Lucy couldn't tell if it was one of hurt or resentment. 'I get it, Lucy. You love your life, just the two of you. Well, don't worry. If I do get my college place I'm sure there will be somewhere I can go and stay. Dex knows a lot of people,' she huffed.

'What? No! That's not what I'm saying at all!' she called after Camille, who raced out of the room and up the stairs.

◆ ◆ ◆

As the days marched on, Lucy found it a struggle simply to stay afloat and breathe, let alone find the voice to speak up. The atmosphere between her and Camille returned to its pre-birthday awkwardness, revealing the short snap of closeness to be a false dawn, and this she found truly disheartening.

It was hard for her, having to bob on the changing tide of Camille's fancy. Trying to please her, Lucy went out of her way, offering to drive her to work when summer showers threatened, buying her favourite foods, and circling snippets in magazines of any fashion item or article that she thought might be of interest before leaving them propped open on her bedside table. Camille never mentioned them or thanked her for them, so Lucy stopped doing it.

The girl's alienation of her was subtle. It might take the form of something as small as only clearing her and her dad's plates from the table, leaving Lucy to take her own and head in Camille's wake towards the dishwasher, while Jonah praised the girl for helping out. Some acts were bigger, more obvious and therefore more hurtful, like discussing fond memories of trips and events that were pre-Lucy, meaning she could only smile and gawp like an outsider, hoping for scattered crumbs of inclusion. Camille also had a knack of only informing Jonah of her plans, meaning Lucy had to constantly enquire as to why she wasn't home for supper or was home late from work. It made her feel like an outsider, on the periphery of the circle and therefore not worthy of sharing information with. It made her feel temporary, and that unnerved her.

'I wish Camille would tell me what she's up to.' She tried subtly to raise the issue with Jonah while unpacking groceries into the fridge and cupboard.

'She's a teenager, love. That's what they do. Her head is in the clouds.' He laughed at this stereotypical behaviour, refusing to entertain the idea that it was in any way calculated. Lucy was aware that to suggest anything to the contrary would make her seem oversensitive and possibly lead to a row, something she was keen to avoid. She chose instead not to mention the fact that he hadn't once properly questioned what it might be like for her to have Camille as a permanent fixture in their home, and this seemed to go hand in hand with his lack of urgency when it came to having a baby of their own.

'I know, but sometimes . . .' She hesitated.

'Sometimes what?' he pushed.

Lucy paused with an avocado in each hand. 'Sometimes I wish I didn't feel quite so excluded.'

Jonah chortled. 'Don't be silly! When are you ever excluded?' He narrowed his eyes.

She opened the fridge and spoke from behind the open door. 'When you two talk about trips and events before I arrived, funny things that have happened, stuff like that.' She hated how juvenile she sounded.

'We shouldn't have to censor our conversation, especially when our shared memories are so few and far between.' His voice was clipped.

'And I'm not asking you to, of course not! I'm not that person, Jonah, but I would like to be involved. It's not like I am ever asked my opinion, or she ever shares with me. It's as if she directs everything at *you* so that *I* feel excluded.'

'That's not the case, Lucy. I think you might need to lighten up a bit.' He stared at her. 'Camille did mention to me she thought you might prefer it if she didn't stay with us if she gets into college. It was something you said.'

Lucy closed her eyes and took a deep breath. 'I said something a while ago, inadvertently, about it being just the two of us. I can't even remember the details, but it was nothing, and certainly no reason for her to be punishing me or trying to escalate a harmless phrase into anything more. I remember she stormed off and has been ratty with me ever since.' She tutted.

'Harmless to you perhaps.'

'Oh for God's sake, Jonah!'

And just like that, the kindling was lit for the row she had been trying desperately to avoid. Lucy slammed the fridge door and swept from the room to hide in the bath, trying to vent some of her simmering anger through the medium of foot stomping, which she did all the way up the stairs.

◆　◆　◆

Tansy had listened over lunch, and now she looked directly at Lucy, stirring her coffee repeatedly.

'Could he be right? Do you need to lighten up? Are you oversensitive?' She twisted her mouth, letting Lucy know that it was a tough subject to broach. Lucy was glad of Tansy's impartiality, despite their friendship.

'I don't think so.' She shrugged and broke the lemon and poppyseed muffin into three, slowly placing an overlarge chunk into her mouth.

'Teenagers are notoriously difficult, finding their feet and all that.'

'I know this, Tansy,' she fired, popping stray crumbs back into her mouth with her finger. 'And that's Jonah's excuse, and I don't mind normal teenage behaviour – I expected it, in fact – but this feels like something more to me.'

'Yes, but the fact that you have been plonked in this situation without any build-up means that you might be taking it a little too personally. Possibly overanalysing things.' Tansy sipped her coffee, grimaced, placed it back in its saucer and reached for another tiny packet of sweetener.

'What do you mean? I had plenty of build-up. We knew she was coming and Jonah told me all about her. I welcomed her with open arms. Literally! Or I tried to, I should say,' she explained, remembering how she had stood in the kitchen with her hug rebuffed.

'That's not what I mean exactly.' Tansy sipped again from the cup before explaining further. 'When you have kids you watch them grow, love them, guide them and have days when you could happily abandon them, but every day is your training ground and every month, every year merges into the next, and it happens fast.' Tansy paused, stirring her coffee, while Lucy's thoughts raged.

I am running out of time! I am running out of time!

'Here's the thing, Lucy. You need to think of it like a new job. The first day is terrifying: you don't even know where the bathroom is let alone the name of the IT guy or how to actually do what you are being paid for, but you pick it up bit by bit until all the things that used to bother you become second nature, you relax into it and everything you learn prepares you for the next stage. Arriving at teenagehood is just another phase for a mum who's been there since the starter pistol was fired, and not only do you have this arsenal of weapons and experience to call upon, but you know your subject inside out. I only know how to handle Michael because I know what makes him tick and how to motivate him, but it's not easy. You, my friend, have gone straight into seventeen years of service, expectations of you are high, but you are really on your first day, you don't know where the bathroom is or the name of the IT guy.'

Lucy got it. This she already knew; she was a late starter in the race. She looked down.

'But I've tried really hard with her. I spent an age getting her room ready, I welcomed Dex into the house—'

'Yes, and that's good, but trust me, that's the easy stuff,' Tansy interrupted her.

'It is?' Lucy swallowed her mouthful of muffin and picked up another large piece. 'It doesn't feel like the easy stuff,' she mumbled.

'Yes, of course it is! If painting a room and making lover boy cups of tea were all it took then all parents all over the world would find the whole thing plain sailing, and yet they don't. You need to think of teenagers as little turtles. They have hard shells that make it seem like they can rebuff most things, but the truth is they are soft on the inside and completely clueless and that hard exterior is just a clever disguise. And the trick is trying to figure out how to get inside their little shells to see the real them, to know what they *really* need, without cracking them open.'

Lucy stared at her friend. 'You are quite good at this parenting thing. Your boys are very lucky.'

'Not really. This advice is easy to give, but when it comes to your own, most mums are quite neurotic.'

She ran her hand over her forehead. 'I had no idea it was going to be this hard. I want to sit her down and tell her that I am not trying to take away her dad and that I want to be her friend.'

'Well then, why don't you?' Tansy boomed. 'You should do exactly that. Follow that instinct.'

'Urgh. It's not that easy. I wish it were. It's like when there's a boy at school who you are crazy about. You can have a million conversations with him in the mirror or in your head and in those situations it's a doddle and you rehearse it until you are confident. But then when you are faced with him in the corridor you fall to pieces.' She placed the muffin in her mouth.

'Actually, this is not like that at all. You are the grown-up and you have a responsibility for Camille's welfare. You need to make the move, have the chat, find the confidence, because she might be seventeen and technically one year away from adulthood, but she's still only a little girl who is probably feeling a bit lost.'

'She doesn't seem that way,' she mumbled through her muffin.

'Trust me: if she is acting out and deliberately excluding you, it's because she feels either afraid or threatened or both.' Tansy nodded assertively.

'I guess so.' This certainly made sense. 'So how do I get Jonah to see it from my perspective and get him to help me, so we present a unified front?'

Tansy laughed loudly and patted the table, before reaching across and stealing the last of the muffin from her friend's plate and shoving it in her mouth. 'Oh, honey, teenage girls, not a problem, quadratic equations or brain surgery, easy peasy, but asking me how to get a besotted dad who can only see the good in his baby girl on board? That's a whole other thing and one that I am definitely not skilled in.'

◆ ◆ ◆

Camille lay on the sofa, flicking through the glossy brochure that she had picked up from City of Westminster College.

'Hey, Cam,' Lucy offered perkily as she kicked off her shoes and shed her suit jacket before placing it on the arm of the comfy chair by the fireplace. 'How did it go at the college? Is that your prospectus?' She sat down on the sofa next to Camille without giving her a chance to budge up.

Camille nodded.

'Have you decided on a course yet?'

'This one.' She pointed at an open page and handed Lucy the brochure. Lucy marvelled at the photographs of a bright, original catwalk fashion show.

'Would you get to design something like this?' she asked with genuine amazement. The garments were structured, beautiful and originally quirky, draped on to models whose faces were emblazoned with flag motifs and who sported wild, mermaid-coloured, backcombed hair.

'Yes.' Camille's smile was genuine. 'That's the end-of-year show. They sell tickets and everything.'

'Wouldn't that be something? Maybe your mum and Jean-Luc could come over?'

Camille retrieved the booklet and placed it on her lap. 'Maybe.'

'Have you spoken to her about your plans? I expect she'll want to talk to your dad.'

'You're not the first, you know.'

'Excuse me?' Lucy had lost the thread, wondering what she might have misunderstood.

'You're not the first girlfriend he's had living here or introduced me to. There's been loads.'

Lucy sat back on the sofa, feeling as if the wind had been knocked from her lungs. She was so uncomfortable that she wished she were anywhere else. Was this repayment for making Camille feel unwelcome with a single offhand comment? Surely not. Fighting her instinct to run up the stairs and lock herself in the bathroom for a hot bath and a glass of wine, she instead drew on Tansy's words of advice.

'Do you know, Camille, if I didn't know you better I'd think that you are trying to be hurtful, to say something to upset me. But then I tell myself that I'm being stupid, I must have made a mistake, because you are not that kind of person, and if you were I would be the *last* person you'd be mean to, as all I have ever done is go out of my way to be your friend, trying to get to know you, introducing you to *my* family and making Dex welcome in our home.'

She noticed the slight tremor to the girl's lip and the reddening of her cheek, as if smarting from Lucy's words of rationalisation.

Camille flicked the edge of the brochure with her agitated fingers and glanced at the door, as if figuring out how to make her getaway.

'I don't want to fall out with you, Camille, in fact the exact opposite.' She softened her tone.

The girl stared at the fireplace. 'I was only saying my dad's had loads of girlfriends. And my mum thinks it's pathetic,' she spat, sounding a lot younger than her seventeen years and looking for all intents and purposes like a child as her leg jumped and her eyes misted with tears of frustration.

'Your dad's a grown man. Of course he's had girlfriends, just like I have had boyfriends, but the big difference is, I'm not his girlfriend. I'm his *wife*,' she emphasised.

'Oh yeah, of course,' Camille retorted with a conviction that threw her completely. 'And I'm sure this time it's *really* different,' she scoffed, as she hopped from the sofa with her brochure under her arm and ran up the stairs.

'Camille!' Lucy called after her, to no avail.

Lucy had barely noticed that the sun had begun to sink, leaving the room bathed in the muted grey of evening. A new range of emotions that felt close to madness confused her; her gut swirled with a sick feeling of inadequacy, and a headache sat behind her eyes. It mattered not that she recognised Camille's venomous words as those of an angry teen, designed to wound, or that she could take comfort from the thin platinum band on her left hand, a sign of Jonah's commitment to her. Lucy felt agitated and inadequate. Both feelings were alien to her and all the more unsettling for it.

'What's the matter with you?' she whispered aloud. Her eyes settled on the bookshelf, staring at the spines of her husband's collection of books on the French Revolution. Dark thoughts came tumbling in like a rolling tide in the dead of night.

Camille hates me, I know it. I don't know how else to try. I thought I'd made headway with her and then this. I'm tired. I want to hide. I can't keep smiling through. I want time to grieve for what I have lost . . . I feel like everything is an illusion, being Camille's stepmother, trying to carry a baby . . . what about Jonah? Is he an illusion too? How many others have sat in this room, waiting for him to come home?

The temperature in the room had dropped; Lucy folded her arms across her chest and tried to muster warmth. She looked up at the sound of Jonah's key in the door. It was a late night for him, having been wined and dined by a glossy London magazine looking for his advertising business.

'Why are you sitting in the dark? I thought you'd gone out and abandoned me!' He flicked on the floor lamp and it cast a honey-coloured glow over the wooden floor.

'No. I'm right here,' she managed.

'Have you been crying?' He studied her face.

'A bit. Yes.' She rubbed her stinging eyelids.

'What's up, Lucy?' His tone was a little more jovial than her mood demanded, and it bothered her that he didn't pick up on this.

She levelled her gaze at him. 'Lots of things, I guess. I'm feeling a bit sorry for myself and possibly overthinking everything. Camille is . . .' She let this hang, noting how Jonah pinched the bridge of his nose between his thumb and forefinger, as if he couldn't stand to hear about another episode.

'Camille is what?' He sighed.

Lucy tried to rehearse the words in her head, hoping that they might come out in a way that was casual and not accusatory. 'How many women have you had living here before me?' she managed, failing miserably.

Jonah loosened his tie and undid his top button. 'What?' He sank down on to the sofa beside her. 'Where's this coming from?' he asked, laughing.

She ground her tseeth together, hating that he was laughing when her sadness was very real. 'Camille said earlier that she'd been introduced to lots of women who had lived here before me and it's made me feel . . .' – she decided to dilute exactly how it had made her feel: grubby, insecure and vulnerable – 'it's made me feel a bit shaky.'

'Well that's absolutely ridiculous!' he boomed.

'Possibly,' she smarted. 'But it's playing on my mind a little.'

'Well don't let it,' he reasoned.

Lucy ran her palm over her forehead. If only it were that easy. She felt her anger stir at how he dismissed her concern with his clichéd response.

'I guess I was feeling a little out of sorts, and I've been thinking about your very smooth courtship. It got me wondering how many others have been given the same treatment.'

'Are you serious? Tell me this is some kind of joke?' He sat up straight.

Lucy placed her arms across her chest. 'It's not a joke. I didn't think you'd been living like a monk, but I guess it never really occurred to me that there might have been others living here, sleeping in our bed before me, meeting Camille . . .'

'I'm nearly fifty! What did you think, that I had a high school sweetheart and then sat back waiting for you?'

'No! I'm not saying that.' She hated the way his words painted her – the way *he* was painting her. 'But Camille said there had been loads and that made me feel uncomfortable.'

Jonah took a deep breath, the kind that might precede any placatory statement. 'There have been a few women, yes,' he confessed. 'Less than ten, more than three, if I had to summarise, but none of them have lived here. Stayed over here, yes, but not lived here. Eaten supper here, yes, but kept a toothbrush here, no. And frankly I resent the suggestion that I have some kind of turnstile on the front door with an endless troop of women coming in and out, to all of which I give a bloody door key. I'm not *that* person!' Jonah shouted, which was rare.

'I'm not saying you are.' She struggled mentally with how else to make her point.

'Well, it sure sounds like it. I don't know what to say to you. I was really looking forward to coming home; I have missed you today and sat through a boring dinner with thoughts of you in my head. This is the last thing I thought I'd be walking into.'

Lucy stared at him, feeling irritated and confused that she had made him feel this way. This was not how she had seen their conversation working out. His words had done little to reassure her and she needed more from him.

He spoke slowly. 'You have been through a lot, my Lucy, and everything is still a little raw.'

'That's true, but I'm tired, Jonah. I'm tired of the way Camille snipes at me, says things that leave me reeling. It's not fair. I can't get through to her. I don't know what her issues are, but I can't take them on.'

'No, it probably isn't fair.' Jonah stared at her. 'But the way you are behaving, it sounds to me like you might be jealous.'

She twisted towards him. 'Why are people saying that to me? Why are you saying that to me?' She yelled now. 'I am not the jealous type.'

'Are you sure? Because it sounds a bit like—'

She cut in: 'I am not jealous, Jonah. I am pissed off! Mightily pissed off!'

'I can see that, but it's ridiculous! Good God, *your* ex has married your cousin. It's only a matter of time before we have some fantastic family reunion and I get to shake hands with him and look him in the eye. You can only imagine how much I am looking forward to that day,' he confided. 'But does it threaten me? Of course not! Because you are my wife! And I love you.'

She drew breath, trying to ascertain just how far to escalate this row and to figure out whether she had the strength for it right now. 'I just don't like to be uninformed. It was the way she said it, "you're not the first". It made me feel like an idiot, as if I was temporary.' There, she had said it, and as she did so the tears of anguish and frustration clogged the back of her nose and stung her eyes.

As Jonah reached out a hand to pull her towards him, the sitting room door opened and Camille walked in, looking cute in her pyjamas and new dressing gown. She had freshly washed hair still damp on her shoulders, a glowing complexion and was smiling quite serenely.

Go away! Please just go away! Lucy urged the girl with her thoughts.

'Oh, sorry, are you two fighting?' she asked, looking from one to the other. Lucy was acutely aware that she would have heard everything; these old houses were not built for acoustic privacy.

'How was your day?' Jonah ignored the question and for this Lucy was grateful.

'Great!' She beamed. 'I think I've chosen my course and it's so cool.'

'Wow! Things are really moving forward,' he stated.

'Anyway, sorry to interrupt you two, but, Dad, is it okay if I call Mum from your phone? My battery is low and I can't find my charger,' Camille said calmly. But for Lucy, even hearing the words 'Mum' and 'Dad' in the same sentence made her feel like a stranger in her own home, a stranger whom no one called Mum.

Maybe Tansy and Jonah are right. Are you being oversensitive, Lucy?

'Sure. Help yourself. It's on the hallstand.'

Camille nodded as she bounced from the room.

Strangely, the girl's intervention had slowed the pace, broken the cycle of their row. The two now sat side by side. Lucy re-evaluated her words and tried to think of a way to change the course of their conversation and bring it back to harmony. She was too tired for anything else. She would again bury her sharpened words and hope that time might blunt them.

Jonah beat her to it. Taking a deep breath, he took her hand into his.

'The thing is, if I could have met you in school, if you could have been my childhood sweetheart, then I would never have loved another. Not only would I have let you braid my hair, but I would have found what I was looking for and I would have been content. But that didn't happen, and I had to kiss a few frogs before I found my princess.'

'I think it's supposed to be kiss a few frogs until you find a prince.' She laughed.

'No, I definitely didn't want to find my prince. I wanted to find my Lucy.' Leaning forward, he kissed her nose.

She looked up at him, his words thawing the ice-laden dread that had filled her up.

'I meant every word I said to you on our wedding day; you are like a glorious second chance that I didn't think I had any right to, and I treasure you every day.' He bowed his head. 'And if you think that after waiting all this time to find you I am going to let anyone or anything put even the smallest dent in our happiness, then you are wrong. I love you, my wife.'

Lucy's eyes teared. She felt infinitely better and tried to ignore the quake of fear she felt when she thought about Camille staying with them permanently.

Jonah whispered in her ear: 'Now, how about we have an early night and you let me hold you tight?'

'Sounds good,' she returned the whisper, kissing the close beard on his handsome face.

The evening had stirred something in her gut that left an unpleasant taste in her mouth. As he placed his arms around her, she couldn't shake the feeling that things were not resolved. Not yet.

High school sweetheart. Jonah used this phrase and, as ever, it set my pulse racing. I sometimes think about that first flash of love and lust that can shape you in ways in which you can never imagine. I have friends who, even as their years advance, have confessed that to escape from the chaos of family life they stop, elbow-deep in suds at the sink or with a mountain of paperwork awaiting them, and stare out of a window into the starry sky above and imagine, just for a second, what a life with that boy might have ended up like. They remember the glorious bubble of happiness that filled them morning, noon and night. The way he smelled, the things he said, the first time he touched their skin and the fact that they knew beyond any shadow of a doubt that no one else in the whole wide world had ever, ever had a love like that before. They were Romeo and Juliet, or Scarlett and Rhett, and they were confident that this unique love would never falter . . .

For me, it's a little different. If I think of his face, I feel a stab of rejection so acute that I place my shaking hand on my gut and pull it away with caution to see if I am bleeding. I smell bleach and feel the plastic of the mask placed over my nose and mouth. My tears come in a rush without warning, a deluge that blinds me, so I have no choice but to sit and weep and try to bury that face, that image, until my tears stop and I can stand up and carry on with my day.

FOURTEEN

Lucy had stayed in close proximity, as requested, hovering in the background in the kitchen while Jonah spoke to Geneviève. She had watched him sweat over making the call to his ex, drawing breath and rehearsing the words. In the end, the woman gave her immediate blessing for Camille to start college at the end of September. His relief had been swift and evident. Lucy, however, had hoped at some level that Geneviève might veto the idea, leaving her off the hook and free from blame should it transpire that Camille had to go back to France.

Lucy had, in light of this new development, adopted a new strategy: avoidance. She hoped that she would feel better about things the more she got used to the idea, but until that point she worked later in the office, gaining nods of approval and praise for her dedication and results on the eco energy project. At the other end of the day, she was up with the lark, pounding the pavements with a new-found energy to her running that helped her to think less. Her mapped run offered blissful moments of escape during which she was able to ignore the background hum of Jonah's bullish antics and the fact that he had stopped mentioning their plan to become parents. All that filled her head was the music from her earphones and the feel of the tarmac beneath her feet.

It was as she ran one morning, while the rest of the world was reaching for its first caffeine fix, that a dull ache spread across her breasts. She decided it was time to invest in a new sports bra; her hatred of shopping meant she would click a few buttons online and get one delivered.

This thought was suddenly replaced with the realisation that her period was due.

Her very next thought was that the prospect of falling pregnant was not nearly so joyous when faced with the possibility of losing this baby or of having to share the news in a house that Camille resided in.

Instantly she berated herself, thinking of the man she loved and recalling how she and Jonah had agreed that a baby would make Camille feel more involved. A new baby to unify them – who could resist that joy? Trying not to get ahead in her thoughts, she slowed her run until it was nothing more than a brisk walk and she arrived home. Jonah had already left for his four days of team building in Scotland. Golf followed by budget planning and sales forecasting were on the agenda. She had smiled through gritted teeth as she waved him off, feeling a gutful of resentment at the fact that he was able to up sticks and go off on his jolly when the house felt like it might explode with all that was being left unsaid.

Camille slept soundly as Lucy pulled off her trainers and ventured upstairs to the bathroom.

The routine was more than familiar. She peed on the little stick – she had secreted a supply of them beneath the cotton wool balls in a basket at the bottom of the cabinet. She let the shower run and peeled the vest and sports bra from her skin, throwing it into a pile in the corner of the room. Then she grasped the spatula and blinked at the window that revealed the result.

Pregnant 1–2

Staggering back, she sat down on the toilet and gripped the little wand to her chest. She felt quite overwhelmed, confused even. There was no doubt in her mind that she wanted a baby, but the situation in the house made her wary of what a positive result might mean.

'Let's try and do this, little one. Let's try and go the whole way, because I am waiting for you and I won't let you down! I won't!' she sobbed, trying to remember a time when she had greeted this result with nothing more than a whoop of joy and an electrifying jolt in anticipation of all the good things to come.

◆ ◆ ◆

Lucy looked up at the sound of her office door opening.

'Goodness me, you are actually smiling! Am I in the right office?' Tansy made a great show of walking back out and checking the name on the door.

'Very funny! And what are you talking about? I always smile.' She laughed.

'Uh-uh.' Tansy waggled her finger in her direction. 'You used to, but more recently all we have had is a half-smile.'

Lucy recalled a similar comment from Fay; it made her feel a little self-conscious.

Tansy continued: 'And that half-smile is the facial equivalent of anyone who works in a shop saying "Have a nice day" when they couldn't care less if you went outside and fell down a manhole. Your expression was the same; necessary, but not always sincere. But *this* smile, this one today' – her friend narrowed her eyes – 'now this is a real one. You are either in love or you've got a secret.'

'Well, you already know I'm in love, so that's not a shocker.' She looked back at her computer screen, trying to find a neutral expression that would mask the joy that fluttered in her chest.

Tansy sat down in the chair on the other side of Lucy's desk and placed her hand on her mouth. 'So that means it's a secret. Hmm . . . promotion?'

Lucy rolled her eyes and tutted. 'Go away, Tansy.'

The two sat in silence for a second, until Tansy gasped and raised her voice.

'Oh my God! You're pregnant!'

'I . . .' Lucy was taken aback, unsure whether to lie or what to say to throw her friend off the scent.

'You are!' She sat forward in the chair, gripping the arms. 'You are aglow and you are knocked up! Tell me I'm wrong!' She beamed, expectantly.

'I . . .' Lucy struggled again to find the words.

'You can't think of a lie quick enough is the answer! Oh my God! You are! You are!' Tansy placed her hand over her mouth and sniffed at the tears that gathered.

'Tansy.' She closed her eyes as her heart raced, feeling a mixture of nerves and a new sense of relief that her secret had been shared. 'I have literally only found out an hour or so ago, I haven't even told Jonah, who's away for a few days, and I certainly wasn't going to share it with anyone else, not for a long while yet.'

Paying no heed to her friend's words, Tansy leapt from her seat and rushed forward, crushing her to her chest in a hug. 'This is the best news in the world! Oh my God! I am so excited. You are going to be the best mum in the world! The best. You can have a girl who will marry Benedict, the age gap will be perfect and we can plan their wedding. I call shotgun on aquamarine for my dress, it's always been my colour, and we will become grannies together and be friends forever! I am so happy!' Tansy clapped as she danced around the room.

'Tansy—'

'Are you taking folic acid? You need to start if you aren't already. I'll get you some.' She tapped her mouth as if making a mental shopping list.

'I am. But, Tansy—'

'And you need to invest in good bras – oh my word, they are vital.' She placed her cupped hands over her chest. 'I didn't bother with

Benedict and I now have a chest I have to roll up at the end of the day like a used sports sock. It's not pretty. They are more like deflated balloons than boobs.'

'The thing is, Tansy—'

'Names!' Her friend clicked her fingers. 'We need to get you a baby book. I feel torn. I want to give you my favourites like Edie and Imelda, but if you use them it means I can't . . .'

'Tansy!' she shouted. 'Please! Just be quiet for a minute.' She briefly closed her eyes and waited while the woman took a seat.

'I'm excited,' Tansy whispered.

'I know, I can tell, and I am too, but I have to curb that excitement.' She took a breath.

'What do you mean?' Her friend sat forward with a quizzical expression.

'It's not the first time Jonah and I have conceived.'

'Oh?'

'I've had a couple of miscarriages, early miscarriages, and so I'm being cautious.' She spoke quietly, wary that even mentioning it might jinx things.

'A couple?' Her friend's expression was one of disbelief and sorrow.

'Yes.'

'Oh, Lucy! I'm so sorry.' She looked into her lap and drew breath. 'It happened to me before Benedict and after Michael, put me off trying for a long while. It happens to lots of people. It will all be okay.' She spoke softly, sincerely.

'I really hope so.' She swallowed, remembering Dr Millard's words that most women who suffered from miscarriage went on to give birth to perfectly healthy babies. It gave her hope.

'You should have told me what you were going through. I can't bear the idea of you facing that alone.'

'I wasn't alone. Jonah has always been brilliant, and this time . . . who knows?' She felt a smile spread across her face. It *was* good news

– the best. She hoped this wasn't a lie, hoped that she and Jonah would reconnect over this wonderful news and be happy. Telling Tansy had somehow made it real. She pictured the wicker hamper on top of the wardrobe.

'I think having a baby will be the making of you, Lucy. I know you are this big exec here and what you've achieved in this shark pool is amazing, but speaking as your friend and not your employee, I really hope that it goes right for you and Jonah. You are two of the best people I know. I think your kids would be a knockout.'

Lucy smiled at her friend. 'I think you might be right. Not a word to anyone, literally, not even Rick. Promise me.'

'I promise.' Tansy raised her hand, unable to wipe the smile from her face, but she seemed calmer now she was armed with this new information. 'And you can have Imelda; that's my gift to you.'

'Thanks for that.' She snorted her laughter and shook her head. This already felt like fun.

◆ ◆ ◆

Dex and Camille were lying entwined on the sofa when she arrived home, something they never did when Jonah was there. There was a beat of awkwardness while she swallowed her unease at them being in the house alone, as well as her desire to question what they were up to and how long they had been there. This was yet another example where if the girl in question were Maisie, Lucy would have called her into the kitchen and suggested that lying on a sofa with her boyfriend was not really the done thing when someone else arrived in the room.

'Hello, guys. How are you?' she breezed, surprised that they made no attempt to sit up, either to offer her a seat or out of a sense of awkwardness that an adult was stood in front of the sofa on which they slouched. It made her feel like an interloper.

'Good, thanks.' Dex smiled, raising his hand in a wave. 'How was your day?'

'Fine. Thank you for asking, Dex. Have you both eaten? I was going to rustle up a stir-fry,' she offered stoically.

'We've got pizza on the way. Wouldn't want to put you out in any way. In your home,' Camille answered casually without shifting her eyes from the TV screen. Her behaviour was different with Jonah out of the house. Firstly she was far more at ease with Dex, lying with his hands in her hair and her shirt a little lifted so her skin was against his. And secondly, it was as if she no longer felt the need to pretend to be a friendly force; her verbal barb was cast carelessly, and Lucy found it almost intolerable.

'It's your home too, Camille, but no worries.' She kept her voice bright, embarrassed in front of Dex, unwilling to again go over the fact that she had inadvertently slipped up before. With something akin to relief, she made her way to the kitchen, where she would prepare a healthy stir-fry and take it up to the bedroom. This prospect of not having to face the teenagers who dominated the sitting room filled her with joy. Without Jonah to crowd her space, she would eat her supper and a dessert of strawberry laces and have a little knit; she was getting close to finishing her blanket.

◆ ◆ ◆

It was a frantic week. Her tenant, Ross, had left the flat on the Thames Path, and Lucy had had to organise an inspection of the property and get the keys retrieved and documents signed. It had been painless, but had still incurred a whole heap of admin that she could have done without.

She did, however, use Jonah's absence to complete a long list of half-finished chores that were considerably harder when he was in situ. She emptied out the larder, attacking the shelves with a sponge and large bowl of soapy water. Returning only the tins and jars that were in date, she managed to throw away several cans of various vegetables that were in excess of three years old, a couple of smeared and sticky jars of spices, bought for some short-lived fad no doubt, and an opened bag of sugar that had gone rock hard. She stood back and admired her handiwork – the contents of the shelves now sat on pristine surfaces in order of height – and was happy to be able to put her mark on the house in any way.

Next, she took the three grocery bags full of Jonah's old T-shirts, sportswear and jeans that had been nestling in the cupboard under the stairs and carried them to the charity shop. Her husband liked to dip into these bags occasionally and rescue a ghastly item that he had out-grown decades ago. At least with them out of the house, that temptation was removed.

By the time Friday arrived and Lucy made her way home from work, the house was neat, the bed linen was laundered and pressed, fresh flowers sat in a ceramic jug on the kitchen table, and two slabs of steak nestled in her grocery bag, along with a whole bunch of organic carrots, a fat Spanish onion, a tin of chickpeas and some heavenly scented fresh tomatoes on the vine, from which she would make a spicy vegetarian Moroccan tagine. Preparing the house for Jonah's return and claiming the evening meal was another small way in which she tried to assert her presence. She hoped that she would beat Jonah home, and she couldn't wait to see him, having decided to share her news after their steak supper and as they climbed between the sheets, hoping it might be the glue that fixed their recent disagreements.

Lucy trod the path to their front door and whistled as she pushed it open. 'I'm home!'

There was no response.

It was only when she opened the kitchen door to find Camille sob-bing into her hands at the table and a rather worried-looking Jonah by her side that she realised she wasn't alone.

She instantly knitted her brows at the sight of her stepdaughter's distress.

'What on earth's the matter?' She kept her tone low, trying to think of all the possible reasons for this level of hysterics. Her first thought was that something terrible had happened to Geneviève. Lucy abandoned the bags of shopping on the worktop, trying not to feel aggrieved at having been robbed of the evening she had planned. Silently berating herself for her selfishness, she took a seat opposite them both, waiting for an explanation.

'Cam's had a bit of bad news.' He grimaced over his daughter's head and continued to pat her back.

'What's happened?'

Camille lifted her head to reveal her face, red and bloated with swollen eyes and a running nose. 'Dex . . .' she started, before breaking away in a loud sob, 'Dex is going away.'

'Going away?' She looked at Jonah.

'He's been offered a job placement in New York for a year and Camille is pretty upset.'

'So I see,' she whispered, angry that the girl had managed to rob her of the reunion she had planned. 'You know, Camille, a year seems like a very long time right now, but it really isn't. It will go very quickly. I promise you that.'

'Stop trying to sound like you are bothered! You don't give a shit! You're just hoping I go back to France so that you two can get back to your cosy life without me here in the way!' Camille spat through her distress.

'Camille!' Jonah was clearly taken aback by the outburst. Lucy was a little reassured by his shock.

'What? It's true, Dad. She doesn't want me here! She more or less said as much,' Camille yelled.

'I . . .' Lucy opened her mouth, genuinely struggling for a response.

'That's not true, Cam. You are just upset because of Dex,' Jonah stated, 'but that is certainly no reason to take it out on Lucy.'

She and Jonah exchanged a look that smacked of alliance. It gave Lucy the confidence to speak freely, relieved that finally they might share a view when it came to Camille.

'To be honest, Camille, when you talk to me like this and treat me this way, you are quite right. I do wonder how we can all live here harmoniously. You don't make it easy for me.'

'Lucy!' Jonah raised his voice in the same way that he had only moments earlier shouted a different name.

She stood her ground, despite the quake of nerves in her limbs. 'No, I'm sorry, Jonah. I am of course sad for Camille that her boyfriend is going away for a little while, but that is no excuse for her to talk to me in that way.'

Camille laid her head on her dad's arm, and he brushed her hair with the flat of his hand. 'Don't cry, love,' he cooed.

Lucy felt her hackles rise. She let her eyes rove the walls of the busy kitchen, resting them on the grocery bags full of items she had lovingly chosen for supper, a precursor to breaking her happy news. Placing her hands on the edge of the table, she pushed the chair away and stood, leaving the two sitting alone. As she trod the stairs, her gut twisted with the feeling of disappointment.

I need some space. Space to think. I want to get away from Camille, away from this house.

It was as she finished showering that Jonah entered the room and lay on their bed.

She stood before him in her white towelling bathrobe with a towel on her head, waiting for him to speak. Feeling, in turn, disappointed and furious.

'I can't stand it when you two bicker. It pulls me in two!' He pinched the bridge of his nose.

'Bicker?' She rounded on his choice of word and the fact that yet again he had let her down with his lack of support. 'I am not her schoolgirl friend, arguing over whose turn it is to wear the high heels. I am her step-mother, and this is precisely the problem. You put us on an equal footing and you can't. She is a child, Jonah, your child. And I am your wife.'

'But don't you see that even by saying that it's as if you want me to choose?' he shouted.

Lucy shook her head and sat on the edge of the bed. 'I *do* want you to choose, but not in the way that you think, not between Camille or me, never that, but how you let her behave. I want you to choose to parent her differently, to let me be a part of it, to set boundaries and not allow her to exclude me or be rude to me!'

'She is absolutely sobbing her heart out down there.' He pointed to the stairs, as if this display in some way justified her behaviour or might be enough to let her off the hook.

'And that's sad, it is. But this is about so much more than a boy-friend going away for twelve months. This is the foundation of our family!' she yelled.

Jonah sat back and looked out of the window, as if the solution might be lurking in the trees that dappled the sunlight through the window.

'I need to go to the flat for a couple of days,' she lied, the idea occurring to her as she spoke, as if the empty flat could give her the space and time out that she craved. 'Ross has moved out, but I need to have a clean-up and sort out the mail and a few other bits and pieces.' She avoided his gaze as she pulled the small suitcase from the bottom of the wardrobe and unzipped it, laying it flat on the bed.

'I'll come with you,' he whispered.

'No.' Her response was firm and instant. 'Camille needs you right now, and I'll be better off left to my own devices. I'll get everything done quicker.' She concentrated on opening the top drawer of the chest and pulling out her underwear, knowing in her heart that all she needed was a couple of nights of solitude, where she could, without distraction, figure out how best to deal with the Camille situation.

The thought of her beautiful, tranquil apartment fuelled her desire to escape. She was grateful that they had decided to wait a while before selling it and using the money to remodel the house.

'How long will it all take, do you think?' he asked with a note of concern.

'Not too long.' She spoke to the contents of the case, absently folding shirts and rolling her pyjamas, almost unable to process this turn of events which couldn't have been more different from the evening that she had been envisaging all day. Lucy had been so excited to share her lovely news. Now, she felt nothing but the waves of disappointment wash over, leaving in their wake a sting of hurt that shook her.

'Do you have to go? Can't it wait for a few days and then we can do it together?'

'No, Jonah, I need to go tonight.' She avoided eye contact and tried to ignore his deep sigh of disappointment.

Finally she stowed her knitting on top of her clothes and re-zipped the bag. Lucy turned to reach for her jeans and a T-shirt that lay on the floor when Jonah called out.

'Lucy!'

'What?' She stood upright. His tone had sounded urgent, and she waited for his apology, his plea for her to stay right there. She knew that if he said the right things, she would unpack her case and fall into his arms, because she loved him. She loved him more than anything.

'You're bleeding.' He pointed at the dark stain that spread on the back of her robe.

Tears pricking her eyes, she hastened out of the room before they spilled. She knew that he would assume this was a regular period, and she did nothing to enlighten him.

◆ ◆ ◆

The dark was drawing in an hour later as Lucy parked her car in the familiar space, just as she had a thousand times before. But tonight she was on edge, her muscles coiled with tension.

'Stay with me, baby, please stay with me.' This she repeated over and over, sending her prayer up into the night air. 'I will lie flat, I'll take it easy, try and relax and I will try to keep you.' She cried, knowing she couldn't cope with a trip to the hospital alone. The fact that the bleeding had slowed she took as a good sign. Deep down, she knew she was putting off having to confront the idea that this baby too might be leaving her.

There had been the odd moment over the last few weeks when she had longed for the solace of this apartment. In fact, there had been occasions over the last year when she had longed for the minimalist order of the space. But tonight neither brought her any comfort.

'It's okay, baby, it's all going to be okay. We can do this.' She rubbed her stomach.

Thankfully, Ross had been a model tenant – just as Tansy had promised when she recommended him – leaving the flat as he had found it. The toilets were bleached, the stove was scrubbed, the floors were swept, the surfaces sparkled, and the vast glass picture window that looked out at the boats and lights that shimmered on the moody Thames was smear free. But the place felt different. She felt different.

The background smell of the apartment was not hers. Gone were the floral notes of her perfume that once lingered in the air, and there was no longer the punchy zing of lemon in the cleaning fluid that she favoured. In its place was the woody, masculine aroma of a dark, brooding cologne, and in and around the kitchen hung the faintest trace of an Eastern spice that was unfamiliar to her. This, like most things in the last couple of hours, made her cry. An empty feeling of loneliness now engulfed her, not only at the fact that she had left the house in Windermere Avenue that had once felt like home, but also that she no longer felt she belonged here. This left the unpalatable question: where did she belong?

Lucy unzipped her suitcase on the double bed and unfurled the sleeping bag she had grabbed from the wardrobe in her rush to leave the house, figuring it would be easier than hunting for bed linen. The crumpled item looked lonely and desolate in the middle of the wide bed in which she and Jonah had consummated their new-found love. She blinked away the image of that first night, full of promise, and placed her hand on her stomach as the gripe of pain tore at her insides. 'Stay with me, baby, please, please, please . . .' she whispered.

Lucy knew the drill by now. Lying back on the cream hide sofa, with her legs propped up on two pillows, she closed her eyes, suddenly aware that the silence carried its own music, and to her ear it sounded a lot like loneliness. She had forgotten the many nights she had spent like this, wondering if she would ever meet someone with whom she wanted to share her life, and she had – she had met Jonah. But what she hadn't envisaged was having Camille in tow, and all the tension that had come with her arrival.

Her bleeding had all but stopped, with nothing more than a spot the last time she checked. 'Please stay where you are, baby. Stay safe and snug and give me a chance, little one. We can do this.' She spoke out loud, fighting to hold in the tears that threatened. She reached down for the book she had placed on the floor by her side. She flipped open the page and read again the words with which she was well acquainted.

Around one in five confirmed pregnancies sadly ends this way. The reasons for miscarriage are many and varied . . .

Drawing back her arm, she launched the book at the wall with all her might, watching as it hit the pristine white paint, leaving a dark grey mark before it hit the floor. 'I can't go through this again, I can't!' She cried then in sadness and frustration, rocking and sobbing, as she lay alone in this place that used to be home.

I told Camille that a year would pass quickly and I meant it. A year passes so quickly that when ten have passed you have to count on your fingers to check that you haven't got your calculations wrong. And then twenty years, two whole decades, now that requires a double-check going over your fingers twice. So yes, it will pass quickly, so much so that when it comes to the end, the speed at which it has gone will leave you completely stunned. Two decades? How is that even possible? Sometimes it feels like no time at all and at others, a whole lifetime . . .

FIFTEEN

Lucy was woken bright and early the next day by the doorbell. It took a full second for her to remember where she was and why. She pulled her sweatshirt over her pyjamas and slid along the pale tiles in her socks. A quick peek through the spyhole revealed Jonah. She felt a quake of nerves at the sight of him. Opening the door, she stole nervous glimpses of her husband, wary of his reaction and intentions, knowing she didn't have the energy for another discussion about Camille, and feeling a flicker of aggravation that he had invaded her space. She placed her hand on her stomach.

'Morning, sleepyhead.' He walked in and swept her into his arms. 'Shit, Lucy, that was a crappy night's sleep,' he whispered against her hair. 'There was no one to chat to me just as I was preparing for sleep and prevent me from nodding off, and no one stealing the duvet in the middle of the night or warming their feet on me. No one disturbing me with noisy trips to the bathroom – where's the fun in that? It was a thoroughly boring, uneventful night. A lonely night, and not one I care to repeat.' He kissed her forehead.

They stood in the hallway as he held her tightly.

'I cried on the sofa and then slept in a wrinkled sleeping bag,' she confessed.

He chortled. 'Well the good news is, I brought breakfast!' Jonah held up a brown paper bag with 'Gail's' written on the side. 'Croissants, muffins, various pastries and bottles of fresh OJ.'

'How lovely. Thank you.' She beckoned him inside, knowing he must have been up with the lark to go to so much trouble and make it all the way across town by now. Yet still she found it hard to soften her clipped tone, knowing deep down that bringing croissants and turning up with a hug wasn't enough to ease the resentment she felt at his treatment of her. If anything, this air of appeasement only reinforced how easily he felt he could dismiss the very real issues that plagued her, as if all it took to make things better were a gift and a giggle.

With the front door closed, he spoke earnestly. 'You can't run out on me, Lucy. This isn't a soap opera that requires a dramatic ending as the music fades. You have to stay with me so we can talk. That's how we do it. Things got out of hand yesterday. I felt pulled. I hated it. But don't ever run out because that puts tiny fissures in the surface of us, and if we're not careful those fissures can become chasms that are impossible to cross. And that would be the very worst thing that I can imagine.'

'I know. I only wanted a bit of time. I couldn't think straight. I thought a different, calmer environment might give me a bit of clarity.' His expression told her he wasn't buying it. 'And I'm glad you prescribe talking because yes, that's exactly what we need, to understand the other's viewpoint and meet in the middle.'

'Yes.' He nodded. She hoped he meant it.

'How's Camille doing?' It was easier to get the topic under way rather than dread it for longer than was necessary.

'She more or less disappeared to bed after you left and she was still sleeping this morning.' He held her eyeline. 'She's very upset – and I know you are too!' He held up a palm, as if trying to keep any hostile response at bay.

'So what's this job Dex has got in New York?' She had been denied the chance to enquire before.

'It's an internship, pretty much, no pay, but with accommodation and expenses, working for a digital recording studio, and it sounds too good for him to miss, but of course Camille feels abandoned and is hurting. I didn't bother trying to justify it to her. She knows it's good for him, but she's just a kid and she's upset.'

'I understand that.' And she did, kind of. 'But no matter how upset she is, that doesn't give her carte blanche to talk to me in any way she sees fit.'

'I know that, Lucy. You are right.'

She was grateful for the admission, happy that he agreed. It felt like progress. She watched his eyes rove the flat in which they had once courted.

'It's strange being here, isn't it?' she asked, as they walked across the cool tiled floor to the spacious open-plan sitting room and kitchen with the magnificent view of the water and the industrial buildings of the docks rising up on the other side of the river.

'I remember the first time I came here,' Jonah recalled, 'and the place was so pristine, with fancy furniture and statement lamps, and I couldn't see how someone like you, a total neat freak, could live in the chaos that surrounds me.' He ran his fingers over the cold grey granite worktop.

'I wondered that too,' she confessed, 'but I realised that being with you and waking up with you in that dusty bedroom of yours with those terrible car pictures was more important than having a sparkling environment.'

'I'm glad.' He reached out and took her hand. 'And what do you mean "terrible car pictures"? They are classics. Anyway, it's *our* bedroom now and I love you.'

'I love you too.' She let her head hang forward on to her chest as her tears fell. It was a sweet reminder that this was their strength, how much they loved each other. 'There's something I need to tell you. I should have said something last night, but I didn't want to add any more drama. I couldn't have coped.' She saw his eyes widen in anticipation. 'I did a pregnancy test last week and it was positive and I've been waiting to speak to you in person, but then when I started bleeding last night . . .' She cried some more.

'Oh God! No. No!' He placed his hand over his eyes, and she watched his chest heave. 'Lucy, you should have told me.' He shook his head. 'I can't stand you going through this over and over. I can't.'

'I don't want to go through it any more,' she whimpered. 'I just want it to go right for us. I want our baby!'

'I know, I know.' He held her in a loose embrace, for which she was grateful. It gave her enough space to breathe and cry. And just like that, everything else paled into the background as they dealt with this, the most important thing. 'Are you still pregnant?' His expression was tortured and she could see that it was hard for him to ask.

'I don't know,' she answered truthfully. 'I haven't bled since last night, so I don't know. It . . . it might just have been a blip, it might be fine.'

'We have to go to the early pregnancy clinic. They run the emergency one at University College Hospital at the weekend.'

She hated that he knew this.

'Get dressed. We'll go right now.' He smiled encouragingly.

'I don't want to.' She looked up at him, wrapping her arms around her trunk. 'I thought about going last night but decided instead to tough it out. I don't want to go through the questions, the process, the sympathy. I don't want to do it. And I don't want to know. I don't feel strong enough to lose another, I really don't.' She shook her head, as her tears fell.

'We have no choice but to go, Lucy. This isn't something we can stick our heads in the sand about, and I will be right by your side every step of the way. I promise. Always.'

'Can't I just stay like this and wait and see?' she whimpered. 'I can't bear the idea of them telling me that it's failed again, I can't! At least by staying here, I can pretend,' she whispered.

He shook his head. 'No, you can't, my darling. You know that, don't you?'

She nodded, reluctantly, knowing this was the right thing to do, but dreading it nonetheless as she went to shower and locate her jeans.

◆ ◆ ◆

It was nearly lunchtime by the time they made their way back to Queen's Park, discharged from the hospital with a cloud of resignation hanging over them. It was a familiar routine. Jonah steered his flashy car through the busy streets as Lucy stared out of the window, her sadness wrapped around her like a rope that anchored her to this moment in time. She tried not to focus on the men with baby slings, the mummies with toddlers, the babyGap stores that lined the high streets, the pushchairs, and the many billboard advertisements for formula and teething gel. It was as if London put on a parade of all the things she could only aspire to have.

'I sometimes think the whole world is pregnant or giving birth or parenting toddlers, except me.' She spoke her thoughts aloud.

'It just feels that way, honey,' he soothed.

'I didn't want to go to the hospital; I didn't want them to tell me. I wanted to keep her for a little bit longer.' She continued to stare out of the window as she spoke.

'I know,' Jonah whispered, 'but you know something, Lucy? We have a lot to feel thankful for; we have a great life.'

'Are you saying we should give up?' She turned in the passenger seat to face him.

'No, no, I'm not saying that.' He met her eye. 'I am saying that I love you and I like the life we have together, and if we get lucky then I will be the happiest man on the planet. And if we don't, I have you, and I consider myself to be the luckiest man on the planet.'

'Is that a roundabout way of saying you don't mind either way? Because I think it needs more commitment than that.' She stared at him, hoping to read the truth in his every nuance.

'Commitment? Jesus, Lucy, you have a way of phrasing things that leaves me cold sometimes. I am committed – that's why I chased across town this morning, and why I didn't sleep a wink trying to think how to put things right. There are only so many times I can tell you that we are in this together.'

'I know, you say that, but words are easy, Jonah. If you are indifferent—'

He cut her off. 'I know you are hurting, but stop putting words into my mouth.'

'I'm not.' She sat up straight. 'I just want you to be honest with me about this. You don't have to sweeten things. I'm stronger than that.'

The way he did a double take told her he doubted this. She felt her stomach flip, knowing he viewed her as weak. And it hurt. She heard him sigh, and when he spoke it was as if a wrapper of well-intentioned deceit slipped from his tongue. 'I don't know how strong you are right now. You are tightly coiled, and I worry that makes you fragile. I do love the life we have, that's the truth, and it's enough for me.'

Lucy stared at him. She felt torn: grateful for his honesty and yet reeling from his words.

'That said' – he glanced at her – 'I think a baby would be an incredible gift to us, wonderful.' He beat his hands on the steering wheel. 'But be under no illusion; every time I see you go through this loss, every time we get back in the car with the veneer of hope scraped from your face and a new reason to feel sad, it feels like shit. And yet strangely each time hurts a little less than the last for me, and I hate how I am getting used to it, expecting it almost. It takes the joy from the pregnancy, and I can only imagine what that must be like for you. I feel torn.'

Lucy heard the catch in his voice. And she nodded at his words of truth. It made her sad beyond belief to hear her own fears voiced so clearly. *'It takes the joy from the pregnancy.'* He was right; it did.

'I want to give you the baby you want, the baby *we* want,' he corrected himself. Lucy thought of Camille and knew how easy it was to let the truth slip out when you weren't watching your words. 'But I am worried that it is a price that is too high to pay. I love you more than I love any potential baby. You are my priority and it's difficult to know when the time to stop is. How many times do we go through this? How many times do we put your body through the strain? How much can you take mentally?' he asked. 'How much can we take as a couple?'

Lucy felt her limbs shake at the prospect of not trying again, and at the same time knew that she couldn't face another pregnancy failing. His words left an imprint in her mind. He was right – how much *could* they take as a couple? The fact that she didn't know the answer caused more hot tears to fall down her cheeks.

She pictured the sonographer earlier, who had, as always, smiled benignly and sounded out the script that Lucy knew better than he did. There was only ever a small variation in the explanation. '. . . no gestation sac, at least not now . . . already lost . . . nothing . . . HCG levels might still read positive, but it would be false . . . not viable . . . gone.'

The process was now so familiar to her that it was hard to imagine it ending any other way.

'Push! That's a clever girl! Nearly there! Push hard now!'

She took a sharp intake of breath which fuelled her next sob.

'I don't know,' she answered truthfully.

Jonah reached across the fancy hand-stitched red leather of the centre console and held her limp hand. 'Me either.'

◆ ◆ ◆

Camille was ensconced on the sofa when they walked through the door. Lucy was happy to see her sitting calmly. She was in no mood for an outburst of any kind.

'Where did you stay last night?' Camille asked, a little sheepishly; this apparently had been her main concern.

'I have an apartment that I rent out, where I lived before I married your dad. It's on the river, very modern. I think you'd like it.'

Camille nodded.

'And Ross, the tenant, has left, so it's empty at the moment while we think of what to do with it,' she explained.

Camille's voice was calm, quiet, as she stood. 'Can I make you a cup of tea?' she whispered the offer.

'Where is my daughter and what have you done with her?' Jonah tried to joke, as he deposited Lucy's small suitcase by the door.

'I'd love a cup of tea, thank you.' Lucy sat down and closed her eyes briefly. Camille came back in with a tray and three mugs of tea. She handed one to Lucy, one to her dad and took one for herself before curling into the chair by the fireplace opposite them and tucking her feet beneath her.

'I'm sorry I flipped out yesterday, Lucy.' Camille kept her eyes on her mug of tea.

Lucy felt Jonah shift his position on the sofa next to her and could sense his delight at this apology.

'It made me feel on edge, unhappy.' Lucy kept her tone friendly yet concise.

Camille nodded and looked down to the floor. Lucy wasn't overly consoled. She had seen this model of behaviour before and knew that contrition from Camille could be replaced in an instant with a demand, a tantrum or an outburst of meanness.

'I want us to be on the same side,' Lucy offered, deciding not to mention that it wasn't only yesterday's outburst that bothered her, but the whole build-up over the last couple of weeks, her snide comments and overreactions. She felt Jonah's hand snake over her thigh to hold her tea-free hand, urging her on.

Camille nodded. 'I can't believe that Dex would ask me to stay here and then go to New York for a whole year.' The girl's tears pooled again, and she wiped them on the back of her sleeve.

'I understand that you are hurt, but it sounds like a big opportunity for him. And you have college to look forward to. Fashion design – it's going to be brilliant.'

Camille nodded again. 'I know.'

'And I think when you love someone,' Lucy began, 'you sometimes have to want what is best for them, even if it might not always be what is best for you.'

Jonah tightened his grip on her hand.

'And you know, Camille, as hard as it is to think about, you are both so very young, and if you are meant to be together you will, and if you are not then someone else will be waiting right around the corner.' She sighed. 'I mean, look at me and your dad. I wasn't looking for a relationship. I went to a christening and the party afterwards, and instead of leaving with a goody bag, I left with a husband.' She tried out a small smile.

'But I don't want anyone else; I want Dex.' Camille looked up with her large eyes full of sorrow, and Lucy felt the stir of sympathy for the young girl who was experiencing heartache.

'I know.' Lucy nodded and sipped her tea.

'I need to go and get showered.' Camille sniffed. 'I'm working at Bill's for a few hours this afternoon. I'm really nervous about seeing Dex.'

'Don't be.' She smiled at the girl. 'If he goes to New York, you will regret every opportunity you missed to spend time with him and talk to him while he was here, so make the most of it.'

'Make the most of every second, Lucy. Before you know it, she'll be gone!'

'Are you okay?' Jonah reached up and wiped the tear that trickled down Lucy's face as Camille left the room. She raised her palm and held his fingers fast against her cheek. Her desire to talk to him, openly and without guile, had always been strong, knowing that confessing everything might help him understand her a little better. But recently the idea of sharing with him something that was still so raw, so damning, so painful, was more than she could bear while things between them were a little fractured. 'Yes,' she lied.

'I think I might go and lie down, have a nap. I'm tired and sad.' She laid her head against his shoulder.

'That's a good idea, my love.' He kissed her sweetly before she stood. 'Can I bring you anything?'

'No.' She shook her head.

Spying the suitcase in the doorway, Lucy laid it flat on the floor and undid the zip. She removed the dog-eared baby book and walked over to the bookshelf, placing it behind the French Revolution titles.

'We are not going to lose heart, remember? We are lucky,' Jonah reminded her.

'I don't feel that lucky right now,' she murmured, as a stab of pain gripped her lower gut. She held her breath until it had passed.

'I was just thinking, we can get a referral now, Lucy – isn't that what Dr Millard said? That is, if you want to. It's up to you. I will support you either way. You know that.'

Lucy nodded, then trod the stairs slowly, not entirely sure that she did know that.

◆ ◆ ◆

Monday morning proved to be a welcome diversion. The routine of preparing for her working week meant she didn't dwell on everything that had occurred at the weekend. The moment she set foot inside the building on Victoria Street, however, she remembered that she had confided in Tansy, and in the next instant there she was, beaming at her and waving surreptitiously from the other side of the foyer.

'Shit,' she muttered.

Tansy walked speedily towards her and then linked her arm around Lucy's, as if they were besties walking into their school prom. She chaperoned Lucy to her office. Lucy shrugged free from her grip as soon as they were inside and walked to the chair behind her desk.

'So? How are we feeling today?' Tansy's voice was higher than usual and reverberated with excitement. 'I've been thinking about you all weekend. It took my mind off the fact that Michael and his friends had invaded the house, playing Call of Duty and staying up until the small hours, making noise that woke Benedict. Oh the joy!'

'I'm not so good, actually,' she began.

'Oh?' Her friend's gaze narrowed.

Lucy looked at her computer screen and concentrated on entering passwords and opening documents while speaking; it was the only way she could guarantee keeping her composure. 'I started bleeding on Friday night and went to UCH on Saturday.' She swallowed and shook her head. 'My pregnancy is not viable, gone, done, so . . .' She bit the inside of her cheek, still without looking up.

'Oh, Lucy! Oh no!' Tansy placed her hand at her chest. 'I am so—'

'To be honest, Tans, I can't cope with you being nice or offering sympathy, so I would really appreciate it if we could not talk about it and just crack on with work. I've got a proposal to look over and some annual leave to okay. I need to get my head down.' She was aware of her dismissive tone, but knew it was that or lose her composure.

'Sure.' Tansy turned and made for door. With her hand on the handle, she smiled at her friend and boss. 'But if you do need to talk, you know where I am.' She paused. 'And I just want to say, and I know this might be hard to hear right now, that there are times when I feel a punch of envy at the fact that your time and your body are your own. I will never get the big office, Lucy, or the big bucks, because my time and my thoughts are divided and sometimes I think I would like to be able to concentrate on one thing and be the best at it that I possibly can be. You know that old expression, "The man who chases two rabbits, catches neither"? That is what it can feel like sometimes, trying to have it all.'

Lucy gave a brief nod. Her friend's words, meant to soothe, caused a flicker of irritation. She returned her eyes to the screen.

The atmosphere in the house in Windermere Avenue was more still than it had been in a long while. It was as if emotions had calmed a little. Camille's broken heart meant she carried an air of reserve and contemplation that Lucy welcomed, considering this far nicer than the petulant mood swings that had been commonplace before. She no longer lived in fear of potential outbursts. When Dex came over, Camille would rush to greet him, as if it were their last contact, holding him with such ferocity it was slightly awkward for any observers. Even Dex seemed a little thrown by it.

As Lucy prepped the asparagus and mangetout that they would have with the herb-crusted side of salmon that baked in the oven, Camille came into the kitchen and sat at the table.

'Hey,' Lucy greeted her, as she busied herself with the mountain of green veg on the worktop. 'I always hear my mum's voice when I'm preparing food; she used to say that we needed over half the plate to be covered in vegetables no matter what the meal, and one day Fay got a tiny plate from her doll's house and put a single pea on it. Job done.' She smiled at the memory.

The girl flopped down into a chair at the table. 'Fay is funny.'

'Yes, she is.'

Camille drew shapes with her finger on the tabletop. 'Do you like your mum?' she asked, out of the blue.

Lucy gave a nervous burst of laughter before answering. 'That's a funny old question. Yes, I like her, I love her, but we are very different people.' This was the most tactful way she could find to say that they weren't close. 'Why do you ask?' Lucy felt a throb of fear that Camille might have witnessed something in her relationship with her mum, quickly calming herself with the fact that she had only ever met her mum at Fay's, where their interaction had been minimal and pleasant.

'My mum doesn't like me.' Camille's whispered aside, spoken to the tabletop on which her fingers fidgeted nervously, caused Lucy to put down the paring knife and walk over to the table.

'What do you mean? You are so close, you and your mum!' She wiped her hands on her jeans. 'Are you fretting because she hasn't called? Because you mustn't. It's probably because she misses you too much and finds it difficult, or because it's expens—'

'No.' Camille cut her off mid-sentence, shaking her head. 'It's neither of those things. I just don't think she likes me.'

Lucy stared at her, at a loss to understand where this sentiment was coming from, knowing by the girl's own admission that she and her mum were the best of friends.

'Do you know, I often felt like that about my mum,' Lucy confided.

Camille looked up at her with interest. 'Did you?'

Lucy continued: 'Yes, absolutely. Fay was always funny and cute and chatty and I always felt that my mum didn't get me.'

'Does she get you now?' the girl asked hopefully.

'No. Not really,' she confessed, and they both laughed. 'It can't be easy for your mum having you over here. It's possible she feels a bit abandoned or that you have chosen your dad over her, and I know that sounds nuts, but when you love someone that much, you can take things to heart and misinterpret them sometimes.' Her words jarred in her mind. Was this what had happened to her and Jonah with Camille?

'I guess.' The girl brightened a little. 'But sometimes, I feel like she . . .'

'Like she what?' Lucy pushed.

'Nothing.' Camille gave a wide if forced grin. 'What's for supper?'

'Oh.' Lucy was a little thrown by the change in topic. 'A side of baked salmon and lots of lovely vegetables and sautéed potatoes.'

'Can I have some salmon?' Camille asked, sheepishly.

'The salmon with a face?' she questioned.

'Yes, but just give me a bit without a face and I won't feel so guilty.' Camille laid her head in her hands.

'You shouldn't feel guilty; you can change your mind whenever you want to. Eat healthy, eat salmon, do what you want; you are seventeen and the whole world is at your feet and the whole of your life is ahead of you and it's going to be a great life, Camille, trust me.'

Lucy stood up to continue prepping the vegetables, but noted the heave of her stepdaughter's shoulders followed by the unmistakable sound of her crying.

'Oh, Cam!' she soothed. 'You could always call your mum, you know, make the first move?' Her suggestion only seemed to make the girl cry even more.

Jonah heralded his arrival by whistling from the hallway. He stopped short of the kitchen door.

'Hey, what's up?' He looked from his wife to his daughter. His stern expression told her of his suspicion that they had been 'bickering' again.

'Cam's feeling a bit low, but the good news is, we are all going to enjoy salmon for supper.' She tried to rally them all with positivity.

'But it has a face?' he queried. 'I thought things with faces were off the menu?'

'Don't you worry about that.' Lucy winked at Camille, who now sniffed into a square of kitchen roll. 'A girl is allowed to change her mind, don't you know?'

I understand why Mum and I aren't close, of course. I was the golden girl, the one with all the hopes and dreams of the things she never got to do stacked neatly on my shoulders. And I didn't mind it, not a bit. I felt special, chosen. I wanted to do all those things and make her proud. Plus, there was something quite comforting about seeing my life plan stretched out before me in an orderly fashion. It meant that no matter what the day threw at me or what boulder landed in front of me, I only had to sidestep it and take a deep breath to be back on track. Fay was the naughty one. The one who asked 'why?', broke the rules, played ball in the house, fed the dog titbits from her plate, ran through the sprinklers in her Sunday best, broke a window, answered back. That was her role. But me? I was the steady hand on the family tiller, the good girl. Or at least that was what my mother believed. I guess that was why she was so shocked, hurt, and why what happened changed the nature of how she loved me. Because it did, without a doubt. It changed it forever.

And it changed me forever too.

SIXTEEN

It was late September. Camille had been ensconced in college for the last two weeks, Dex had departed for life on the other side of the pond, and, after her most recent setback, Lucy's body seemed to have found its rhythm.

She sighed at the sight of the wilting brown heads on the potted geraniums that lined the wall of the garden. They were confirmation that summer had ended. It always made her feel a little down, this rather grey time between the glorious warmth of the summer months and the beautiful burnished hues that autumn brought with it. Autumn was her favourite season; for her it held close associations with real fires, hot toast, mugs of cocoa and starchy meals eaten by lamplight from the comfort of the armchair with warm socks on her feet to ward off any chill.

The house stood forlornly in the encroaching darkness; it was as if, with Jonah away, it mourned a little for his cheery presence, as did she. It felt very different climbing between cold sheets without him close by for comfort. He had been gone for a week, already halfway through his business trip to China, an expanding market for vehicles just like the ones he sold. He was set on opening a garage in that faraway land, and his enthusiasm for the project was infectious. She had watched him come alive when detailing their dive into the unknown.

'I shan't be away for long, I promise,' he had consoled her before he left.

'Whereabouts will you be?' She liked to picture him.

Taking her by the hand, he had led her up to the study and pulled the dusty globe down from a shelf. He turned it gently. 'Here.' He pointed to a spot on the vast land mass.

This ball that represented the whole of the earth fascinated Lucy. She had placed her hands on its surface and let her fingers dance over continents separated by vast swathes of sea.

You are somewhere on this tiny planet . . .

'Penny for them?' he had asked.

'I'm going to miss you. That's all.' She had forced a smile, unwilling to admit that she pictured their planet spinning on its axis, going faster and faster, with her still no closer to having her baby. It had felt like more than she should burden him with as he left home to travel so far away.

'Oh, my Lucy, it'll fly by. You'll see.' He had kissed her passionately on the mouth.

Her feet ached. She felt as if she had been running all day, and she couldn't wait to get inside, kick off her heels and sink under the bubbles of a full bath, with a cup of tea cooling on the side and her music on for company. Even picturing the next hour of abandon filled her with a warm, happy feeling. With no sign of life at any window, she quietly hoped that Camille had gone out with some of her new college friends, though the girl's descriptions of them had been a little lacklustre: 'She's okay' and 'He's all right, I suppose.'

Jonah was confident that time would prove to be the magic balm, and that by the end of term Camille's pining for Dex would have waned, and some other handsome beau with a penchant for fashion would be cluttering up the sofa and devouring their snacks. She hoped he was right, but worried that he might be underestimating the pull of that first love. Lucy saw the way her stepdaughter leapt up at the sound of the postman, rushing to the door to see if Dex had written – which he had, once or twice, to supplement his daily email.

The little blended family of three had settled into a routine of sorts. Camille seemed more at home. She had put up some pictures in her room, including the framed card that Lucy had given her for her birthday, and on her chest of drawers stood a jewellery rack holding her vast collection of vintage beads and bangles, all of which gave the sand-coloured wall an alluring splash of colour. She had also added patchwork cushions to her bed, picked up for a song from a backstreet stall in Camden Market. These too helped Camille put her own stamp on the decor.

Lucy jostled her bag on her knee and waved to the lady with the dogs down the street before putting her key in the door. A bundle of post had been pushed to the wall. She stooped to gather it in her hands, visually dismissing the unappealing brown envelopes and flyers for the usual nonsense, food delivery services, gardeners with a good daily rate, and a new window-cleaning service. It was as she straightened and cast her keys on to the sideboard in the hallway that she heard the unmistakable sound of sobbing.

'Hello?' she called into the darkness, her heart racing. 'Camille?'

Making her way into the sitting room, she noted that the chairs and sofa were empty, so where had the sound come from, upstairs? She flicked on the lamp on the table by the sofa and her eyes immediately flew to the corner of the room.

'Jesus!' she shouted, her breath coming in short bursts as fear leapt in her throat and turned her bowels to ice. As her eyes adjusted to her surroundings, she realised that the hunched figure lying in the small gap on the floor between the sofa and the wall was Camille.

Even without the sound of her crying, it was obvious from the shake of the girl's shoulders and her laboured intake of breath, muffled by the wet wheeze of tears and snot, that she was consumed by her distress.

'Camille?' she spoke softly as she rushed towards her, wondering what might have caused this breakdown. Slowly the girl unfurled her arms and legs and it seemed to take superhuman strength for her to pull herself into a sitting position.

Lucy took a step closer and sank down on the floor next to her. She placed her hand on Camille's back. 'What is it, Camille? What on earth is wrong?' She swallowed, fearing the girl's response as her mind raced. Had someone hurt her? Had they been in the house? Was Jonah okay? Her tone was kind and yet pressing.

'Talk to me, love. What's happened?' It occurred to her then that it must be Dex. Her muscles slackened a little and she sat back, fully expecting to hear that Dex had ended their relationship. The girl was taking it hard, and this level of heartbreak took Lucy right back to herself at a similar age.

I never want to wake up . . . she had yelled in all sincerity.

Her stepdaughter opened her mouth to speak. Lucy watched as the next torrent of tears fell, and Camille battled to compose herself.

'It's okay, you take your time, try and get your breath,' she cooed. 'There's no rush.'

The two of them sat still, waiting. It was some seconds, though it felt like an age, before Camille managed to compose herself enough for speech. The two shifted to get comfortable on the cold wooden floorboards. Camille raised her head to reveal her blotchy, tear-stained face, her skin mottled with purple dots of anguish.

'It's . . . it's true what I said about my mum . . .' she began. 'She, she doesn't want me there. She's never wanted me there, and the older I get the worse it's got.' Her eyes filled with tears again.

'I'm sure that's not true. You said yourself that you and your mum were great friends, your trips to the cinema – goodness me, I never did anything like that with my mum. You are lucky.'

'I'm not lucky,' she countered. 'We never went to the cinema.' Her tears forced her to pause. 'We never did anything. I made it all up.'

'Oh, Cam.' Lucy narrowed her eyes and let her head drop. It was the saddest thing. She was full of self-recrimination for not seeing the boasts for what they were: the wishes of a very insecure little girl.

Camille continued. 'My stepdad, Jean-Luc, he's really nice, but if he says one nice thing to me or offers to give me a lift, or anything, she flips and . . .'

'And what?' she coaxed.

'When my mum's drunk she says terrible things – that I'm a slut and that I am after Jean-Luc! Jean-Luc! He's been my dad since I was a baby.' She shook her head at the absurdity of it and banged the floor in frustration.

Lucy felt her gut flip with the horror of her stepdaughter's words and could not imagine what it must be like trying to manage that situation. Camille was, after all, still a little girl.

'He doesn't know what to do. He loves my mum, they've been together forever, but when she's drunk it's so horrible in the house . . . and I couldn't stand it any longer so that's why . . . that's why I wanted to come here.' She caught her breath.

'Oh, Camille, you poor love.' She would never confess to the slight relief that there were no darker implications to the girl's revelation. Her mum's jealousy, however, was still a horrible thing. 'Your mum doesn't mean it. That's just the drink talking.' She heard her words, leaping to the defence of a woman she had never met and whom she judged harshly. She was, however, aware that all that mattered was Camille's view on the situation, and she hoped these words would make her feel a bit better. 'Come and sit on the sofa with me. You'll get a numb bottom sitting down there and that will never do.'

Lucy slowly stood and Camille followed, flopping down against the wide arm of the sofa, facing her. Lucy decided to keep the light low and pulled the faux-fur throw from the back of the sofa and placed it on the girl's legs. Camille nodded her thanks, and ran her palm over the soft fur as though it was a pet offering comfort.

Her voice quavered. 'And my dad was all I had. Even though I didn't see him all the time, he was my escape. I used to think about coming here and living with him when I'd finished school, and it was getting closer and closer and I thought about all the adventures we would have. And then he married you and it changed everything for me, everything.'

Lucy nodded. This she understood.

'And when you said about it being just the two of you, how much you loved your life, I felt like crap. I'd imagined coming here for so long. I thought it would make everything better and instead I felt like you didn't want me here or couldn't wait for me to leave.'

'Oh God.' Lucy felt a jolt of guilt at the words.

She jumped up and grabbed a tissue from the box on the table and gave it to the girl, sinking back down on to the sofa next to her. 'I wish you had told me this sooner; all I ever wanted to do was to get to know you. I want us to be great friends, I really do. I didn't want to detract from the life you had before I arrived. I wanted to add to it!' She tried out a small smile.

'I don't know what to do, Lucy.' Camille shredded the damp tissue in her fingers. 'I don't know where I fit in. I feel like I'm floating, like rubbish on the sea.' She cried anew.

'You fit right here! And you always will. This is where you live for as long as you want it to be. I think we could have fun together, if you let me in. But never doubt that you will always, *always*, have a home here with your dad, who loves you more than anything in the whole wide world, and he always will.'

Camille looked up at Lucy and her tears seemed to slow. She took a breath and tilted her chin upwards. 'I don't know if he *will* always want me here.'

'Camille, I give you my word. It doesn't matter how much time you have spent apart, you must believe that he loves—'

'I'm pregnant.'

'You're . . . What?' Lucy thought she might have misheard.

'I'm pregnant.'

Camille's words tore open a box of shock and concern. Thoughts of worry and surprise were sent flying up into the air like newly released bats that swarmed around their heads, spreading a sense of panic that fogged all rational thought.

Lucy heard the blood rushing in her ears. Camille, this seventeen-year-old girl, currently in her care, was pregnant. Her mouth felt dry with nerves, and it reminded her of being sixteen again, knowing what she wanted to say, but not having the confidence to say it. She prayed, as she had then, for a steady hand on the tiller, someone that could take control and guide her through these choppy waters. She wished that Jonah were by her side. She had had no training, Tansy was right, and she felt sick at the prospect of saying or doing the wrong thing.

'Are you . . . are you sure you're pregnant?' She was aware of the stunned tone of her enquiry; even saying the word out loud felt alien. It hit her with force in the gut. She had thought it likely that Camille and Dex were having a physical relationship, but full, unprotected sex? It had not really occurred to her, not in this day and age with contraception so freely available and encouraged that she thought it would be a given. She also knew that had she and Camille been closer, discussion of such a thing would have been so much easier. This was another terrible example of her holding back where her stepdaughter was concerned.

Camille averted her gaze, looking down at the throw on her lap, displaying the embarrassed signs of a seventeen-year-old who was still bashful about sex because it was new, and who was still tinged with the guilt that Lucy remembered feeling.

'Yes, I'm sure. I had my scan today. I knew I was, already, but I had kind of blocked it out, but it was confirmed today.'

This little girl was pregnant. Having a baby.

She felt the bile of jealousy leap into her throat. Lucy felt numb.

'You had a scan?' Lucy pictured Camille treading the shiny, sanitised floors that were so familiar, lying on the couch in a room where the memory of her own misery lingered, and awaiting the sonographer's words as Lucy had done so many times, only for it to end in the same way, with her tears and an awkward drive home, as she and Jonah silently pondered what might have been.

Camille nodded.

'Does Dex know?'

'Not yet. I don't know how to tell him.' She started crying again. 'It's such a mess.' Finally she looked up.

'Oh, Cam, it is a bit of a mess, but not the end of the world. It really isn't.'

'It feels like it,' the girl managed.

Lucy hardly dared ask her next question. 'How far are you, did they say?'

'Thirteen weeks.'

Thirteen weeks . . . she had made it to thirteen weeks.

Camille slid from the sofa and stood, arching her back to reach into the pocket of her jeans. As she did so, Lucy saw the unmistakable swell of a bump beneath her T-shirt. She hadn't noticed it before, partly because she hadn't been looking and also because the loose layers that Camille favoured did much to disguise any shape. But there it was. *Oh my God, a tiny bump . . .* She instinctively placed her hand on her own stomach and felt another punch of resentment that the thing she had yearned for and coveted most, the thing she had failed at, seemed to have fallen unrequested into the lap of this girl.

Camille sat back on the sofa and handed her a grainy black-and-white image. Lucy held the matte, square photograph towards the arc of light from the lamp and could quite clearly see the image of a baby.

She touched her fingertip to the outline of the large head, a rounded stomach and the legs bent up towards the chest. The arms appeared to be up and folded behind the head, as if the little thing was relaxing on a lounger. Lucy's smile was almost involuntary; her happiness to see such a special picture was evident. But it was coupled with an ache in her chest for this to be her baby.

'It's a little boy,' Camille added. Lucy had almost forgotten she was there and jumped when she spoke.

'A little boy,' she repeated.

'Yes.'

'Have you told your mum?' she wondered, as she handed back the picture.

'No.' Camille shook her head. 'I don't want to tell her, not until I have to. She will only go crazy and I can't cope with that right now.' She sniffed.

'You will have to tell her, but you and your dad can decide on how and when. Try not to worry about it right now.' Lucy considered what it might feel like being present when Jonah and Geneviève shared this news. Their daughter was having a child. She looked ahead and could only see more exclusion from this ever-growing family that she had hitched her wagon to.

Camille nodded. 'Can you tell my dad for me?' She started crying again.

'Oh, love. I need to think about it, but right now, I'm not sure.' Her hands fidgeted. 'I think it might be best if we do it together. I can say the words, but you should be there and it will be fine,' she soothed.

'But supposing it's not fine? Supposing he throws me out? I don't know what I would do! Where would I go?' She raised her voice with an edge of hysteria.

'That's not going to happen, trust me.' She felt a leap of nerves, wondering exactly how Jonah was going to react and what would be the best way to orchestrate the time and place of discussion. 'Have you'

– Lucy thought carefully of how to couch her next question – 'have you made any decisions, Cam, about the future, about the baby?'

'I'm keeping him. No matter what. I'm keeping him.' She raised her chin, speaking with a sense of clarity and assuredness that Lucy recognised. It fired a bolt of admiration right through her heart.

'Your maturity and confidence are wonderful.' She smiled, hoping that her expression was enough to mask the many concerns that leapt into her mind. Not least of which, how was this young girl going to cope with the demands of motherhood? How would she cope financially, emotionally and practically?

'I'm scared,' Camille whispered.

'Of course you are.'

The two sat in darkness, both quiet for very different reasons as the reality of the situation in which they found themselves began to permeate.

It was Camille who eventually spoke.

'Sometimes I feel okay, and I think I can do this, and I picture me and Dex and this baby and it makes me feel happy. And then others, I think about what will happen if Dex doesn't come back from New York or just dumps me when I tell him and I will be on my own and I don't earn any money and I can't picture what my life will be like!' Her breathing once again came in irregular bursts and her tears fell.

Neither can I . . .

'Have you thought about where you might want to live, how this might work?' She gestured towards the girl's stomach.

Camille shook her head.

Sweet Jesus!

Lucy stared at the girl who most of the time was averse to doing the most basic of chores. She pictured Adam and Fay, who ran around at the behest of their kids, the relentless parenting tasks that filled their very long days, and she wondered how Camille would fare. She thought of tired Tansy, who moaned about sleepless nights, Benedict's teething and the strains of parenting while working. Even with two incomes coming in, money was still tight for her and Rick. Camille yawned, as if on cue, and Lucy felt a swell of sympathy for her, picturing her life being shaken upside down at a time when she was trying to navigate the rocky, obstacle-strewn path from child to woman. And now, on top of her hormone-driven outbursts, the immature rants of a girl brimming with self-doubt and a lack of worldliness, she would have to cope with the demands of motherhood. She hoped that Camille was strong enough.

Lucy pictured herself at sixteen: almost entirely ignorant of the reality that lay beyond the front door of her family home and yet entirely convinced of her own invincibility, believing she could take on the world and win. Was that blind faith, or sheer ignorance? She wasn't sure. She thought about her mum, who had always been there to help her navigate that rocky path.

'Why are you crying?' Camille whispered.

Lucy touched her palm to her cheek; she hadn't realised that she was. 'I guess it's just a very emotional time.' She chose not to heap anything more on to the shoulders of this fragile girl.

Lucy watched as Camille ran her hand over the slight swell above her waistband. What she felt was again a dash of envy but mainly pity for this young girl who was about to be thrust into adulthood and all that it brought with it. She found it hard to see her so distressed at this time.

'There are some things you need to be doing, Camille, like taking folic acid.' She decided to offer practical advice, a positive action that might boost the girl's confidence.

'I already am. I read that on the Internet,' she whispered.

'Good, that's smart.' Lucy smiled. She stood and walked over to the bookshelf, reaching deep behind the French Revolution to find her baby book.

'I think you might find this interesting.' She sat on the sofa next to Camille and opened the book. 'This is the first page and so I always thought it must be one of the most important messages.' She gave a small cough and then read aloud, by lamplight, though it clearly wouldn't have mattered a jot had she not been able to see the words, since Lucy knew them by heart. '"It is a known medical fact that stress in a mother can be rather harmful to the unborn child. It can raise the baby's own level of stress hormone, and this has been known to contribute to babies being born prematurely. It is therefore highly recommended that mothers-to-be avoid stress wherever and whenever possible."'

Camille sniffed. 'It's funny, isn't it? It's telling me not to get stressed and yet I don't think I have ever felt so stressed and so scared in my whole life. I will try, though.'

'Shall we have a cup of herbal tea?' Lucy knew she certainly needed one. She handed the book to Camille, who followed her into the kitchen, where Lucy switched on the light and filled the kettle and set it to boil, before grabbing two mugs and placing a rose-scented teabag in each.

Camille leant on the worktop; her eyes were almost swollen shut as a result of her intense sobbing.

'Do you think I could get an apartment if I, like, went to the welfare office or whatever? Would someone give me a home?'

'I don't know, honey. I'm not sure how it works, but I think it would be unlikely.' Again the girl's naivety brought a lump to her throat.

Camille flicked through the baby book, reading aloud: '"At week ten your baby is growing fast and could weigh up to eight grams. Despite being so tiny, all its vital organs are now in place, including its brain, lungs and bowels." It says, "Your baby is moving around a lot but you will not be able to feel it just yet." Gosh, I'm over thirteen weeks, so mine will be doing even more than that, won't he?'

'Yes. Yes, he will.' Lucy closed her eyes briefly as she reached into the fridge for the milk.

◆ ◆ ◆

The two of them sat at the table with a hot mug of tea each and a shared plate of crusty bread, slathered with butter and strawberry jam.

'When I came down here on my birthday morning, I couldn't believe what you had done for me, Lucy. Those big balloons and pancakes and a whole stack of presents and cards – it was so cool. My mum has never made me a birthday breakfast like that, never really got me a cake. I couldn't believe it, and now I think about that and realise that it was the day I was born, the day she got me, and she doesn't seem that bothered. It makes me feel terrible.'

23 January at 11.10 a.m. The date and time leapt unbidden into her mind.

'Maybe she is suffering too, Cam? Maybe there are things going on with your mum that you don't know about, but that might be difficult for her.'

'Like what?' Camille grabbed a slice of thick-cut sourdough from the plate and took a bite.

'I don't know,' she replied after some thought.

'Well, thanks for that,' Camille quipped, and they laughed at the ridiculousness of it all.

'I love that you are determined, Cam, and I think you have made a difficult decision all alone and that's admirable . . .' She paused. 'But there is a lot to consider.'

'I know.'

'I'm not sure you do know,' she pressed. 'A baby is a wonderful thing, a gift, goodness knows that's what I believe, but a baby will change your whole future. It will become your future, taking the space of any thoughts or ideas you might currently have. It doesn't mean you can't have the things you have planned for, but it means they will undoubtedly be harder to achieve, and it means you can't put yourself first. That's before you even consider the practicalities, like how you can earn a living and where you might live. You need to think these things through, Lucy; you need to understand that this will change *every* aspect of your life. It's not like it is in the babyGap ads, not all smiling and easy. It will be hard, harder than you can imagine.'

Camille stared at her, her expression blank, whether in shock, fear or resentment it was hard to tell. She suspected it was a measure of all three.

'You called me Lucy,' Camille pointed out.

'Did I?'

The girl nodded, and again they both felt a snicker of nervous laughter that went some way to lighten the mood.

'I know you are right. I know there is so much to sort out and so much to think about, but I will do it and if things take longer for me or I have to go about them in a different way, then that's just how it will be.' She shrugged.

Lucy nodded at her brave, easy words of justification.

'Is it okay if I use the computer in the study? I want to look up some stuff about being pregnant and I want to look into any allowances that I might be able to get, but my iPad cuts out sometimes if I want to download anything. It's quite old.'

'Yes, of course you can. You don't have to ask.' She smiled, gladdened by Camille's proactivity.

Camille yawned. 'I feel exhausted.'

'Me too, honey. Me too.'

My stepdaughter fell pregnant, and I can tell you: it felt bittersweet having a pregnant woman in the house who wasn't me. I didn't have the chance to tell my husband immediately. I thought it would be unfair to do so while he was so far away on a business trip, but the fact that I knew this thing about his daughter was a horrible burden and one I disliked. It felt disloyal. My stepdaughter was adamant she didn't want her mum to know, and with greater understanding of the strained nature of their relationship, this made more sense.

I would wake in the middle of the night and think about the thirteen-week marker, picturing the scan picture of that little baby, and I'd put my hand on my tum, before waking more fully and remembering that it wasn't me that was pregnant and it wasn't my child. I'd lie back on my pillow and cry myself to sleep. That sadness was always lurking and manifested itself in a variety of ways. I couldn't bear to see former colleagues come into the office, passing around a new baby like a prize – which of course it was, a prize of the very best kind. Far better they think me off, aloof, work-obsessed or disinterested as I scuttled past the gathering in the reception, trying to block out the oohs and aahs of the instantly besotted, hopeful women who jostled for a better look, running their fingers over the rounded, rosy cheeks of the baby and thinking of the day it would be their turn. I wanted to remind them that for some people the universe had a different plan, that it might never be their turn. But of course I didn't. I kept my eyes on the file in my hands and quietly closed my office door.

SEVENTEEN

Lucy arranged the large glass jug of flowers on the table in the sitting room, while Camille paced the wooden floor in front of the fireplace.

'You need to try to keep calm,' she reminded her, while trying to ignore the slick of sweat on her own palms and her flustered pulse.

'I feel sick and I don't know if I can do this. Can't I just hide upstairs and come down when you've done it?' Camille pleaded, as she folded and unfolded her arms.

'No. If you and I sit side by side, it not only shows that you are supported, but that you are strong enough to sit and face him. I know it isn't an easy thing to do, but it's exactly those qualities that will get you through this tricky time. You are stronger than you think.' She twisted the Peruvian lilies so that they looked their very best, and she stoked the fire with the wrought-iron poker before returning it to the little stand on which it hung next to a mini shovel. She then popped another seasoned log on to the glowing embers, ensuring a warm welcome for her husband in every sense.

'I need the loo again.' Camille rushed from the room.

With perfect timing, no sooner had Camille locked the bathroom door on the floor above than Jonah's taxi pulled up outside the house. Her heart lifted at the sound of his voice thanking the driver.

She raced to the hall and opened the front door, pulling her cardigan around her form and trying to ignore the whistle of cold air that came in from the street. She waved at him as he paid the cabbie and grabbed his suitcase.

'Hello!' he called out, grinning at his wife as he made his way up the front path.

'Hello, you,' she responded, as he abandoned his case and wrapped her in his arms. 'Two weeks is a very long time,' she whispered against his ear.

'It felt like a lot longer. I missed you.' He pulled back and kissed her face. Time apart had softened the tension between them; it felt good to have him back. She tried to calm the nervous swirl in her stomach over what was about to unfold.

'So how was China?' she asked eagerly, as she held the door open and ushered him into the familiar warmth of home.

'Well, the bit I saw' – he looked up and shook his head, as if searching for the words – 'was vast, exhilarating, fragrant, modern; the people were kind and welcoming and the weather warm and dry. I think you need to go more than once or travel more widely to fully appreciate it, and I think we should go together. I can be your guide.'

'I'd love that.' She smiled.

Jonah walked ahead into the sitting room. 'Oh, the house looks lovely. A fire! Perfect. Tell me there's a steak somewhere with my name on it and a large glass of red wine and I will be the happiest man alive.'

'Close – a roast chicken and chilled white, but I did make a pudding.' She was aware of the celebratory tone of their conversation and decided to pull back on the jollity, as if she might in some way be able to set the mood for what was about to happen. 'How about a cup of tea?'

'Sounds good! Where's Cam? How's college going? Has she settled in?' He unzipped his computer bag as he spoke, and pulled out a light green silk kimono robe, decorated with pale grey cranes standing in azure pools with a large pink moon hanging hauntingly behind them.

'Oh, Jonah!' she gasped. 'That is so beautiful.'

'I'm glad you like it.' He held it up to reveal the full beauty of the gossamer-like silk. When she reached for it, it slipped through her fingers like water.

'I shall treasure it.' She smiled as she draped the light fabric over her arm and then stowed it on the arm of a chair. 'Thank you for my gift. I'm glad you're home.'

Lucy made her way to the kitchen and put the kettle on, placing three mugs on the worktop and making the tea in silence.

'Are you okay?' He sidled up behind her and kissed her neck.

She nodded.

'Thought we might have an early night, so you can show me just how much you have missed me,' he whispered, kissing her again.

'Yes.' She turned, offering him a brief smile, as she once again concentrated on making the tea.

'Have you and Camille had words again? Something's up, I can tell,' he pushed. She gave a small smile at this assumption and felt her stomach roll in anticipation.

'Hi, Dad.'

He turned at the sound of his daughter's voice in the hallway. 'Hey, Cam! How are we doing?' He walked towards her and hugged her loosely. 'I got you a present; boring old perfume I'm afraid. I'll grab it in a bit. I didn't know what to get, so I picked a bottle up at Heathrow. Hope it's the right one. I have to confess, they all look and smell remarkably similar. The assistant thought it was hilarious that I could only describe it as being in a glass bottle with a funny-shaped lid.'

'Thank you.' Camille dusted the floor, moving her socked foot in an arc.

'Here we go, three teas.' She handed a mug to Camille, holding her eyeline, and then gave one to Jonah, who had gone quiet, matching the mood that enveloped him.

'Let's go and sit in front of the fire.' She took a deep breath and shuffled behind the other two as they made their way to the sitting room. Jonah took the chair, stretching his legs out in front of him, as she and Camille sat next to each other on the newly plumped sofa cushions.

Jonah took a sip of his tea and exhaled, happy to be home.

'So, what have I missed?' He smiled, drumming his fingertips on the side of the mug.

Lucy exchanged a glance with Camille and sat up straight. 'Well, we've had quite a fortnight.'

'Work busy?' he interrupted.

'Yes.' She nodded, not wanting them to get distracted with small talk.

'Well, it's tough at the top.' He winked. 'I've already told you: quit your job and come and work for me. The pay will be rubbish but the perks, fantastic!'

Camille sat forward slightly on the seat. 'The thing is, Dad . . .' She paused.

'Oh no! You don't want a job too? Lucy we can cope with. Setting up in China, a piece of cake. But you, Camille?' he joked. 'I don't think Jonah Carpenter Motors is ready for that!'

Lucy stared at him, wishing he would sit quietly and let them speak. She decided to take the bull by the horns. 'Jonah—'

'Oh shoot! Just give me one sec and I promise that I will be all ears. I told Rod I'd let his wife know about his train arrival time. Apparently he was low on battery. Let me just fire off a quick three-word email. I'll only be a second.' He jumped up and hurtled up the stairs.

Lucy placed her hand on her stepdaughter's arm and gave her a squeeze of reassurance and a nod of encouragement, her message loud and clear: *You can do this!*

Less than a minute later Jonah appeared in the door with a wide grin on his face. 'Oh, Lucy!'

She exchanged a look of confusion with Camille.

'What?' She turned to face him, trying to read his emotion, watching as he shook his head in disbelief.

'Do you know,' he went on, 'I knew something was up.' He waggled his finger at the two women. 'I could feel it. My mind's been racing and I suspected it was bad news, but I've just found this, propped up on my screen! I can't believe it!'

She felt her stomach drop and her eyes widen as she caught sight of the grainy square image in his hand. A scan picture of a beautiful, healthy baby boy at a little over thirteen weeks. They had never had a scan picture, never made it that far.

'You clever girl!' He rushed forward and crouched on his haunches in front of her, placing his hand on her lap. 'I'm in total confusion over the dates, goodness knows it's been easy to lose track, but look!' He stared at the picture. 'Here we are. How about that, Cam? You are going to be a sister!'

Lucy stared at Camille as the blood drained from the girl's face.

'No, Dad.' She swallowed. 'No, I'm not.'

'Now, don't be like that. This is a wonderful thing. You need to get on board and be happy. If only you knew the journey that Lucy and I have been on to make this possible,' he offered earnestly, now gripping his wife's limp hand. She opened her mouth, but no words came. It was as if time had slowed.

'I'm not going to be a sister, Dad.' She swallowed. 'I'm going to be a mum.'

There was a beat or two of silence while Camille's words, spoken with eloquence and serenity, filtered into their consciousness.

Jonah threw his head back and let out a loud laugh as Lucy and Camille stared at him. 'Very funny!' He straightened and placed his hands on his hips.

'It's true, Jonah.' Lucy knew it was her time to speak.

He poked out the tip of his tongue and placed it on his top lip as the smile on his face faded and he looked from one to the other.

'This is a joke,' he stated.

Lucy shook her head. 'No, it's not. Camille is . . .' She swallowed. 'Camille is pregnant.'

He laughed again. 'I don't . . .' he huffed, and turned towards the fireplace, where the flames flickered. 'I can't . . .'

Lucy stood and placed a hand on his back. 'Sit down, darling. It's very important for everyone that we all stay calm.' She watched as he half staggered to the chair and sank into it, loosening his tie and undoing the top button of his shirt, as if he needed air.

'Is this true?' He looked at Camille, who had shrunk back against the sofa.

She nodded as her tears welled.

'Sweet Jesus!' He ran his hand over his face. 'So this . . . ?' He looked at the picture in his hand.

'Yes, that's my scan,' the girl whispered.

'Camille is being very brave, Jonah,' she added with a warble to her voice, speaking quickly, as if this might put a lid on the head of steam she could see building. 'I wanted to talk to you, we both did, but you were so far away, and we decided there was no point in worrying you while you were in China. We thought it best to wait until we could all sit down like this and talk things through, calmly.'

Jonah shook his head, looking first at the floor and then back to his daughter.

'Where's that boy?' he spat.

'Dex?' Lucy didn't know why she felt the need to qualify, knowing perfectly well who he meant.

'Yes! Dex! Who else?' he shouted. 'That kid who lay on my furniture, ate my food, sat in my company, celebrated her birthday! Him!' He had raised his voice, and this was the cue for Camille's tears to fall.

'He's in New York, Dad,' she warbled.

'I bet he bloody is!' He bit down on his bottom lip and his fingers formed a fist that he rested on his thigh. 'Does he think I can't get to New York? I can be there before he wakes up!' he shouted.

Camille snivelled and sniffed. 'He doesn't know. I haven't told him yet because I didn't know what to do or what to say and Lucy said I needed to get my head straight and it's still not straight,' she managed, running her fingers over her forehead.

'What did Geneviève say?' His tone was curt.

Camille looked down. 'I haven't told her either. She'll just freak out.'

'Well, maybe this is the time to freak out. Maybe she has every bloody right to freak out!' He stood and paced the room.

Lucy sat next to her stepdaughter.

Jonah wasn't finished. 'She sent you over here to straighten you out, said she was worried about your behaviour.'

'I didn't need straightening out!' Camille shouted, finding her voice.

'Oh, well I think that's up for debate, don't you?' he fired back.

'You don't know what she's like!' Camille shouted, gripping the arm of the chair.

'You might be right, but I do know that we have bent over backwards to accommodate you, redecorating your room, cooking your vegetarian food while that fad lasted, helping you find a job, sorting out college, not batting an eyelid when you said you wanted to stay permanently. Good God, we even let that boy come into our home, and this is how you repay us? This is your idea of a future?' he yelled now.

'Please, Jonah, we can't all get angry. We don't want to say anything that we might regret, and it's no good for Camille and it's certainly no good for the baby.' Lucy tried to calm everything down. Her palms were slick with sweat and her breathing a little irregular. Despite the different setting and a new set of players, this was a familiar exchange, and the memory left her flustered.

'Jesus H Christ, can you hear yourself? No good for the baby?' He gave a loud, insincere chortle. 'What's going on here, Lucy? How can you be so calm? You have been one of Cam's biggest critics – all of her slovenly habits and lack of gratitude – and yet here you are waving the flag for this ridiculous situation!'

She shrank from his words, embarrassed and angry that he had raised this in front of Camille, exposing confidences she had shared with him, especially now she and Camille seemed to have bonded over the pregnancy. It angered her that Camille might feel less than supported by her at a time when she would need all the support she could get.

'She's a child! My little girl!' He pointed at her. 'How the hell is this going to work? Where does a baby fit in? How does she support it? Where do they live? Jesus Christ, she is ruining her life!' he yelled. Lucy and Jonah stared at each other, aware of how he had asserted his parentage. It hurt.

Lucy closed her eyes and could hear the phrase, screamed an inch from her face: *You are a child! And you are ruining not only your child-hood but your future too! What have you done? What on earth have you done?*

'She's not a child, Jonah. She is young, granted, but she is a young woman, a young woman who is pregnant and who needs us. She needs our support,' she rationalised with a measure of dignity that belied their exchange and his hurtful accusation.

'Oh God! How can you be so calm? She is only just seventeen, a few weeks ago she was in full-time education in the south of France, and after five minutes here she's running wild and is pregnant by some little prick who has run off to New York!'

Camille placed her hands over her ears and closed her eyes. 'Please stop! Please just stop! I didn't mean it to happen and I'm sorry! I'm so sorry, Dad!' she sobbed.

'I'm sorry! I'm so sorry, Mum!'

Lucy cocked her head and smiled at the tearful little girl in the corner of the sofa. She might have been looking at Camille, but it was herself she saw, curled into a ball in her school uniform with her heart beating fit to burst and her distress threatening to drown her. 'She wasn't running wild! She fell in love, that's all. She fell in love and she was unlucky!' She shouted her response, caring little who could hear.

'Unlucky, I'll say! Bloody unlucky! Geneviève said she was getting out of hand. Maybe this is what she meant.'

'No, Jonah!' she yelled. 'That's not how it was.'

'What do you mean "no"? How do you know?' he spat. 'How do you know she fell in love and slipped up? How do you know this wasn't exactly what her mother was talking about?' His face was red with anger.

'Because it happened to me! It happened to me,' she screamed.

It felt as if the air had been sucked from the room. Wrapping her arms around her shaking form, she looked at Jonah and then Camille, who both stared at her. 'It happened to me. I was sixteen when I had a baby. My little girl.'

Jonah let out an involuntary laugh of incredulity. 'Is it true?' he asked, slowly.

'Yes.' Lucy lowered her head, letting her chin fall against her chest as she cried. She could feel the heated stares of her husband and step-daughter boring into her. Camille was struck dumb.

'Your . . . your little girl? You have a child?' Jonah managed. It was as if the fact just wouldn't sink in.

'Yes.' She looked up finally and nodded at him.

'I don't believe it,' he breathed, followed by a silence that seemed to carry physical weight. 'How could you not tell me something like that?' he whispered, before staggering backwards until his legs found the chair by the fireplace and he sat down.

Lucy watched as he placed his head in his hands before looking up at her with an expression that she was unfamiliar with – it bordered on dislike. To see him look upon her in this way caused her insides to shrink. He looked like a stranger. Lucy let her eyes close briefly and recalled the words he had spoken in love as they sat on the damp ground. *'What I am trying to say is that you are like a glorious second chance that I didn't think I had any right to, and I will treasure you every day . . .'* It felt like a thousand years ago.

'Who *are* you?' he asked. She jumped at his words and stared at him. 'I said who the hell are you? Because I sure as hell don't know!' he yelled now.

'Don't shout at me!' she responded. 'I have had enough! I can't cope with that.' She took a deep breath. 'I refuse to feel any more shame for the fact that I fell in love at the age of sixteen and was unlucky. I got pregnant! I got caught out, that was my crime, but right now, I can tell you I feel more shame in the fact that I have never found the courage to say the words out loud, not until now.'

Jonah looked away.

Camille's sobs filled the air. Lucy stared at her, knowing the best thing she could do was remove herself from this situation. Her presence was like the fuel that fed the flame. It would be better for Jonah, and certainly better for Camille, if she were to leave; the last thing the girl needed at this difficult time was to watch the two of them explode.

She left the room, making her way on shaky legs to the bedroom, where she once again gathered her suitcase and unceremoniously dumped clothes, a few belongings and her make-up bag into it. It took great effort to lug it down the stairs; her limbs, in fact her whole body, felt weakened by the earlier exchange. Taking a deep breath, she walked forward, hovering in the door frame. Neither Camille nor Jonah had moved. Both seemed to be sitting in quiet contemplation. Jonah still held the scan picture in his hand.

She addressed her husband. 'I'm sorry – sorry that I'm not the person you thought I was. And I am sorry that you feel unable to support me when that is what I need more than anything right now.' She waited for a second, almost subconsciously waiting to see if he tried to stop her. He did not. And with that one sentence hanging in the air, she walked out of the room.

◆ ◆ ◆

Lucy lay on the wide bed in the pristine bedroom of the flat that looked out over the Thames Path. With neither the energy nor desire to move, she drifted in and out of sleep, wishing, not for the first time, that she wouldn't wake up.

There she lay for forty-eight hours. Apart from reluctant trips to the bathroom and to take sips of water, she lay very still, almost comatose.

The grief that rendered her thus was as fresh as it had been on the day she gave her daughter away, only now it was wrapped in the memory of the way Jonah had reacted, the things he had said and thoughts of her mum. She saw her sitting in the armchair, crying into her palm, her face contorted, mumbling regret and recrimination of how this might have happened. Lucy recalled the visceral punch of concern she had felt for Camille at her announcement, and again she saw her mum, all those years ago, doubled over with her head in her hands.

'I'm so lost,' she wailed into the darkness. 'I love you, Jonah, and I'm sorry for not telling you, but you have no right to punish me further. Don't you think I have suffered enough? Because I can tell you I have. I have . . .' She cried, beating her pillow with her fist until, overtaken with exhaustion, she slept once again.

I am nearly forty-one, but saying those words out loud, admitting for the first time ever that I had you, took me back to that time when I was a frightened girl. I felt instantly guilty for sharing it, after swearing that I would never tell a soul. I felt the hot, uncomfortable cloak of shame that I had worn for all these years, but right then, it was no longer hidden under layers of laughter, achievement or any other number of diversions. It was a brightly coloured shame, there for all to see. Now, it feels as if a burden has been lifted and I want to shout at the world: 'I was sixteen when I had my baby, when I had you, my little girl!'

EIGHTEEN

The hot shower went some way to restoring her body; it brought feeling back to her hollow limbs, but could do little to stop the gripping sadness that sat in her gut and the feeling of weakness that clung to her, dragging her down. Lucy stood facing the warm deluge, trying to block out the intrusive thoughts of self-recrimination. What would Jonah do now? Where did this leave their marriage? And what would Camille think? How was she coping alone in the house with only her angry dad for support?

Working her hair into shampoo lather, she lifted her arms with some difficulty and tried not to think too far ahead. It was only when she felt the wrinkly touch of her finger pads to her face that she switched off the tap and stepped into her towelling robe.

She pictured the beautiful green silk kimono that she had left on the arm of the chair, wondering if she would ever get to feel it against her skin. After this short window of time, mere hours, the house in Windermere Avenue and the things in it already felt like another life, and one that she could hardly relate to. With her head in a towel, she padded across the floor to the kitchen and searched the cupboards, where she was delighted to find a sealed packet of ground coffee, courtesy of Ross. She set the cafetière to brew on the stove and picked up her phone for the first time in nearly two days.

She felt sick when she saw that there was no attempt at contact from Jonah – sick and disappointed. There were numerous missed calls from work, which could wait; she considered she had done enough, sending the relevant people an email explaining she needed emergency leave. There were also several news updates from various alerts she had set. They all seemed trite compared to her own situation: a meteor of truth and confession had landed on her marriage and she could hardly see or think straight for the debris and dust that it had kicked up. Lucy cleared the screen without a second thought; she could not have been more disinterested in what was happening anywhere outside of the flat. Her voicemail icon pulsed. She switched the phone to loudspeaker and placed it on the empty worktop, listening to the messages. The first was from Fay.

'Hey! Pick up your phone! What's going on? I called you at home and Jonah was a bit curt and said you were at the flat. Don't tell me you have had a lovers' tiff already? If you have, this is way too soon! You are supposed to be married a good long while before they start. Anyhow, call me, need a favour – do you still have that black dress with the strappy back? Adam's got a rugby dinner and I have to dress up, yuck, and I'm darned if I'm going to splash out on something I'll never wear. Anyway call me . . . it's your sister by the way.'

Lucy felt the threat of tears at hearing her lovely sister's voice. The next message was from the effervescent Tansy.

'Lucy, HR said you had taken some leave, hope all is okay, give me a ring if you need anything or if you fancy some company. I have wine. Nuff said. Speak soon!'

The coffee burbled in the percolator. She poured a big mugful, gulping down the dark, restorative blend before slumping on the white leather sofa and staring at the large picture window, which the rain trickled down. It felt like the whole world was crying, and that suited her just fine.

She was considering another cup when the front doorbell rang. Misery gave her the gait of the elderly or infirm as she limped to the door and placed her eye on the spyhole.

Jonah stared at the door.

This time there was no smile, no brown paper bag full of breakfast, no encircling arms, no laughter and no promise of forgiveness, and just the memory of that previous visit was enough to make her tears pool. She opened the door and he stepped inside, eyes trained on her face. She stared at the man who had become a stranger in such a short space of time and closed the door, gathering her robe around her frame.

'Come through,' she offered, walking slightly ahead with her eyes downcast, until she found the familiar territory of the sofa and sat down, already further weakened by the exchange. Jonah sat too and they stared at each other. Her own face, she knew, bore the hue of an insomniac, with two dark shadows of fatigue sitting below her eyes, which were swollen, reddened and small. She noticed his uneven stubble, the fact that his face looked thinner, his sunken eyes and his expression of hopelessness. He too looked like he was grieving.

'How's Camille doing?' she asked with a croak to her voice.

'She's . . .' He breathed out and shook his head, looking out of the window at the grey rain and dense cloud. He lifted his hands and let them fall into his lap, whether unwilling or unable to talk about his daughter, she wasn't sure. 'I was going to call but thought this might be easier, face to face.'

She nodded, hating the finality of his phrase. '*This* might be easier' sounded like the beginnings of goodbye, and her heart flipped.

'I don't know where to start.' He rubbed his palm over his beard. 'I feel sick. I'm shocked, upset . . .' He closed his eyes, as if words failed him.

Lucy could do nothing to help him out; it wasn't like any other day, when he had forgotten the name of a client as he often did and was clicking his fingers until she threw in suggestions – 'Mr Potter? Mr

Noakes? I give up!' Or when he would fire a question – 'Where was that place we ate, near High Street Kensington tube, with the great veg? You know it!' – accompanied by the clicking of his fingers. 'Maggie's!' she would chime. 'Yes, that's it! Maggie's.' And he would beam at her superior memory for such details.

She stared at him, waiting for him to speak. Feeling a shiver along her limbs, she reached for the faux reindeer fur that sat on the arm of the sofa, wanting to pull it over her shaking limbs. But she realised the instant her hand touched the cool hide that the throw resided in the house in Queen's Park, the home with the soft arcs and plush furnishings, the dusty corners and the worn wood, unlike here, where everything was sharp, cold and angular. She had thought she liked living like this, until Jonah had shown her the alternative and she realised that she didn't, not at all.

'I can't sleep,' he confessed.

She nodded. *Me neither . . .*

'I keep replaying that moment.' He looked towards the window. 'I was reeling from the news about Camille; that information was swirling around my mind and I was waiting for you both to give in and tell me it was a joke.' He shook his head. 'I was tired from my trip, still am. I saw the scan picture and I was . . .' He paused. 'I was elated, and then to hear it was my grandchild, not my son . . . it was hard to take in. And then to top it all, you dropped a bombshell.'

'I have wanted to tell you – more than I have ever wanted to tell anyone.'

'So why didn't you?' he asked, holding her gaze.

'Because I have never told anyone.'

'But I'm not anyone – I am your husband!' he interrupted with passion.

She closed her eyes, knowing she didn't have the strength for another fierce row. 'I know. And I know it's hard to accept or even understand, but the thing is, Jonah, no one in the world knows apart from me and my mum. We even kept it from Fay, arguing silently behind closed doors and keeping her in the dark. That has been one of the hardest things for me over the years, the fact that she was an unwitting outsider.'

'Tell me about it,' he interjected.

'My mum made me swear, and I have spent so many years being so afraid of people finding out that I never considered it might be okay to break that promise I made her, to admit to what I had done.' She felt her lip quiver. Her mum's voice was loud in her ear: *You never tell a soul! No one, ever, do you understand me? Because if you do, you'll be finished!'*

'So what changed? Why the sudden confession the other night?'

She shrugged. 'I guess it was the right time.'

He gave a short snort at this. 'Oh God.'

She continued. 'You can snort, Jonah, but you have no idea of what I went through, what I continue to go through.'

'You are right,' he fired, 'because you kept it from me!'

She decided not to get sidetracked into another fight. 'I watched Camille shrink from your words; she had her fingers in her ears and her eyes screwed shut and I remembered what it felt like on the night I told my mum.' She took a stuttered breath as her tears gathered. 'My dad had already died, and she said it was a good job as he would have died anyway of the shame. I never forgot that. And I still think about it sometimes. I was so frightened, more frightened than I had ever been in my whole life, and usually when you are afraid, if you are very lucky, you can go to a parent, who will make everything feel better, but she didn't.' She picked at the belt of her bathrobe. 'She made me feel dirty; her words filled me with self-loathing and shame. For her, it seemed to be more about the fact that I had had sex than the fact I was expecting a baby.'

There was a moment of silence while they both digested the new gobbets of information being shared. It was Jonah who coughed and broke the silence. 'Your words are heartbreaking, they are, but it's like you are talking about a stranger.'

'I'm not a stranger, Jonah. It's me!' She placed her hand on her chest.

'When I met you, Lucy, and we sat up late on the sofa in front of the fire, chatting and asking questions and getting to know each other . . . I thought you were perfect. Not because you were without flaws. Who is?' He gave a fleeting smile, as if forgetting for a glorious second the situation in which they found themselves. 'But perfect because you were so open, honest. I had never met anyone like you, and I knew you were the woman I wanted to marry, the woman I would be happy introducing to Camille as my wife. I'd never been that happy.'

She pictured those magical nights on which the foundations of their relationship were to be built, and her heart ached. 'Me either.'

'But now I feel like I don't know you,' he whispered.

'You do!' she cried. 'You know me, Jonah.' She was aware of the weary tone of her words. How many times did she need to express this?

'I'm not sure I do, and that realisation is as terrifying as it is sad. I didn't know this one thing about you and it's not a small thing, like pretending you like football or saying you like my cooking; it's a bloody big thing. The biggest. You had a baby! You have a child in this world somewhere.'

Lucy felt the creep of tears over her cheeks; this she already knew. *My daughter . . .*

But Jonah wasn't done.

'You cried to me only a month or so ago, saying how you felt as if you were being excluded, and it ripped me apart, the idea that you thought there was some conspiracy to hide something from you, make you feel left out, even if it was done at a subconscious level. I beat myself up about that. And all the time, you had this big, big secret. Talk about exclusion!'

'I know it's hard to understand, but—'

He cut her off. 'You're right; it's hard to understand. I feel as if you have ripped my heart to shreds. It's so unfair, Lucy, so unfair to have kept this from me. I thought I was worth more than that, deserved more than that.'

'You do.' She tried to offer a verbal balm that might help them move forward.

'And the thing that really gets me, the one thing that has gone around and around in my head since you left, is that we were trying for a baby, trying hard.' He stopped talking to rectify the catch in his voice. 'The hours I have spent holding you, telling you it was all going to be okay, believing we could get through anything, anything. The endless trips back and forth from the hospital . . . It has killed me to hold you while you cried, to see your blood and your expression when yet again you were faced with that loss. It has killed me to see you so excited and to watch it fade to nothing while you knitted away, knitting all the love and hopes you carried into those bloody baby clothes!' He sniffed his tears to the back of his throat. 'And all the time, all the time, Lucy, you chose not to tell me that you had had a child, a baby girl. How do you think that makes me feel?'

How do you think it makes me feel? she echoed.

She felt her body fold as she wept. He made it sound so simple. As he spoke, she realised that something had been broken between them that couldn't be fixed. His lack of sympathy made her muscles coil. A thought occurred: that maybe he wasn't the man she had thought he was. This very idea struck her as final and left her with a new layer of sadness to sit atop her grief.

'I'm sorry, Jonah. For everything, for this situation.'

'Me too.' He shifted on the sofa until he was facing her.

'I can see how angry you are, but you haven't once asked how I am feeling or what it's been like for me. This is not all about you. It's about *us*, all of us.'

There again was the uncomfortable beat of silence.

'Who was the father?' he whispered.

His question came out of the blue and floored her a little. It wasn't one that she had been expecting. By the set of his jaw, she could see that despite so many years having passed there was still a flicker of jealousy, and she understood a little. He was curious as to who had managed to succeed where he felt he had failed to give her a healthy full-term baby.

She shook her head. 'Just someone.'

'No,' he boomed. 'You don't get to leave it like that. You can't keep cherry-picking what aspects of your life you get to share – you just don't get it, do you? I need you to be open with me, Lucy, for my own peace of mind.'

'The trouble is, I think that no matter what I say, you are only going to get madder. I feel like I can't win!'

'Try me.'

She took a deep breath and pictured the boy in the year above her at school. It felt difficult to dig into the past and pull out the facts that Jonah craved, but she knew she had to try.

Her hands fidgeted in her lap. 'His name was Scott. He was a year older than me. Not popular or particularly good-looking and I can't think of one thing that singled him out, apart from the fact that I loved him. And I did, as far as you can when you are sixteen and think that the world can be like a movie and everything will work out fine.'

'Were you seeing him for long?' he asked, as his leg jumped against the sofa.

'Not really, six or seven months. We got the same bus and we became friends and my dad had just died and he was kind to me. That was it really.'

'Are you still in touch?'

She let out a loud burst of nervous laughter at the idea, angered by this unfounded, ridiculous obsession with the boy. 'No, Jonah. I was a kid. He was kind to me and we used to have sex in his house when his mum and dad were at work.' She saw him wince at her matter-of-fact statement, and a small part of her was glad that she had wounded him a little in return. 'There was nothing glamorous or exciting. It was as if we were playing house and I couldn't see beyond how to wear my hair at school the next day to make me look nice for him.'

She thought about Scott, who had been just a boy, a clever boy, a maths whizz who was working hard towards his exams, hoping for a better life than the one his parents had, living in their damp little house with a scrawny backyard and having to scrabble down the back of the couch for their bus fares at the end of the month. The couch on which she and Scott had made a baby. She remembered the damp smell of their house and immediately thought of Camille, wanting more for her than a life of hardship with a baby in tow.

'I want more for you, Lucy, than this! This is not the life your dad and I planned for you. We have worked so hard!'

Her mum's words were loud in her head. She had never fully considered how she might raise her baby, unable to see past the romantic ideal of becoming a mother, wrapped up in her desire to hold the little thing that grew inside her and wholly diverted from the grief of losing her dad. She recalled another conversation between her and her mum, with Jan calmer and more quietly spoken: *'You are in no position to care for a child, Lucy, and you are giving this couple the greatest gift. They are going to give her a wonderful life and you are like an angel to them . . .'*

'So did he take off, like young Dex?' He spat the boy's name, pulling her out of her memory.

Lucy delivered her words slowly and calmly; she didn't want to argue with him but knew this point was important. 'Dex doesn't know about the baby. Cam hasn't told him.'

Jonah twisted his jaw and said nothing, breathing heavily through his nose.

'And no, Scott didn't take off, because I never told him. As I said earlier, the only people that knew were my mum and me. It wouldn't have served anything telling him, but it might have messed up things for him too and I didn't want that. Thankfully my mum wasn't hell-bent on punishing him and so he was free, ignorant of the thing that has been such a big part of my life.'

'A big *secret* part of your life,' he corrected her.

'Yes!' she agreed. 'But I am trying to put that right. And this is what I mean about your response. You are confusing me, making me feel worse when all I am trying to do is explain to you just what it was like. I think all of the time about the day I had her, but strangely I never think about Scott. He faded from my mind almost instantly and now he is almost invisible.'

Jonah sighed and seemed to relax a little, as if comforted by this new information. 'I had this terrible thought in the middle of the night that maybe you were in touch, and that added a whole new layer of deceit for me.'

'Good God, Jonah, no, no, not at all. Give me a bit more credit.' She placed her hand on his arm, and noted how he stiffened involuntarily. She removed her fingers and coiled her hands against her throat. This one act of rejection showed her how far they had drifted, and it left her feeling bereft all over again. It made her feel dirty.

'How did you keep it from everyone? Your pregnancy.'

Lucy drew a deep breath. 'By the time I plucked up the courage to tell my mum, I was nearly six months, but I was very sporty, skinny, and I didn't really show that much at that stage. And my mum told the school I had glandular fever, and that's what she told Fay, who was told to keep away or she'd get it. It was all part of the deceit. And then I went to hospital in Guildford, not that far from where we lived, and I had the baby and I gave her away and then I went home. And two weeks later I went back to school and caught up on what I had missed, industrious and quiet as ever. And Scott ignored me and I didn't really care.' She wiped her tears on the sleeve of her robe. 'I was a different person. It was like part of me had died, and if I cried I said it was because I missed my dad, which I did, very much. It was really hard.'

'Don't cry,' he offered softly.

She whimpered at his show of kindness, and it angered her to be so in need of any crumb of affection he scattered.

He nodded at her briefly. 'I don't know how to feel,' he admitted. 'I love you, I do. That's not something I can switch off and I wouldn't want to, but I am finding it really hard to get past the fact that you didn't tell me. I am your husband; it was you and me against the world! That's what I thought.' He looked straight ahead.

'That's what I want!' she urged.

'But it's not only about what you want, Lucy. It never was,' he stated, coolly. 'Can I ask you something?'

'Yes.' She nodded.

'Did you try to keep her?'

Her tears turned to sobs that left her fighting for breath. 'How can you ask me that? I was a little girl! I was sixteen, a young sixteen who had only ever known school and homework and Saturday nights at home with my family. I'd never worn make-up or been out much after dark. My mum said what we ate, what we wore, what time we went to bed, everything. I was a child and my mum made the decisions and I went along with it and it never ever occurred to me that I might have any other option. I didn't have a voice!' she howled. 'But if I could go back – oh my God, if I could go back,' she heaved, 'I would fight, Jonah. I would fight for her, I would, my little girl.'

He reached across and patted her back, a gesture that was so much less than she deserved at the height of her distress that she wished he hadn't bothered. It felt conciliatory, insulting.

'I fought back in my own little way. They told me not to feed her, but I did. I did.' She sobbed, looking up at him briefly. 'And I will never forget it. Never.'

'What . . . what did you call her?' he asked, visibly shaken by her words.

'Bella. My daughter is called Bella May.' Despite the desperate circumstances, to say her name aloud felt like the most wonderful thing in the world. 'And I haven't seen her since she was three days old.'

'Bella May,' he repeated. 'How old is she now?'

Lucy pushed her long hair behind her ears and fought for composure, as she looked at her husband. 'She is twenty-four.'

'And where is she?' he asked.

'I don't know!' Lucy screamed. 'I don't know! I don't know! But I miss her. You have no idea how much, Jonah. I miss her so much that it hurts!'

I heard them talking in the corridor. And with hindsight the fact that so many decisions were taken and so much planning was done without my consent, it seems inhuman, staggering. But at the time, I was used to being told what to do at school and at home, and this was just another big municipal building full of adults who all told me that they knew best and I didn't question anything. I didn't know I could. But when you were only hours old, I overheard a nurse saying to my mum, 'It's best that she doesn't feed her. It won't do either of them any good to bond in that way.' Hearing these words fired something inside me. That was it, my one chance for us to bond, for me to imprint myself on to you, and even though I was little more than a child myself in so many ways, I was determined. And I did it. I held you close and I fed you, Bella, and it was . . . it was something that I think about in my darker moments. It hurt, but I thought that was part of my punishment and it didn't matter. I overlooked the discomfort and stared into your beautiful, big blue eyes and I willed you to remember me and more importantly to remember just how much you were loved by me, your mum, in the short time we had together.

NINETEEN

Lucy had watched as Jonah slowly rose from the sofa, waiting for his words of invitation for her to come home to Queen's Park and having mixed feelings at the prospect. She tried to picture where in the flat she had placed items that she would need to gather up and throw into her overnight bag, remembering her dirty pyjamas behind the bathroom door and her work laptop, still in its case in the hallway. Yet at the same time she was angered by his lack of sympathy, trying to imagine how she would have reacted to a similar level of distress from him. She knew she would have been kinder, and that thought alone made her glad when he had kissed her lightly on the forehead, as one might an ailing relative, and left as quietly as he had arrived. Alone.

Their exchange was that of strangers, and this left her feeling quite numb. This, and his refusal to open up about Camille, left her with a familiar sensation. She had experienced it with previous boyfriends, including Richard: that what she had perceived to be a lifetime relationship was in fact a temporary thing, and the golden, shining future she had seen stretching ahead into the sunset was instead a wrong turn that led to a dead end. She pictured Richard with his face split into a grin as he proudly showed off Dominic Drake. The humiliation at having to make a one-hundred-and-eighty-degree turn and start walking again, on legs weakened by humiliation and heavy with sadness, was far from easy to take. What made it all the harder now was that unlike with any previous beaus, what she felt for Jonah was a deep, all-consuming love, which is why he was the one she had married.

She spent the rest of the day and most of the next night sitting and waiting, for what, she wasn't sure, but she found herself paralysed with indecision and sadness. Her distress was, however, tinged with a small amount of relief. It felt quite amazing to have shared her secret after all these years. Whatever the outcome with Jonah, it felt good that some-one knew about Bella; it helped make her real. She put the television on and stared blankly at soap operas, the news, a movie, anything to help occupy the minutes that ticked by. Before falling asleep, she fired off a text to Camille.

I am here if you need me or if you want to talk. Just say the word and I'll be there. Take good care of you, Cam. I am thinking about you. Lucy Xx

She woke the next day with a new-found clarity, wanting more than anything to talk to her mum. Reaching for her phone from the bedside table, her heart lifted to see there was a text waiting for her. She hoped it was from Camille. Closer inspection revealed it was from a pizza company local to Queen's Park, offering a three-for-two deal for the weekend, which she deleted aggressively, angry with them for getting her hopes up.

After showering and stepping into her jeans and a jersey, she grabbed her handbag and jumped into her car. With the radio on, she made her way out of town, passing through the busy streets at a snail's pace as traffic clogged the arteries of the city, until eventually the car sped up, the air tasted sweeter, the houses were not quite so squashed together and she found herself in the leafy suburbs of Surrey where everything looked a little shinier.

As she turned her car into the quiet cul-de-sac in which she had grown up, she pictured her dad standing in the front garden of a summer's evening with his shirt sleeves rolled above the elbow, watering his shrubs and pulling any weeds that might mar his perfect borders.

Her heart sank as she recognised Fay and Adam's car in the driveway. She had been hoping to find her mum alone. She sat in the car, toying with the idea of leaving without going in, wondering if she could execute a speedy three-point turn and disappear. This was beginning to feel like the best idea when her plan was foiled. Her sister spotted her car from the lounge window, robbing her of anonymity as she ran to the front door, flinging it open and smiling broadly.

Lucy took a deep breath and parked the car.

'Well, what a shocker! Didn't expect to see you here today! Bagsy not sharing my pudding with you – we only have three. Mum's bought individual chocolate pots for the grown-ups and there's no way I'm giving you mine!'

'You can keep your pudding!' Despite the heaviness of her heart she was happy to see her sister, who sounded about as far from a grown-up as you could get.

Fay greeted her with a hug. 'To what do we owe this honour? Are you lost? Have you taken a wrong turn on your way somewhere far more exotic?'

Lucy held her tight and closed her eyes. Her sister had no idea just how much of a wrong turn. 'Very funny.' She walked into the house and hung her bag on the banister before making her way into the large kitchen-diner where everyone was congregating.

'Keep the noise down.' Fay pointed upstairs. 'Adam's just putting Maisie in her cot for a nap.'

'Oh, Lucy! What a lovely surprise. Have you eaten?' Her mum looked at the chicken pie on the worktop.

'I haven't, but don't worry. I'm really not hungry. Fay has already broken the news that there are not enough chocolate pots for me.' She saw the relief spread across her mum's face.

'Hiya, trouble!' Lucy walked over to the table where Rory sat with his tongue poking out of his mouth as he coloured in a picture with his array of pencils. 'What's that you're doing?' She bobbed down to the level of the tabletop.

'I'm colouring in this scene from *Star Wars*,' he replied without looking up, with a slight impatience to his tone, as if what he was doing was quite obvious and he would prefer not to be disturbed. 'Is Camille coming here?' His eyes suddenly brightened at the prospect.

She shook her head. 'Afraid not, Rory. She's busy.'

His noisy sigh told her all she needed to know.

Lunch was the diversion she needed. While everyone else eagerly tucked into the pie, Lucy picked at a large bowl of salad and nibbled on a baked potato. The conversation flew back and forth across the table, with Rory telling all in great detail about his new invention for a flying car with stealth capabilities and an ice-cream dispenser.

'I think there would be a big call for those, Rory.' Lucy nodded. 'I would definitely buy one.'

'Maybe Uncle Jonah can sell them in his posh showrooms, eh?' Adam winked at his sister-in-law and she smiled, ignoring the flip in her stomach at the very mention of his name. She felt sad that Jonah was so integrated into her family, so loved, and yet his links to them were looking more and more fragile by the day.

It might have been Lucy's imagination, but it was as if her mum sensed all was not well. It was possible that she noticed the fatigue etched on her daughter's face, the straining of her neck muscles or the way her fingers strummed the tabletop as she waited for the opportunity to speak to her alone.

Lucy held her gaze a couple of times, her eyes unsmiling.

It was as the three adults dug into their chocolate pots with gusto and Rory was enjoying a less sugary children's version that a faint bleating came from the worktop.

'Oh, great timing, Maisie!' Fay stared at the baby monitor and hurriedly placed the spoonful of dark dessert into her mouth before pulling the spoon out clean and placing it down as she prepared to leave the table.

The time had come.

'You finish your pud. I'll go,' Lucy chirped. 'Mum, give me a hand?'

'Oh!' Jan looked taken aback. Her eyes darted to the busy table that she felt required her presence. 'Yes, of course. You go and grab her. I'll be one sec.'

'Are you sure, sis? She might need changing.' Fay pulled a face.

'Of course I'm sure.' Lucy hurried from the kitchen and up the stairs to her mum's bedroom, where Maisie's travel cot had been placed in the corner of the room. The little girl lay pulling at her feet, which were up in the air, and she part whimpered, part chatted. She was a happy little thing.

'Hello, Maisie! Hello, you gorgeous baby! Look at you – you look so big!' She reached in and lifted the smiling child into her arms, loving the solidity of her against her chest, inhaling the wonderful fresh scent of a newly woken infant, and ignoring the flash of hurt that this was not her child. 'How have you been, beautiful girl? How's things in the world of Maisie, hey? Pretty good I would imagine.' She kissed her several times on the face, and in response the little girl batted her away with her chubby hands. 'Right, let's get your wet bum changed.' She laid her on the changing mat that had been propped by the side of the bed, and rummaged around among the bags and baby paraphernalia, looking for a nappy.

'I can't find anything!' She laughed at Maisie, who found the whole thing amusing. 'It's not funny! I can't send you down without getting you changed or your mum will know how useless I actually am. And that would never do.' She lay her palm on Maisie's tum and bent over to kiss her. She found her irresistible.

'The nappies are in the side pocket.' Her mum's voice drifted from behind her.

'Oh, thanks.'

Her mum bent down and reached for a nappy, passing it to her.

She decided to cut to the chase. 'Jonah and I have had a massive row.'

'Oh no, I am sorry to hear that, Lucy. I did think it was strange that you pitched up here unannounced and alone. You are of course welcome anytime, but that kind of spontaneity is not really you.'

'I guess not.' She ran the wet wipe over Maisie's soft skin and reached for the talcum powder.

'Well, I do hope you get it resolved quickly. He's a good man and he's good for you. Nothing is worth falling out over, not really,' she remarked.

'I told him about Bella.'

At the sound of the name, which neither of them had spoken aloud in over twenty years, her mum seemed to sway a little. She took a step towards the bed, sitting sharply on the edge, as if to stop herself from falling.

'You did?' Her voice was a whisper.

'Yes.' Lucy nodded. She let this fact permeate for a second or two before speaking again, waiting for a response from her mum that didn't come. 'He knows, and so does Camille, and so I suspect will others over a period of time. People like having secrets or, more specifically, they like telling secrets.' She nodded at this universal truth.

'I thought you had put it behind you, after all this time . . .' Her mum's voice was shaky.

'Put it behind me?' Lucy laughed a little louder than she had intended. 'I had a baby, a little girl, just like Maisie here, and she was beautiful. And you took her from me when she was three days old and it ripped my heart in two and it has never healed, not properly. How could I *possibly* put that behind me?' It felt surreal after all these years to finally be able to voice the words that had hovered in her throat on so many occasions. She watched her mum's mouth twist.

'I didn't take her from you.' Her mum's eyes filled with tears. 'You were sixteen. It was for the best.'

'The best for whom?' she asked, rhetorically, as her own tears matched her mum's. 'I'm not sure. I don't know if it was the best for Bella, who has grown up thinking that I didn't want her. And certainly not the best for me, who has ached every single day for my daughter, not knowing where she lives, how she is, who brought her up or even if she is still alive!' Her tears fell fast, and Maisie, alerted by the change in atmosphere, began to cry. Lucy picked her up from the changing mat and cradled her into her shoulder. 'Shh . . . it's okay, little one, don't cry, my darling,' she cooed, while her fat tears slipped into Maisie's fine cap of blonde hair.

'You were just a little girl, Lucy, and your dad had just died. It was a terrible time for us all.' Her mum reached up her sleeve for her hand-kerchief and dabbed at her eyes before blowing her nose. 'I spoke to the social workers and the doctors. They said it was likely you wouldn't have been able to cope. They said it was in the baby's best interest and I agreed. They said the baby—'

'Stop calling her "the baby". Her name is Bella, Bella May! That's the name of your eldest granddaughter. Bella May!'

'I know! I know her name and I see her little face all the time, and if you think that was an easy decision for me, then you are wrong, but I could only think about you, *my* daughter, *my* little girl, and what I thought was best. I didn't want that one mistake to ruin your life.' Her mum reached for a wet wipe from the dispenser on the bed and blotted at her eyes and nose.

'I was sixteen, Mum, and I was old enough to get pregnant, and that one mistake, as you call it, did ruin my life, but not because I brought a child into the world, but because my choices were taken away from me!'

'You have no idea, Lucy, no idea at all what it was like. I was hanging on by a thread. I was trying to make things the best they could be for Fay, who had just lost her dad too, money was tight, I was grieving and then that happened to you.' She shook her head, her voice tight with distress, as her tears fell. 'I couldn't see any other way. The social worker who interviewed you said you were a very young sixteen-year-old, and you were. She said you were vulnerable, fragile. You weren't worldly, you wouldn't have had the first idea about the pressures and stresses of raising a child, and I didn't want you to have to find out. I thought I could restore your childhood and leave you free to have a life, a good life, and you have!'

Lucy tried to imagine arriving back from the hospital, walking into her childhood home with a baby in her arms, and strangely she couldn't.

She thought of Camille and her tone became calmer. 'I was probably more worldly than you thought, and I have had a life full of holes. Bella-shaped holes that get bigger with every day that passes.'

'How, Lucy? How would you have cared her for? Paid for her? How would it have happened?' Jan pushed.

'I . . . I don't know,' she admitted. The words of her conversation with Camille came flooding back. *A baby will change your whole future. It will become your future, taking the space of any thoughts or ideas you might currently have. It doesn't mean you can't have the things you have planned for, but it means they will undoubtedly be harder to achieve, and it means you can't put yourself first. That's before you even consider the practicalities, like how you can earn a living and where you might live . . . This will change every aspect of your life.'*

'No. I don't know either, love.' Her mum's voice was soft. 'If money had been no object and we had had the space, we could have considered it, but things were terrible for me, for us all. You were already frail, broken over your dad, and I can't imagine how much worse it would have been if you'd had to leave school and get a job and care for a child.' She shook her head.

Lucy opened her mouth, but had no response. She pictured Camille, and for the first time saw a life with her own child that wasn't happy and carefree; instead she saw poverty and struggle, and it sent a shiver along her limbs.

Lucy gently rocked Maisie, who had stopped crying. The sound of the creak of a floorboard in the hallway caused both her and her mum to turn their heads. Fay crept into the room with tears streaming down her face. She calmly walked over to the baby monitor that was set on the sideboard and turned it off before making her way over to Lucy. She placed her arms around her and held her tight, while they sobbed. Her mum leapt up and held both her girls, as the three generations stood locked together, united by a common sadness. Lucy cried loudly, 'I miss my dad!'

Fay pulled away and spoke to her big sister. 'I miss him too, and for the record I have never thought you were useless. I have always, always, thought you were absolutely brilliant.'

◆ ◆ ◆

Fay and Adam went home, leaving Lucy and her mum sitting opposite each other at the kitchen table.

'I love you, Lucy,' Jan began.

Lucy felt lighter, relieved and hopeful. 'I love you too.'

'Well that's a very good start.' Her mum swiped the pad of her index finger under both eyes and sniffed. 'You have always been fascinating to me, Lucy. I find it incredible that this little baby I had is such a strong, capable, clever woman.'

She felt her heart twist at the compliment that left her feeling a little light-headed. To hear these words from the woman she had felt closed off from for so many years was the most wonderful gift imaginable.

'But you weren't always this way.' Jan shook her head. 'You were a daddy's girl when you were little, clinging to him and waiting for him to come home, and when he walked into a room you lit up. It was wonderful for me to see two of the people I loved most in the world feel that way about each other.'

Lucy felt the creep of tears at the memory of her beloved dad and how safe he had made her feel. She pictured him poking his head around her bedroom door. She would make out that she was asleep and he would whisper into the darkness, *'Sleep tight, Lucy. Have the sweetest of dreams'*. How she wished she had not feigned sleep, but had instead leapt out of bed and held him tight, asking him question after question, getting to know him better and making sure he knew just how much she loved him. She hadn't known her time with him was about to be cut short. She thought she had all the time in the world to chat to her daddy.

Her mum continued: 'And when he died, part of me died too, and Fay was openly devastated, but you . . .' She paused. 'You seemed to clam up like a little nut. Everything about you was muted. You didn't smile so much, you didn't talk as much . . . it was like you weren't really present and I didn't know what to do for the best, didn't know how to handle it. I was in the middle of my own grief, which didn't help. We lived in a fog.'

'I remember that time. I kept thinking I would wake up and Dad would be in his chair or in the garden. I hoped I would wake up.'

'I know.' Her mum clasped her hands on the tabletop.

'And then I started talking to Scott and he didn't know about Dad and so there wasn't the pressure of having to talk about him or have him ask me if I was okay. He made me feel happy, made me feel good, took my mind off things. I had never really kissed a boy before him, not properly, and yet I was uninhibited like I was someone else. I think I wanted to be someone else.'

'I can understand that,' her mum whispered.

'When I found out I was pregnant' – Lucy stopped speaking and looked up at the ceiling – 'I could not believe it. I didn't think for a second that it would happen to me. Having sex with Scott and actually having a baby seemed about a million miles away from each other.'

'It often does,' her mum confirmed.

'But then once I understood what was happening to me, I looked forward to becoming a mum, couldn't wait to get my hands on that little baby.'

'Weren't you afraid? Because I was.'

'Not really, Mum. Only about giving birth, but not afterwards. I thought it would be lovely.'

Jan placed her fingers over her lips and took a deep breath. 'I was so, so scared for you. I could only see struggle ahead, for us all. I was certainly battling the onset of depression. I was lonely without your dad. I still am.' She closed her eyes. 'I was figuring out how to pay the mortgage without your dad's income, wondering how to get a job and what kind of job I could get. I was desperately worried for you and Fay and how it was all affecting you both, trying to keep things as normal as possible, trying not to let my fears become infectious, and then you told me you were pregnant.' She shook her head. 'It felt like the final straw.'

Lucy thought about the impact Camille's news had had on Jonah, whose life was on an even keel; she could only imagine what it must have felt like for her mum, whose life had been crumbling.

'I never really thought about what it must have been like for you,' she admitted.

'Oh, Lucy, it wasn't me I was worried about. Things were tough, yes, but my only concern was what this would mean for your life. All the things you were capable of would be curtailed because your life would have been one of struggle, and when you are struggling and things are tough all choices go out of the window; you don't have that luxury and you can't plan. Life becomes about meeting your immediate needs, doing what you must, unable to think further ahead than the now. I didn't think that level of struggle would have been fair on you or Bella.' Her lip wobbled as she spoke the baby's name. 'That wasn't a life I wanted for you.'

Lucy nodded, beginning to understand, and she recalled many of Camille's outbursts that seemed to have little reason to them. Had she been the same?

◆ ◆ ◆

It had been a day that Lucy would never forget. A day of openness and a day of healing. Later she settled back into the bed in her childhood room, where memories lined the walls. She thought about Scott, the bookish boy she had loved, and wondered how his life had turned out. Was he happy, fulfilled, a father again?

Did he have the right to know, as she believed Dex did?

Her mum knocked on the door and entered. She sat down in the chair in which Lucy had studied for her exams.

'How are you feeling?' Jan asked.

Lucy looked up at her. 'I'm okay. Drained, but I feel a bit better, Mum. Just to be able to talk about her is a good thing, I think.'

Jan looked into her lap. 'I tried to talk about her soon afterwards.'

'I don't remember that,' she confessed. 'In my mind it was like I was forbidden from mentioning her.'

'No, it wasn't like that, not at all, but I understand that you might not remember things that accurately. You were so zipped up, hurting and withdrawn, and I didn't know how to get through to you. I will never forget the look you gave me when I sat you down and tried to ask you how you were feeling. It was one of pure hatred, and I understood, but I never wanted you to look at me like that again, and I thought I was taking your lead by staying silent about it and burying what happened.'

'Burying Bella.'

'Yes. I suppose so. I thought it was easier than bringing up the subject, opening up the wound again and again. I figured what you wanted was to put it behind you, and the more years that passed without her being mentioned, the more it seemed that it was for the best. I honestly didn't know how to start.' Her mum shook her head from side to side, as if even the memory of that time was painful.

'You told me not to tell anyone. You made me promise to keep it a secret,' Lucy reminded her.

'Yes, because you were at school! And they would have ripped you to shreds. You would have become *that* girl, the one who got into trouble, the one who had a baby, and you were already so fragile, paper thin, grieving for your dad, and I didn't know how much more you could take. I was afraid for you, Lucy, and I only ever wanted to keep you safe.'

'I think I was already *that* girl, Mum. I was already broken.'

'Oh, Lucy.' Jan ran her fingers over her face. 'I want you to know that I only ever did what I thought was best. I went with the professional opinion, I read their reports, and maybe, looking back, if I hadn't been so wrapped up in my own grief, I might have acted differently, but I couldn't and I didn't and I am sorry.' She bowed her head then, crying yet more of the tears that seemed to be constantly hovering near the surface.

Lucy let her hand creep over the floral chintz duvet and rest on the back of her mum's. 'It's okay, Mum. It wasn't your fault. It was a horrible situation that has left its mark on me, but it wasn't your fault, just like it wasn't mine. It was just how it was.'

Her mum bowed her head. 'You have no idea how long I have waited to hear you say that.'

They sat in quiet contemplation for some time.

'There is something that I have been thinking about for a while now.' Jan swallowed her nerves.

'What?'

'I'm sure you know already, but there are these agencies you can apply to, both as a parent who has placed a child for adoption and as a child who has been adopted, once they reach eighteen. Both can register an interest to be found. Thousands of people are reunited in that way. I've read about it.'

Lucy looked up with eyes full of sorrow. 'How could I, Mum? How could I look her in the eye and tell her that I was fit and young and healthy but I gave her away? Do you think she would understand that I had very few choices?'

'I don't know, darling,' Jan answered in earnest. 'But you would find a way. And I know that with Jonah by your side, you can do anything.'

'But he's not by my side. He's barely talking to me and things between us are horrible.' She sniffed.

'Don't give up, Lucy, and don't close down or run away. Talk to each other. You two have such a special thing.'

'Maybe.' Lucy wasn't so sure. 'Camille is pregnant.'

'She is?'

'Yes, she's having a baby, a little boy.'

'Oh my word.'

She watched as her mum sat back, digesting this new piece of information.

'Well, if anyone can guide that girl in her time of need, it's you, Lucy. You better than anyone know what she is going through. And Fay is right, you are absolutely brilliant.'

Her mum's words were like music, sweet and welcome in her mind, and though she knew it would be a while before they could sweep away all the memories of hurt and things said that couldn't be unsaid, this was definitely a wonderful start. Lucy looked at her mum and felt lighter, as if a large chunk of the boulder she hauled around in her gut had been chipped away.

'And you should never ever forget the joy you brought to the door of the couple who adopted her. A woman who couldn't conceive and would not have had a daughter were it not for you.'

A woman like me . . . She let the thought bob to the surface of her mind.

She lay back on the pillow and pictured again the woman who had become Bella's mum, imagining the moment the woman was handed the swaddled child.

I bet she cried. I bet she held her to her and kissed her little face . . .

Leaving the hospital without you was the most horrific thing that I have ever had to do and, I am certain, ever will have to do. They told me you were going into temporary foster care; I think they were worried I might change my mind. Oh, if only I had known that I could! I felt empty, hollowed out, and that's a feeling that has stayed with me. You went from foster care to your adoptive family when you were just three weeks old and I knew very little about them other than how happy they were, this married couple, to be given such a gift. My mum said once that I must have seemed like an angel to them and I know I would feel the same if someone gifted me a child. At the time, however, I remember placing my head on the pillow and feeling wave after wave of anger, because you weren't a gift, not from me. In my mind you had been stolen, and that was something very different. It was weeks later that someone from the court came to see me and explained that now you were six weeks old, the formal adoption process could begin. My mum sat by my side, scared, I guess, that I might say or do the wrong thing. I signed the document and I could barely see the dotted line through my tears. And I'm crying now and the feeling is as fresh today as it was then. By my own hand, I denied my heart and I signed you away, my Bella May.

TWENTY

Lucy had been back at work for a couple of weeks, returning seamlessly to her role and ignoring numerous enquiries from Tansy as to why she had been away. She did what she had always done: compartmentalised her work and home life, presenting her normal, friendly, yet efficient self so that none of her colleagues would ever guess what was going on at home. She and Jonah had exchanged a couple of emails; reading their mundane content had been like taking a dagger to her heart.

'You have had a delivery, looks like books, should I forward to flat?' he wrote.

And her response. 'Thank you, yes.'

He had also texted her late one night; she suspected from the spelling and grammar that it was probably after a few glasses of wine: 'Were are yoru my Lcuy?' She replied instantly: 'I am right here and I miss you.' His sober reply came three days later: 'I need some time.' His words sent a bolt of frustration through her.

'You know what, Jonah?' she announced to the empty walls of her bedroom. 'To steal a phrase from you, this is not all about what you need.' She pulled the duvet over her shoulder and threw the phone further down the mattress.

◆ ◆ ◆

One night, Lucy arrived home from work and switched on the dazzling recessed LED lights. They lit up the entire apartment and made all the glossy surfaces shine, mirroring the shimmering array from the buildings across the river. It was beautiful, the apartment she had always dreamed of, and yet still her heart twisted at the thought of a seat on the squidgy sofa in front of the real fire in Windermere Avenue.

After showering and changing into her pyjamas and robe, she sat on the sofa with her hair in a messy topknot and casually scrolled through her emails. Without the routine of family life, and without Jonah to chat to of an evening, her working week was fluid, and it was now normal for her to work until she fell asleep.

The knock on the door made her jump; she wasn't expecting anyone. She tightened the belt on her robe and stood close to the door to reach the spyhole, and her heart leapt when she saw through the little glass-covered hole that it was Camille. Reaching down she eagerly slid the bolt and twisted the deadlock to greet her stepdaughter.

There were times when Lucy's desire to become a mother slipped into the background of her life. There were days, even weeks, when she would be so preoccupied with the task in hand that she could, for a while, thankfully forget the debilitating yearning that dogged her. And then there were times when something small, a reminder, would hit her with such force that she felt the blow against her breastbone, and the air would leave her lungs as if she was winded. As the door opened to reveal Camille standing there, this was one such moment.

Lucy quickly looked from Camille's face to her stomach, as if magnetically drawn to the slightly swollen, tiny rounded bump of her profile. The waistband of her thermal leggings dipped low beneath her tummy, and her grey V-neck T-shirt sat tightly over her form.

'It's getting bigger, isn't it?' Camille ran her hand self-consciously over her taut skin.

Lucy shook her head. 'It's . . . It's beautiful.' She stepped forward, feeling a mixture of nostalgia and inadequacy as she stared at Camille's small bump, the mark of a successful pregnancy.

'I think so too,' she whispered. This in itself was a sign of how far Camille had come in accepting and enjoying her altered state.

'Come in, come in!' Lucy ushered Camille into the hallway and closed the door. 'Is everything okay?' Her thoughts rushed to the idea that something bad had happened to Jonah or that Camille might be in trouble, and her pulse raced accordingly.

'Yeah, everything is kind of okay.' She paused. 'But not perfect.'

'Right.' Lucy was a little confused by this vague response.

'I hope you don't mind me just turning up at this time of night. Am I disturbing you?' Camille fiddled with the neckline of her T-shirt.

'Not disturbing me at all. I am glad of the break from work, and of course I don't mind. It's so lovely to see you. Does Jonah know where you are?' The question in itself was a reminder that while Camille might be expecting a baby, she was still a young girl living under her dad's roof.

'I left him a note.'

'I'm really glad you came.' Lucy reached forward and embraced her stepdaughter.

'The truth is, I've been having a bit of a panic.' The girl exhaled.

'What about?' Lucy asked, placing her hand on her arm.

'Everything!' She placed her fingers in her hair, as if this was where some unseen pressure lurked. 'I still haven't told Dex about the baby and I can't go to college because someone there will tell him. Plus I'm worried about actually having the baby. I've had a look at some pictures and stuff on the Internet and I don't know if I can do it.'

'I wouldn't recommend looking at anything about it on the Internet. You know it's like those health sites where you log in with the smallest of aches and according to all the posts you have three weeks to live. I bet it's a bit like that – probably only the horror stories make the grade. Remember that millions of women all over the world have babies every second of every day. You will be absolutely fine.' She dug deep to find her most reassuring smile.

'I guess that's true.' Camille seemed to breathe a little easier.

'I'm sure it is.'

'Dad is barely speaking to me and my mum is definitely not speaking to me and I'm really worried about everything.'

'It's okay, Cam. Keep taking deep breaths and we'll work through each thing. But the most important thing is to try to keep calm and stress-free, okay?'

'Okay.' Camille nodded before taking a deep, deep breath.

Lucy guided her into the apartment and sat her at the breakfast bar.

'Wow! Look at this place!' Camille gasped as she twisted in her seat, taking in the wide sweep of the apartment and letting her eyes settle on the vast window and the urban landscape beyond. 'It's so cool! Very swanky!' She pulled an impressed face at Lucy.

Lucy filled the kettle, trying not to think too deeply about the many times she had performed this task in Windermere Avenue in the cosy kitchen that she loved. The fact that they were now in her flat confirmed all of her worst fears; she had been a guest, a visitor, just passing through, although the reasons for this state of affairs were none that she could ever have guessed at.

'So, apart from feeling a bit anxious, are you feeling healthy?' Lucy asked, taking in the beautiful bloom to Camille's cheeks and the lustre of her tawny hair, which made her question redundant. 'You certainly look very well.'

'I think so. I'm eating healthily and doing all the right things. I do feel a bit sick in the mornings, and if I smell something strong, like perfume or fried food, it makes me retch, but apart from that, all good. I have another scan at the end of next week.' Camille turned and smiled at her, and Lucy saw in her expression the happiness and excitement that she had so often felt in anticipation of what might be revealed. She tried to block out the sound of the sonographer's words, heard so many times in a variety of ways: *'I am so sorry . . .'*

'That'll be exciting! It's really lovely to see you, Cam. Although a bit of notice would have been good – I'd have cooked for us and got out of my pyjamas!' She smiled.

'That's okay, I'm not hungry, and besides, I'm used to seeing you like that at home.' Camille's words carried a note of affection that made Lucy's stomach flip with longing. If only she could turn back the clock and start over with Jonah. It killed her that if there had just been a little more confidence and honesty on both their parts, she might still be with him. With the tea half-made, Camille spoke earnestly.

'It's not the same in Queen's Park without you there.'

'Well, I miss being there. I miss you and I miss your dad. How is he?' Lucy stared at the girl, trying to pick up any clues that might lie in her expression about how Jonah was faring.

'He's a bit rubbish really. Working a lot, but when he's home he's very quiet. I think he's upset and angry at us both.'

'Probably,' Lucy agreed. 'But he shouldn't be angry with you. That's not what you need right now.' She thought about how one kind word, one shoulder of support, would have made all the difference to her in her time of need. 'And in fact he shouldn't be angry with me. I deserve more from him.' She levelled with the girl, this admission a mark of their new closeness, allies now rather than enemies.

'I know.' Camille drummed her fingers on the cold granite surface. 'I wanted to come here tonight to tell you that I'm sorry, Lucy,' the girl whispered as she held the end of her long beaded pendant and toyed with its central tassel.

'What are you sorry for?'

'For so many things.' She flicked her gaze towards Lucy and then away again, as if ashamed. 'Mainly I'm sorry because you and Dad have fallen out and it's all because you were being kind and trying to stick up for me.' She held Lucy's eye. 'It's been a long time since anyone has defended me like that.'

Lucy recalled the girl's tearful confession of her turbulent life with Geneviève and Jean-Luc. 'It's not your fault, Cam. It is a difficult situation that has changed things, but it wasn't your fault, just like it wasn't mine or your dad's, not solely. We all contributed in our own way. That's just how it is.' She shrugged. 'But not how I want it to be. I can see that I should have trusted your dad with my secret and I should have been more open. I guess at the back of my mind I thought I would tell him one day, but it was hard to find the right time, and the longer I left it, the harder it became. I wish I had found the courage sooner before it became wrapped up with everything else that is going on. Right now it feels like a tight knot with several strands. I am so saddened by his reaction; he seems to have cut me off, says he needs time, but it's also about my needs.' She twisted her mouth. 'Never settle, Cam, for anything other than what is right for you. Always put your needs high on the list; know your worth. Okay?'

'Okay.'

'I also feel strangely better because it's out in the open. Not only has it meant that my mum and I have smoothed things over, but it's as if a burden has been lifted. Secrets become heavy weights when you carry them around.'

'I'm glad too,' Camille whispered. 'I know that more than anyone you get what I'm going through, and I felt like the most stupid girl in the world to get into this mess, but you did too, and you are one of the smartest women I know.'

Lucy walked over and placed her arms around the girl's shoulders, feeling a flush of motherly love for her stepdaughter.

'I'm scared, Lucy!' Camille cried against her, gripping the back of her robe with clenched fists.

'Don't be scared, darling. You are not alone,' she whispered as she smoothed Camille's hair.

At the sound of the doorbell, Lucy released her. 'I've never had so many visitors.'

She opened the door and stared into the face of the man she loved.

'Jonah!' She touched her hand to her hair which was looped on top of her head, trying to tame it a little.

'Hey. I got home and Camille had left a note,' he said hurriedly. His chest heaved. He looked like he had been running. 'Are you both okay?'

Lucy saw the way his eyes danced across her face with concern and she felt her eyebrows meet in confusion. 'Yes, yes, we are fine.' She looked over her shoulder towards where Camille sat in the kitchen. 'She pitched up a while ago. I was just making us some tea. I think she might have been having a wobble.' Her heart raced to be talking to her husband face to face. His physical presence confirmed how much she had missed him.

'Jesus!' He placed his hands on his hips. 'I've driven like a crazy thing to get here as quickly as I could. Her note suggested there was an emergency and that she had to get over to you. I've been imagining all sorts.' He ran his palm over his chin.

She felt a surge of happiness that he was this concerned, caring for Camille in this way.

'Come in. Please.' She hated the formality of having to invite him over the threshold.

He made his way across the hallway and called to his daughter the moment she came into view. 'What on earth's going on, Cam?' He looked at her quizzically. 'I have been worried sick. Your note said you needed to get to Lucy urgently. I didn't know if one or both of you were in trouble.'

Lucy felt a flicker of joy to know he had thought he might be coming to *her* aid.

'I don't know.' Camille shrugged. 'I guess I must have made a mistake.' She stood and continued where Lucy had left off with making the tea, avoiding her stepmother's puzzled stare.

'You made a mistake?' His voice had gone up an octave in disbelief.

'Yes.' Camille nodded. 'I maybe shouldn't have said that I *needed* to get to her, just that I *wanted* to, and not urgently, but I'm very pleased to see her.' She turned from the worktop, apparently searching for milk.

Lucy stood like a spectator, trying to figure out what was going on. Jonah stared at his daughter, seemingly at a loss, before turning to face Lucy.

'How are you?' he asked, folding his arms across his chest.

'I'm . . .' She tried to think of the words that best described the sense of loss she felt at not being with him and Camille, in their house. 'I miss you.' She opted for the simplest explanation and stood looking up at him, as her tears trickled down her face.

Jonah strode forward and placed his arms around her. 'You have no idea how overjoyed I was to see you open that front door. No idea.' He held her tight. 'I have wanted to talk to you on so many nights. I even drove over and sat in your parking bay, looking up at the apartment and trying to figure out how to say sorry. I'm so embarrassed by my behaviour. I should never have let you leave that night. I meant what I said; this isn't a soap opera that requires a dramatic ending, as the music fades. I should have paid closer heed to that. I should have made you stay with me so we could talk. That's how we do it, remember? I hate being away from you. I don't want those tiny fissures developing into cracks that mean we end up losing what we have. That would be more than I could bear.'

She pulled away from him and nodded, overcome with emotion, and she saw that his tears now matched her own.

'I'm sorry, Lucy. I should never have said the things I did. I was a shit, insensitive and cruel, and I don't know where it came from,' he cried into her ear. 'I was so angry, and jealous. I regretted my words the moment I said them, but I didn't know how to take it back or make it better. I messed up with Camille and I messed up with you.'

'You didn't mess up with me, Dad,' Camille whispered.

'I did. I did.' He nodded. 'I should have tried harder to see you when you were little, should have worked harder at being your dad and not tried so hard to be your friend. I will do better, Cam. I will.'

Camille beamed.

Lucy kissed his wet cheek. 'You need to be my husband, my friend, not my judge. I need to know that when I need it, you have got my back.' She beat her fists gently on his chest. 'I need that, Jonah. I need you to let me be free to open up to you without fear of censure, without jealousy – unconditional love.'

'I know, I know.' He hung his head. 'I had you on a pedestal of perfection and I now know you are human, and the thing is' – his distress was making speech difficult – 'I still love you just as much. I do. I love you, my Lucy.'

Camille coughed. '*Now* it's perfect.'

It had been with an air of relief and quiet contemplation that they had packed her meagre belongings into the suitcase and loaded up the car. It was now late in the evening as the three sat in amiable silence in front of the fire, which crackled and snapped, sending orange flames upwards as they licked the sides of the chimney.

'Welcome home,' Jonah whispered, as Lucy lay her head on his shoulder, and he stroked her hair. Camille sat on one of the floor cushions, leaning back against the sofa with Lucy's baby book open in her hands as she flicked from page to page, looking at the diagrams and reading aloud snippets.

'I'm between sixteen and seventeen weeks pregnant, and it says my baby will be about fourteen centimetres long. And he has his own unique set of fingerprints – how amazing is that? Hear that, baby? You can't commit a crime, you'd get caught.' She rubbed her stomach, before returning her attention to the book. '"Your baby is secreting a thick, white, greasy fat called vernix, and small buds are forming in your baby's jaw that will eventually form his first or 'milk' teeth." Isn't that amazing?'

'It really is,' Lucy agreed.

'Is it as hard for you to hear this without thinking of our own pregnancies?' Jonah asked.

She nodded and nestled against her husband, grateful for his comfort as he held her tightly.

'I can't believe I am nearly halfway. I don't know if this next bit will go quickly or slowly. Can you remember what it was like for you, Lucy?'

Lucy looked from Jonah to her stepdaughter. She felt a surge of love for Camille, who was giving her the greatest gift: the chance to talk about Bella without awkwardness, without shame and yet still with a pain in her heart, as if it were only yesterday that she had signed her away. She felt overcome by the moment. 'Erm . . . I think the whole thing went very quickly. If I remember rightly,' she whispered.

'When was she born?' It was Jonah's turn to ask a question.

'Wait here,' Lucy murmured softly, as she shrugged free of his embrace before walking slowly up the stairs. She was beyond happy to see her new silk robe, her gift from China, hanging on the back of the bedroom door, and her perfume and toiletries just where she had left them on the dresser. Her bedside table, too, was just as it had been on the night she left, with a reading book, tissues and her water glass, all in place, waiting for her to come home.

Reaching up to the top of the wardrobe, Lucy pulled down the precious wicker basket. She carried it carefully down the stairs.

'Ah, the knitting basket,' Jonah noted, as Lucy placed it on the rug in front of the fire and slowly undid the leather straps, easing open the lid with its irritating squeak.

'It's actually a little bit more than that,' she informed him.

Jonah and Camille gathered around, watching in the firelight as Lucy fingered the edge of the white tissue, which was yellowing around the edges. They waited as she peeled it back layer by layer to reveal tightly packed bundles of clothes, tiny pairs of socks, bonnets, cardigans, dresses and the beautiful, newly finished blanket. Reaching in, she tentatively removed the little items and laid them in neat, lacy, beribboned piles on the floor.

'Oh, look! This is all so cute! And so pretty! There's tons of it,' Camille gasped, as she let her fingers dance upon the fruits of Lucy's labours.

'I've been knitting these things for a very long time.' She looked over at Jonah, who exhaled before wiping his eyes. It was evident that he recognised many of the items that had been intended for their babies who had left them too soon. The little promises made of love that grew wings and took flight before they had the chance to become anchored in this world. His sob was loud and heart-wrenching.

'Sorry,' he mumbled, embarrassed by this show of emotion.

'Don't be sorry, darling.' She smiled at him.

With lightness to her touch, Lucy pulled the fine layers of tissue from their home and laid them next to the clothes. Her face broke into a smile as her eyes fell upon a slightly out-of-focus photograph, taken with a Polaroid camera. It was instantly recognisable by the wide white band that sat along the bottom, upon which someone had written 'Bella May, 23 January 1994'.

'She was born on 23 January 1994 at ten past eleven in the morning.'

Lucy lifted the image slowly and felt her resolve collapse, as it always did when she saw the little face peeping back at her. There she was – her perfect, beautiful little girl with big eyes, a dainty mouth, full cheeks and a knowing expression.

Touching the image to her cheek, Lucy could instantly recall the smell of that room, the way the plastic mask had felt as they placed it over her nose and mouth, the strong scent of bleach that hung heavy in the air and, most important, the way Bella had felt in her arms. She had been light, angel-like, almost weightless, and yet she knew in that instant that the feel and memory of this baby girl would weigh her down for eternity. The idea of this child would sit like a rock in her gut, and having to wake and carry this with her, every day, would make life harder than she ever thought possible.

Sitting beneath the photograph was a small scrap of lined paper, torn from something larger. There was no need for Lucy to read the words; they were etched in her mind, imprinted, branded on her subconscious, allowing for perfect recall whenever the mood took her. The words, written in a social worker's unremarkable script, were these:

No forwarding address is to be given and we ask that they do not make contact in the weeks leading up to full adoption, unless it is absolutely critical, and only then via the relevant agency.

It still hurt now, after all these years, that those in power, the adults she had had no option other than to trust, had made certain that any avenue that might lead to her changing her mind was closed off.

She knew that if things had been different, it was quite possible that she would now be in possession of a box of photographs, snapshots of her daughter's world. A precis of Bella's history might sit in Lucy's hands, maybe even regular updates, the odd letter, and that would have been something wonderful! As it was, she had nothing of her baby girl, and neither, she suspected, did Bella have anything of her birth mother, except perhaps a host of conjured images based on nothing more than her imagination.

She handed the photograph to Jonah and watched as he squinted at the adorable little face of her daughter. 'Oh my.' He swallowed, looking at the child his wife had given birth to. 'I can't imagine how hard it must have been giving her up, Lucy. Can't imagine what it was like for you when you were so young.'

Very carefully, Lucy extracted a single tiny pink knitted sock and placed it in the palm of her hand. She inhaled its scent and felt its texture against her face. This little sock was more precious than any she had knitted. More precious than anything else she owned. It had been in contact with Bella's skin, had covered her tiny toes until Lucy had stolen it, hiding it in her palm, understanding even in the storm of emotional turmoil in which she sat that it would be a thing to hold dear, more precious than gold. She inhaled the scent again, picturing her daughter's minute, perfect foot inside its confines.

'This was Bella's.' She smiled, handing it to Jonah, who gently took it. As if it was a thing too delicate to risk touching, he cupped his palms and held it in them, cradling it and keeping it safe. His deep sigh of sadness filled the room.

'Every birthday, I wonder if she thinks about me. I picture her mum making her a cake and putting balloons by a big stack of presents.' She smiled at Camille. 'Or worse, I think she might be with a mum who doesn't bother celebrating her birthday, and that fills me with a cold sadness and a desperate longing to give her a nice day. Christmas is the same. I wonder who she spends it with, and if she is happy. Maybe she dozes the afternoon away in a comfortable chair, watching the same movie as me on TV.'

Camille sniffed and Jonah made a strangled sound. She looked up to see him crying for the second time that evening. Finally, she pulled a thick white envelope from the basket. Taking the sock from his palms and returning it to the tissue nest, she handed the envelope to him.

'Every year, on her birthday, I draw a kiss – one single large kiss – and then I put the date in the corner and pop it in this envelope. I say out loud, "Happy birthday, Bella. Happy birthday, darling." And then I pop it in here. I sometimes think that one day, I might be able to give her all these birthday kisses that I have saved up for her. Wouldn't that be a wonderful thing?'

'How . . . how many are there?' he managed, running his finger through the little white cluster of paper squares.

'Twenty-four.' She bit her lip and smiled. 'There are twenty-four of them.'

'I'm so sorry, Lucy. Sorry I reacted how I did. I understand now how hard it was for you to keep that secret and how brave you were to break it. You are so brave.'

'I won't ever recover from the fact that I gave my baby away, never. I spoke to Mum about it only recently, after I had told you, and I can see that she thought it was for the best. She believed that anything else would have thrown up so many challenges that I was ill-equipped to handle. I get it much more now, how it would have affected my life.' She cast a glance at Camille, hoping not to frighten her. 'But I long for my baby. I ache for her.' She ran her fingers over the piles of knitted clothes.

'I feel . . . I feel very lucky to have you and Dad to support me right now.' Camille cried and hugged her knees to her chest.

Jonah dropped to the floor and held his child. 'And you have got us, Cam. Always. You are not alone.' He kissed her scalp.

'You are never alone once you become a mum,' Lucy said softly, 'and even though I didn't get to raise Bella, I have kept her with me every day, carried her here.' She touched her shaking fingers to her chest. 'I think of her all the time. I see her little fingers gripped around mine as she slept, as if I could keep her safe, but I knew I couldn't. I knew my time with her was nearly up and it took all of my strength not to pick her up, run out of the door and keep running. But I was sixteen, a child in so many ways. Still at school, and in those days my mum's word was the law. I believed she knew best, and I now think that is probably true. How would I have managed? What would I have done? I have to believe that, otherwise it makes everything pointless and that is too hard for me to even consider. But things will be different for you, Cam. You are going to be a great mum and we are going to be here to help you.'

Jonah stood up and blew his nose. 'I think this evening is a cause for celebration.' He dried his eyes and walked to the kitchen to fetch a bottle of champagne. 'Only juice for you, Cam, but don't worry – Lucy and I can celebrate enough for the three of us.'

Camille picked up one of the bundles of knitted baby clothes and handed it to Lucy to put back in the hamper. 'No!' Lucy shook her head and placed her hand over the basket.

'Oh!' Camille looked a little taken aback. 'I'm sorry I touched them; I thought—'

'No, darling, that's not what I mean. I have spent hours and hours making these clothes, poring over every stitch, and there is no point in keeping them wrapped in tissue and shut away, not any more. I don't want them to languish in this box, gathering dust. I want you to take them for your son. I want you to let him wear them and make sure he knows that they were made by me, with love.'

Camille held the beautiful, delicate matinee coats against her chest. 'Oh! *Ils sont si beaux!* Thank you, my stepmum. Thank you.'

◆ ◆ ◆

Lucy woke to a burst of winter sunshine dappling the bedroom ceiling through the trees.

'Good morning, Mrs Carpenter.' Jonah was propped on his elbow, watching her.

'How long have you been awake?' she asked, sleepily.

'About eight hours.'

'Oh, shut up!' She batted at him. 'I love waking up with you. I'd forgotten just how much.'

'Ditto. I've missed you, Lucy. I never want to feel like that again.' He ran his thumb over the inside of her arm.

'Me either,' she agreed. Lucy sat up in the bed and gasped, as if a sudden thought had occurred.

'What's the matter?' he asked.

'I've just realised that I'm going to be waking up with a grandpa very soon!' She pulled a face at him.

'And me with a granny! Who'd have thought?' He laughed.

'I am not going to be just any old granny. I'm going to be the best granny on the planet,' she stated, muffling her sadness at the fact that she might well be skipping motherhood. She *was* going to be a granny, something that in recent times had felt beyond her reach.

'I think you might be right.' He smiled.

'In fact, I am going to start today.' She jumped out of bed and grabbed her silk robe from the back of the door, fastening it around her waist.

'Oh God, what have you got planned?' He grimaced.

'We are going to empty out that bloody study of yours and make a nursery for our grandson.' When she turned back to the bed, Jonah had thrown the duvet over his head, as if he could hide from her suggestion.

'And don't think you can escape by hiding in bed – you know me better than that!' she called from the doorway.

'I do.' He peeked out from beneath the covers. 'I do know you better than that.'

She smiled at him over her shoulder, feeling a wonderful surge of optimism about their future.

I thought long and hard about what my mum said, about there being agencies that you might have contacted, wanting to get in touch, and even the thought of this fills me with such a burst of happiness it is quite hard to describe. It feels like the night before Christmas when everything you have wished for might come true. Equally, I have considered the thought that you might not have registered with them and I would understand this too. As hard as it would be for me, I would accept it.

Oh, Bella. I know nothing about you, and the chance to know something, anything at all, would be more than I have any right to hope for, and yet it would fill the rest of my days with happiness! Any snippet, no matter how small, would for me be a big thing. Are you still called Bella or did your parents give you a new name? Did your eyes stay blue? Do you still have a button nose? Have you been happy? What's your favourite colour? What was your favourite subject at school? Do you play an instrument? Do you have an accent? Do you have brothers and sisters? What's your favourite food? The list of questions I have for you is long and always growing. My thirst to know all about your life could never be sated. I don't want to interrupt your life or cause you any pain or a single moment of worry. I wish for you nothing but happiness and good, good things. I wonder if you even know about me? I shall stop writing now and get these ramblings of mine sealed and sent off. And then the waiting game will begin. Strangely, writing down these thoughts, ideas and my innermost feelings has helped me feel close to you. Even though we are in one sense strangers, I am still your mum. I am your mum! And that one fact fills me with more pride than you could ever know.

With love,
Lucy
X

TWENTY-ONE

With Camille's latest scan picture framed and resting on the chest of drawers, Lucy covered the whole thing with a greying dust sheet before dipping the roller into the pale blue paint and climbing the stepladder to better reach the ceiling.

'This is looking great!' Camille clapped her hands. 'I love it!'

'Wait until I add the clouds; it's going to look awesome.' She smiled, enjoying being part of the transformation of the room from a dusty office to the baby's very own space, trying to keep at bay the thought that this room and this design had always been destined for her baby. The plan was for Camille and the baby to stay with them until she had a clearer view of what came next. She and Jonah had decided that while it was tempting to scoop Camille and her baby up and keep them close, it wouldn't be the best thing to help Camille grow into the woman she needed to become. They would instead parent Cam from a safe distance, ready to catch her if ever she fell.

'What do you think of Nelson as a name?' Camille asked, as she dipped the narrow brush into the white gloss and continued to tackle the woodwork.

Lucy spat her laughter.

'Okay, we'll take that as a no. What about Hudson?' Camille suggested.

'As in the river?' Lucy asked.

'Oh yes, good point.' Camille was quiet for a second or two. 'How about Chester?'

'Are you determined to name this child after a monument or a river or a place? Why can't you go for an ordinary but gorgeous name?' she suggested.

'Like what?' Camille stared at her.

'I don't know, Cam. How about Jonah?'

'Oh God, no!' The girl pulled a face of disapproval.

'How about Jonah what?' Her husband poked his head in from the landing. And this time they both laughed.

'We're just thinking of names, darling.' Lucy smiled sweetly at him.

'Oh, I rather like Hector,' he suggested.

'Hector?' they both shrieked.

'Yes! That was my grandfather's name and he was a fine man.' Jonah defended his choice.

'Think I prefer Nelson,' Lucy whispered.

'What was that?' Jonah cupped his hand over his ear.

'Nothing, darling!' She and Camille laughed once again.

'Well, I can see I am being ganged up on. I shall leave you two to it.' He smiled at his wife with a look of sheer delight and left the room.

'I think because he now understands how crappy things were for you when you were pregnant, that's why he's being so great with me. I know he loves me and I don't think he wants me to go through anything similar.' Camille spoke to the wall as she painted.

'He does love you, very much,' she confirmed. 'Have you thought any more about telling Dex?' She broached the subject, which was still a little thorny.

Camille sighed. 'I think about it all the time. I don't know what to do. I want him to know because I think he has a right to, but I don't want to ruin his time in New York, this one chance he's got to do something that he has always wanted to do. In fact, I've stopped texting and emailing him. It felt too odd – asking about the weather and what he's had for lunch when I am sitting here like this.' She pointed at her stomach. 'I think it's probably easier if I just let him drift away. And then tell him in the future, maybe, when things are calmer.'

'But what about what Dex wants? What about if he wants you and you are not giving him that chance? Have you thought about that?' she urged.

Camille gave a small, resigned smile that was heartbreaking to see. 'Plus . . .'

'Plus what?' Lucy stopped painting and looked at her stepdaughter.

'Plus, I don't want him to be with me because he feels he should be, out of duty or because he feels guilty. I want him to be with me because he loves me, and once he knows about the baby I won't be able to tell which it is. And there is always the chance that he will just ignore me and tell me to get on with it. What did Bella's dad do when you told him?'

Lucy pictured Scott and briefly closed her eyes. 'I . . . I never told him.'

Camille whipped around. 'What, never? Are you saying he doesn't know?'

'No.' She shook her head. 'He doesn't know.'

'Wow! I hadn't thought about not telling Dex at all – I was trying to work out how and when – but if you think that's best—'

'No, Camille. No, I don't think that it's best at all.' She shook her head and climbed down the stepladder to sit close to the girl. 'I can tell you hand on heart that it was a mistake. He did have a right to know; I should have told him. Not because I wanted anything from him, not even a relationship. We were just kids who found comfort in each other – whatever we shared had truly run its course. But I can see now that not telling him was disingenuous.' She bit her lip as she acknowledged this truth.

'I'll think about it,' Camille promised, as she resumed her painting.

◆ ◆ ◆

A fortnight later the grand celebration for the new nursery and combined baby shower was in full swing. Music filled the house as the playlist shuffled between her favourite eighties pop and Jonah's preferred soft rock.

'This poor baby is going to have no taste in music,' Camille moaned, as she cradled her bump.

'Don't worry about that, darling,' Jan reassured her. 'My husband played nothing but Carly Simon during both my pregnancies and neither of my girls has ever favoured the music.'

'Who's he?' Fay wrinkled her nose.

'See what I mean?' Jan tutted and rolled her eyes.

Lucy could see and feel the seismic shift between her and her mum. Gone were the staccato conversations, the nervous suggestions, the feeling that they were walking on eggshells and the self-conscious awkward embraces that had plagued every arrival and departure for as long as she could remember. Jan now looked at her in the way she did Fay, with ease. It was a blessed relief.

The family were crowded into the kitchen. As the sandwiches were passed around, a fancy cake from Pru Plum's was topped with a sugar-paste baby lying on a blue-and-white blanket. It was beautiful and simple. The tea flowed from the pot and everyone fussed over Camille and her burgeoning bump. Lucy smiled to negate the flame of jealousy that threatened to ignite. How she would have loved this day for herself.

Her stepdaughter delighted in every gift, laying tiny denim dungarees over her rounded stomach and confessing that she was struggling to imagine a little person bringing them to life in a little over three months. Fay had, as ever, put a lot of thought into her gift and presented Camille with a white basket filled with creams, potions and lotions to help moisturise skin, cure cracked nipples and provide bubbles to soak in when weary muscles might need a spot of rejuvenation. The whole thing was wrapped in cellophane and finished off with an enormous blue bow.

'Thank you, Fay!' Camille grinned.

'You're welcome, and it's the least I can do for my niece and Rory's favourite cousin.'

She saw Camille beam; being part of this family was good for her.

Geneviève and Jean-Luc had sent a card, which sat in pride of place on the mantelpiece, and a packet of muslin squares.

'They're an essential!' Fay nodded at the gift.

Camille had started a dialogue with her mum, and with Lucy's encouragement had even managed a FaceTime chat. She noticed an easing of her stepdaughter's stress after this interaction and understood this only too well.

She gave Jonah the nod and he made his way to the shed, coming back into the kitchen with a pushchair and baby seat travel system in a gorgeous lime-green design on a pale grey background with chunky tractor-like wheels. Camille would never know how Lucy had stood in the shed in the dark of night with her hands gripping the handles, sobbing, as she stared at the empty pram, feeling a pulse of longing at what was not to be.

'Oh God!' Camille placed her hand over her mouth. 'It's so cool!' she cried. 'It's brilliant. Thank you!' She looked at Lucy and Jonah. 'I don't know what I'd do without you both.'

'Well, luckily you'll never have to find out.' Lucy smiled, guessing by the way Camille rubbed her tum and blotted her tears that her thoughts were with Dex. She silently resolved to try once again to encourage her to make contact with him and tell him what was going on.

Later, the party headed up the stairs to admire the nursery, which looked spacious now all the clutter had been removed and the cot stood in one corner with the changing station opposite. The ceiling was peppered with clouds. It was beautiful and peaceful. Folded neatly in the top drawer of the chest of drawers were Lucy's hand-knitted baby clothes. Handing over her crop of baby clothes had felt to Lucy like an admission that she was never going to need them, and just the thought of this brought tears to her eyes and a sting of loss to her heart.

But the jolt of joy she felt to think that a baby would finally grace them – even if it wasn't to be her own – almost outweighed the feeling of despair.

Fay and Adam stood on the landing, peering in at Lucy and Camille's handiwork.

'I love what you have done in here!' Jan clucked approvingly.

Camille beamed. 'We wanted something that was a bit quirky and cool, something neutral, but not cold – like a linen or a light khaki.'

'Did Fay tell you to say that?' Lucy screeched.

'Yes!' Camille laughed. 'I have no idea what it means.'

'It means my little sister likes to have the last word and thinks she's so cool!' Lucy thumped her on the arm, playfully.

'You were lucky, Cam. When she knew you were coming, Lucy toyed with the idea of giving you a pink feature wall! You should be thanking me. I saved you from that horror.' She poked out her tongue in disgust.

'I love my bedroom. I love every bit of it. I couldn't believe that she had done that all for me!'

Lucy beamed. This was good to know.

They all made their way down the stairs, apart from Jan, who hovered next to Lucy as she ran her hand over the cot where her hand-knitted blanket lay on top of the little mattress.

'I have always been proud of what you have achieved, darling – your amazing jobs, your beautiful apartment. It all came to you because you are smart and work so hard, but the truth is' – Jan composed herself – 'all I ever really wanted was for you to find the courage to be truly happy.'

'I am happy, Mum.' She spoke with a thick throat. 'I think I'm learning that maybe you don't get everything in life, but you can be happy with the gifts you have.'

'I think that's true, but doing all this for Camille' – she waved her arm in an arc around the room – 'it can't be easy for you.'

'It's not, but it still feels good to do the right thing for her, to support her. After all, she's having my grandchild.' She smiled.

'I am so proud of the woman you became.' Jan spoke with misted eyes. Lucy stepped forward and fell against her mum for a hug. She closed her eyes and wrapped her arms around her mum, holding on and savouring the contact that she had craved.

'Also . . .' Lucy began.

'What, darling?' Jan released her daughter and gripped the side of the cot, as if bracing herself for bad news.

'I thought about what you said and I have written to an agency to see if Bella has registered an interest to get in contact. I wrote her a long letter, poured my heart out really, and I don't know if she will ever get it, but I am glad I've done it.'

'Oh, Lucy!' Jan reached up and took her baby girl back into her arms. 'I shall keep everything, everything crossed!' she cried, as she crushed her to her.

◆ ◆ ◆

Christmas had come and gone and had been a relatively quiet affair. She and Jonah had agreed that they would have been perfectly happy to skip the season this year and jump straight into the new year when the baby's arrival would be getting closer. The whole family had congregated for a stunning festive lunch at Fay's house, where Lucy was barred from the kitchen, all had worn flimsy paper hats and sung carols, and Camille had played endless board games with Rory.

In Lucy's view, the best evenings of the holiday period had seen the three of them sat in front of the fire at home, making plans for the new arrival. It was only in the early hours, when drowsy from sleep her hand snaked to her stomach in dreamlike confusion, thinking it was her baby they had been planning for, that her sadness struck.

It was one wintry day in that twilight time between Christmas and new year that she and Jonah bustled in from the cold. The coffee and cake they had eaten at Gail's had fuelled them all the way home. Camille was in her room, napping no doubt. Lucy stooped to gather the post from the floor where it had been pushed against the wall, while her husband went ahead and flicked on the lamps. She leafed casually through the uninspiring envelopes, until the last envelope in the stack caught her eye. She placed the bundle on the sideboard, but kept this envelope in her hands.

'Jonah,' she called softly, as she made her way into the sitting room. He was crouched on the floor, setting the fire with kindling and piling up the logs to ensure a cosy temperature. 'Jonah,' she repeated, as her finger slid along the gummed edge and flipped it open.

Lucy gasped and sank down on to the rug, collapsing in a heap, as her tears made reading impossible. 'Oh my God! Oh my God! Help me! Jonah, help me!' she cried, handing him the page she had extracted with trembling fingers.

Jonah stood and took the sheet from her. He smoothed it in his palm and read aloud. His words danced in the air and settled on her like sparkling fairy dust.

◆ ◆ ◆

Dear Lucy,
Hope it's okay to call you Lucy. 'Mrs Carpenter'
sounds too formal and 'Mum' a little weird.

Jonah paused to control the catch in his voice and sob in his throat. For Lucy it was as if time stood still. She held her breath, scared to move in case she woke up and found that this glorious moment was merely a dream.

Jonah coughed and continued:

> *It was an extraordinary thing to receive your letter –
> wonderful and alarming at the same time. In answer to
> one of your questions, my name is Bella. My parents kept
> my name and I have always liked it.*
>
> *My mum and dad, Ivy and Graham, have told me
> as much about you as they could remember and any other
> bits of information that they picked up. Like the fact that
> you had long dark hair and you had one sister. My mum
> told me that your mum, my nan, I guess, seemed lovely.
> These details have remained vivid in my memory, and
> so I guess, with these snippets in mind, I was not wholly
> surprised to receive your letter. I think it's important to
> tell you that I had a wonderful childhood and I have a
> good life. I am happy. My mum also said that she always
> had the feeling that giving me up for adoption was not
> an easy decision for you and that she thought you would
> always carry me with you. Throughout my life, this idea
> has given me a really nice feeling . . .*

Lucy's sobbing was loud and invasive. Jonah stopped reading and dropped to his knees to hold her. 'Don't cry, darling. Please don't cry. This is such a wonderful thing, a letter from Bella!' He smiled as he kissed her.

Lucy shook her head and braced her arms against his for support, it was some while before she could speak. 'No, Jonah, you don't' – she gulped – 'you don't understand.' Her face crumpled again until she managed to compose herself a little and continue. 'The baby I mourn, the newborn I picture, she's gone. This is a letter from a grown woman and it's made me see that I have lost her. I lost her, Jonah! My baby, my little girl – she doesn't exist any more, does she?' She slumped forward into her husband's arms.

'No, my Lucy, she doesn't exist. She is all grown-up, but she has grown up happy!' He pulled his arm free and again unfurled the sheet of paper. '"I had a wonderful childhood and I have a good life. I am happy",' he read aloud. 'That's what it says, right here, and that is the most you can ever ask for where your children are concerned.'

She looked up at him, her tears slowed and her heart stopped racing. 'She is happy,' she repeated.

'Yes!' he pressed. 'She is happy and she has a lovely life and that means you made the right decision. You did the right thing. You gave her security. You gave her happiness.'

'I did. I gave her happiness. My beautiful Bella.'

Lucy sat back on the rug and stared at her husband, wiping away her tears with the back of her hand. 'You are right. All these years I have spent worrying that she might be cold or hungry or scared. I have pictured every horrible scenario you can imagine, and the feeling that I couldn't get to her, couldn't make it better, has haunted me. But she was happy.'

'Yes! She was happy, "a wonderful childhood",' he read again.

Lucy felt the beginnings of a smile twitch on her lips. She looked up at the window as a shard of winter sunlight pierced through the trees and fell in front of her, bringing light into a dark place.

'There's more, darling.' He read on, and Lucy sat with fists clenched, listening to every word. The second half of Bella's letter, however, cut Lucy to the core, dashing her hopes and sending her spiralling into a dark place of self-recrimination and regret. She learned that Bella was a statistician who worked for a bank and was engaged to a quiet man, Tom. But it wasn't these facts that bothered her. Those were not the words to be analysed and pored over in the dead of night. It was another seven or so lines that caused her heart to sink into her boots.

I do not think there would be any value in us meeting or indeed exchanging further correspondence. I am of course grateful for the life you gave me and for the brave decision you made to give me up for adoption. I have a wonderful family and I fear any further involvement with you might unsettle the people I love the most and might unsettle me too. Thank you, Lucy, for getting in touch. I shall treasure your letter and like to think that you might do the same with mine.

With very best wishes,
Bella

Lucy read the words again and again, until she knew them by heart, and the more she recited them, analysed them and considered them, the more something unexpected happened. The words blunted and became easier to digest, until Lucy finally reached a point of acceptance. Bella had a good life. A good life! And if that wasn't the goal for her daughter, then she wasn't sure what was. It was as if with this realisation the cloak of guilt, worry and shame that had weighed her down for all these years was lifted. It felt good.

◆　◆　◆

The next three months passed by in a blur of excitement and anticipation of the baby's arrival. By the time the end of March and Camille's due date drew near, every blanket they could possibly need was folded and ready, and nutritious breastfeeding snacks filled the cupboards and freezer, leaving Lucy free to focus on keeping Camille's stress levels to a minimum.

In the early hours one morning, Lucy was sleeping soundly with Jonah's arm cast over her shoulder when she became aware of a light rapping on the door.

'Hello?' She sat up, reaching for the bedside lamp and rubbing her eyes.

Camille crept into the room and held on to the end of their bed. 'Lucy?'

'Yes, darling? Are you okay?' Her adrenaline began to pump and she reached a state of full alertness very quickly.

Camille shook her head. 'I need you to call Dex.' After speaking his name, she whimpered, and her tears fell. 'I need you to tell Dex that I need him and that I love him and that I am having our baby. Can you do that for me?'

'Oh, sweetie, don't cry! Please don't cry. Yes, I can do that for you if you really want me to, but I think it would be better coming from you, and you don't need to worry about it right now. Your sleep is too important,' she soothed.

'Lucy is right, Cam. You and Dex should have that conversation,' Jonah added from the pillow where he now lay awake. 'But she can sit right by your side if that helps?'

'No.' Camille shook her head again and bent forward a little. 'I can't call him. It's too late because I am having our baby now. Right now.' She leant heavily on the bed.

'Oh shit!' Jonah jumped out of bed and gathered his jeans from the floor. Lucy swung her legs in an arc from the mattress, leapt out of bed and placed her arms on Camille's shoulders. She remembered the ice-cold knot of fear that had gripped her when in the first throes of labour; she had only been able to think of what lay ahead and the horror stories she had heard.

'Sit down, Cam.' The girl did as she was told. 'Now, you are going to keep calm and everyone is going to look after you and this is going to be fine, okay?'

'Okay.' Camille nodded at her, her face pale with fear.

'Your bag is already packed, so we just need a minute to get dressed and grab the car keys. Okay?' she asked again, trying to keep her own nerves at bay.

Camille nodded.

'Are you having contractions?' Lucy asked, as Jonah rushed to the bathroom with his shoes in one hand.

'Yes. And they're getting stronger.' She closed her eyes.

'Good, that's great!' She smiled to mask her own turbulent flurry of pain, envy and regret. 'We will stay with you, Cam, and you have nothing to think about or worry about other than keeping calm and delivering this baby.' She kissed her forehead, which was a little clammy.

'Please, Lucy, please' – she winced a little as a sharper pain bit – 'please tell Dex!'

'I will. I promise.' She felt her stomach drop at the prospect, as they made their way to the car in the dark of night.

◆ ◆ ◆

As Jonah held Camille's hand and the nurse pushed her wheelchair from the lift up to the delivery suite, Lucy hovered in the reception and used Camille's phone to call Dex.

'Cam! I was wondering if you would call me. It's been a while. Thought you were ignoring me.' He sounded excited to hear from Camille after her imposed radio silence, and Lucy considered this a good sign. It had been a delicate battle, trying to encourage Camille to confide in the boy, while being wary of imposing anything on her. Lucy knew above all else how important it was that her stepdaughter felt like she was in control during this tumultuous time.

'Dex, it's Lucy here, actually, Cam's stepmum?'

'Oh, hi, Lucy. How are you? Is everything okay?' He was smart enough to know that if his on-off girlfriend's stepmother was calling him from the other side of the world at ten o'clock at night, his time, the chances were that something was not okay, and in this assumption, he was correct. 'You'll have to speak up. I'm in a busy street and there's cars and people – it's a bit crazy!' he informed her.

Lucy pictured him on a New York street, living a life that she was about to alter. She held the receiver to her mouth and spoke slowly and clearly, knowing that for Dex things were about to get a whole lot crazier.

'This is going to come as a bit of a surprise, but the thing is, Dex . . .' she began.

◆ ◆ ◆

Standing alone in the lift that took her up to the delivery floor was a strange experience. Each time she had entered this hospital in various stages of pregnancy, this had always been the goal: to enter this lift, with her ID sticker firmly in place and the beat of an intensifying labour in her groin. And yet here she was, alone, coming to assist as another woman gave birth. She closed her eyes and concentrated on the task in hand: being there for Camille at this time.

Wandering out of the lift was like stepping from a time machine. It could have been a winter's night in 1994. There were smiling nurses and busy midwives, nervous, pacing dads, some beaming into phones as they shouted the facts they considered to be of the most interest down the line: 'A girl! Six pounds seven ounces . . . she's beautiful! Yes, yes, doing well, both of them . . .' To listen in, albeit accidentally, felt like an intrusion on their precious moment.

Lucy pictured the person at the other end of that line, gasping and crying and giving thanks for this new little life that had come into their family, before going off to tell another in a similar call, in a glorious game of Chinese whispers.

The sound of newborns mewling in side rooms was sweet and evocative; she felt her heart beat in her throat.

'Don't cry, my baby . . . It'll all be okay . . . I've got you . . . These are our moments together, this is our time, and I promise you that I won't forget a single second of it.' And true to her word, she hadn't.

'There you are!' Jonah called to her as he strolled up the ward. 'How did it go?' He rubbed his palms together, as he did when he was a little anxious.

'I got hold of him okay. He was very quiet and it was a little hard to hear. There was a lot of background noise. But he did say to give her his love.'

'Was that it?' He screwed his face up.

'Yes. That was it. What did you expect?' She was curious.

Jonah shrugged. 'I don't know, something more, I guess, but I don't know what.'

'I think it's right that he knows, but it's important we remember that he is just a boy himself really, only eighteen and on the other side of the pond on his big life adventure. He is probably in shock. But we shouldn't judge him, Jonah. Only the future will reveal his character.'

He nodded. 'I guess so. Anyway, right now it's all about Cam and she is asking for you.'

'For me?' she questioned, quite overwhelmed by the prospect of being there at the birth of her grandson, but also at the beautiful connection she now felt with Camille.

Jonah nodded.

'Okay, then.' She smiled at him. 'Let's do this!'

He gripped her shoulders. 'Are you sure about this? Because if it's too much—'

'I'm sure, Jonah,' she interrupted him. 'I can do it.'

He kissed her lightly on the mouth before she turned and walked towards Camille's room.

'See you on the other side!' She turned towards him and gave him a smile of reassurance that hid the quaking in her limbs.

◆ ◆ ◆

'Lucy!' Camille called out with obvious relief as she walked into the room.

'Here I am.' She took a seat next to the bed and smiled, trying to look calm and confident, when inside she felt anything but.

She remembered a kindly nurse looking in on her. *Are you nervous, sweetie?* she had asked.

'Did you speak to Dex?' Camille's tone was urgent. She lay back on the pillows in the loosely tied hospital gown, rubbing her stomach and breathing deeply, trying to counter the waves of discomfort that Lucy knew she would be feeling. Her womb pulsed in sympathy at the memory.

'I did.'

'What did he say?' Camille lifted her head, and her heart rate monitor suddenly pushed out mountains on to the screen.

'He said to give you all of his love.'

'Did he say anything else? Was he angry or happy? What did you think?' she asked desperately.

Lucy took her hand. 'He sounded shocked and surprised, as you would expect, but definitely not angry.'

'Okay.' Camille lay back against the pillows. 'Good. That's good. My contractions are getting stronger' – she held her breath – 'and it hurts, Lucy!' A lone tear trickled from her eye and over her face, on to the pillow.

'It hurts!'

Lucy remembered how she had screamed out and the nurse had leant over her and lied – with the best of intentions, she liked to think: *'This is as bad as it gets, love, and it'll be over before you know it. Take deep breaths, that's a good girl . . .'*

Lucy gripped her hand and spoke the words she knew would have made a difference to her. 'This is the time to be strong, Camille; you need to be strong for this baby. You need to be the best mum you can possibly be, and it starts now. And I give you my word that you will not be facing this alone. Not now and not in the future. You are loved and we are going to be right by your side. Come what may.'

'Thank you.' Camille grimaced through her tears and leant forward with her chin on her chest and her knees raised, as another contraction built. 'Thank you, Lucy.'

Lucy patted the back of her hand, overcome by the impact a few heartfelt maternal words could have. 'Now, take a deep breath, Cam, that's it. Keep breathing!'

◆ ◆ ◆

Lucy was exhausted. She cleaned her teeth, and with eyes half-closed she climbed between the sheets that she had leapt out of twenty-four hours before.

Jonah was already horizontal. 'I called Geneviève,' he told her. 'Spoke to Jean-Luc, who sounded relieved more than anything that all was well. And they said they would come over when Camille comes home and is settled.'

'That's good. I'll sort out the futon for the nursery. They can sleep in there.'

'You want them to stay here?' He sounded surprised.

'It'll be fine.' Lucy snaked her hand across the mattress and patted her husband. 'I didn't like leaving Cam in the hospital on her own.'

'Me either, but she's not on her own; she's with her boy. Plus she's tired, even though she's on cloud nine. She'll sleep,' he reminded her.

Lucy knew he was smiling; she could tell by his voice.

She sighed. 'What a day. How beautiful is that baby?'

'I can't believe it. It doesn't seem possible that my little girl is a mummy!' He twisted his arm until his fingers found hers and they knitted hands, fingers entwined, palm against palm.

She swallowed a gulp of sadness at the fact that her dad never got to say these words.

'Did you see how competent she was, holding him confidently, feeding him, and so composed, a natural.' She spoke in awe, ignoring the tears that slipped over her temples and on to the pillow. It hurt so badly that, for the second time in her life, she had left the delivery suite without a child of her own.

'Yes, she really is.' Jonah squeezed her hand. 'And how are you doing, my brilliant girl? I don't know what Cam would have done without you there today.'

She beamed at his compliment, knowing that in it lay a kernel of truth. She had been there for Camille in her time of need, like any good mum. 'I'm tired, but happy. This is Cam's time, Cam's baby.' She opened her eyes and looked at the wicker basket on top of the wardrobe.

'I love you.' He squeezed her hand.

'I love you too.'

'I wonder what he'll be when he grows up . . .' Jonah murmured before sleep pulled him under. 'He's got big hands – maybe a boxer?'

'Happy. That's what I want him to be: happy.' She too yawned, as she drifted off to sleep at the end of an extraordinary day, listening as her husband broke into a gentle snore.

She and Jonah arrived back at the hospital bright and early to find Camille sitting up in bed, looking serene, happy, and holding her son in her arms. He was wearing a little bobble hat that Lucy had knitted and he looked really cute.

'Oh, now the fun starts,' Camille whispered to him. 'Here come your grandparents.'

It was something Lucy hadn't properly considered – how the arrival of this little man would bind them together. It had been hinted at, but this new level of unity overwhelmed her. She felt the punch of love in her gut when she looked at the little man, newly arrived on the planet. It was as overpowering as it was unexpected.

She and Jonah had decided around Christmastime to stop trying to conceive, both agreeing that they should focus on each other and the amazing life they had rather than become consumed by a different kind of life they did not. Lucy knew there would always be that visceral punch of sadness at what she had lost, but their decision meant she was able to look forward with clarity and optimism, rather than waiting each month on tenterhooks, preparing for the next bout of heartache or disappointment. Just making this decision gave them strength, the feeling that they were back in control. In a strange way, it was as if a pressure had been lifted from her shoulders.

She and Jonah hadn't managed to become parents but, for this little guy, they would always be granny and grandpa together. It felt lovely, a small reward in a sea of regret.

Jonah chuckled and, after kissing his daughter, peered into the wrapped bundle that lay in her arms. 'Here, you hold him, Dad.' Camille lifted the baby gently as Jonah dipped down and took him from her, holding him awkwardly, as if he were slippery china.

'I think I'd better sit down,' he murmured.

Lucy guided him backwards into the armchair by the side of the bed. He stared at her, his eyes brimming, and she knew that he, like her, was imagining what it might be like to hold one of their babies who had left them too soon.

'How did you sleep, Cam?' she asked, trying to keep the atmosphere bright.

Camille bit her lip and stared at her son, as if still shocked that he belonged to her. 'Not great. He was awake a lot of the night, but I remembered what you said and I am going to be the best mum that I can possibly be. Anyway, it wasn't exactly a hardship, getting to chat to him in the middle of the night. It was really nice.'

I bet, you lucky thing . . .

'Well, I was awake in the middle of the night worrying about you – were you sleeping, were you comfortable? I should have come over . . .' Lucy suddenly trailed off, looking at her stepdaughter, and a smile spread over her face. She laughed, a warm glow of joy thawing her icy sadness and filling her up. It was a simple notion, but one that had nonetheless not occurred to her until now: she didn't need to have given birth to a child to experience motherhood.

'I got on the phone at the crack of dawn this morning,' Lucy began again, laughing. 'I've spoken to Mum and Fay, and last night your dad spoke to Jean-Luc. Everyone is over the moon and sends you all their love, and they all want to book in for cuddles. I don't think you are going to be short of a babysitter or two.' She smiled.

Despite trying to battle her fatigue, Camille slipped into a doze, while she and Jonah took turns to hold their grandson. Lucy inhaled the scent of him, kissing his crown and running her finger over the side of his cheek. Her tears fell freely, as her nipples tightened with the desire to feed him and her whole being ached with longing. But he was not hers. She would be content to have any part to play in his life no matter how small. She would treat it as the privilege that it was.

The baby started to get a little restless, batting the air with his tiny, scrunched-up fist and wriggling slightly, seeking food with his dainty mouth, and Camille sat up straight, as if programmed to stir at the sound of his cry.

'Oh my, is it that time again already?' She placed her hand over her nose and mouth as her tears fell.

Lucy stared at Camille, wondering if this was a case of baby blues. 'Hey, hey, it's okay, darling, he just needs a little feed. That's all. You are probably feeling a little overwhelmed, but everything is okay,' she cooed, as she handed the little boy to Camille, knowing that when emotions ran high and milk was coming in, these mini-meltdowns were to be expected.

Camille shook her head. Her sobs made speech impossible. 'I just miss Dex. I think it's a shame he's not here to see this.'

'I know, darling,' she soothed, watching as Camille pulled her head back every few seconds to stare at the face of her baby son.

'I don't know if I can do this on my own,' Camille stuttered. 'I . . . I love my baby so much. I want everything to be perfect for him and I feel as if I have already let him down.'

'Are you kidding me?' Lucy boomed. 'You only need one person in life who has got your back, and this little fella has at least half a dozen. He is one lucky boy.'

Lucy watched as Camille kissed her son gently while giving him the nourishment he sought.

Jonah stood from his chair. 'Well, the only reason I feel sorry for the little fella is because he hasn't got a name yet.'

Camille laughed through her tears. 'Do you still want to call him Hector, after your grandfather?' She rolled her eyes.

'Yes. Hector is a Trojan champion and that takes strength and guts. I like the name.' He again nodded his approval.

◆ ◆ ◆

Lucy and Jonah smiled at each other as they waited for the lift.

'She's doing fine. It's only natural that she should be a little tearful. Her body has been through a lot and her hormones are going haywire,' Lucy pointed out.

'Yes. I'm glad she seems to be warming to the name Hector.' Jonah rocked on his heels.

'Hector Carpenter-Babineaux sounds like a right mouthful, that is, if he takes Cam's surname. If they add Dex's in too he'd be Hector Carpenter-Babineaux-Williams. It's a bit much – poor child would need two lines on the school register.'

'What poppycock! It sounds great.' He laughed.

Lucy slipped her arm through his and rested her head on his shoulder.

They drove home from the hospital in an amiable bubble of silence, and Lucy made plans to spring-clean Camille's room, buy fresh flowers to put in her window and move the cot to the side of her bed where they could have time and space to get settled as a family.

Jonah put the key in the door and stepped back, ushering her inside on this cold, bright March day. 'Come on, Grandma. A nice cup of tea awaits.' He patted her bottom as she walked past him into the hallway.

Jonah lit the fire and the two of them sat on the floor listening to the logs crackle and basking in the orangey glow of the flames. It was a while before Lucy broke the silence that bound them.

'I need to think about my girl's future. We need to help her in any way we can.' She sidled closer to her man.

There was a second of silence before Jonah offered his response.

'You can of course write back, if you want to, see if Bella might reply, but I don't want you to be disappointed, darling. She sounded quite resolute in her letter, and—'

'Sorry, no, Jonah,' she interrupted him. 'You misunderstood me.' She looked up at her man, lit by the glow of the blaze. 'I was talking about Camille.'

TWENTY-TWO

Two years later

It was a warm, sunny afternoon in Queen's Park as Lucy walked slowly to the end of the garden to retrieve Hector's ball. Her long ponytail hung down over the shoulder of her smocked white shirt as she crouched down into the shrubs and dug around with her hands to find the ball.

'I mean it, Hector. This is absolutely the last time I am fetching this for you!' Her threat was a little diluted by the big smile that accompanied it.

Hector clapped and ran in a circle, holding in one hand the little brown woollen rabbit Lucy had knitted him, while he chased after his cousin Maisie. He knew full well that he only had to shout 'Bibbit, get it!' and off Lucy would trot. No one knew where the name 'Bibbit' had come from, but it had stuck.

Lucy and the little boy shared a wonderful relationship, where Hector made demands and Lucy did his bidding. She adored him and relished every second of the times she got to spend with him, which weren't nearly as frequent as she would like, not with Camille now living with her best friend, Alice, in Poitiers.

Their little flat was quaint. It was a stone's throw from the Place du Maréchal-Leclerc, a bustle of activity among the beautiful historic buildings. Camille and Hector shared a room and Alice lived in the second. Both girls worked their shifts at the busy Café Populaire. Camille's were timed around Hector's childcare, and Jean-Luc and Geneviève stepped in when needed to care for their grandson on their sprawling farm.

Lucy and Jonah had enjoyed some wonderful trips to the region, most notably in the summer months when they took their grandson to paddle on the shallow banks of the Clain, picnicking by a bend in the river while Camille regaled them with her plans to go back to college when Hector started school; her love of fashion hadn't waned. They were both so very proud of her independence. She lived mainly off her wages and managed to keep her head above water, just. Lucy and Jonah happily made sure that Hector had all that he needed – a little bike, new shoes, anything that would lift the financial burden from Camille while at the same time giving them the huge joy of purchasing things for the boy they loved.

'We all know you don't mean it! That child only has to shout and you jump. He has you wrapped around his finger!' Fay called out, clinking her beer bottle against Jonah's wine glass as they ribbed her from the terrace. Lucy smiled broadly at her sister.

'Yes, but Hector doesn't know that!' she replied, laughing.

'Err, I think he does actually!' Camille chuckled from the table where she sat next to Geneviève and Jean-Luc, who had travelled over with their daughter.

'What is this, pick on Lucy day? Give me a break.' She giggled, making her way back towards the house.

She looked up, still bowled over by their home's grand makeover, funded by the sale of the flat, a gesture that proved she no longer had need of a fallback. The extra floor and the wide open-plan kitchen that led out to the terrace made the house spacious, easier to live in and certainly a whole lot fancier to entertain in. It looked stunning, and she had decided a while ago never to confess to Jonah that, while the house was indeed grander and more streamlined, she kind of missed the dark, cobwebby corners of the narrow corridors that had added so much character.

Camille fetched the jug of iced tea from the kitchen and wandered down the steps of the terrace with Rory by her side, his preferred place to be. 'Who wants some iced tea?' she called out, clearly as at home here as she had ever been.

'Oh yes, please!' Lucy smiled, giving Hector back his ball before going to stand next to her beautiful stepdaughter. Lucy felt nothing but admiration for the way the girl handled her situation, showing maturity beyond her years.

Dex remained a key figure in their lives. He clearly loved Hector, and they were at present planning his next visit when he was back from New York for a spell. Camille felt nothing but affection towards the boy who now called America home as he chased his dream of success in the land of opportunity. Lucy had on one occasion suggested that Camille might like to rekindle her romance with him; to this, Camille had confessed that she could no longer envisage a romance with him, showing a level of understanding Lucy respected. Dex had been just a boy, a year older than Camille. A good-looking boy she had loved. Well, as far as you can love someone when you are sixteen and think that the world can be like a movie.

'What about in the future?' Lucy had pushed. 'Do you think you and Dex might make a go of it?'

Camille had smiled, slowly. 'The thing is, Bibbit, I've been taught never to settle for anything other than what is perfect for me, to always put my needs high on the list, and to know my worth, and I don't know if Dex fits that equation. Okay?'

'Okay.' Lucy smiled.

◆ ◆ ◆

Lucy had, after much soul-searching, written to Scott. Tracking him down with ease, she gave him all the information she had about Bella. It was now up to him as to whether he made contact. She hadn't yet received a reply.

It seemed to her that Camille had a good grasp of things that had taken Lucy years to figure out. She still thought of Bella, of course, but was no longer haunted by the idea of the baby she had given away. Receiving her letter had been poignant. *My mum thought you would always carry me with you. Throughout my life, this idea has given me a really nice feeling . . .* ' Even just recalling these words made her smile and brought her peace.

'Iced tea for you, Maman?' Camille raised the jug, calling to Geneviève and pulling Lucy from her thoughts.

'Might as well. I need to drink something!' The woman smiled at Jean-Luc, who squeezed her hand, clearly liking his newly teetotal wife. The two were slowly reconnecting with Camille, and having Hector around had undoubtedly helped with this. It made Lucy happy to see the support network that her stepdaughter enjoyed, knowing that you could never have too many people looking out for you.

'Actually, Cam, there's something I wanted to show you, upstairs.' She took her stepdaughter's hand into her own and guided her through the now spacious house, where oversized vases stuffed with glorious blooms filled the rooms and the new neutral colour scheme on the walls was indeed sophisticated and yet cool.

They trod the stairs and walked into Lucy and Jonah's bedroom. Camille sat on the bed and giggled. 'This is all very mysterious.'

'I wanted to give you this.' Lucy reached up and lifted the nearly empty wicker basket from the top of the wardrobe.

'What? Not your wicker hamper! That's your most precious thing!' Camille sat back and watched as her stepmother opened the lid of the box with its irritating creak and pulled out the envelope and the little pink sock.

'I'll keep these,' Lucy whispered.

'How many kisses are in there now?' Camille asked, quietly.

'Twenty-six,' she replied, before touching the sock to her cheek and then placing the two items in her bedside drawer. 'I want you to have it, use it to store your special things, keep them safe. Letters, memories, whatever – this box is a good keeper of secrets.'

'Do you think' – the girl paused – 'do you think I'm doing okay?' She looked up, biting her bottom lip.

'Oh, Cam, you are doing more than okay. You are incredible. Just look at Hector – he is so happy and that is down to you, that's all that matters!' she enthused.

'Thanks, Bibbit.' Camille smiled. 'I really don't know how I would have coped without you.'

Lucy batted away the compliment.

'Yes,' Cam insisted, 'I have you to thank for everything. I thought you would blow my family apart and instead, look at us, all sat on the terrace drinking iced tea, while my son plays on the grass with his cousins. You did the opposite; you brought us all together.'

Lucy felt the emotion rise in her throat. 'I am very proud of you, Camille. I admire you,' she confessed. 'And I love you.' The words now tripped easily from her mouth.

'I love you too. Thank you for the hamper. I shall treasure it.' Camille ran her fingers over the creaky wicker lid. 'I was going to ask you . . .' She hesitated.

'What?' Lucy prompted. 'You can ask me anything.'

'Do you think you might teach me how to knit?'

Lucy heard her gran's words loud and clear in her head, as if she was standing next to her. *Something magical happens, Lucy, just by adding more loops, and with more twists of the needle you can make all kinds of wondrous things! Like scarves for people you love, and most important – baby clothes.*

'I'd be honoured to.' She swatted the tears that cascaded down her face.

Jan popped her head around the door.

'Well, my darlings, here you are.' She spoke quietly and gave a small nod. 'What are you two plotting?'

'Nothing.' Lucy sniffed. 'We were just talking about knitting.'

And for some reason, this struck the three of them as very funny, and they chuckled.

'People are asking after you. I think everyone's getting a bit peckish. I told them that if they were all really lucky, you might rustle up some of those chicken Kiev ice lollies that you make so well.'

'Very funny!' She pulled a face at her mum. 'Come on. Let's get back to the party.' Lucy reached out and took Camille's hand and the two walked slowly down the stairs behind Jan.

Jonah was in the kitchen, putting on his apron and preparing to impress their guests. 'I don't know about anyone else, but I think it's about time we cracked open that champagne!' he boomed. A ripple of laughter spread among them. He greeted his wife with a smile. Jan and Camille ambled on to the terrace, where the family happily sipped their drinks, laughing. Fay and Geneviève were deep in conversation about shopping. Camille winked at Lucy as she sat down between her parents across from Rory. This was quite some occasion.

Jonah placed his arm around his wife's shoulders. 'What are you thinking about, Bibbit? You look lost in thought.'

'I was just thinking how happy I am, and how very lucky.' She smiled.

The duo stood in front of the kitchen cupboards, their doors covered in things that Hector, Maisie and Rory had made. Her grandson's little handprints were smeared across a page in red and blue paint, and there was a colourful Christmas picture with sparkles and glitter all over it. Rory had drawn them a rocket, and Maisie had gifted them a collage – it was a riot of colour with pom-poms and bits of macaroni stuck randomly on.

Lucy looked up at the pictures, these glorious creations that would turn any house into a home, a home with a love of children at its heart. And that was most certainly the home she wanted to live in.

'Bibbit!' Hector called from the lawn.

'Yes, come on, Bibbit! You are needed out here! That ball isn't going to fetch itself,' Camille yelled.

Lucy and Jonah moved to the wide patio doors and gazed out over the garden at their family.

'Would I do, Hector?' Jan asked hopefully. 'Can Great-Granny fetch it for you?'

'No!' Hector stamped his foot. 'Bibbit!'

Jonah laughed loudly. 'Oh boy, he takes after his mum. Stubborn and wilful!'

Camille tutted, as Geneviève rolled her eyes. *'C'est vrai.'* She nodded, smiling at her ex-husband. *'C'est vrai.'*

Jonah looked at his wife and bent close to her face. 'I don't think I have ever been prouder or loved you more than I do right now, Mrs Carpenter.'

'The feeling is entirely mutual.' She laughed.

'Bibbit!' Hector's call drew her attention.

'I think you are needed.' Jonah kissed her nose.

'On my way!' she called.

Lucy made her way out into the garden with a spring in her step. She was indeed very lucky. She really did have it all.

ACKNOWLEDGMENTS

I would like to express my sincere gratitude once again to my fantastic editors, Sammia and Ms Tiffania Teaseblossom.

Thank you once again for your insightful, clear, genius ideas that massively enhance my stories. Working with you feels far more like fun than I'm sure it should! I would also like to thank the whole incredible team at Amazon, all of whom brilliantly produce their piece of the jigsaw, ensuring that when we put it together at the end it is just about as perfect as it can be.

I send love as ever to my family, who support me and love me unconditionally as I do them. I send special love to my husband, Simeon, who has shared the loss of all our little babies who left us too soon. Our grief made us stronger.

BOOK CLUB QUESTIONS

1. Did Lucy's story alter your view of miscarriage? If so, how?

2. Which member of the Carpenter family did you most sympathise with and why?

3. Has *The Idea of You* changed you or broadened your perspective? If so, how?

4. For you, what was the book's main message?

5. In a movie, who would play each of the characters?

6. Lucy and Jonah reach a number of emotional crossroads. How do you think that they coped at these times? How well do you feel they supported each other?

7. Did any parts of the book make you feel uncomfortable? If so, which parts and why?

8. What will be your overriding memory from *The Idea of You*, the one incident or paragraph that will stay with you?

ABOUT THE AUTHOR

Photo © 2012 Paul Smith of Paul Smith Photography at
www.paulsmithphotography.info

Amanda Prowse likens her own life story to those she writes about in her books. After self-publishing her debut novel, *Poppy Day*, in 2011, she has gone on to author sixteen novels and six novellas. Her books have been translated into a dozen languages and she regularly tops bestseller charts all over the world.

Remaining true to her ethos, Amanda writes stories of ordinary women and their families who find their strength, courage and love tested in ways they never imagined. The most prolific female contemporary fiction writer in the UK, with a legion of loyal readers, she goes from strength to strength. Being crowned 'queen of domestic drama' by the *Daily Mail* was one of her finest moments.

Amanda is a regular contributor on TV and radio, but her first love is and will always be writing.

You can find her online at www.amandaprowse.com, on Twitter at @MrsAmandaProwse and on Facebook at www.facebook.com/ amandaprowsenogreaterlove.